P9-CFP-003

Praise for Kat Martin

"Martin revs the power from page one…. Fans of romantic suspense won't be able to put [*The Deception*] down until the final page is turned."

—*Publishers Weekly*

"An un-put-downable page-turner…sure to satisfy fans of romance and thrillers alike."

—*Kirkus Reviews* on *The Deception*

"Drugs, lies, corruption, and long-held secrets are at the core of this hard-hitting romance and well-done series opener."

—*Library Journal* on *The Conspiracy*

"Martin keeps the twists and turns coming in the sensuous and spirited first Maximum Security romantic thriller…. Readers will find it hard to wait for the next book in this tantalizing series."

—*Publishers Weekly* on *The Conspiracy*

"Kat Martin is a fast gun when it comes to storytelling, and I love her books."

—#1 *New York Times* bestselling author Linda Lael Miller

"[Kat] Martin is a terrific storyteller."

—*Booklist*

"It doesn't matter what Martin's characters are up against—she dishes up romantic suspense, sizzling sex and international intrigue."

—*RT Book Reviews*

"[A] master of suspenseful romance…Martin doesn't hold back on the page-turning thrills or steamy love scenes."

—*Publishers Weekly*

KAT MARTIN

THE DECEPTION

HQN

If you purchased this book without a cover you should be aware
that this book is stolen property. It was reported as "unsold and
destroyed" to the publisher, and neither the author nor the
publisher has received any payment for this "stripped book."

HQN®

Recycling programs
for this product may
not exist in your area.

ISBN-13: 978-1-335-09025-6

The Deception

First published in 2019. This edition published in 2020.

Copyright © 2019 by Kat Martin

Shadows at Dawn
First published in 2019. This edition published in 2020.
Copyright © 2019 by Kat Martin

All rights reserved. No part of this book may be used or reproduced in
any manner whatsoever without written permission except in the case of
brief quotations embodied in critical articles and reviews.

This is a work of fiction. Names, characters, places and incidents
are either the product of the author's imagination or are used fictitiously.
Any resemblance to actual persons, living or dead, businesses,
companies, events or locales is entirely coincidental.

This edition published by arrangement with Harlequin Books S.A.

For questions and comments about the quality of this book,
please contact us at CustomerService@Harlequin.com.

HQN
22 Adelaide St. West, 40th Floor
Toronto, Ontario M5H 4E3, Canada
www.Harlequin.com

Printed in U.S.A.

CONTENTS

To my sister, Patti, for her years of love and support.

THE DECEPTION

CHAPTER ONE

Dallas, Texas

"I'M SORRY, MS. GALLAGHER. I know this is terribly difficult, but unless there's someone else who can make a positive identification—"

Kate shook her head. "No. There's no one else."

"All right then, if you will please follow me." The medical examiner, Dr. Jerome Maxwell, a man in his fifties, had thick black hair finely threaded with gray. He started down the hall, but Kate stopped him with a hand on his arm.

"Are you...are you completely sure it's my sister?" She smoothed a hand nervously over the skirt of her navy blue suit. "The victim is definitely Christina Gallagher?"

"There was a fingerprint match to your missing sister. I'm sorry," he repeated. "We'll still need your confirmation."

Kate's stomach rolled. Her legs felt weak as she followed Dr. Maxwell down a narrow, seemingly endless hallway in the Dallas County morgue. The echo of her high heels on the stark gray linoleum floor sent a sweep of nausea through her.

The doctor paused outside a half-glass door. "As I said before, this is going to be difficult. Are you sure there isn't someone you can call, someone else who could make the identification?"

Kate's throat tightened. "My father's remarried and living in New York. He hasn't seen Chrissy in years." Frank Gallagher hadn't seen either of his daughters since he and his wife had divorced.

"And your mother?" the doctor asked kindly.

"She died of a heart attack a year after Chrissy ran away." For Madeleine Gallagher, losing both her husband and her daughter had simply been too much.

The doctor straightened his square black glasses. "Are you ready?"

"I'll never be ready to see my sister's murdered body, Dr. Maxwell. But I'm all Chrissy has, so let's get it over with."

The doctor opened the door, and they walked out of a hallway that seemed overly warm into a room that was icy cold. A shiver rushed over Kate's skin, and her heart beat faster. As Dr. Maxwell moved toward a rollout table in front of a wall of cold-storage boxes, Kate could see the outline of a body beneath the stark white sheet.

Emotion tightened her chest. This was her baby sister, only sixteen the last time Kate had seen her two years ago, before she had run away.

The doctor nodded to a female assistant in a white lab coat standing next to the table, and the woman pulled back the sheet.

"Oh, my God." The bile rose in Kate's throat. She swayed, and the doctor caught her arm to steady her.

"Is this your sister, Christina Gallagher?"

The body on the table in no way resembled the beautiful young girl who had been her little sister. At only eighteen, this young woman was gaunt, her cheeks hollow, her skin chaffed and sallow and clinging to her bones. Her closed eyes were dark and sunken. Bruises covered her face, shoulders and chest, all Kate could see of the body.

Tears welled and slipped down her cheeks. "It's her." It wasn't Chrissy in any way Kate remembered her, and yet there was no doubt she was the thin, brutalized, lifeless form lying on the stainless-steel table.

The doctor nodded at the assistant, who drew the sheet back over Chrissy's face. Dr. Maxwell kept a firm grip on Kate's arm as he turned her toward the door and guided her out of the room, back into the hallway. Her legs were shaking, her throat too tight to speak.

"I'm sorry for your loss," the doctor said, finally letting her go.

"Thank...thank you."

"We have your contact information. You'll be notified when the body has been released."

She swallowed, wiped at the tears on her cheeks. "Do you...do the police have any leads on the killer?"

"I'm sure they're working hard to find whoever was involved."

Kate nodded. Without saying more, she started back down the hallway. The doctor didn't follow and she was glad. There was nothing left to say, nothing more he could do.

Tears blurred her vision and her head swam as she walked out into the sunlight and crossed the parking lot to her car. She wouldn't be returning to her office today. She needed time to deal with her crushing emotions, the sense of loss and pain. The terrible sense of failure.

She needed time to grieve.

Kate slid in behind the wheel and shoved her key

into the ignition. Fresh pain struck so hard she couldn't breathe. Instead of starting the engine, Kate put her head down on the steering wheel and started to weep.

CHAPTER TWO

JASON HAWKINS MADDOX sat at the old-fashioned long bar in the Sagebrush Saloon, a country-western hangout with a live band for dancing on the weekends and a jukebox that served the same purpose the rest of the week. The place, out I-30 on Bruckner Boulevard, was a spot Jase had been to before but not for a couple of years.

He was there tonight on business, meeting an informant he hoped would give him a lead on the fugitive he was hunting.

Randall Darren Harding, a cement contractor, had been arrested for the brutal murder of his ex-girlfriend. He'd been out on bail when he'd decided to flee instead of standing trial, where most likely he would have been convicted.

On the outskirts of Dallas, he'd had a firefight with police, shot two sheriff's deputies and escaped. The guy was tough. He wouldn't go down easy.

From what Jase could find out, Harding was a rotten, self-centered, mean-tempered bastard, the kind who could wind up killing again. He'd strangled his girlfriend in a fit of rage, but a fancy lawyer had gotten him out on bail.

Jase had a warrant for Harding's arrest—rearrest, technically, since the guy had already been charged

with murder-one, the premeditated kind that could earn
you the death penalty in Texas.

The reward for catching him was a fat 15 percent
of his million-and-a-half-dollar bond. Jase planned to
collect.

Thus his meeting with Tommy Dieter at the Sagebrush Saloon.

It was relatively early, a little after 9:00 p.m., but the
place was already more than half full. A big dance floor
dominated the interior, surrounded by a sea of wooden
tables. Being Wednesday, there was no band, but the
juke was belting Willie Nelson so a few couples two-
stepped out on the floor.

It was a decent place, not one of the rat holes he occasionally frequented for information, the crowd a mix
of cowboys and bikers, couples of various ages, and
a smattering of tourists, there to try some real Texas
line dancing.

From the mirror in the carved oak back bar across
from him, Jase could keep an eye on the front door
and watch for Tommy's arrival. Between a row of liquor bottles, he could see himself on a bar stool next to
a little guy in a blue Texas Rangers baseball cap. The
little guy made Jase look even bigger than his six-foot-
four-inch, 210-pound frame, a size that in his job often
came in handy.

So far Tommy hadn't shown, but he wasn't due for
another few minutes. In the meantime, Jase was enjoying the local scenery, his attention fixed on the tall
blonde with the pretty face, sexy curves and amazing
cleavage, but then half the guys in the bar were watching her.

In a short denim skirt, a pair of cowboy boots and a
bright pink tank top, she had danced to five songs in a

row. Jase figured as long as her stamina held out, she wouldn't lack for partners. If he weren't there on business, he might have asked her for a turn around the floor himself.

The blonde finished the dance and sat back down on a bar stool a ways down from him. He noticed she was drinking tequila shooters. Looked like someone was going to get lucky tonight. Hearing the throaty purr of her laughter, he felt a tug in his groin and couldn't help wishing it was him.

The front door swung open and Tommy Dieter walked in. Jase tossed money for the Lone Star he'd been drinking on top of the bar. Time to go to work.

Tommy spotted him and walked over to the bar. "Hey, Hawk." It was a nickname Jase had picked up thanks to his middle name. They called him the Hawk because he swooped down on his prey and always got his man. Or so the story went.

"Tommy." He was a slender guy in his early twenties with carrot-red hair, not a bad sort, but he hung with a bad crowd, which gave him access to a lot of dirt, and he was hungry enough to deal the info for money.

Jase nodded toward an empty table at the back of the bar, and the two of them made their way past a pool table where a couple of cowboys clacked balls across a sea of green.

Tommy and Jase both pulled out chairs and sat down at the battered wooden table. Jase didn't ask Tommy if he wanted a beer. It wasn't healthy for an informant to spend too much time with a guy who hunted people for a living.

"You got something on Harding for me?" Jase asked.

"Yeah. Randy has a girlfriend in Houston," Tommy

said. "Mexican girl. No papers. She keeps him happy. He pays her rent."

"What's her name?"

"Rosa Diaz. She's got a brother in town. A mechanic named Paulo."

"You think Randy's still in Houston? I figured he'd leave the state, head for Arizona, maybe, or New Mexico."

"Word is he's got the serious hots for Rosa. According to Randy, she's a great piece of ass."

The words sent Jase's gaze back to the blonde who had returned to the dance floor with a lanky biker too short for her, too skinny and a few years too young.

She wasn't meant for the boy biker, but she was just Jase's type, luscious, with legs that went on forever. And, as she slid her arms around the boy biker's neck and he pulled her close, clearly uninhibited, it didn't take much to imagine the way she'd feel moving beneath him.

Jase ignored a surge of heat and forced his mind back to business. "If Randy's that close, you'd think the cops would already have him in custody."

"I don't think the cops know anything about the girl."

Probably not. They had their hands full without having to arrest the same guy twice.

Jase reached into the pocket of his black T-shirt, plucked out a folded-up hundred-dollar bill and slid it across the table to Dieter. "Let me know if you come up with anything else."

Tommy snagged the hundred. "Good luck," he said. "I hope you nail this prick. What he did to that girl… fucker deserves to fry."

Jase made no comment since he completely agreed.

One of the perks of the job was bringing dicks like Harding to justice.

As Tommy walked away, Jase noticed his seat at the bar was still empty. Since he wasn't ready to leave, he picked up his beer and headed back the way he'd come.

He watched the blonde as he passed the dance floor. He'd been watching her all evening. The good news was, she'd been watching him, too.

When the song came to an end, she left the boy biker and walked toward him, stopped right in front of his bar stool, the heels on her boots pushing her closer to his height.

She smiled. "You like to dance, cowboy?"

"Depends."

"On what? The song?"

"Who I'm dancing with."

A dark blond eyebrow went up. "Is that right…"

"That's right, darlin', and you'll do just fine." Without waiting for a reply, Jase swept her onto the dance floor. She felt good in his arms, fit him just right. She was a good dancer, but so was he. He was a Texan. He'd done all the usual things a Texas boy did. Played football, drank beer down on the river, rode horses and two-stepped.

"What's your name?" he asked as he whirled her around the floor.

"Kate." She smiled. "You're Hawk."

So she'd heard Tommy greet him. "I prefer Jason or Jase."

Her smile widened into a grin that etched a dimple into her cheek, and he felt jolt of heat. He realized she was on her way to drunk, but so far, he didn't think she'd crossed the line.

"I like Hawk," she said. "It's sexy."

"You think so?" As the song came to an end, he drew her off the dance floor into the shadows, took a chance she wouldn't slap his face and kissed her.

She softened against him and kissed him back, and he took it a little deeper, felt the rush hit his system. Since they were standing in a bar full of people, he didn't let it go too far.

Kate ran a finger along his jaw. "You looked like you'd be a good kisser and you are," she said.

"We can go outside and I'll show you just how good I can be, but it's gotta be up to you."

Something flickered in her big brown eyes, and for an instant her bright smile faded. "I need that. Just this once, just for tonight." Her grin returned. "Come on, cowboy, let's go."

She left him long enough to grab her purse off the bar. When she led him outside, he didn't resist, just followed her out the door and pulled her back into his arms. She tasted better than good and he deepened the kiss, sinking into those plump pink lips, inhaling her soft perfume.

Kate was right there with him, taking the hot kiss deeper, pressing her full breasts into his chest, turning him rock hard and making him reckless.

"My house or yours?" he asked. He wasn't into one-night hookups, not usually, but this woman hit every hot button he had.

For the first time, Kate looked uncertain. "I might want you, big boy, but I'm not dumb enough to leave with a total stranger."

He leaned down and kissed her. "Smart girl." Pulling the keys to his big black Yukon out of the pocket of his jeans, he clicked the locks, flashing the lights, and

gave her the keys. "So you know I'm not going to drag
you off somewhere."

She looked down at the keys, then over at the SUV
parked in the dark at the edge of the lot. In his job, it
paid to be careful. Kate slid her arms around his neck
and kissed him again, hot, wet and deep, and the last
of her reservations seemed to fade.

"I need this," she softly repeated, speaking more to
herself than to him. Grabbing his hand, she pulled him
over to the SUV. Jase jerked open the backseat door,
climbed inside and hauled Kate in behind him.

He lifted her, settled her astride his lap, one of her
knees on each side, making her short skirt ride up on
her thighs. He tried not to wonder what she was wearing underneath, which, with any luck, he was about to
find out.

Sliding his hands into her long, thick, honey blond
curls, Jase kissed her until both of them were breathless, until she was squirming against his hard-on and
moaning.

She shoved up his T-shirt, and he stripped it off over
his head. He pulled off her tank top, unfastened the
front hook on her lacy white bra and slid it off her shoulders, filled his hands with her luscious breasts.

"Beautiful," he said, admiring the soft globes that
perfectly fit his big hands. He kissed the side of her
neck, and Kate tipped her head back to give him better
access. He trailed kisses over her shoulder and took a
rosy nipple into his mouth. Breathing hard, Kate ran
her hands over the muscles in his chest.

"I love your body," she said, leaning down to kiss
him. "Please... Jason."

"I'm all yours, baby." He was reaching between them
to unzip his fly when he heard a young couple walking

toward the SUV. The girl was laughing, a soft, sweet sound more like a teenager than someone old enough to be drinking.

Kate's whole body went tense.

"Easy," he said, pressing his mouth against the pulse beating in her neck, kissing his way down to her shoulder. "They'll be gone in a minute."

Kate dragged in a shaky breath. A noise came from her throat that sounded something like pain.

"It's all right," he said. "They're just kids. They aren't going to bother us." But she was already moving off him, reaching for her bra and sliding it on, hooking the front, grabbing her tank top and pulling it over her head.

"I'm… I'm really sorry," she said as she slid off his lap. "I'm not like this. I don't do this kind of thing."

"You're a grown woman, Kate. You can do whatever you want." He wanted to be mad. Nothing worse than a tease, but the pain in her eyes leashed his temper.

She cupped his cheek, and when she looked at him, he realized there were tears in her eyes. "Something bad happened today. My sister was killed. I couldn't… I can't get the image of her dead body out of my head."

"Jesus, honey."

"I just… I just wanted to forget for a while."

Jase pulled her back into his arms and she let him, her body softening against his. She started crying and he tightened his hold. He knew a lot about death. He'd been a marine. Now he was in law enforcement. He knew a lot about grief.

"It's all right," he said. "It just takes time."

"I'm sorry." Her hand shook as she wiped tears from her cheeks. "I made a fool out of myself tonight."

"I don't think you're a fool, Kate. And everybody does things they regret once in a while."

She drew away from him, opened the door and climbed out of the SUV. Jase grabbed his T-shirt and pulled it on, followed her out and she handed him back his keys. He was still hard as a brick, aching with every heartbeat. He couldn't remember wanting a woman so badly.

"My name's Maddox. Jason Maddox. Give me your number and I'll call you. We'll start over, go out to dinner or something."

She just shook her head.

"At least tell me your name."

She smiled sadly. "It's just Kate. Thank you for being so nice about…tonight."

Nice wasn't a word often used in connection with the Hawk.

"Good night, Jason."

"You shouldn't be driving. Let me take you home."

"I'll call an Uber." Turning away, Kate dug her phone out of her purse as she hurried off toward a hot-looking black-trimmed white Camaro sitting under a light in the parking lot. Jase watched her until an Uber car appeared out of nowhere, she climbed inside and the car drove away. Opening the door of the Yukon, he slid in behind the wheel and fired up the powerful engine.

She wouldn't give him her name or her number. She didn't want to see him again. Or at least that's what she'd said.

He told himself to forget her. She was just a pretty blonde, and Dallas was full of pretty blondes. But there was something special about this one, and it wasn't just her amazing cleavage.

He had some things to finish in Dallas before he could head down to Houston to look for Harding.

The following day he found himself returning to the

Sagebrush Saloon. Kate's flashy white Camaro was gone. Turned out *Just Kate* occasionally came in to dance on Friday nights with her girlfriends, occasionally came alone. No one seemed to know her full name, but according to the bartender, she never left with a guy, just danced, had a few drinks and went home.

Jase knew he could find her. Finding people was what he did. But he wasn't a stalker. If she'd wanted to see him, she would have given him her number.

Still, when Friday night came around, he found himself on a bar stool at the Sagebrush Saloon.

Unfortunately, *Just Kate* never showed up.

CHAPTER THREE

AFTER HER MELTDOWN at the bar, which still embarrassed her, Kate spent the following week hounding the Dallas Police Department.

Chrissy's case had been assigned to a homicide detective named Roger Benson, an older guy with thinning brown hair and a bad attitude. She'd done a little digging, found out he had previously worked in the sex crimes unit, an unabashed misogynist who acted as if he believed all women were whores and was completely the wrong person to be handling cases in that department—which was probably why he now worked in Homicide.

She tried to give him the benefit of the doubt, figuring the crimes he had worked had changed him into the man he had become. Or maybe he had always been like that. Either way, Kate didn't like him.

"Your sister was using the name Tina Galen," he told her when she appeared in his office demanding answers for the fourth day in a row. "She was a heroin addict and a known prostitute."

Her heart squeezed, though the police had already told her those things. "She was murdered, Detective. Her killer needs to face justice."

"I'm sorry for your loss, Ms. Gallagher. We're doing everything we can to locate the person who killed her, but in circumstances like these, the odds of finding him aren't good."

"The killer must have left evidence. Fingerprints or DNA. Something."

"We're working on it. We believe Tina hooked up with a john who liked rough sex. That night, he got carried away, beat her worse than he meant to and killed her. If that's the case, he may have assaulted women before."

"So you'll be able to find him."

"Like I said, we're working on it. You need to let us do our job, Ms. Gallagher. Coming down here every day and badgering us isn't going to help. Now if you don't mind, I've got things I need to do. Your sister's case isn't the only one on my desk."

She glanced over at the stack of files on the detective's desk and bit back a sharp retort. "Yes, I can see that." And clearly, arguing with Benson wasn't going to get her anywhere.

As she left the police station, it occurred to her there was a good chance nothing she said or did was going to get the answers she was determined to get in regard to Chrissy's death.

She needed someone to help her. A detective who worked directly for her and strictly on her sister's murder case.

At twenty-nine, Kate was the owner of Gallagher and Company Consulting, an up-and-coming management consulting firm. And though there were only two other analysts in the office so far, plus a receptionist who acted as her personal assistant, she had built a solid reputation during the time she'd been working in Dallas, and the company was making money.

She could afford to hire a private investigator.

Arriving in the lobby of the five-story building on North Akard near McKinney where the Gallagher and

Company office was located, she waved at one of the security guards, a big guy named Clay, as she passed.

Kate's stomach tightened. Clay didn't have the thick dark hair and gorgeous blue eyes of the man she had nearly had sex with in the parking lot of the Sagebrush Saloon, but he was almost as tall, with the same rock-solid body. Seeing Clay, who was older and not nearly as good-looking, made her think of Jason "Hawk" Maddox, and she felt a combination of embarrassment and a ridiculous rush of heat.

Dear God, she had never been more turned on in her life. When he'd hauled her out on the dance floor and into his big, powerful arms, it occurred to her for the first time, she might really go through with the hookup she had only imagined when she'd seen him in the bar that night.

Maddox really knew how to dance. And he could kiss. She could have kissed him for hours.

Thank God, she had come to her senses before it was too late. She didn't do hookups, especially with hot, muscle-jocks in jeans and scuffed boots. She didn't have sex with strangers.

But after she'd left the morgue, she had gone a little crazy. Crying hadn't done a lick of good and eventually she had managed to pull herself together, but the terrible feelings of guilt and failure would not go away.

It didn't matter that she and Chrissy, her parents' surprise baby eleven years younger than Kate, had never been close, that by the time Chrissy was in high school, Kate had moved from the small Texas town of Rockdale to Dallas.

She was working full-time for Bain Consulting as a junior member of one of their teams when Chrissy began having problems with drugs and alcohol, and behaving promiscuously with boys. Kate had gone back to Rockdale to talk to her, but it hadn't done any good. A few months later, her sister had run away from home, and though the police had done everything in their power to find her, Kate had never seen her again.

Not until the police had called with the terrible news of her murder and Kate had gone to the morgue.

How she'd wound up half drunk at the Sagebrush Saloon still wasn't completely clear. She'd just been desperate to get the image of Chrissy's battered and bludgeoned body out of her head, and for a while in the backseat with Jason, it had actually worked.

It was impossible to think of anything but those big hands on her breasts and the thick ridge beneath the fly of his jeans. God, she had never known that kind of want before.

The elevator dinged its arrival on the third floor of the building, and Kate shoved the memory away.

There was a small reception area in the front of the office. Her assistant, Laura Delgado, an attractive Latina woman in her twenties with long straight black hair clipped back at her nape, sat behind a computer, clicking away on the keyboard. Kate waved and kept walking.

Beyond the reception area were three private offices and a conference room. None were large, but the dark blue-and-gray motif was sleek and sophisticated and gave the impression of success—imperative in the consulting business where an analyst's job was to give advice on how to make more money.

Kate closed her office door, took a seat behind her glass-and-chrome desk, turned on her computer and started scouring the internet. It didn't take long to come up with a list of security firms that handled private investigation. The firms were star-rated by reviews.

An hour later, she had narrowed her choices down to three. At the top of the list with the highest reviews was a company called Maximum Security, owned by an investigator named Chase Garrett. Kate knew who he was. Chase and his two brothers were megarich, the co-owners of Garrett Resources, a Texas-based oil and gas company.

The middle brother, Reese, ran the business while Chase and Brandon had chosen careers in law enforcement. The Garretts were Dallas elite, and were frequently featured in local news articles. Kate jotted down the address of Maximum Security, as well as two alternate choices. Might as well start with the best and work her way down.

Kate grabbed her purse and headed out the door.

IT HAD BEEN one helluva week, Jase thought. He'd spent the last few days in Houston, trying to locate Rosa Diaz or her brother, Paulo. Trying to hunt down Randy Harding.

The closest he got was finding the garage where Paulo Diaz worked, Ray's Auto Body. Apparently Paulo didn't like Harding any better than anyone else, so Jase didn't have to press too hard to get information.

"The no good *pendajo* left town three days ago. He knocked the crap out of my sister, but she still went with him." Paulo spit on the ground outside the metal shop door. He was a little guy, black hair and a few tattoos, probably a lot tougher than he looked. "*Women.* I do not understand them."

"Neither do I, Paulo, and we probably never will. Does Rosa know what happened to the last woman Harding lived with? She know that after she left him, Randy broke into her house, beat her and ended up strangling her to death? Does Rosa know he's wanted on murder charges?"

"She says he did not do it. She says Randy ended things with the woman after he met Rosa. She says he only hits her because he is jealous. It means he loves her."

"Yeah, right. You got any idea where they went?" When Paulo didn't answer right away, Jase held up a hundred-dollar bill. One thing he'd learned—money talked and bullshit walked.

"If I knew, I would tell you," Paulo said. "You would not need to pay me."

"I guess I don't have to tell you not to let your sister know I'm hunting him."

"I won't tell her. Rosa is a fool when it comes to Harding."

"Sooner or later, I'll find him. I just hope for Rosa's sake, it's sooner."

That was two days ago. Now he was back in Dallas, digging into Randy's past, looking for something he might have missed. He needed to figure out where Harding was now that he'd left Houston and taken Rosa with him.

He looked up as the glass front door opened. The Max, the guys called it, a single-story brick building on Blackburn Street, was a great place to work. The décor was masculine, kind of Western, like the Sagebrush Saloon only nicer, with a tufted dark red leather sofa and chairs in the waiting area, oak desks, and antique farming tools on the walls.

The woman who had just walked in was sophisticated and modern from the sleek blond knot twisted at the nape of her neck, to the burgundy skirt-suit she was wearing with gold jewelry. He couldn't see her face, but she was tall and curvy. Even the business clothes couldn't hide her spectacular figure.

"I'd like to see Chase Garrett," she said to the receptionist. "I'm hoping he's here."

"Do you have an appointment?" Mindy Stewart, a petite brunette, flashed her trademark smile.

"I'm afraid I don't." That voice...like whiskey and cream and sexy as hell.

"May I have your name?"

"Kathryn Gallagher."

She turned a little and Jase came out of his seat. *Just Kate* hadn't been at the Sagebrush Saloon Friday night, but she had just walked into The Max. He hadn't pursued her. Instead, she had come to him.

The bad news was she was looking for another man.

Jase strode toward her. Kate spotted him, and the blood drained out of her face. For an instant he thought she was going to turn around and run back out the door.

"Hello, Kate."

She swallowed so hard her throat moved up and down. He remembered pressing his mouth against the spot where her pulse beat frantically at the base of her neck.

"Jason..." The sound of his name on her lips sent a rush of heat straight to his groin.

"We'll be in the conference room," Jase said to Mindy, taking a firm hold on Kate's arm. She resisted a moment, then let him lead her in that direction.

He closed the conference room door behind them. "It's good to see you, Kate."

She glanced around as if she were looking for a way to escape. "So you...you work here? You're...you're a private investigator?"

He avoided the question. "Is that why you're here? You want to hire a private detective?"

"That's right. My sister was murdered. I mentioned it...that night."

His mind was beginning to function again, and he remembered she had told him that her sister had died. She hadn't said the girl was murdered.

"I remember." He remembered a lot of things. *Everything.* "Why don't we sit down? You can start at the beginning, tell me what's going on."

She looked over her shoulder toward the door as if she still might run. "I was hoping to hire Mr. Garrett. He's supposed to be very good."

"I'm very good, Kate. And I know you. I want to help you." He rolled out a chair at the long oak conference table, and she eased down onto the seat.

Jase took out a chair and sat down beside her. "So your name is Kathryn, not Kate?"

"Kathryn Gallagher. I use Kathryn in business but my friends call me Kate."

"Kate then." Surely they were friends. He knew the exact shape and size of her pretty breasts, the weight of them in his hands. He knew the softness of her lips and the way they tasted. "All right, Kate, let's start at the beginning. Tell me what happened to your sister."

She took a deep breath, but remained perched on the edge of her chair. "Her name was Christina. We called her Chrissy. Two years ago, Chrissy ran away from home. She was...she was only sixteen. The police say she was murdered, but they don't...they don't know who did it. They say there's a good chance they won't be able to find out."

"So you want to know what happened to your sister."

She seemed to collect herself. "That's right. I want

to hire a private detective, someone who'll help me find out who killed her. Are you a private detective?" she asked again.

"I'm licensed. I'm also a bail enforcement agent. That's how I make most of my money."

Her dark blond eyebrows arched up. "You're a bounty hunter?"

"That's right. That's why they call me the Hawk. I hunt criminals for a living, and I'm good at it. Very good. You want to find the man who killed your sister? Finding people is what I do."

Silence fell. Neither of them moved. Jase was afraid if he wasn't very careful, he would scare her away for good.

"Let me help you, Kate," he said softly.

"I don't...don't think it's a good idea. We have a certain...history. What happened could get in the way."

He never let pleasure interfere with business. He wouldn't do it now. Seeing Kate again only doubled the attraction he felt for her, but pursuing her could wait until the job was done.

"I won't let anything that's happened between us interfere. You won't, either. We'll find out who murdered your sister, and I'll help you bring them to justice."

She looked at him for several long moments, trying to gauge his sincerity. Since she could see he meant every word, Kate relaxed back in her chair.

"I believe you will," she said. "All right, Hawk Maddox. If you want the job, you're hired. But you have to forget that night in the parking lot. You have to pretend it never happened."

Amusement touched his lips. "I won't forget it, Kate. But I'll put it aside—for now." Color slid into her cheeks. "We'll get this done and go on from there. That work for you?"

She looked nervous again. "I'm not...not completely sure."

"Why don't we try it for a while and see?"

Some of the stiffness eased from her shoulders. "Fair enough."

He had the job, Jase thought. Now all he had to do to gain Kate's trust was to find her a killer. A look passed between them, and the air in the room seemed to thicken and heat.

The sooner he got the job done the better.

CHAPTER FOUR

KATE COULD HARDLY believe it. Jason Maddox, the last man in the world she wanted to see, was sitting right beside her. Worse yet, he was the man she had just hired to help her find Chrissy's killer. What the unholy hell had just happened?

"So…um…where do we start?" she asked, accepting whatever circumstances fate seemed to have set in motion.

"I need to take some notes," Maddox said. "I'll be right back." He rose from the swivel chair next to hers, and she tried not to think how good he looked in a yellow knit pullover and dark blue jeans.

But the pullover stretched over his powerful chest and an amazing set of biceps, one with a tattoo of an eagle perched on a globe and the words *Semper Fi* inked beneath it. She had noticed it that night in the parking lot.

She blocked the thought as he walked away and tried not to notice his long legs, broad back and round, muscular behind. She felt like fanning herself. Just looking at all that hard masculinity made her face feel warm.

He disappeared out the door, returned a few minutes later with a lined yellow pad and sat back down at the conference table.

"In my line of work you have to be pretty tech savvy, but writing things down helps me focus and gives me something solid to look at." He clicked the end of his pen and settled back in his seat, stretching those long legs out in front of him.

"Tell me about Chrissy."

She forced herself to concentrate, thought of her sister as a child, and warm memories slipped through her.

"She was a beautiful little girl. By the time she was a teenager, she was gorgeous. Blond hair and big blue eyes. She was always popular in school. In her freshman year, she was a cheerleader."

Kate told him how she and Chrissy had been raised in Rockdale, a tiny town northeast of Austin, how Chrissy had always hated it and wanted to move to the city. "I left for college as soon as I finished high school, and as she grew older, she got so envious. She couldn't wait to be old enough to leave."

"Were the two of you close?" Maddox asked. Kate forced herself to think of him that way, as Maddox, not Jason, not the man she had kissed, then seduced in the parking lot, not the man who had held her when she cried.

"She was eleven years younger, so no, we were never very close. By the time Chrissy was in high school, I was working in Dallas. By then, Mom and Dad were fighting all the time. That's when Chrissy started having trouble with drugs and alcohol. When Dad left home, things got worse."

"In what way?"

"Mom couldn't control her. She was constantly in trouble at school. I tried to talk to her, but it didn't do any good. She was sixteen when she ran away. My dad was remarried and living in New York. Mom blamed herself. She died later that year." And Kate missed her every day.

"The cops never came up with any information on your sister's whereabouts?"

"The police did everything they could to find her, but it was like she had vanished into thin air. I never saw her again, not until I went to the morgue." She glanced away, the pain still close to the surface. "If I'd known she was in Dallas, maybe I could have found a way to help her. At least talked to her, done *something*."

"Maybe that was the reason she came here. She wanted to see you again."

A lump swelled in her throat. "There's a chance, I guess, but it never happened. I wish it had."

Maddox made notes on the yellow pad, but she thought he was using it more as a tool to connect with a client than a way to jog his memory.

"I need to see the police report," he said. "See what they've got on the case so far."

"They said she was using the name Tina Galen. According to Detective Benson, she was a heroin addict and a prostitute. God, just saying it hurts."

"Benson's the lead on the case?"

"Yeah. He seemed like a real dick, but I guess I could be wrong."

Maddox's lips twitched. "You're not wrong. Benson's definitely a dick. I still need to talk to him, see what I can find out." They continued for a while, Maddox asking questions about Chrissy, anything she could remember that might help him. He asked her to get him a photo, the most recent one she had.

"I'd like to get started on this," he said, rising from his chair.

Kate stood up, too. "I want to help. I'll take some time off so we can work on this together."

"You can trust me to handle this, Kate. You don't have to get involved."

She straightened her shoulders. "That's not an option. I failed Chrissy before. I won't do it again. I'm going to do everything I can to help find her killer and bring him to justice."

Maddox studied her face. She could almost see his mind working behind those intriguing blue eyes. "All right, we can do that. As long as we're just digging up information and following leads. But if things get dicey, I take over and you stay out of it."

Kate didn't argue. Arguing hadn't worked with Benson, and she had a hunch it wouldn't work with Maddox. It didn't matter. Whether he approved or not, she wasn't stopping until Chrissy's killer faced justice.

"You parked in the front or the back?" he asked.

"I'm out front."

Maddox walked her to the front door of the office. "I'll need your contact information." A corner of his mouth kicked up. "*Just Kate* isn't going to work this time."

A memory arose of those lips moving hotly over hers, and desire clenched low in her belly. It was ridiculous. She tried to tell herself it was just that she hadn't been with a man in over six months, not since her breakup with Andrew. But the truth was, she was wildly attracted to Jason Maddox.

She forced herself to concentrate. Pulling a business card out of her purse, she turned it over and wrote her personal information on the back, including her address and cell phone number. She handed Maddox the card.

"'Gallagher and Company Consulting,'" he read. "Owner and Management Analyst." He glanced up. "What's a management analyst do?"

She smiled. "We study a company's efficiency, its systems, that kind of thing. Then we recommend ways to increase productivity and make it more profitable."

"Sounds useful." He pulled out his cell and punched her number into his contacts. "Your turn," he said, then rattled off his number and waited while she added it to her phone.

"I researched your rates and how all of this works," Kate said. "Don't you need money up front? A retainer of some kind?"

A smile lightened the blue of his eyes. "Are you good for it?"

"Of course, but—"

"I'll call you as soon as I talk to Benson. With any luck we can meet up again tonight."

Her breath caught. *Meet up again tonight?* She hadn't thought that far ahead, but she hadn't imagined seeing him again so soon.

"If I have something, that is," he added. "Like I said, I'll call you." Maddox pulled open the door, and waited for her to walk out onto the sidewalk.

Kate headed for her car and didn't look back. For the first time it occurred to her that what had happened with Jason that night in the parking lot wasn't the problem.

It was the temptation he posed in the days ahead.

JASE LEFT THE office still reeling from the stroke of good fortune he had been handed. Kate Gallagher was more than just a hookup that hadn't actually happened. She was a successful businesswoman. She was beautiful, smart and determined. She appealed to him on a half dozen different levels, attracted him in a way few women ever had.

She wanted to help with the case. Letting her work with him would give her a chance to get to know him.

Which was good news and bad.

Jase wanted Kate in his bed—no question about it. He wanted to have sex with her for hours on end. Make that days on end, possibly weeks.

But he wasn't a relationship kind of guy, at least not for any length of time. He led a hard, fast life and always had. There was no place in that kind of life for a woman.

He shook his head, amazed he had gotten as far as even thinking about it. But with her sister dead, Kate already had more than her share of trouble. She didn't need more from a guy like him.

On the other hand, Kate needed his help. She was determined to find the man who had murdered her sister, and Jase didn't believe she'd give up until she did.

But hunting a killer was dangerous. In his line of work he'd learned that firsthand. He'd known Kate only briefly, but holding her while she cried made him feel protective of her. No way was he trusting Kate's safety to someone else.

Jase left the office, his first stop the morgue. According to Kate, Dr. Jerome Maxwell was the medical examiner who had handled her sister's case.

For a bounty hunter, the right contacts meant the difference between success and failure. Jase knew Jerry Maxwell. He'd helped him locate his grandson, who had dropped out of school and was hanging around with a bad crowd. Jase had found him, talked to him, helped set him straight. The boy was back in class and doing well.

"Hawk," Maxwell called out as Jase walked through the door. "It's been a while. It's good to see you."

"You, too, Jerry."

"Have a seat." Maxwell sat down at his desk, and Jase sat down in the chair beside it.

"What can I do for you?"

"I need information on a dead girl named Christina Gallagher. Died a little over a week ago."

Maxwell nodded. "Homicide victim. I remember her sister, Kathryn. Beautiful woman."

"Yeah, well, according to Kate… Kathryn… Christina was beautiful, till she started doing drugs."

Maxwell located the file, set it down and slid it in front of Jase. He flipped it open to the photos of the victim. Pale, emaciated, eyes sunken in, Chrissy Gallagher looked nothing like her older sister.

"Cause of death was blunt force trauma," Maxwell said. "She was very badly beaten. There was bruising on the torso and face, but it was a blow to the head that killed her. Looks like it was made with a bat of some kind, or something shaped that way."

"What else?"

"Needle marks indicate heavy drug use. Multiple fractures and contusions, some several years old, others recent."

Jase looked up. "She left home at sixteen, been missing two years. The cops told Kathryn that Christina was a prostitute." He looked down at a photo of Chrissy's bruised and battered body. "Whoever was pimping her out wasn't kind." He glanced over at the doctor. "What about DNA?"

"No skin under her nails, nothing like that. Probably too drugged up on heroine to fight back."

"Recent evidence of sexual intercourse?"

"No semen. The guy used a condom, so again no DNA, but there was a great deal of bruising around the vagina."

"So the sex wasn't for pleasure."

"Not unless she liked it rough, which could be the case. There were ligature marks on her wrists and ankles. Both old and new."

Jase frowned, thinking of the pretty young girl who had left home at sixteen and the broken young woman in the photos. "Maybe she wasn't working the street by choice."

Maxwell pushed his black-rimmed glasses up on his nose. "It's possible."

"She was young when she left home. She would have been a likely candidate for trafficking."

"It's also possible being tied up was her specialty. Johns pay extra for certain kinks." Maxwell sifted through the photos, pulled up one Jase hadn't noticed. "She had an interesting tattoo on her neck right here." He pointed to a photo. "Red. Just behind her left ear."

"Shaped like a pair of lips…or more like a red lipstick mark left from a kiss." Jase pulled out his cell and took a photo of the tattoo. "Ever seen a tat like that before?"

"No."

He went through the rest of the file, his mind spinning with possibilities. None of them good. He wished he didn't have to tell Kate.

He stood up from his chair. "Thanks, Doc. I appreciate your help."

"No problem."

Jase left the building. Maybe there was more going on here than a john roughing up a whore and accidentally killing her, he thought. But first, he needed to talk to Detective Benson.

THE DALLAS POLICE station on Lamar in downtown Dallas was a fifteen-minute drive on I-35 from the medical examiner's building out on North Stemmons. The female officer working the front desk called upstairs so Benson knew Jase was coming. He crossed the bull pen, waved to a couple of cops he knew on his way to Benson's desk.

"Maddox." The detective didn't bother to stand. "Since when are you working a murder case?"

"The client's a friend. The dead girl's her sister."

Benson grunted. "Kathryn Gallagher—the royal pain in the ass. It's her, right?" Benson was one of those people who was always in a bad mood. It fit with his perpetually wrinkled suit, and the lines in his face that made him look like an English bulldog.

"It's her," Jase said, his own irritation growing.

"Figures."

"Why? Because you know what a pain in your ass I'm going to be if you don't give me what I need?"

"Take it easy. What do you want to know?"

"I'd like to look at the file."

"Not gonna happen."

"Fine. I talked to the coroner. Cause of death was blunt force trauma."

"That's right, she was beaten to death. Probably a john who got carried away."

"Maybe. She had a tattoo of a kiss on her neck. You ever seen one like it?"

"No."

"ME says there wasn't any semen so no DNA."

"Nope."

"What about prints?"

"Remains sat outside all night. It was rainy, muddy. Got nothing we could use."

"Where was the body found?"

"Old East Dallas. Alley behind Mean Jack's. You know it?"

"I know it. That the primary crime scene or was she killed somewhere else?"

"The body was moved. We haven't found the primary yet."

"What about her phone? Did you find it?"

"No. She had a webpage with a customer contact number. Number belonged to a burner."

"Give me the number."

Benson looked down at the file and rattled it off.

"Anything else? What about a john in the area who liked to knock girls around?"

"We've banged some doors, talked to a few people in the neighborhood, working girls, couple of pimps. Came up with squat. If they knew her, they aren't saying."

"She had ligature marks on her wrists and ankles. Maybe the girl was being trafficked. You find anything that points in that direction?"

"Look, Kathryn Gallagher might not want to face it, but her sister was a whore. She wasn't tied up in some basement somewhere."

"What makes you so sure?"

"If there was a trafficking ring in the area, we would have heard something by now, seen some kind of evidence. The girl was working the streets and one of her johns killed her, which means we've got one less hooker to worry about. Maybe we'll come up with something that'll lead us to the guy who offed her, maybe not. Either way, the only one who cares is Kathryn Gallagher."

"You're a real piece of work, Benson. You know that, right?"

The detective just smiled. "I'll let you know if we get a break in the case."

"You do that." Jase walked out of the bull pen. He liked Roger Benson even less now than he had before he walked in, but he wasn't surprised at the detective's lack of interest. The homicide division had a shit ton of cases to solve. A prostitute's death wasn't a high priority.

If Kate wanted answers, she had made the right decision in coming to The Max. An even better decision when she had hired him for the job.

Now all he had to do was stay focused, think with his big head instead of his little one. At least until he had solved Chrissy Gallagher's murder.

CHAPTER FIVE

THE INTERCOM BUZZED in Kate's apartment at eight o'clock that evening. After the stress of the day, she was beyond bone-tired. For an instant she wondered if Maddox would show up without calling. *Surely not.*

She hit the button and heard the voice of the security guard in the lobby. "Good evening, Ms. Gallagher. Mr. Bradley is here to see you." The guard knew Andrew Bradley. Kate had dated him for nearly a year.

Her stomach knotted. She and Andrew had "taken a break from each other" six months ago. They needed a little time apart, he had said. Kate had taken the breakup badly. He had dumped her, no matter what he called it.

At the time, Kate had been hurt and upset. But two weeks after the breakup, she'd been amazed to discover the emotion she was mostly feeling was relief. She hadn't realized how controlling Andrew had been, how restricted her life had become.

The only parties they attended were those Andrew deemed important to their careers. He carefully chose which couples they spent time with, who was invited over for dinner, which charity benefits they attended. Kate had to be careful, he said, to protect her business image. It was understood she was not to drink more than a glass or two of wine when they went out, and they had never gone dancing.

After Andrew left, she felt as if she'd been let out of

a cage, that her life was once more filled with unlimited possibilities. She felt free as she hadn't since before she had met him.

When her two best friends, Cece Jacobs and Lani Renton, asked her to go to the Sagebrush Saloon, she agreed. She had always loved country-western music, but according to Andrew, it wasn't good for her to be seen in those kinds of places. The first time she joined them, she drank tequila and danced till midnight. It was the best time she'd had in years.

The three of them began to meet regularly on Friday nights. Kate had even gone to the bar by herself a couple of times—as she had at the end of the worst day of her life. The night she'd met Jason Maddox.

Her body flushed with heat just thinking about him and what they had done.

"Ms. Gallagher?" the guard repeated over the intercom, jerking her back to the present.

Kate took a deep breath. She had said goodbye to Andrew six months ago. She had no interest in seeing him again. But Andrew Bradley was CFO of Capital Management, a company that sent her a good deal of business.

"Send him up," Kate said.

Her nerves stretched taut as she awaited his arrival. When his knock sounded, she took a deep breath, pasted on a smile and pulled the door open. "Hello, Andrew."

"Kate, it's so good to see you." He leaned over and brushed a kiss on her cheek, closed the door behind him. "I've missed you." He was six foot two—tall, she'd thought, until she'd met Jason.

"Have you?"

"Of course I have." With his black hair and brown eyes, he was handsome, with a trim, athletic build, a smart man, and always perfectly groomed. "You look even more beautiful than the last time I saw you."

In a pair of stretch jeans and a Dallas Cowboys T-shirt? Hardly. Andrew always expected her to be as well groomed as he was. "If there was something you needed, Andrew, you could have called."

"Actually, I called your office this afternoon. Your assistant said you were taking some time off. She said your sister had passed away. I wanted to be sure you were okay."

There was something more. She could see it in his calculating dark eyes. "That was kind of you, Andrew."

"I know you and your sister were never close, but losing a family member is always painful."

"Yes, it is. I appreciate your stopping by." She didn't move away from the door. She had no intention of spending the evening with him.

"I could use a drink. Considering the circumstances, you could probably use one, too."

He wanted to stay. And Kate had a feeling she knew why. She didn't budge from the entry. "I'm sorry. I'm not really in the mood for conversation."

He reached out and took hold of her hand. "I came for another reason, Kate. I was hoping—now that we've had some time apart—you've realized what a good thing we had. I know I have. As I said, I've missed you. I came here hoping I could convince you that we should start seeing each other again."

Kate almost laughed. "That isn't going to happen, Andrew. We're over. I've moved on. I thought you had, too."

He looked surprised. "So you're seeing someone else?"

Before she had time to answer, the intercom buzzed again.

"Busy night," Andrew said grimly, clearly unhappy with his plans being interrupted.

Kate hit the intercom button. "Yes, Gordy?"

"Ms. Gallagher, there's a Jason Maddox here to see you. He isn't on your approved visitor list, but he says you're expecting him. Is it all right to send him up?"

She looked at Andrew and caught his irritated expression. He'd been so sure she would take him back. He'd been certain she'd been pining for him for the last six months. He probably needed a bedmate, at least until he found someone new.

She thought of Maddox and the look on Andrew's face when Jason walked into the apartment.

"Send him up," she said.

JASE STEPPED OUT of the elevator on the tenth floor of the condo building nicknamed the Glass Menagerie because it was mostly glass. He reached up to knock on Kate's door, but it swung open before he had the chance.

"Jason! Come on in."

He was surprised at the friendly greeting. He hadn't called first because he thought she might not want to see him again so soon. She didn't want to get involved on a personal level. Jase didn't blame her. They'd probably both be better off if she stayed the hell away from him.

Kate smiled at him a little too warmly, and he noticed there was someone else in the room. He caught the look on her face as she turned to the black-haired man in the expensive pin-striped suit, and Jase had a feeling he understood.

"Jason, this is Andrew Bradley. He's an old...friend." *Once, maybe*, Jase thought, *not anymore*. "We haven't" seen each other for a while. He dropped by to pay his respects on the death of my sister." When Kate took Jase's arm and led him farther into the living room, he knew he had read the situation correctly.

"Andrew, this is Jason Maddox." She didn't move away or drop her hold on his arm. "We're working together to find my sister's killer."

The guy's black eyebrows shot up. "Killer? Your sister was murdered?"

"That's right," Kate said. "Jason is helping me find out who did it."

Andrew turned to Jase and drilled him with a glare. "What are you? Some kind of private detective?"

Jase just smiled. "Close enough. Mostly I'm a bounty hunter. Kate wants to find her sister's killer. Finding people is what I do."

Andrew looked like he was going to choke on his own saliva. "You can't be serious, Kate. If your sister was murdered, you need to let the police handle it, not some muscled-up cowboy who hunts people down and drags them out of their houses in the middle of the night."

Jase glanced down at his cowboy boots, and Kate's eyebrows went up. He wondered if she thought he was going to go for good ol' Andrew's throat.

"It's a little more complicated than that," he drawled, letting his gaze drift intimately over Kate just to irritate the guy a little more. "Since Kate and I were already… acquainted, it was only logical she come to me for help."

Andrew's face turned beet red. "I can't believe this."

"Believe it," Jase said, moving even closer to Kate.

"We need to talk, Kate," Andrew said. "I'll call you tomorrow."

Kate made no reply, just walked over and opened the door. "Thanks for stopping by, Andrew."

He stepped out into the hall, and Kate closed the door behind him. As she returned to Jase, the corners of her mouth tipped up. "Thank you for that."

"Old boyfriend, I take it."

"We broke up six months ago. He wants us to start seeing each other again."

Jase didn't like the sound of that. He had no hold on Kate, and yet he felt strangely possessive. "That what you want?"

She shook her head. "Not a chance."

He relaxed. "Good choice. Somehow I can't see this guy with the girl I danced with at the Sagebrush Saloon."

"You're right. We don't fit. It took me a while to figure that out."

"He's a good-looking guy. Probably successful. I can see why he'd appeal to a woman."

"We're both business people. That's what kept us together. But he wasn't interested in the person I really am."

But I am, Jase thought. He didn't say it. They had a murder to solve first. "I talked to Detective Benson and the medical examiner, Dr. Maxwell. I thought you'd want to know what I found out."

She nodded. "You want a beer or something?"

"A beer sounds good."

While Kate went into the kitchen, Jase checked out her Uptown, loft-style apartment. Hardwood floors, high ceilings, walls of glass that looked out over the city. The views were spectacular.

"Nice place," he said as she handed him a Lone Star. But a little too exposed for him. He didn't like people looking in his windows, even if they were ten stories above the ground. Too many years in the marines, too many guys dead from snipers bullets.

She led him into the living room, and they sat down on a cream sofa trimmed in black in front of a glass-topped coffee table. The place was modern, and it looked expensive, though he knew the building was older, not as high rent as Kate had managed to make the apartment appear.

"You talked to Benson and Dr. Maxwell," she said, picking up the conversation where they left off. "What did they tell you?"

"You sure you're ready to hear this, Kate? Because the facts in this case are going to be brutal."

"I know," she said softly. "I've thought about it. Whatever the facts, they can't be worse than what I'm imagining. I need to know what happened. I need to know the truth."

Jase tipped up his beer and took a long swallow, set the bottle down on a black granite coaster. "When I was going over the info, a couple of things stood out to me. First, the body was found in an alley behind a bar called Mean Jack's. It's in Old East Dallas. But Benson said she was killed somewhere else."

"Do they know where?"

"Not yet." He filled her in on what the police had done so far, which wasn't all that much. "Second, she was badly beaten, but the actual cause of death was blunt force trauma from a blow to the head. Doc says the weapon could have been a bat or a club of some kind, something like that. That doesn't sound like a john to me, even one who likes his sex rough. They get their jollies out of beating a woman, but they aren't usually trying to kill her."

"So you think there was a different motive? Not just a john who got violent?"

"I think it's possible. Although it could be the john was a regular. Maybe he got jealous, didn't like her turning tricks with other men. That kind of thing." It could have been a lot of things, but he didn't want to overwhelm her.

"We need to know more about your sister," he said. "To do that, we need to dig up as much info as we can, then talk to people she might have known or worked with."

"Other prostitutes, you mean."

"That's right. And anyone else who might have known her. But there are things we might be able to learn about her on the internet. Benson mentioned Chrissy had a webpage for Tina Galen. I didn't press him about it. I figured we could find it ourselves. You got a computer?"

"Of course. It's in my home office." She got up from the sofa and led him down the hall. As they passed the master bedroom, Jase glanced inside to see a room filled with pink. Pink draperies, a pink ruffled bedspread piled with pink throw pillows. The dresser was covered with pink knickknacks. There were even a couple of pink stuffed animals on one of the shelves.

"There you are," he said with a grin. "The Kate I danced with at the saloon. That's your bedroom, right?"

Kate looked back at him, her face turning a shade that matched the drapes. "So I like pink. So sue me."

He smiled. "I like it, too, honey. It suits you."

She looked at him as if he couldn't have said anything that would please her more. "Andrew hated pink. I redid the bedroom after we broke up."

Nothing turned him on more than a smart, feminine woman. "That when you got the Camaro?"

"As a matter of fact, it is. I was sick to death of the Prius."

Jase bit back a laugh. He could imagine Kathryn driving a Prius but not Kate. As she continued down the hall, he took in her perfect round ass in the tight-fitting jeans and ignored a rush of heat that went straight to his groin.

Her office décor mirrored the sleek ivory and black of the living room. She sat down and booted up her computer, brought up Google, and they went to work.

"Let's start with Christina," Jase suggested. "She was in high school before she ran away. Her social media might still be on the web."

"It is," Kate said. "I checked periodically to see if she'd posted something that might give me a clue where to find her."

"That was smart."

"She never posted anything after the day she left home."

"She didn't want to be found."

"No. She hated living in Rockdale. She wanted to be a city girl."

"I guess she got her wish."

Kate glanced away. Exhaling deeply, she turned back to the computer and pulled up her sister's Facebook page. The photo of Chrissy looked exactly as Kate had described her. A young, fresh-faced blonde with big blue eyes and a wide, innocent smile.

They checked her Twitter account, Instagram, Pinterest, Tumblr, Snapchat, everything teenagers liked to use. The postings on those accounts all stopped two years earlier, when Chrissy had run away.

"You got a good firewall on this thing?"

"Exceptional," she said. "I've seen what can happen to a business that doesn't keep up with the changing times."

"Let's look up Tina Galen."

Kate started typing. Tina Galen wasn't hard to find. She had a webpage with a photo of her nearly naked, nothing but a little red swatch of lace that barely covered her.

"Oh, God." Kate looked up at him and her eyes filled. "I can't believe that's her."

"We can stop right here, Kate. You don't have to do this. You can let the police handle it."

She wiped away the tears. "You really think the cops will find the killer?"

"They might get lucky."

"That's it? They might stumble onto something?"

"I won't lie to you. The death of a drug addict and prostitute isn't a high priority. So, yeah, that's about it."

Kate released a shuddering breath and sat up a little straighter. "Then we keep going."

"Check out her contact information," Jase said, hoping for something new, but the phone number listed on her page was the same one Benson had given him. They kept searching, went back to Facebook. Tina Galen had a page there, too. In her profile picture she was wearing a skintight sequined red dress that just covered her ass and plunged so low only her nipples were covered.

Kate reached out and touched the picture on the screen. "Chrissy was always so pretty. She looked like the girl next door, you know? Like the cheerleader she was in her freshman year. Here she looks ten years older."

"Drugs will do that." And the brutal work done by a

prostitute. But he didn't mention that. "Your sister had a tattoo on the side of her neck, just behind her left ear. It was red, like the lipstick mark from a kiss."

"I didn't notice it that day at the morgue. I'm sure it wasn't there the last time I saw her, a couple of weeks before she ran away. My mother would have gone ballistic."

"I've got a friend who does ink. Tomorrow I'll go talk to him, see if there's anything he can tell me about it."

"Did he do the eagle on your biceps?"

"Yeah. I got it after I got out of the service."

"Marines, right?"

"Yeah." He didn't say he was a special operator. A lot of women were impressed by that, but he wanted Kate to like the man he was now, not the guy he was back then. Though there were times it was hard to tell the difference.

"I want to go with you," Kate said.

He nodded. "All right." So far they were just asking questions, gathering information. The danger revved when they started getting answers. They checked the contact info Tina's Facebook page and found the same phone number, then Jase traded places with Kate and sat down in front of the screen.

He typed in *Craigslist Personals*, looking for any ads that might link to Tina's webpage.

"Are you kidding me?" Kate said, shock clear in her voice. "Twenty-five hundred pages of advertisements for different kinds of kinky sex?"

"Sex sells, darlin'. Always has." He scrolled backward by date, going to the days before Chrissy was killed. They both studied the ads, but nothing jumped out.

He typed in *Erotic Services Dallas*, and dozens of

sites popped up—links to erotic escorts, strip clubs, exotic massage, sex shops. He followed a few of them. He didn't think Tina would be linked to any kind of escort service. She was too ravaged by the drugs she was using.

"Look at this one," Kate said. "'Don't pay for services. Date a married woman instead.'" She looked up at him. "I didn't know this kind of stuff existed."

Jase felt a trace of pity. "Still not too late to change your mind."

She just shook her head.

He returned to the Craigslist pages.

"You think Tina Galen could be listed in one of those ads?" Kate asked.

"It's a good place to look but with this many listings, we're going to need some help." He closed down the screen. "It's getting late." He rose from the chair. "We'll can work on it again tomorrow."

Kate led him back to the front door. She looked tired and beautiful, and he wanted to lean down and kiss her, sink into those plump pink lips. But they had a deal. He wouldn't break it.

"I'll pick you up at ten," he said. "Black Spider Ink should be open by then."

"Black Spider Ink. I've seen the sign. It's next door to the place I went with my friend Cece."

"You got a tattoo?"

Her face flushed. "Cece dared me. It was after Andrew and I broke up."

Jase's mind slid straight into the gutter. He hadn't noticed a tat in the parking lot when he'd stripped off her top, but it was dark in the Yukon. Maybe it was someplace even more intriguing. "You gonna show me?"

She shook her head. "No way. Seeing my tat isn't part of the deal."

The corner of his mouth kicked up. "Yeah, well, we may have to renegotiate. I'll pick you up at ten." Trying not to imagine Kate Gallagher's tattoo—or where he might find it—Jase left the apartment.

Forcing his mind back to business, he mentally went over the info they had so far and what they could do to add to it.

Tomorrow night, he would hit the streets of Old East Dallas, see what he could find out about Tina Galen. He'd make a stop at Mean Jack's, see if he could find a connection between the bar and the body that had been dumped in the alley behind it.

In the meantime, he'd try not to remember how good Kate looked in a pair of tight-fitting jeans.

CHAPTER SIX

KATE AWOKE AT the first gray light of dawn. As she tossed back the covers, she realized the sheets were damp, her body hot and tingling all over. She wasn't sure what she'd been dreaming about, but she had a hunch it had something to do with Jason Maddox.

The man was sex personified, from the top of his thick dark hair, cut not-quite military short, to the soles of his size thirteen cowboy boots. She would never forget the look on Andrew's face when Jason had walked through the door.

She owed Maddox for the favor, even though he had clearly enjoyed every moment of Andrew's discomfort. Counting the night in the parking lot when she had cried on his shoulder, it was the second time he had come to her aide.

She sighed as she rolled out of bed. If they didn't have a business relationship, she might consider sleeping with him, just see if it was as good as she imagined. She'd never been interested in one-night hookups. If it hadn't been for Chrissy's murder, she wouldn't have come close that night at the Sagebrush Saloon.

Maybe finishing what she had started that night would get Maddox out of her system. *Maybe.* But until the man who had murdered Chrissy was behind bars, that wasn't going to happen. She needed to focus and so did he.

Which meant she shouldn't continue to let him call her *honey* or *darlin'* or anything else. Wasn't there some kind of feminist taboo about that? Then again, Maddox didn't seem like the kind of guy who gave a rat's behind about taboos.

And the truth was she kind of liked it. Andrew had never used endearments. He thought they were demeaning. She wouldn't like it in a work environment, but when Jason used those terms, it made her feel feminine.

Blocking any more thoughts of him, Kate went into the kitchen and brewed herself a cup of coffee, then showered and dressed for her visit to Black Spider Ink, choosing black skinny jeans, knee-high, mid-heeled black boots, and a silky white wrap-top that showed a little cleavage. Hey, she was going with Hawk Maddox. There was no rule that said she couldn't look good.

She walked into her home office and sat down at her computer. Thinking of the websites they had visited last night, she was glad she had first-rate virus protection. She cleared her search history so she wouldn't have pornographic websites popping up all over the computer, then typed *Jason Maddox* into the Google search bar—as she had meant to do last night before Andrew had showed up.

Maddox had a Facebook page, but there wasn't much on it beyond a basic profile. He was thirty-three years old, born in Lubbock, went to community college before joining the marines. Currently he worked at Maximum Security as a licensed investigator and bail enforcement agent.

Clearly he didn't use Facebook for social purposes. She figured it was a tool to gain access to other pages where he searched for information on the people he hunted.

Curiosity kept her digging. She followed links on Google to articles about him, captures he'd made and the bounties he had collected, which were often surprisingly large.

There was an article in the *Houston Chronicle* about a serial killer he had arrested called the Alpha Man who had escaped from a police vehicle on its way to his sentencing hearing. Maddox had tracked him through a connection to a half brother unknown to authorities. The arrest had earned him a two-hundred-fifty-thousand-dollar reward.

In the *Lubbock Avalanche-Journal*, she found a photo of Jason in marine dress blues, so handsome it made her toes curl. The article mentioned he'd been an honor student at South Plains College in Lubbock, graduating a year early to join the marines, where he'd been honorably discharged from special operations after being wounded in action. He'd received a silver star and a purple heart.

Wow, she thought, and leaned back in her chair. An honor student. Which made sense. You had to be tough to get into special ops, but you also had to be smart. Her friend Cece's uncle was a navy SEAL. He spoke five languages and was an expert in communications, everything from Morse code to satellite systems.

Apparently Jason Maddox was a lot smarter than the muscled-up cowboy Andrew had dismissed him as. Kate found herself grinning.

She glanced at the clock, grabbed her cell and phoned her office. Her assistant, Laura Delgado, picked up the phone.

"Hi, Laura. Everything under control?"

"Bruce got that consulting job with Mission Textile he's been after. He'll be starting tomorrow." Bruce Bernstein was one of the two consultants who worked for her. Robin Murdock was the other.

"That's great news. I'll call and congratulate him later."

"Other than that, it's business as usual," Laura said. "I'll let you know if anything important comes up. In the meantime, you don't have to worry about coming back until you're ready."

She thought of Chrissy lying dead on a slab in the morgue, the reason she was taking time off, and tears burned her eyes.

"Thanks, Laura." Kate ended the call and blinked back the wetness.

They would be continuing the search again today. If she was going to succeed, she couldn't start crying every time she thought of what had happened. If she wanted to find Chrissy's killer, she needed to keep her emotions out of the equation or she would be a hindrance to Maddox's investigation instead of a help.

She was getting ready leave when the intercom buzzed. She checked the time, ten o'clock, and her stomach floated up. Maddox was in the lobby.

Kate took a deep breath, grabbed her purse and headed for the door.

JASE PARKED THE Yukon in front of Black Spider Ink on Main in Deep Ellum. He and Kate both walked up on the sidewalk in front of a window with a big black widow etched into the glass.

"I hate spiders," Kate said, shuddering. "Just looking at a picture of one gives me the creeps."

"I've seen some as big as dinner plates," Jase said.

"When you were in the marines?"

"Yeah."

"Where were you?"

"West Africa." He didn't say which country. He didn't talk about his deployments except in generalities. "Mostly I was in Afghanistan." He pulled open the door and waited for Kate to walk inside. She was wearing a pair of black skinny jeans tucked into tall black boots, her golden hair loose around her shoulders. She looked good. Damned good.

He noticed a couple of bikers watching her. He hoped the fat guy leaning against the wall didn't say what his lewd expression said he was thinking. Jase didn't want an excuse to smash a fist into the guy's ugly face.

"Keep going," he said. "Will's in the back." The place was clean, not cluttered like a lot of tattoo parlors, but the walls were covered floor-to-ceiling with framed photos of tattoos done by the ink artists who worked there.

Jase paused to look over the designs, but didn't see any red lipstick kisses like the one behind Chrissy Gallagher's left ear. He flicked a glance at a bearded biker waiting for his turn in one of the chairs and set a hand at Kate's waist, urging her toward the booth at the back of the parlor.

The owner, Will Rizzoli, was a skinny guy with a zillion tattoos, prematurely silver-gray hair and a long pointed nose that fit his narrow face.

"Hey, Hawk! Dude, it's good to see you!"

"You, too, man." They did a handgrip, leaned in and brushed shoulders. "Kate, this is Will Rizzoli. He's a good friend and a true artist."

Kate smiled. "It's nice to meet you, Will." Her glance went to the sleeve of tattoos on each of Will's long arms, mostly landscape scenes of waterfalls and ocean waves crashing up on the beach. "Your work is amazing."

Will smiled shyly. "Thanks." His gaze went over Kate in a professional scan of her body. "You've got nice skin. I could design something special for you, anything you wanted."

"Thanks. I'll...um...give it some thought."

Jase figured she would pass—one tat was probably enough for Kate. He'd caught a glimpse of her wild side at the Sagebrush, but the woman who owned Gallagher and Company and dressed in business suits had a conservative side, as well. He was a little surprised to find both sides appealing.

"So what can I do for you?" Will asked him. "You ready for something new?"

"I need information, Will." He took out the photo of the tattoo he had taken at the morgue, and held it up for his friend to see. "Look familiar?"

"Is that a...*body*?"

"Yeah. The girl was murdered. We're trying to find the guy who killed her. We were hoping the tattoo behind her ear might give us a lead."

Will looked down at the picture on Jase's iPhone. "The kiss tattoo isn't that uncommon. Lot of women have them. But I've never seen one placed behind an ear."

Jase pocketed the phone. "Any idea who might have done the work?"

"Like I said, it's a fairly common tat. Could have been anyone. No real skill required to put it there."

"You said the location is unusual," Kate said. "Maybe that could turn out to be something?"

"Could be. I guess investigating a crime, you never know what's gonna be useful." Will smiled at Kate. "If you change your mind about that tat, I'll give you a good deal. Any friend of Hawk's and all that."

Kate smiled back. "I'll remember that."

Jase led her outside and they climbed into the Yukon. "What's next?" Kate asked.

He cranked the key and fired the engine. "I've got a friend. She's a genius at digging up info. I called her this morning. She's expecting us."

Tabitha Love, The Max's computer whiz, lived in Richardson, not far from the university. He could have phoned but he preferred to stop by, reinforce personal connections whenever he could.

After a thirty-minute drive, he pulled up in front of an older redbrick single-story house. They got out of the car and walked up on the porch, and Tabby opened the door.

"Hey, Hawk. Come on in."

Jase looked at Kate. "Tabitha Love, meet Kate Gallagher."

Tabby smiled. "Nice to meet you, Kate." Both women stood around five-nine. While Kate's hair was long and golden blond, Tabby's was black, cut short, sheered on the sides and moussed on top. A silver hoop glittered in one dark eyebrow, and a row of tiny hoops circled the side of one ear. When she smiled, a tongue stud flickered.

"Nice to meet you, too," Kate said.

Tabby was unique in every way, and one of the smartest people he had ever known. They followed her into a living room that needed another window, decorated in a thrift shop version of chic. Tabby kept walking, leading them across the brown shag carpet down the hall to her bedroom office, which was exactly the opposite of the rest of the house, ultramodern, with the best computers and high-tech equipment money could buy.

"Welcome to my humble abode," Tabby said to Kate. "Jase told me about your sister. I'm sorry for your loss."

"Thank you."

He didn't generally reveal a client's personal information, in this case that the dead girl was Kate's sister. But Tabby was practically family, someone he trusted.

She turned to Jase. "What can I do to help?"

"We know Chrissy Gallagher was using the name Tina Galen. The cops never found her phone, but we got her contact number off her website. Detective Benson said the number belonged to a burner. He said they tried to ping the last location, but it bounced around Russia and a bunch of other countries and they wound up with zip."

"Give me the number. It might take a while, but I'll see what I can do."

"Thanks." Jase handed her a slip of paper with Tina's cell number written on it. "Also, her body was found in an alley behind a bar called Mean Jack's in Old East Dallas. Cause of death was blunt force trauma. I need the names of men with arrest records for assaulting prostitutes, preferably in that area."

"I can do that. Anything else?"

He showed her the photo of the tat on his phone. "This was behind her left ear...in case you run across a connection."

Tabby nodded. "I'll call or text as soon as I come up with something useful."

"Sounds good. Thanks, Tab." They made their way back out of the house into the bright sunlight. It was only the first week of May, but the temperature had already reached the low nineties. After the stifling heat in Afghanistan, it seemed downright cool.

"You think she can help us?" Kate asked as they climbed into the Yukon.

"If anyone can, it's Tabby. Like I said, she's a genius."

His cell phone rang just as he pulled away from the curb. Jase checked his screen and recognized Tommy Dieter's number. He put the call on speaker as he pulled into traffic. "Tommy, what's up?"

"Hey, Hawk, I got something for you on Harding. When can we meet?"

It was already past noon. "Where are you now?"

"I'm at the Mustang." A dive bar downtown.

"I can be there in an hour. That work for you?"

"That's great. I'll see you then."

Jase ended the call, signaled and pulled out to pass a slow car in front of him. "That was one of my informants. He's got info I need on another case I'm working."

One of Kate's eyebrows hiked up. "What do you mean another case? You're supposed to be working for me."

"There's nothing more I can do for you until tonight. I'm heading down to Old East Dallas. I'll stop in at Mean Jack's, see what I can find out. In the meantime, Dieter has a lead on Randy Harding. He's a bail skip lowlife I'm hunting. Beat his girlfriend and strangled her to death, missed his court date and went on the run. I tracked him to Houston, but he'd already left town. I need to find him before he hurts someone else."

Some of the stiffness went out of her shoulders. "I'm sorry. Of course you have other cases besides mine."

He checked the rearview mirror as he reached over and squeezed her hand. "You don't have to worry, Kate. Finding Chrissy's killer is my first priority. But working a case takes patience. We've talked to Will and Tabby. We're putting feelers out. We'll keep doing that until we turn up something that points us in the right direction."

Jase pulled onto Highway 75 and headed back to Dallas. At Kate's apartment building, he pulled up under the portico in front and stopped at the entrance.

Kate cracked open the passenger door. "Good luck with your informant."

"Thanks."

"I'll see you tonight. What time will you be picking me up?"

Jase shook his head. "Sorry, darlin'. Too dangerous. You'll have to wait this one out."

She gave him a saccharine smile. "I don't think so, *darlin'*. I'm going with you to Mean Jack's—that was our deal. Either you take me or I'm going by myself."

His temper inched up. "I don't think you understand how this works, Kate. You hired me to find the man who killed your sister. That's what I'm going to do. You need to stay home where you'll be safe."

Her features tightened. "I'm tired of playing it safe. I'm in this all the way. Either you're in it with me, or I'll find someone who is."

He wanted to shake some sense into her. Her sister was dead. The kind of people Tina Galen associated with were the scum of the earth. He didn't want anything to happen to Kate.

"I'm going," she repeated, and his temper cranked again. Good thing he'd never laid a hand on a woman and never would, or Kate Gallagher's sweet little ass would be in danger.

She shifted, gently touched his arm. "I can help you, Hawk. Let me do this. *Please.* I should have been there when Chrissy needed me, but I wasn't. I need to do this for my sister. And I need to do it for myself."

He heard the guilt in her voice and his anger deflated. He knew a lot about guilt. He wore a tat on his calf with the names of the three men in his unit who had died while he had lived.

The low rumble of the engine muffled his sigh of defeat. "All right, I'll take you. But you do what I say, all right? No questions asked, no arguments. Understood?"

She gave him a blinding white smile that hit him like a punch in the gut. "I'll do whatever you say. I promise." She made a cross over her heart.

She looked so cute Jase shoved the Yukon into Park, leaned across the seat, cupped her nape and pulled her in for a quick, hard kiss.

"Behave yourself, Kate Gallagher," he said, his voice a little husky. "I'll see you tonight."

Kate opened the door and slid out of the SUV without looking back. In seconds she'd disappeared through the glass doors into the lobby.

I must be out of my mind, Jase thought, somewhere in the rational part of his brain. He didn't take women into seedy sections of the city, particularly not beautiful, sexy women.

But the lust-filled part of his brain that was keeping him hard after that brief-but-incredibly hot kiss was selfishly glad he'd be seeing her again tonight.

CHAPTER SEVEN

KATE STEPPED OUT of the elevator and made her way down the corridor to her apartment. Her face felt warm and her insides still quivered. One kiss? It was impossible.

She walked into the living room, closed the door firmly and blew out a shaky breath. She didn't trust herself when it came to Hawk Maddox. She had never been this physically attracted to a man before.

Kate sighed as she headed for her home office. If she could turn back time, she would stay as far away from Maximum Security as she could get. She didn't need a man in her life. After Andrew, she didn't want the complication. Particularly not a man who drew her the way Jason Maddox did.

That attraction had been the cause of her first mistake—seducing him at the Sagebrush Saloon. It had seemed so safe at the time. A one-time hookup with a hot-bodied guy who made her stomach flutter with a single kiss. And those amazing blue eyes. She shook her head. Why not? Other women did that kind of thing.

Now she was working with him, exposed to all that hot masculinity on a daily basis till they found Chrissy's killer.

Another sigh slipped out as she sat down at her computer to do a little more research. She could handle it.

She was a grown woman. Besides, she really had no choice.

As the screen lit up, her cell phone rang. Kate dug it out of her purse, checked but didn't recognize the number. "Kathryn Gallagher."

"Katie…sweetheart, it's your father."

Her stomach instantly knotted. She could see him in her mind, a tall, slender man with silver threads in his dark hair.

"It's good to hear your voice," he said.

Her fingers tightened around the phone. She hadn't seen her father since her parents' divorce. They'd spoken a few times while the police searched for Chrissy, but her sister had left a note so there was no doubt she had run away. He had called again when her mother got sick. She had heard from him only twice since her mom had died.

"Hello, Dad."

"I should have called you when I first heard the news, but I… I just couldn't."

His words and the regret in his voice surprised her. Maybe he actually did care about his daughter, at least a little.

"What do you want, Dad?"

"I know you and Chrissy weren't close, but she was still your sister. I want to know if you're okay."

Her eyes burned. A lump formed in her throat. "No, Dad, I'm not okay. Chrissy's dead. She was murdered, and the police have no idea who killed her. So no, I'm not okay."

"I'm sorry, sweetheart, I truly am. I wasn't a good father to you or your sister. I regret that. I want to make it up to you. I'm coming to the funeral. I just need to know where and when."

"They haven't…they haven't released Chrissy's body yet."

Seconds passed. "I assume you're making the arrangements. You're handling the funeral?"

God, she hadn't even thought about it. She was too consumed with finding Chrissy's killer.

She took a deep breath. "I'll be taking care of it, yes." And now that he'd asked, she realized she wanted Chrissy to be buried next to their mother. The plot had already been paid for, once meant to be for her dad—which was never going to happen now. "I'd like her to have the place next to Mom."

"Yes, of course. I should have thought of that myself. Are you…are you going to be all right?"

"I've always been able to take care of myself, Dad. I'll be fine."

"All right, then. Just call and let me know what day the service is going to be held, and I'll be there."

"You don't need to do that. Rockdale is a long way from New York."

"I want to see you, sweetheart. It's been far too long."

"You're married, Dad. You have a family. I'm all that's left of your old life." The lump returned to her throat. "I understand, I really do."

"Katie, listen to me—"

"I've got to go, Dad. I'll email the date and time." She hung up before he could say anything more. Fresh tears threatened. She told herself to compartmentalize. She had learned to do that over the years, separate the parts of life that needed to be dealt with now from the painful parts that could be dealt with later. At the moment, she needed to compartmentalize the loss of her sister, separate the Chrissy of the past from Tina Galen,

the woman who had lived on the streets and been bru-
tally murdered.

She could do it, she told herself. Just like with Maddox. She didn't really have any choice.

JASE SHOVED OPEN the door to the Mustang Bar and
stepped into the darkened interior. He took a moment
for his eyes to adjust before walking farther into the
room. You never knew who might be waiting, and you
never gave your enemy the advantage.

He spotted Tommy sitting at the bar, his carrot-red
hair glowing in the neon beer sign in the mirror above
a row of liquor bottles. Jase walked up to the bar beside
him and ordered a Lone Star.

"Over there." Jase pointed to an empty table at the
back of the room. When the beer arrived, he left money
on the counter for Tommy's tab and his own, and they
carried their beers over and sat down.

"What have you got?" Jase asked, tipping up his
bottle and taking a long refreshing drink.

"Got wind Harding's in Waco. Got Rosa with him.
Word is he's jacking cars and dealing drugs." Tommy
had his own information chain. In this case, someone
connected to Ray's Auto Body in Houston likely knew
someone in Waco involved in a carjacking ring.

Ratting people out for a living was a dangerous
racket, but so far, Tommy had managed to survive.

"I need a name," Jase said. "Someone to talk to when
I get down there." Which might not be for at least a few
more days, depending on what he came up with tonight.
He'd meant what he'd said. Chrissy's murder came first.

"There's a guy named Pete Rodriquez. Hangs out
at a joint called El Sombrero. That's the best I can do."

Jase slid a wad of greenbacks across the table. He

liked to keep Tommy happy. An informant who trusted you with information was worth every dime.

Jase took another long swallow of beer and got up from the table. "Thanks, Tommy." He headed for the door.

Unless the police caught up with Randy Harding in Waco, there was a good chance Jase would be able to bust him and collect the 15 percent fee from Harding's million-and-a-half-dollar bond. Just depended on how good a carjacker Harding was—how long he managed to get away with it without getting caught. Either way, sooner or later, Randy Harding was going down.

From the Mustang, Jase headed for his office, hitting the McDonald's drive-thru for a burger, fries and a Coke to quiet his growling stomach. It was late afternoon, but he still had plenty of time before his trip to Mean Jack's tonight.

The Max was humming when he walked through the door, guys working on their laptops or checking their cells. Bran Garrett waved from behind his desk, his phone pressed up against his ear. The door to Chase's office stood open. Harper, Chase's pretty blond wife, perched on the edge of her husband's desk, their heads together, the two of them laughing.

Jase had never expected to see his best friend happily married. For years, the Garrett brothers had been the most eligible bachelors in Dallas. In a way, Jase envied his friend. But the settled-down life wasn't for him. He had never been in a serious relationship, never been in love. Until Chase and Harper, he'd been fairly sure there was no such thing.

He'd only been ten years old when his mother had run off with a pharmaceutical salesman, leaving him in the care of his drunken father. His dad had gone from a sloppy drunk to a mean one, until Jase got old enough to stand up to the big bastard. Fortunately, he'd never had to actually kick his old man's drunken ass.

He'd toughed it out at home until he was sixteen, then moved into an apartment with a friend and got a job, finished high school, then put himself through junior college. He'd graduated early and joined the marines.

Aside from his brothers in the military, *love* wasn't a word in his vocabulary.

He paused for a moment to speak to Chase as he walked out of his office. Chase liked to be kept in the loop so Jase brought him up to speed on his current cases, then walked down the hall to the employee lounge and sat at the round oak table to eat his lunch. He inhaled the burger and fries, and was stuffing the wrappers back into the bag when Bran Garrett walked into the room.

The youngest Garrett brother was thirty-three, same as Jase, same dark hair and blue eyes. Bran was about six-three, with a lean, hard-muscled build. He was former army spec ops, which gave them a bond. And they just flat-out liked each other.

Bran poured himself a cup of coffee and sat down at the table opposite Jase. "I hear you stole one of Chase's clients." Bran grinned. "I also hear she's a sexy blonde with a dynamite body. Nice work."

"We'd met before."

One of Bran's dark eyebrows went up. "That's it? 'We'd met before.' End of story?"

"Okay, I met her and I liked her. *A lot.* Her sister was murdered. She needs help and that's what I'm going to do."

Bran sobered at his serious expression. "Maybe I can help. What have you got so far?" Bran's specialty was personal protection. He was one of the most sought-after bodyguards in Dallas. Since the Garretts were rich as Croesus, he could pick and choose his clients.

He was also a licensed PI who kept his ear to the ground, same as Jase.

"Haven't got much so far." He filled his friend in on Chrissy Gallagher aka Tina Galen and what he'd been able to come up with, which was mostly a big fat zero.

"Tonight I'm going down to Mean Jack's, see if I can find someone who knew Tina, maybe figure out why the killer would dump her body in the alley behind the bar."

"You want company?"

"Unfortunately, I've already got company. Kate insists on being involved in this. She managed to con me into taking her with me."

Bran laughed. "Dude, you got it bad."

He grunted. "Yeah. Hopefully, once this is over and I take her to bed, I'll get my head on straight again. Both of them."

Bran laughed. "Mean Jack's can be rough. Not a great place to go courting."

"That's what I told her, but Kate's got a stubborn streak a mile wide."

"Just like you. No wonder you like her." Still smiling, Bran took his coffee and rose from the chair. "Let me know if you need some help."

Jase rose, too. "I will." Heading for his desk, he sat down and made some phone calls, then set up his laptop, caught up on his email and started digging on the internet again, clicking around on erotic websites to see if Tina Galen popped up anywhere interesting.

When nothing came up, he thought about calling Tabby, but she'd get back to him as soon as she could, and there were other things he needed to do.

The office officially closed at five thirty, but the men and women who worked there, being independent contractors, were in and out at all hours. Jase finally packed up and headed out to the Yukon. As dumb as it was, he was looking forward to his evening with Kate.

CHAPTER EIGHT

KATE TURNED IN front of the mirror, inspecting the fourth outfit she had tried on for her trip to Mean Jack's. Satisfied with the ultrashort silver miniskirt, silver midriff-baring top she'd pulled on over a pushup bra, and sky-high silver heels, she put away the black leggings and black leather vest she had considered, along with her high-heeled black boots.

Returning to the bathroom, she made a final check of her makeup and hair. She had teased her heavy curls into a big-hair look. Too much glittery eye shadow, too much mascara and too much rouge turned her into the hooker she was pretending to be. She figured Maddox could get up close and personal with a lady of the night, but that didn't mean the woman would tell him her secrets. But perhaps another streetwalker could get one of them to talk.

Imagining what Maddox would say when he saw her, she bit back a grin. She was sure he was going to go ballistic, but she wasn't backing down. Maddox could just get over himself.

The intercom buzzed. Jase was waiting in the lobby. She grabbed her small silver purse and slung the chain over her shoulder. Adjusting her top, she pulled it down far enough for her cleavage to bulge to near overflowing.

She grabbed a lightweight trench coat from the hall closet and put it on. She still had a business to run and an image to protect. Besides, Maddox would be easier to deal with if she revealed her outfit after they were already at the bar. *Hopefully.*

She walked out of the elevator, the coat flapping around her legs as she strode toward him. He was definitely in the game, wearing black jeans and scuffed black cowboy boots, a black T-shirt under a black leather vest with an American flag on the back.

Her stomach fluttered. The man had some serious macho working for him.

"You sure you want to do this?" he asked, clearly hoping she would say no.

"Absolutely." She turned and walked ahead of him out of the lobby to the Yukon parked out in front. She didn't think he'd noticed her heavy makeup or the way she had teased her hair, or if he had, he was too polite to mention it.

"I don't think it's going to rain," he said, eyeing the trench coat.

"I'll leave it in the car."

He didn't ask why she was wearing it. He would certainly figure it out when she took it off. Kate grinned.

They got into the Yukon and started the fifteen-minute ride to Old East Dallas.

"I dug around a little more on the internet," Jase said. "Didn't find anything useful."

"I didn't come up with anything, either."

As they closed in on their target, the area began to degenerate further and further. Run-down strip malls, seedy motels, mini-marts whose windows hadn't been washed in years. Every third building was a liquor store: Johnny's, Rueben's, an Express drive-thru beer mart. The Puff and Stuff Smoke Shop sat next to J.B.'s Pawn Shop.

Her stomach tightened as she began to notice the girls standing beneath the lights at intersections, quietly displaying themselves for sale. Every age, shape and skin tone, all dressed scantily to catch the buyer's eye.

Her heart beat faster. Her sister had been one of these girls.

"We're almost there," Maddox said.

Mean Jack's was a stand-alone, flat-roofed building with a dirt parking lot out front and a sign above the door. A gas station and convenience store with a motel behind it were the closest nearby structures. Beneath the overhead gas station lights, a couple of women strutted up and down the pavement.

The lot was full of cars when they pulled in, not all of them beaters as she had expected. A couple of motorcycles sat off to one side, older models, the paint faded and the bodies dented. There were a couple of women out in front, both dressed in short tight skirts and low-cut tops. One wore a see-through blouse that showed bare breasts under the gauzy fabric. Another wore a pair of cutoff jeans too short to cover the pale globes of her behind.

Looking at them, a customer pretty well knew what he was getting.

Jase turned off the engine and got out of the Yukon. Kate took off the trench coat as he walked around to her side of the vehicle and opened the door.

With a steadying breath, she climbed out, tugging her skirt down as her heels hit the ground. She swallowed. Another inch shorter and her butt would be showing. Her cleavage bulged over the top of her bra. For the first time, she felt uncertain.

Maddox zeroed in on her, and those blue eyes turned hard as steel. "What the fuck!" His outrage pinned her where she stood. It was the first time she had ever heard him use that word. His gaze ran over her head to foot, so sharp it could have sliced through stone.

"So I guess you don't like my outfit," Kate said with a stab at humor, hoping to diffuse the situation.

"Goddammit, Kate."

"We need answers, Jase. I'm going to help you get them."

He just stared at her, his jaw tight, fighting to control his temper.

"Give me a chance. I can do this."

He studied her face, must have read how important this was to her. Some of the tension eased from his powerful shoulders. "All right, fine, we'll try it your way. But you need to stay close and don't fight me, no matter what I say or do."

She nodded. She could do that, let Maddox establish his claim, which would hopefully be enough to protect her. But as they shoved through the door into a dark, smoke-filled interior that smelled like sweat and sour whiskey, she got her first real glimpse of the customers inside and her courage wavered.

Maddox wrapped a big hand around her waist and pulled her to his side. When they reached the bar, he lifted her up on a bar stool, caught her jaw, leaned over and kissed her, deep and hard. Shock hit her, followed by a rush of heat and a curl of pure lust.

The kiss went on and on, a hot, wet kiss that left no doubt she belonged to him—at least for the night. When she looked into Maddox's eyes, she saw that same heat and lust reflected—the instant before he turned away.

"Jack rocks for me. Tequila for the lady." Her drink of choice at the Sagebrush Saloon. In the background she heard one of the men whisper *lady* as if it were a joke. She turned to see which one, spotted a big man with a thick, square body, shiny bald head and tattooed arms bulging with muscle. He sat at a table across from a man with coal black hair, a dark complexion and a pockmarked face.

"Do not be insulting, Cueball," the black-haired man said. He was ugly. Really ugly.

"Keep your mouth shut, Paco," the bald man said.

A jukebox played but no one danced. The bar was full of hard, tough-looking men like Cueball and Paco. A bunch of leather-clad bikers sat around a table in the corner, another group huddled nearby, men who lived one step up from the gutter. There were women there, too, worn and tired from the hard life they led, but Kate didn't think they were prostitutes.

She turned back to the bartender, a reed-thin man with leathery skin. He set a shot glass in front of her. No lemon or salt, just straight tequila.

He set a shot of Jack Daniel's in front of Jason. "I remember you," the bartender said to him. "You've been in before. You're Hawk Maddox."

"That's right."

"So who are you hunting this time?"

"I'm not working tonight. I just needed some company." He reached over and cupped her breast, gave it a suggestive squeeze. Kate thought she might fall right off the bar stool. "Looks like I found it," Jase said. The gaze that met hers held a hint of humor tinged with retribution.

"Sure does," the bartender agreed. He turned to Kate. She hoped her face wasn't as red as it felt. "You're new to the neighborhood. What's your name?"

"I'm… I'm Kitty." Grasping the first name she could come up with, she smiled a little too brightly. "Like kitty cat, you know? I'm just here to visit a friend." She shifted on the bar stool and tugged down her skirt. "You might know her. Tina Galen? I heard she worked the area."

The bartender's gaze shot to Jase then slid back to her. "You haven't heard? Your friend, Tina...she got killed."

Her hand flew up to her mouth. "Oh, my God. I didn't know. What happened?"

"Don't know much about it. One of the guys on the cleanup crew found her body in the alley early one morning. Cops came sniffing around, asking questions. Far as I know, they never found out who done it."

"We were like sisters," Kate said, catching a look from Jase. "Like family, you know?" He tossed back the shot of whiskey in his glass and let her run with it, which she hadn't expected.

"Did Tina have friends in the area?" she asked. "I'd really like to talk to them."

"She hadn't been 'round here long, only seen her a couple of times. Come in with a girl named Lollie. They call her Lollipop. Works out of the gas station next door. She's there most nights."

"Thanks, I'll look her up." Kate took a sip of tequila, the burn calming her nerves and bolstering her courage. "You been real nice." She smiled. "What's your name?"

Not wanting to poach another man's territory, the bartender shot a wary glance at Jase. "I'm Dizzy. Good to meet you."

"You, too, Dizzy."

"Time to go, babe." Jase helped her down from the bar stool. "You got work to do."

Her face heated again at the lewd glance that slid over her body, but she managed to stay in character.

She smiled. "Come on, big boy. Kitty's got just what you need."

Jase wrapped a possessive hand around her waist and steered her toward the door. They had almost made it when the big bald guy named Cueball stood up from the table and stepped in front of them, blocking their escape.

"Be smart and get out of my way," Jase warned.

Cueball's mouth thinned into a hard line. "I need some fresh meat. You'll have to wait your turn."

Oh, my God!

Jase's whole body tightened. "I said get out of my way." When the man didn't move, Jase didn't hesitate, just hauled her behind him and threw a punch that landed square in Cueball's bulldog face.

The man's big head snapped back and one of his silver earrings went flying, but he just looked at Jase and grinned. Cueball swung a blow that could have been lethal if Jase hadn't ducked. He came up swinging, and this time he wasn't kidding around. He was a big man, almost as big as Cueball, and in amazing physical condition. The punch he threw came straight from the shoulder and sent Cueball flying backward over a table, crashing to the floor.

Paco charged, throwing punches, dodging the blows Jase threw, a lean, hard man, not as easy an opponent as he looked. Two more men stepped into the fray. Kate screamed as a table went flying, glasses shattered on the worn board floor—and all hell broke loose.

JASE HATED ALWAYS being right. It was a bad idea bringing Kate to a dive like this. He knew it, Bran knew it, Kate had probably known it, but the woman had a knack for slipping beneath his defenses and getting her way.

Launching a hard right hook at Paco Camacho, a well-known drug dealer in the area, he glanced in her direction. Kate was safe for the moment, but the distraction cost him. He took a punch from Paco that split his eyebrow, found an opening and drove a fist into the guy's midsection, doubling him over, took him out with a right that sent him smashing into the wall.

The good news was, he was winning. The bad news was there were half a dozen other guys ready and eager to take him on. Worse yet, a big badass black dude was dragging Kate toward the front door. If he got her outside, she was in trouble. *Big trouble.*

Jase jammed an elbow into the face of a guy with a ponytail and he went down, but two more men came out of nowhere and began throwing punches. The bartender was on the phone dialing 911, but even if the cops showed up—which in a place like this was iffy—it would be too late.

Kate was kicking and scratching, fighting like a wildcat, but she was losing the battle. The badass slapped her, and fury burned through him. Jase fought his way toward the door, trying to get to her, fear for her coiling in his stomach.

Then suddenly Kate was free and the badass dude was on the ground moaning. From the corner of his eye, Jase caught sight of a familiar figure, and relief poured through him. Bran Garrett was in the fight. Which meant the fight would soon be over.

Bran took out the two guys who were on Jase, took out a dumb fuck who thought he wanted a piece of the action. Jase finished off the guy between him and Kate, grabbed her and shoved her out the front door, staying close behind her. Bran followed them outside, kicking and punching, keeping them covered long enough to reach the Yukon.

When Kate stumbled in her sky-high heels, Jase scooped her into his arms and carried her the rest of the way. Pulling open the passenger door, he tossed her onto the seat, sprinted around and jumped in behind the wheel. Bran piled into his black Jeep Wrangler and they tore out of the lot, wheels spinning, dust powdering the air, driving hell-for-leather back to safe territory.

"You're bleeding," Kate finally said, which wasn't exactly a surprise.

He flicked her a sideways glance. "Yeah, that can happen when half a dozen sleezeballs are trying to beat the crap out of you."

"You were…you were amazing."

Some of his temper eased. She had a way of powering him down. Besides, what happened wasn't her fault. Well, not exactly. Hell, she was the hottest, sexiest hooker he'd ever seen. He'd wanted to drag her out of there himself, do exactly what the badass wanted to do to her.

"You okay?" he asked. She was shaking, a red mark on her cheek. So no, not okay.

Kate took a deep breath. "More or less. Bran showed up at just the right time. How did he know we'd be there?"

"I talked to him this afternoon, told him about your sister, mentioned we were going to Mean Jack's." His gaze sliced to hers. "He thought it was a bad idea."

Kate glanced away, a guilty flush creeping into her pretty face, making the red mark stand out and pissing him off all over again. "I…um…didn't see him, and then he was just…there."

Jase powered himself back down. "He was probably

already inside when we got there. Bran has a way of making himself invisible."

"So you guys are friends?"

"That's right. Bran's a bodyguard, former special ops. We look out for each other."

Kate glanced behind them, saw the Jeep's headlights following the Yukon. "Where are we going?"

"My place. I need to get cleaned up."

She flinched. "I'm… I'm really sorry you got hurt."

He wiped a trickle of blood from the corner of his mouth. "Yeah…we'll have to find a way for you to make it up to me."

When her eyes widened, he almost smiled. Kate fell silent and stayed that way till they got to his town house in the historic district, downtown on Marilla.

He pulled into his garage while Bran drove up out front. Jase went around to Kate's side of the vehicle, and they went into the town house through the door into the kitchen.

"Come on," he said. "I'll introduce you to your savior."

Kate stopped him with a hand on his chest. "*You* were my savior in there, Jason." She went up on her toes and kissed him gently on the mouth, being careful not to hurt his swollen lip.

Hunger roared through him, sank into his groin. Jase reached for her, but Kate backed away before he could pull her into his arms and kiss her the way he'd wanted to since she'd left him that night at the Sagebrush Saloon.

The doorbell chimed. *Saved by the bell*. For the second time that night, Bran had come to his rescue. Jase crossed the living room and pulled open the door.

CHAPTER NINE

THE KITCHEN IN Jase's three-story town house was modern and surprisingly clean for a guy, Kate thought, no dirty dishes in the sink, no trash that needed to be taken to the garbage. But Jase had been in the military, she reasoned, and the lessons he'd learned had apparently stuck.

The living room was a nice surprise too, beige carpet, navy blue sofa accented with beige and navy throw pillows and armchairs upholstered in a navy-based plaid. The coffee and end tables were pine, and an antique pine sideboard sat against one wall, everything well put together.

Unease slipped through her. She wondered who had helped him with the décor, wondered, as she hadn't before, about the women in his life. She had never really considered he might be married. Hawk Maddox didn't look like a marrying kind of guy.

"Kate, meet Brandon Garrett," Jase said as she walked up to the two men. "Bran, this is Kate Gallagher."

She thought of her outrageous hair and makeup, spike heels and bulging cleavage, and felt the heat creeping into her face. "Nice meeting you, Bran. I don't… I don't usually dress like this. We were trying to…um… get information…"

"Yeah, I figured that out," Bran said, careful to keep

his eyes on her face. She thought it was probably a guy thing, not wanting to ogle the woman who was with his friend.

"Thanks for what you did back there," Kate said. "If it hadn't been for you and Jase, I don't know what would have happened."

"Glad I could help," Bran said. He was only an inch or so shorter than Jason, maybe six-three, with wide shoulders and what appeared to be a lean, rock-solid, V-shaped body. Clearly both men stayed in top physical condition. Bran was ridiculously handsome, might have even been pretty if it weren't for the hard, edgy look in his eyes, which were a more intense blue than Jason's.

Maddox's deep voice rumbled to life. "I don't even want to think about what could have happened to you," he said. "Maybe you'll listen to me next time I tell you it isn't safe."

Her chin went up. "We got a lead, didn't we? We got the name of a woman who knew my sister."

Maddox's expression softened. "I'll admit you did good in there. Better than good." His mouth edged into a smile. "You're a real wildcat when you get riled up."

Kate returned the smile, though her cheek still stung where the guy in the bar had slapped her.

"How about a beer?" Jase asked. "I could sure as hell use one."

"I could go for that," Bran said.

"Me, too," said Kate, and they all headed into the kitchen. As Kate and Bran sat down at the pine table, Jase took three Lone Stars out of the fridge and passed them around.

"So you got a lead?" Bran asked, getting back to the subject.

Jase nodded. "Kate got the name of a woman who knew her sister."

"Lollie's her name," Kate said. "She's a prostitute who works out of the gas station next to Mean Jack's. We need to talk to her."

"*I'll* talk to her," Jase corrected. "I'll follow up on it tomorrow night."

"I'm going with you. I know you don't want to hear that, but we both know it'll be easier if I'm there."

Jase started to argue, but Bran cut him off. "She's right, and you know it. She's Chrissy's sister. If Lollie was Tina Galen's friend, that'll mean something to her. Way better odds the woman will open up and give you something you can use."

Jase cast him a hard glare. "With friends like you, who needs enemies."

Bran laughed.

Kate reached over and touched Jase's arm. Hard muscle bunched beneath her hand. "We won't be going into Mean Jack's tomorrow night, and I won't be dressed the way I am."

Jase's eyes drifted down to her cleavage. He blew out a breath. "I don't know why you bothered to hire me. You're the one making all the decisions."

"I hired you because I need your help. I wouldn't have even known about Mean Jack's if it weren't for you."

He rubbed the bruise on his jaw. "Yeah, and look how that turned out."

"Thank God you were with me tonight," she said. "I know things got a little rough, but it was worth it."

Their eyes met and held.

Finally, Jase nodded. "All right, tomorrow night we go back and find Lollie."

Relief washed through her. "Thank you," she said softly.

When they finished their beers, Bran headed for the front door. "Let me know if you need backup."

"Will do," Jase said. "But we should be all right. Like Kate said, we're not going back to Mean Jack's."

Bran waved over his shoulder as he left. Jase closed the door behind him, and went back to Kate. "You want another beer?"

What she wanted was to do was drag him upstairs to his bedroom, do what she had almost done in the backseat of his Yukon. It wasn't going to happen, though. Not yet.

"Thanks, but I'd better get home. I still have an office to run, and we'll be going out again tomorrow night." She glanced around the apartment, her interest in his life returning. "Your place is really nice. One of your girlfriends help you with the décor?"

He smiled. "I managed to struggle along on my own. I'm glad you like it."

"So no girlfriends, old or current?"

"Not at the moment. I've got my eye on a tall, sexy blonde."

Her heart jerked. She wasn't prepared when he pulled her into his arms and kissed her even more thoroughly than he had at Mean Jack's. Kissed her until her knees went weak and her mind went muzzy.

Her fingers dug into his thick shoulders and she kissed him hard, her tongue in his mouth, their bodies pressed together. She could feel his arousal, thick and hard against the fly of his jeans. She wanted to feel him inside her.

She was shaking, breathing too fast when she pulled

away. "We c-can't," she said, dragging in air. "Not yet. If…if we do, it'll change everything."

"I hope so." Jase kissed her again. "You got any idea how much I want you?"

If his erection was any measure, at least as much as she wanted him. She rested her palms on his heavily muscled chest. "Please, Jason. I have to finish this first. I can't think about pleasure when my sister is lying dead on a slab in the morgue."

He released a deep, shuddering breath and stepped away. "You're right. I'm sorry."

Her eyes met his. "Me, too."

When she started to turn away, he pulled her back into his arms. "When this is over, you're mine."

Kate looked at his hard, handsome face. "Yes," was all she said.

CHAPTER TEN

IT WAS LATE afternoon the next day when Tabby called Jase at The Max. "I got those names you wanted," she said. "Guys with arrest records in the last two years for assaulting prostitutes."

"Good work, Tab."

"Three guys look like possibles. The first two were charged with assaults that happened in the East Dallas area. All three are currently out of jail, either served their time or were arrested but never convicted. I'll send the info to your phone."

"Give me their names." He knew a lot of scumbags. It was essential to the job.

"Guy named Marco Bandini beat a hooker nearly to death with his fists just for fun. The woman wouldn't press charges. DA didn't have enough to pursue the case without her."

"Sounds like a real nice guy." And not a scumbag he knew.

"The second is a high-priced accountant named Preston Wells. Works for Crocker, Reynolds & Associates, CPAs. Good ol' Pres was into S&M. Big-time into bondage. Tied the woman up and beat her with a belt, pushed it too far and she ended up in the hospital. Because the sex was consensual and he had an expensive attorney, he got the charges dropped."

He hadn't met that scumbag, either—not yet.

"Guy number three is Terry McCollom. He liked them young, liked to put them in a studded collar, slap them around and do them doggie style. Hurt one of them pretty badly and went to jail. He got out a couple of weeks ago."

Right around the time Tina Galen was killed, which definitely made him a suspect. "I'll check them out. Thanks, Tab."

Jase ended the call and brought up the info Tabby had sent him. The last known location for Terry Mc-Collom was closest to the office, but when Jase arrived at the apartment, McCollom wasn't there. The landlord said he'd tossed him out for unpaid rent before he went to jail, and hadn't seen him since.

He mentioned a friend of McCollom's named Toby Doyle who lived around the corner, said Doyle might know where to find him. Jase paid Toby a visit and for a few bucks, the guy gave him McCollom's new address.

McCollom wasn't home, but the landlord verified he was a tenant. The day was shot, and since Jase had plans with Kate for the evening, he decided he'd go back to see McCollom tomorrow.

It was 11:00 p.m. when Jase pulled up beneath the portico in front of Kate's apartment building. He'd considered picking her up earlier, taking her out to dinner before they headed back to Old East Dallas to find Lollipop. But until her sister's murder was solved and he could pursue the attraction they shared, the less time he spent with her the better.

Kate stirred him up in ways a woman never had, arousing his curiosity, his protective instincts, his surprisingly possessive nature, and sure as hell arousing his libido.

Half the time he was with her he had a hard-on. She

was trouble he really didn't need, and yet he had promised to help her find her sister's killer. He was determined to do that no matter what it took.

He glanced through the glass front doors into the lobby as Kate stepped out of the elevator, breathed a sigh of relief that she wasn't wearing her hooker garb. Instead, she wore a scoop-neck pale blue top, and black jeans tucked into low-heeled, knee-high black leather boots.

He almost smiled. Maybe she figured the boots would be easier to run in if she needed to make another quick getaway.

Kate's long blond hair, woven into a single thick braid, swung across her shoulders as she opened the SUV door and slid into the passenger seat. He itched to wrap a hand around that sexy braid and drag her across the seat into his lap. Damn, the woman turned him on.

Reminding himself to behave, Jase started the engine and pulled out onto the road to Old East Dallas. He glanced over at Kate. She looked tired. But then, bar fights with an army of drunks had a tendency to wear you out.

"Rough day?" he asked.

Kate sighed. "Andrew came by to see me."

Jase tensed. He didn't like Andrew Bradley. He liked him hound-dogging Kate even less. "What'd he want?" As if he didn't know.

"He asked me to go to the Dallas Symphony on Saturday night. Mozart's Piano Concerto."

He cocked a dark eyebrow. "You into that kind of thing?"

"I enjoy classical music." She grinned. "I'd rather go country-western dancing."

Jase smiled, told himself he didn't feel a sweep of

relief. "Good to know." His gaze slid back to the road. "So, you going out with him?"

"Hell no. Been there done that. Not interested in doing it again."

Even better.

"What about you?" Kate asked. "Make any progress on the case?"

He hit his turn signal and passed a beater Toyota loping along the road in front of him. "Tabby called. Came up with three names, guys arrested for assaulting prostitutes." He told her how he'd already tracked the location of one the men and planned to see him tomorrow.

"I want to go with you," Kate said. "I want to be there when you talk to him."

She'd told him from the start she wanted to be involved. Talking to a suspect shouldn't be as dangerous as going to Mean Jack's or even as risky as what they were doing tonight. *Shouldn't* being the key word. You never knew what could happen when you were dealing with scum like these guys. On the other hand, a deal was a deal.

"I figured. I'll pick you up at ten. That'll give us both time to check in at work."

It wasn't long before he was cruising the same street they had been on last night. Mean Jack's was up ahead, the lot more than half full. Next to it sat the Sunshine Station, gas and convenience store, a run-down, glass-fronted structure with a wide awning out front that extended over a pair of outdated gas pumps. The Sunshine Motel sat behind it.

Tall lampposts in the parking lot cast light on a pair of rough-looking men who leaned against the gas station wall smoking cigarettes or maybe joints. At the moment, there were no women around.

Jase pulled up to one of the gas pumps and turned off the engine. "I don't see anyone in the store except the guy behind the counter. I'll gas up while you go see what you can find out."

She looked surprised he would let her go in by herself, but he'd rather be outside where he could keep an eye on things. He used his credit card to start the pump, jammed the nozzle into the tank and began filling up.

He glanced over at the men. He didn't like the looks of the big dark male, clearly not a customer, who appeared to be waiting for someone. He didn't like the tall, skinny dude beside him any better.

But then pimps were never his favorite people.

KATE MADE HER way to the convenience store. The Texas night was warm and damp, a moist wind drifting over the landscape. Beyond the glass door, the air smelled like lube oil and cloying perfume.

Kate walked over to the Coke machine, filled a cup with ice and Diet Coke, then went up to the counter to pay for it. Her eyes widened at the sight of a fishbowl filled with foil-wrapped condoms. A handwritten sign on one side read $.50 CENTS. Her gaze flashed to the man behind the counter, narrow-faced, with fine brown hair and a bald spot at the back of his head.

He just shrugged. "They're big sellers here."

Her stomach tightened but she managed to smile. "I'm looking for a woman named Lollie. I hear she works in the neighborhood."

His filmy blue eyes slid over her like cold grease. "I wouldn't have picked you for the type."

It took a moment to realize he thought she wanted a sexual encounter with a female. Kate raised her chin.

"I didn't see any women outside. Do you think she'll be here tonight?"

"So eager." A lecherous grin curled his lips. "Maybe a man can give you what you want. I'd be happy to try."

Her irritation grew. She propped her hands on her hips and drilled him with a glare. "I asked you a question. Do. You. Know. If. Lollie will be here tonight?"

The guy seemed to wither. "Take it easy, okay? Lollie's here most nights. Sometimes she works somewhere else. You never know with a whore." He flicked his unshaven chin toward the door. "You can ask Snoopy—the tall, skinny guy outside. He's her pimp."

The man she'd seen when they drove in. Had her sister been one of Snoopy's women, too? It made her sick to think of it. But if it were true, he could be involved in her murder.

She paid for the Diet Coke then walked out the door, saw that Jase had pulled the Yukon away from the pumps and parked it in the lot. He was standing over by the wall, talking to the two men.

The big, dark-skinned man tipped his head in her direction as she approached, but spoke to Jase. "What you need with Lollipop when you got a white bitch looks like that?"

Kate answered for him. "I'm into women." She flashed a phony smile. "Both of us are. Sometimes we like to share."

She caught Jase's flash of amusement before he turned back to the men. He pulled out a pair of twenties tucked into the pocket of his black T-shirt and handed them to Snoopy. "We'll be back to see Lollie tomorrow night."

"You sure it's gotta be her?" Snoopy asked. "Here

comes Kiki. She's an even hotter bitch than Lollie. Take good care of you both."

Jase just shook his head. "We'll be back for Lollie." Turning, he waved to the men over his shoulder as he led Kate back to the Yukon. Until that moment, she hadn't noticed the outline of the small semiautomatic pistol shoved into his front jeans pocket, but she felt better knowing it was there.

Her college boyfriend had taught her how to shoot a gun. She'd thought it might be a useful thing to learn. As she climbed into the vehicle and cast a last glance around the seedy area, she figured she might have been right.

Across the lot, a couple of working girls approached the two men, one African American, short and overweight, with frizzy orange hair, the other a young Latina. From their gaudy, barely there skirts and low-cut blouses, clearly they were prostitutes.

"You don't think one of those women could be Lollie?" Kate asked, her pulse picking up at the thought.

"Lollie's a white girl. Snoopy says she's working, pulling an all-nighter at the motel. She'll be available tomorrow night at ten. I promised him triple her usual fee."

Kate looked back at the women. The younger girl, so thin she looked anorexic, had to be on drugs. Kate thought of her sister and a soft pang moved through her.

Jase fired the engine and started to drive away, slowed before they reached the street, and Kate realized he was watching the bigger of the two men. The guy was shaking the Latina girl, slapping her again and again.

"He's hitting her!" Kate said. "We have to help her."

She cracked the door, but Jase caught her arm and dragged her back inside.

"It's part of the life and none of our business. If you want to find out what happened to your sister, you need to stay out of it. Besides, you'll only make it worse for her after we're gone."

Anger had her trembling. She took a steadying breath, knowing Jason was right. If they made an enemy of Snoopy or one of his friends, they would never get the information they needed. And after they left, her pimp might hurt the girl even worse.

The two women were standing together now, the punishment over. Jase pulled out of the lot. Kate fastened her belt and glanced back out the window.

"That guy's big and he's strong," she said. "We know Snoopy is Lollie's pimp but maybe the big guy was Chrissy's... I mean Tina's. Maybe he beat her and ended up killing her."

He nodded. "Zepeda's definitely on the suspect list. But we can't move too fast. Let's talk to Lollie first, see what she knows, find out if Eli's involved. We don't want them all clamming up or disappearing before we get the info we need."

"*Eli.* You sound like you know him."

"I know him, didn't recognize him at first. Elijah Zepeda is a real bad mother. He's half Mexican, half black and hard as nails."

Kate fell silent. They had a lot of murder suspects, and all of them were very bad news. Maybe tomorrow night, Lollie could help them narrow down the list.

CHAPTER ELEVEN

JASE PICKED KATE up the following morning, and they headed for the first stop on their suspect list—Terry McCollom. McCollom was just getting out of bed when they arrived at around ten thirty, his red hair sticking straight up, three or four days' worth of rusty whiskers on his slack-jawed face.

"Who the hell are you and what do you want?" Terry asked, scratching his bony, naked chest. At least he'd had the sense to pull on a pair of baggy jeans.

"Name's Jason Maddox. We'd like to talk to you about a girl named Tina Galen." He flicked a glance at Kate. "The lady was her friend."

"You a cop?"

"I work private."

"Yeah? Let me see your badge."

Anticipating this kind of day, Jase reached into the pocket of the navy blazer he was wearing, pulled out his badge wallet and flipped it open, displaying his PI license. Same as last night, his little .380 semiauto rested comfortably in the right front pocket of his dark blue jeans.

"Fine, so you're not a cop. What do you want?"

Jase reached back inside his jacket and took out a photo he had printed off the internet of Tina, bare-breasted, in nothing but a tiny red thong. Kate made a sound in her throat when he flashed it at McCollom, but there was no help for it. "She look familiar?" he asked.

"No. I been in jail for the last six months. Get the hell out of here and leave me alone." McCollom tried to slam the door, but Jase blocked it with his boot.

"You've been out three weeks. Plenty of time to enjoy a pretty young thing like Tina. You sure you never knew her?"

"She's blond. I go for redheads." His lips curled. "I like to pretend she's my sister. Now leave me alone."

Disgust curled in the pit of Jase's stomach. He stepped back and the door slammed closed. Unfortunately, he believed the son of a bitch. The guy liked young redheads, not blondes. When he turned to Kate, the color had leached from her face.

"Come on." He set a steadying hand at her waist. "Let's get out of here." Kate made no reply, just let him guide her back to the street, around to her side of the Yukon, and help her climb into the seat.

He closed the door and went around to his side of the car. "I'm really sorry, honey. I can see how hard this is on you. Why don't you let me handle things from here on out? I give you my word, I'll do everything in my power to find your sister's killer."

Tears leaked from her big brown eyes and ran down her cheeks. Kate wiped them away with a shaky hand. "I knew there were people like that in the world, but it's different when you actually meet them, hear the terrible things they say, the awful way they treat other people."

"Baby, you don't have to do this. Let me take you home."

Kate just shook her head. "I started this. I'm going to finish it. Let's go."

Jase silently cursed. Shoving his key into the ignition, he started the engine and buckled his seat belt.

"What's the next name on your list?" Kate asked, stoic once more.

He sighed. "Guy named Preston Wells. He's an accountant, works for a company called Crocker, Reynolds & Associates. Wells is into S&M. Arrested for beating a hooker with a belt. Hurt her bad enough to put her in the hospital. Hired a fancy lawyer and got the charges dropped."

"Crocker, Reynolds is a very prestigious firm. I'm surprised they'd have a guy like that on the payroll."

"Like I said, he was never prosecuted."

"Maybe he learned his lesson and stayed out of trouble after that."

"Guy with a serious kink usually ends up a repeat offender, but I suppose there's always a chance."

Kate settled back in the seat. "Let's find out."

Jase punched the company address into the Yukon's GPS and pulled out into the street. Crocker, Reynolds was located in a high-rise building in the 700 block of St. Paul Street. Jase pulled into the underground garage and found a parking space.

Kate rode quietly beside him as the elevator rose to the eighth floor, which was entirely occupied by the accounting firm. The doors dinged open into the plush reception area, with steel gray carpet, dark wood paneling, expensive sculptures on the tables and seascapes on the walls.

Jase stepped back, allowing Kate to take the lead. This was her kind of gig. He figured a businesswoman might get further than a bounty hunter, even if he was currently working as a private dick. And she was dressed more conservatively today, in a pair of khaki pants, sandals and a short-sleeved blue print blouse.

She headed for the receptionist's desk and gave the small, dark-haired older woman behind the counter a smile. "Hello. My name is Kate Gallagher. I'd like to see Preston Wells."

"Do you have an appointment, Ms. Gallagher?"

"I'm afraid not. I was hoping Mr. Wells might be able to fit me in. I only need a few minutes." Kate opened her purse, pulled out a business card and handed it over.

"'Gallagher and Company Management Consulting,'" she read. "I'll let Mr. Wells know you're here. Perhaps he can spare a few minutes."

Kate smiled. "Thank you."

As the woman walked away, Jase walked up to Kate. Anticipating this particular visit was the main reason he had worn the blazer and button-down shirt he had bought at Neiman Marcus. He had a fairly extensive wardrobe. When he was hunting a skip, he had to blend in. At least today he looked more like a PI than a bounty hunter.

The receptionist returned. "Mr. Wells has a few minutes between appointments. If you'll please follow me." The woman turned and started walking. Kate flicked Jase a sideways glance, and they both fell in behind her.

Preston Wells was a tall, attractive man, with thick brown hair, brown eyes and a salon tan. He wore an expensive Italian suit and didn't look anything like the pervert he actually was. Jase had no problem with a guy's personal kinks—as long as nobody got hurt.

Wells walked around his desk to greet Kate, his eyes running over her head to foot. Jase wanted to punch him.

"Ms. Gallagher? I'm Preston Wells. What can I do for you?"

"Thank you for seeing us. This is Jason Maddox. He's a private investigator. I hired him to look into the murder of my sister. She was using the name Tina Galen. I thought you might know her."

He frowned. "You thought your sister was one of my clients?"

"Actually," Jase drawled, "we thought you might be one of hers."

"My sister was a runaway, Mr. Wells," Kate explained. "She was working as a prostitute." Her mouth edged into a smile that really wasn't. "Word is you enjoy a working girl's talents on occasion."

Wells looked offended. "I don't know what you're implying, but—"

"We know you were arrested for assault," Jase said. "Beating a woman so badly she ended up in the hospital."

Wells's mouth thinned. "Those charges were dropped. What happened is none of your business, but because I don't want any more trouble, I'll tell you this just once. Heather and I were engaged in consensual sex. She liked it when I used my belt, and I wanted to give her pleasure."

"You put her in the hospital," Kate said. "That doesn't sound like pleasure to me."

His shoulders moved in a shrug beneath his expensive jacket. "Accidents happen." His gaze ran over Kate. "Have you ever been punished for pleasure, Ms. Gallagher? Perhaps your big friend, here, would do the honors. Or if you prefer, I would be happy to oblige."

Jase lunged forward, grabbed Wells by the lapels of his coat and hauled him up on his toes. Kate stepped between them, blocking the punch he wanted to throw and saving Wells a couple of missing front teeth. She set a hand on his chest, and he was sure she could feel the anger vibrating through him.

"It's all right, Hawk," she said. "Preston isn't my type. In his case, I'd prefer he was the one getting the beating."

Jase let him go. "Step aside and I'll gladly make it happen."

Kate turned back to Wells. "So you never knew Tina Galen?"

"Never heard of her. And unless she was into the S&M scene and a willing participant, I never would have."

"Where were you on the night of April 29?" Kate pressed.

"I was at a company function—which, if you'd checked with Detective Benson, you would have known."

Jase's back teeth clenched as he worked to rein in his temper. Good to know Roger Benson had actually done some legwork on the case.

"Let's get out of here," Jase said. Kate linked her arm with his, not quite trusting him not to bash Wells in the face, and led him toward the door. They didn't stop until they were back in the elevator, the doors sliding closed behind them.

"Do you think Wells was telling the truth?" Kate asked.

"So far there's no evidence to suggest Tina was into the S&M scene. According to the ME, the cause of death was blunt force trauma. Looks more like killing her was some sort of retribution or maybe someone was delivering a message."

"Punishment or a message," Kate said. "Like what Eli Zepeda was doing to that girl at the station."

"Could be." He pressed the button for the parking garage, and the elevator began its decent.

"Which brings us back to Tina's pimp," Kate said. "If she had one, we need to know his name."

"With any luck, we'll find out when we talk to Lollie tonight. In the meantime, just to be sure we don't leave any loose ends, I'll check with Benson, make sure Wells's alibi's been verified."

When the elevator doors slid open, they headed for the Yukon. Since the day was pretty much shot to hell and they were planning a trip to the Sunshine Motel that night, he drove through a Burger King to get something to eat, then took Kate home.

"I'll see you later." He walked her across the lobby, couldn't resist leaning down to brush a kiss over her lips.

He ran a finger down her cheek. "I don't like seeing you with filth like that. I wish you'd let me work the case on my own."

She just shook her head. "Not gonna happen, big guy. Besides, look what an education I'm getting."

He liked that she could bounce back from trouble the way she did. He still wished he could convince her to let him handle things.

Since he knew her mind was made up, he just nodded. "Later," he said, turned and walked away.

CHAPTER TWELVE

KATE'S CELL PHONE rang as she walked through her apartment door that afternoon. She smiled at the her friend's name on the caller ID, her dark mood lifting. She pressed the phone against her ear.

"Hey, Cee, how are you?"

"I'm fine, but Lani and I have been worried about you. I knew you were taking a few days off to handle the…um…arrangements for your sister, so I was hoping you might be at home. If you can handle some company, I'm only a few blocks away."

"I'm home. Just walked through the door. I'd love to see you. Come on up." Kate ended the call, then used the intercom to let the front desk know she was expecting a visitor. A few minutes later, the doorbell rang and Kate hurried over to welcome her friend.

Cece leaned in for a hug. "It's so good to see you. I've really been worried." She was several inches shorter than Kate, with shoulder-length dark brown hair cut in a bob, and moss-green eyes. "How are you holding up?" She was pretty, with a fabulous figure.

"I'm doing okay." Kate led her farther into the apartment. "A lot's been going on. How about a Diet Coke or a glass of iced tea, or something?"

"Diet Coke sounds great." They went into the kitchen and Kate pulled two diet sodas out of the fridge. Filling glasses with ice, she joined Cece at the breakfast bar and set the glasses and cans on the counter.

Cece poured Diet Coke into her glass, sending up foamy bubbles, eyeing Kate over the rim as she took a sip. "You seem a lot better than the last time I talked to you."

"If I seem better, it's because I'm doing something to find my sister's killer. I hired a private investigator… well, he's actually a bounty hunter, but he's also a detective. His name is Jason Maddox."

One of Cece's dark eyebrows went up. "You hired a bounty hunter?"

"That's what he does most of the time. Either way, he finds people, which is the kind of help I need. We met kind of by accident at the Sagebrush Saloon. I ran into him again at The Max. It's a security company. Maddox sort of took a…um…personal interest in my sister's case."

Cece sipped her drink. "Has he made any progress?"

"Things are moving along. I insisted he let me help with the investigation. We're going out again tonight to interview a prostitute who might know something about the murder."

Cece knew that Chrissy was a runaway who had ended up on the streets. She studied Kate with speculation. "You've been spending time with this guy, Maddox, right?"

"I told you we're working the case together."

"So this bounty hunter slash detective? What's he look like?"

Kate could feel the heat creeping into her cheeks. "Well, he's…" *The sexist man alive?* "Jase is a good-looking guy, but I wouldn't have hired him if I didn't think he could help me."

Cece grabbed her purse and whipped out her cell phone, started digging around on the internet. *Jason Maddox*, she typed, her fingers flying. She glanced up. "Middle name Hawkins?"

"That's right."

"Oh, my God—that's him?" She turned the phone around so Kate could see the photo she had pulled up.

Jase, of course, looked amazing. You could even see his gorgeous blue eyes. "That's him. Hawk Maddox."

Cece's gaze remained on the photo. She pulled up a couple more, one that showed him next to a swimming pool in a skimpy Speedo swimsuit. "Wow! That dude could definitely lift *my* spirits."

Jason in a swimsuit. Kate took a good long look herself. Long, powerful legs, sculpted chest and amazing biceps. Heat scorched through her just looking at him.

Cece's gaze swung back to Kate. "Just how well do you and Mr. Hot Bounty Hunter know each other?"

Kate snorted a laugh. "I haven't slept with him, if that's what you're asking."

"Why not?"

Good question. "Because we need to solve Chrissy's murder first. But if things work out, I intend to."

"No kidding." Cece took a long swallow of her drink and glanced back down at the picture. She fanned her face. "I'm getting a hot flash just thinking about it."

Kate laughed. Cece always made her smile. "I'm really glad you stopped by."

Cece leaned over and hugged her. "Me, too." She took a drink of soda. "So fill me in on what's been happening with the case. Especially the part where you're going to end up in bed with Hawk Maddox."

Kate found herself smiling again, a welcome change

from the terrible sadness she had been feeling since she'd found out about her sister.

Kate told her about the visit to Mean Jack's, the fistfight, and the creepy men she and Jason had been questioning. Her friend seemed fascinated but also worried.

"Investigating a murder…it's got to be dangerous, Kate. Are you sure you shouldn't let the police handle this? Or maybe this Maddox guy?"

"I need to be involved. I can't just sit around and do nothing."

"I hope you're at least being careful."

Kate didn't mention her hooker outfit, or the guy who had slapped her and tried to drag her out of the bar. "Of course I am."

They talked a little longer before Cece had to leave. She managed a restaurant called The Turtle, an upscale bar and grill where she worked a split shift.

As soon as her friend was gone, Kate went back to the plans she was making for Chrissy's funeral in Rockdale.

The moment the phone was answered at the Rockdale Mortuary, any joy she had been feeling slipped away.

IT WAS LATE afternoon when Jase walked into The Max. Mindy Stewart, their receptionist, stopped him as he passed on the way to his desk.

"A guy named Tommy Dieter has been calling you all afternoon, Jase. He says your phone goes straight to voice mail, and he needs to talk to you right away. I tried to call you myself, but I couldn't get through, either."

Jase pulled out his cell. He'd turned it off before they went up to see Preston Wells. He didn't like to be interrupted during an interview, but he'd been so damned mad when he left, he'd forgotten to turn it back on.

"I'll take care of it. Thanks, Mindy." He checked his messages, saw a string of them from Tommy, punched the number and the kid picked up right away.

"Hawk, I got trouble," Tommy said.

Any guy who ratted on rats for a living was asking for trouble. Apparently Tommy was just now figuring that out. "What's going on?"

"Someone told Randy Harding I been keeping tabs on him. He's coming after me, Hawk. I don't know what to do."

Tommy was over twenty-one, but still just a kid and not the brightest bulb on the string. "Come on down to my office. I'll stake you enough to get out of town. You need to lie low for a while, till I can get Harding off the street. Once he's in jail, you should be okay."

"Thanks, Hawk. I won't forget this. I owe you. I'll make it up to you, I promise."

The call ended and Jase went back to work. He phoned Detective Benson, who verified Preston Wells's alibi. Benson hadn't spoken to Terry McCollom, or to Marco Bandini, the other name Tabby had come up with.

"From what you're saying, doesn't sound like Mc-Collom's our guy," Benson said. "I'll talk to him and Bandini, but unless the guy gives us something new, we've just about reached a dead end."

It wasn't good news, but it wasn't a surprise. Benson had a stack of murder cases to solve, and the stack grew bigger every day. A dead prostitute wasn't a top priority.

"I'll let you know if anything turns up," Jase said. If Benson didn't come up with something, he'd talk to Bandini himself. He liked to get his own take on a suspect. And he didn't trust Benson not to brush a possible lead under the carpet.

Time slipped past. Mindy left for the day, along with Chase and Bran and anyone who had plans for the evening. Jase and a PI named Jax Ryker were the only ones still working.

It was after seven when the front door swung open and Tommy Dieter rushed into the office. One of his eyes was black, his lip cut and bleeding, his plaid shirt torn and hanging open to expose his skinny white chest.

"Hawk!" Breathless, he staggered toward the desk. "You gotta help me!"

Jase rose from his chair, his gaze shooting toward the door.

Ryker also came to his feet. He moved to the window, careful not to stand in front of it to check outside. "I don't see anyone out there."

Jase focused on Dieter, who was breathing hard, his eyes darting back and forth between Jase and the door. "Take it easy, Tommy. Tell me what's going on."

"It's…it's Harding. When he found out I was tipping you, he sent…sent two of his buddies after me. They followed me out of The Liberty—you know, that little bar downtown? Dragged me into the alley and started punching me in the face. I got lucky, saw this police car and started yelling. The cops came running and I—I managed to get away. I came straight here. You said… said you'd help me."

Ryker headed for the back door. "I'll check around, make sure he wasn't followed." Jax was a former navy SEAL, six feet tall, short dark hair, built like an armored tank. A good guy Jase could always count on.

He nodded as Ryker made his way toward the rear of the office and disappeared out the back door.

Tommy glanced wildly around. "I don't think they followed me, but I don't…don't know for sure."

Jase opened his desk drawer, opened the locked box inside and took out a money clip stuffed with bills. Keeping a butt-load of informants on the payroll was expensive, but in his line of work, it was worth it. Plus Tommy was basically a good kid. Jase didn't want something bad happening to him.

He peeled off three hundred-dollar bills and handed them over. "So Harding's back in Dallas?" he asked.

Tommy folded the money with shaking hands and stuffed it into the pocket of his jeans. "I'm not sure. These guys said Randy was a friend. Said they'd heard I was passing info on his whereabouts. They started beating me, said they'd show me what happens to a guy who interferes in other people's business."

Jase didn't say what he was thinking, that the kid was lucky to be alive. From what he'd heard, Harding had some tough-ass friends. "You think he could still be in Waco?"

"I think there's a chance he is. They mentioned Ray's Auto Body in Houston. Said I shouldn't have told anyone Harding was there. Harding probably thinks he's still safe in Waco."

That was good news. Jase set a hand on Tommy's shoulder. "Come on, I'll follow you out of town. Make sure no one gives you any trouble. You got family, someplace safe you can stay for a while?"

"My sister lives in San Antonio. I can stay with her."

"Once I get Harding off the street, you should be able to come back." But currently, he was working on Chrissy Gallagher's murder case. With Tommy in danger, he might have to rearrange his priorities. Jase wasn't looking forward to having that conversation with Kate.

Ryker walked back into the office. "All clear. Nobody out there."

If Jax said it was clear, it was clear. "Thanks, bro."

"Anytime," Ryker said.

While Tommy went out front and climbed into his little red Toyota pickup, Jase went out back and loaded into his SUV. Tommy pulled into the street and Jase drove up behind him, checking his surroundings and keeping an eye on his rearview mirror as they rolled off down the road. Tommy made several evasive turns to make sure he wasn't being followed, then finally drove onto I-35 and headed south out of town.

It was dark, the wind picking up, blowing papers along the gutters in the street when Jase turned back toward his town house. He had enough time to go home and grab a bite to eat before he picked up Kate, maybe lift a few weights, burn off some of the restless energy he felt just thinking about her.

He tried not to imagine what she might be wearing to their interview with a prostitute, but his mind shot back to that night at Mean Jack's. A memory arose of the soft white cleavage bulging out of her indecently low-cut top, the short skirt that outlined her perfect ass, and he started getting hard.

Jase sighed as the Yukon rolled along. He needed to find Tina Galen's killer. He needed to take Kate Gallagher to bed and put his obsession with her to rest.

He pondered the notion. Tommy should be safe for at least a couple of days.

Maybe changing his priorities could wait.

CHAPTER THIRTEEN

KATE WORE HER denim skirt with a sleeveless pink top and a pair of sandals to their rendezvous at the Sunshine Motel. She didn't want to look like a streetwalker tonight—or any night in the future.

Jase pulled the Yukon into the lot in front of the motel, which was only two stories, a total of twelve rooms. Room 8, where Lollie was supposed to be waiting, opened off the walkway upstairs.

Jase parked his SUV in front, and they both got out. Neither Eli nor Snoopy was around, which, if Lollie was actually there waiting for them, was a relief. As they walked toward the motel, the door to room 8 on the second floor swung open, and a slender blonde woman in a short, see-through lavender nightgown stepped out to the railing that overlooked the parking lot.

Kate and Jase headed for the stairs. The woman didn't back away as they approached along the upstairs walkway.

"You must be Hawk," Lollie said when they reached her, giving Jase a practiced come-on smile. Her gaze cut to Kate, then back to him. "Snoopy told me you'd be bringing a lady to join in the fun."

At the woman's fake enthusiasm, pity curled in Kate's stomach. "I'm Kate," she said, extending a hand. "And you're Lollie, right?"

"That's right, honey. Lolita's my real name." She

accepted the handshake, clearly surprised by the gesture. She was a little too thin, her eyes slightly sunken, hair short and curly. Her fake black lashes were heavily mascaraed, her cheeks brightly rouged. She looked old beyond her twentysomething years, but she had once been pretty.

"Come on in." The woman stepped back and Kate walked into the room, Jase a few steps behind her.

Lollie closed the door, her gaze moving from Jase, who took up way too much space, to Kate, who was way taller than Lollie, to the sagging queen-size bed.

"It's all right," Kate said gently. "We aren't here for sex."

"We're paying Snoopy for your time," Jase said, "but we only want to talk to you, ask you some questions."

Relief flickered over her face, followed by wariness. "What kind of questions?"

Kate managed to smile. "My last name's Gallagher. The girl you knew as Tina Galen was my sister, Chrissy."

Lollie glanced away, her eyes clouding. "I heard what happened. I'm real sorry. I liked Tina. We were friends."

"Yes, that's what we heard," Kate said.

Jase shifted, probably feeling claustrophobic in the close confines of the tight, seedy motel room. "We're hoping you can help us figure out who might have killed her, Lollie."

The woman started shaking her head. "I don't know anything. I told the police that when they came knocking at the door."

"Do you know if she might have had a john who liked rough sex?" Jase asked.

"She might have. She never mentioned it."

"What about a regular customer who might have started getting a little too possessive?"

"Not that I know of."

"Can you tell us a little about her?" Kate asked. "My sister ran away two years ago. She was only sixteen. My mom and I tried to find her, my father, too, in the beginning. We never heard from her again. I never knew where she was until I got a call from the Dallas Police Department asking me to identify her body."

Kate's throat tightened. "I'll never forget the way she looked lying on that stainless-steel table. My sister was beaten to death, Lollie. Someone needs to pay for what they did to her."

Lollie sank down on the mattress, her hands clasped together between her thin legs. "I didn't know her for very long. We only just met a few weeks before she was killed." A wobbly smile touched her lips. "For some reason the two of us just hit it off right away."

"Sometimes that happens," Kate said, sitting down on the bed beside her. "I'm glad she had someone who cared about her."

"She wasn't from Dallas. I don't know where she came from—Tina never said. She'd only been working the area a couple of nights when Eli spotted her on the street. She was in his territory, you see? You can't just work like that on your own. You gotta have a protector."

"So Eli Zepeda became her pimp?" Jase asked.

"Eli didn't give her any choice. And the truth is, Tina needed him. She was in bad shape when she got here. She was hungry. She needed a place to stay, and…"

"And…?" Jase pressed.

"She needed a fix. Eli takes care of that for all his girls."

Kate and Jase exchanged glances. The track marks on Lollie's arms were impossible to miss.

"What else can you tell us?" Kate urged gently.

"Tina went to work for Eli, but she was determined to get out of the life. She told me she had family in Dallas." Lollie looked at Kate. "She must have been talking about you."

The lump in Kate's throat grew more pronounced. She swallowed. "I moved to Dallas before Chrissy was in high school. Why didn't she call me? I'm her sister. I would have helped her. Surely she knew that."

"She wanted to see you—very much. But she wanted to be clean and sober before she called, wanted to straighten herself out first."

Chrissy had been trying to turn her life around. Kate blinked against the tears burning behind her eyes.

"She wanted a better life, but she was murdered before she got the chance," Jase said.

Lollie shook her head. "That isn't what happened. A few days after she started working for Eli, Tina found out about the rehab center. It's a place called New Hope, a big old house just around the corner. Tina talked to the people who worked there, told them she was ready to change her life, but she needed their help. They don't take many girls, but they agreed to take Tina. The day she moved in—that's the last time I saw her."

Silence fell in the shabby motel room.

"So Tina was living in the rehab center when she was killed?" Jase asked, while Kate was still trying to wrap her head around the fact that her sister had been trying to get clean, that she had wanted to see Kate again.

"I'm not sure if she stayed there. They have strict rules. Most of the girls who try to get clean don't make it. Maybe the folks over at the center will know more about what happened."

"Did you tell this to the police?" Jase asked.

Lollie shook her head, moving her short blond hair. "Snoopy doesn't want me talking to the cops." She looked at Kate. "But you're Tina's family. I figure she'd want you to know."

Jase walked over and placed a wad of folded bills on the dresser. "Snoopy expects you to get three times your usual fee. The extra's for you."

Lollie picked up the bills and started counting. She stashed the money in the drawer and looked up at him. "Thank you."

Kate walked over and hugged her. "Take care of yourself, Lollie."

The woman made no reply. There was really nothing else to say.

Kate and Jase left the motel. All the way back to her apartment, Kate thought of her baby sister.

Her eyes burned. So far she'd been able to compartmentalize, keep the emotion she was feeling under control. After talking to Lollie, knowing her sister had wanted to reach out to her, emotion tightened her chest.

She thought of the short, terrible life Chrissy had lived. When she'd found herself in trouble, why hadn't she called home? Surely she knew her family loved her. Even if Kate hadn't been there for her, Chrissy had to know their mother loved her.

What had happened to her after she'd run away? How had she ended up a prostitute? Kate was desperate to know.

As the Yukon turned down her street, her insides ached with the awful sense of loss and grief. She blamed herself, blamed the system that had somehow failed a sixteen-year-old girl, knew she wouldn't be able to get the terrible things she had learned out of her mind, and suddenly she wasn't ready to face the long night ahead.

She wiped tears from her cheeks and turned to Jase. "Do you think you could…? Would you…come up for a while? Just for a while. Maybe have a beer or something?"

His beautiful blue eyes held a trace of pity. "I could use a beer," Jase said, though she doubted he was looking forward to such dismal company. Instead of pulling up in front, he parked in a visitor's space in the garage, came around and helped her out of the Yukon.

She rode the elevator upstairs in silence, her mind spinning with troubled thoughts. Guilt and regret made her heart hurt. If only Chrissy had called her, somehow reached out to her. Together they could have beaten her addiction. Chrissy would still be alive and she would be safe.

Her chest tightened as they walked into her living room and Jase closed the door. His eyes ran over her, took in the track of tears that had dried on her cheeks. He was standing so close she could feel the heat of his big, hard body.

"You want that beer?" he asked, his gaze locked on her face. "Or do you want something else?"

The last time she'd felt this terrible pain was the night she had met him. That night she had wanted him to take away the awful ache she felt inside. To make her forget, if only for one night. She wanted that same thing now.

"I want something else," she said softly, her arms sliding up around his neck. "I want you, Hawk. You're what I want tonight."

AROUSAL BURNED THROUGH him. Jase was already hard by the time he pulled Kate into his arms and kissed her.

She needed him tonight, and he damn well needed her. Had since that night at the Sagebrush Saloon.

He forced himself to slow down, to kiss those soft full lips, taste the heat and need he had seen in her eyes, a hunger that matched his own. Desire rose up, thick and pounding, strengthening his arousal, running hot in his blood.

His hands slid over the perfect round globes of her ass and he settled her in the vee between his legs, let her feel how much he wanted her. Her body was toned and strong, and yet her skin felt soft as silk wherever he touched her.

He kissed his way down the side of her neck, claimed her mouth again, delved deep, took what he wanted. Her fingers dug into the muscles across his shoulders, and Kate took the kiss even deeper.

He wasn't sure how they managed to reach the sofa, but it was exactly where he wanted to be. Her panties were gone by the time he sat down and pulled her on top of him, her knees straddling his lap, the powerful erection beneath the fly of his jeans pressing into the sweet spot beneath her short skirt.

He'd lived this fantasy a dozen times since she'd left him that first night, imagined what it would be like to finish what they'd started, imagined the pleasure.

He stripped her soft knit top off over her head, unfastened the hook on the front of her lacy white bra and slid it off her shoulders, filled his hands with her magnificent breasts, ached to put his mouth there. He bent his head to the task, his tongue running over the pebbled crest, laving and tasting, satisfying at least one part of his fantasy, would have enjoyed taking more time if his need hadn't been so strong.

Kate pulled his T-shirt off and tossed it away, pressed

her lips against his heated skin, trailed kisses over his chest and shoulders.

Jase groaned. Reaching between them, he unzipped his fly and freed himself, felt the dampness between her long legs. She was ready for him, and he was more than ready for her.

He managed to dig his wallet out of his back pocket and pull out a condom. Kate took it out of his hands, opened the foil packet and sheathed him. Jase kissed her as he lifted her, and she eased down on top of him with a soft, sexy purr. Cupping his face between her hands, she bent and settled her mouth over his.

Kate kissed him deep, kissed him hard, and desperate hunger burned through him. She was riding him now, slow and easy at first, then faster, deeper, harder. The lust he'd felt that night returned tenfold, and he clamped down hard to stay in control. Even those efforts didn't last long.

Kate braced her hands on his shoulders, fitting their bodies together, moving in perfect rhythm. Her climax struck, her passage tightening around him, and Kate cried out his name. Gripping her hips to hold her in place, he drove into her again and again, drove into her until she came once more.

Need clawed through him, so powerful his jaw clenched, and release hit him hard, his muscles going rigid, pleasure burning through him, hot and fierce. All consuming.

"Kate…" he whispered, saying her name like a vow, a promise of things to come.

Because one thing Hawk Maddox now knew—having her once wasn't going to be nearly enough to get over his obsession with Kate.

CHAPTER FOURTEEN

KATE AWOKE LATER than usual the following morning. As events of the night came rushing back, her gaze shot to the other side of the bed, but Jason wasn't there.

Relief filtered through her, followed by uncertainty. She sat up in bed, feeling aches in places that had never ached before. Maddox had done that, driven her to heights she had never experienced. Doubt swelled. She wasn't sure how she felt about what had happened, had no idea how it would affect the job she needed done.

Sunlight streamed through her bedroom curtains as she came to her feet, grabbed her robe and headed for the bathroom. Jason was already gone. She hadn't heard him leave, wondered if he had left to avoid the always difficult *morning after* conversation.

Whatever the reason, she would never forget the night they had shared. Instead of lonely hours filled with grief and regret, he had swept her into a night of passion, a place where sadness didn't exist, just heat and need and pleasure.

She had known he would be a demanding lover, hadn't expected him to also be generous and attentive. His lovemaking had been unlike anything she had experienced before. It was impossible to regret what had happened. Or at least not so far.

On the other hand, she had no idea what Jase would expect from her now, or if he was the kind of guy who was mostly about the conquest, the kind who would be moving on after spending a night in her bed.

The smell of coffee reached her as she emerged from the bathroom, drawing her toward the kitchen. A white mug with a yellow daisy painted on the side sat next to a freshly brewed pot of coffee on the counter. A few words scribbled on a piece of paper sat beside it. She reached for the note. Pick you up at ten, it read. Nothing more than that, nothing personal. Part of her was disappointed, though she had no idea what she would have liked him to say. Far more important, he wasn't going to ignore his pledge to help her, even if their relationship had taken a major turn.

Even if things were uncomfortable between them.

Kate poured the mug full of coffee. Whatever happened last night, Jase wasn't to blame. Having sex had been her idea. He had simply done what she'd asked him. He'd just managed to do it far better than she ever could have imagined.

Kate took a sip of the thick dark brew, which had turned strong and bitter while she had been sleeping, and grimaced at the taste. Without time to brew another pot, she carried the mug into the bathroom to shower and get ready for Jase to pick her up.

As she turned on the water and waited for it to get warm, an odd mix of excitement and trepidation slid through her. She had no idea what to expect from him. On a personal level, they needed to go back to where they were before last night, to focus on solving Chrissy's murder. They needed to talk to the people at the New Hope Rehab Center, to Elijah Zepeda, and also to Marco Bandini, the last of the three men arrested for assaulting a prostitute.

As she brushed her hair and applied her makeup,

she tried not to think about last night. When that failed, she tried to convince herself she didn't want it to happen again.

But when she walked into the living room a little before ten o'clock, she found herself in a pair of sexy skinny jeans, heeled sandals and a formfitting, cap-sleeved, scooped-neck blue top that showed some cleavage.

It wasn't blatantly sexy, but it wasn't a pillowcase, either.

Her stomach fluttered when the intercom buzzed and the front desk announced Jase's arrival in the lobby. Kate slung her purse over her shoulder and headed for the elevator. When the doors slid open, he was waiting. In jeans, boots and a dark blue T-shirt that hugged his amazing chest and showed the tattoo on his biceps, the man was definitely eye candy. A sliver of heat curled low in her belly.

His gorgeous blue eyes ran over her. "You okay?" he asked.

Was she okay? She wasn't exactly sure. She felt different, as if making love with him had changed her in some fundamental way.

"I'm ready to go to work on the case, if that's what you're asking."

A corner of his mouth tilted up, and she knew what he was thinking. "Glad I could be of service."

Memories arose of the things he had done to her, and heat rushed into her cheeks. "I'm sure spending the night with a distraught woman wasn't your top priority, so...thank you."

As they reached her side of the SUV, he caught her shoulders and turned her to face him.

"I stayed with you last night because being in your

bed was exactly where I wanted to be. That hasn't changed this morning. Neither has my commitment to finding your sister's killer." He pulled her hard against him, and his mouth crushed down over hers. Heat and wild hunger roared through her, the instant before he broke away.

"We've got work to do," he said gruffly. "Let's go."

Still shaken, her body still humming, Kate climbed into the passenger seat and closed the door. She hadn't seen things going in this direction. She hadn't been sure he'd be interested in a repeat of last night, wasn't sure he'd want to get involved on more than a superficial level.

Hawk Maddox wasn't a relationship kind of guy. Exactly the reason she had chosen him that night at the Sagebrush Saloon. After inviting him into her bed, she felt out of control and out of her depths, and she had no idea what she should do.

Her lips still tingled as Kate fastened her seat belt and leaned back in her seat. Sitting behind the wheel, Jase cast her a burning glance and started the engine.

Kate drew in a shaky breath. For the moment, she would focus on what she most needed to do—concentrate on finding a killer.

JASE FLICKED A sideways glance at Kate in the passenger seat. He hadn't been sure how he would handle the morning-after conversation he always dreaded, but the moment he'd seen the same uncertainty on Kate's pretty face, any reservations he'd had fell away.

She was no more sure what rules they were playing by than he was. He wanted more of her—that much he knew. From the way she'd responded to him last night and again this morning, Kate wanted more of him, too.

Where that would lead, he had no idea. He'd never had a serious relationship with a woman, never really wanted one. But Kate wasn't like any woman he'd ever known. She was smart, loyal, brave, and just looking at her made him hard.

He wasn't sure what to do about her, but eventually he'd figure it out. His mind shot back to the hours they had spent in bed, to finding her secret tattoo, a tiny butterfly on the cheek of her ass. He had laughed, it was so cute. Unfortunately, the tempting sight had left him with a new fantasy that involved Kate on her hands and knees.

His groin stirred and he shifted in his seat. *Not going to happen.* They had work to do.

Jase pulled the Yukon up in front of the address on Reiger he had found on the internet that morning for the New Hope Rehabilitation Center. The old gray house with white trim sat on a big corner lot with a pair of gnarled oak trees standing guard out front. The house stood two stories high, with wraparound porches on both levels.

He and Kate got out and walked up on the porch. Jase knocked on the door, and a man in his midfifties, with silver in his hair, pulled it opened. A tiny dark-haired woman stood beside him. Jase recognized the couple from their photos on the website as Jim and Vera Lockwood.

"May I help you?" Vera Lockwood asked. She looked a few years younger than Jim, a few wrinkles, not many.

"I'm Jason Maddox. I'm a private investigator. This is Kate Gallagher. We'd like to ask you some questions about a girl who lived here named Tina Galen."

The woman's expression turned solemn. "Yes, Tina was with us for a short time. How can I help you?"

"Tina was my younger sister," Kate said softly.

The woman's hand flew to her mouth. "Oh, I'm so sorry about what happened. Please come in."

They stepped over a doormat that read GOD BLESS THIS HOME and into a hallway with gleaming hardwood floors. Mrs. Lockwood led them into an old-fashioned parlor, and they sat down on a burgundy sofa with lace doilies on the rounded arms.

"We're the Lockwoods. I'm Vera and this is my husband, Jim. Would you like some coffee or perhaps a cup of tea?"

"Thank you for offering, but we're fine," Jase said.

The couple took seats across from them. Jase could hear female voices somewhere in the house and footsteps on the stairs.

"My sister's real name was Christina Gallagher," Kate said. "Jason and I are trying to find out who killed her. We're hoping you can help."

"Tina was a lovely girl," Vera said. "So sweet. And so young. She told us she was only eighteen."

"That's right," Kate said. "Chrissy ran away from home two years ago. We tried to find her, but she just seemed to disappear. I had no idea what had happened to her until the police called to tell me she was dead."

"Such a tragedy," Vera said, shaking her head.

"A friend of Tina's told us she came to you and you agreed to take her in," Jase said.

"That's right. We're a Christian faith–based organization. Jim is a minister. We focus specifically on girls who end up on the street. We don't have a lot of room, but if the girl is truly needy, willing to follow our rules and we believe she is sincerely determined to change her life, we try to find room for her." She smiled sadly.

"Your sister wasn't with us long, but she was making very good progress."

"Do you have any idea what happened?" Kate asked.

"I can tell you about your sister, but I don't really know what happened to her."

"Please…anything you can tell me will be more than I know now."

Vera nodded. "Well, I mentioned our rules. I know they may sound harsh, but we've learned they provide the best chance for the girls. The applicant must agree to stay for one full year, during which time they must forgo all family ties. They have to give up cell phones and social media. There is no smoking, no alcohol, absolutely no drugs. They completely forfeit their privacy during that year."

"And my sister agreed?" Kate asked.

"That's right. She was very sick at first as the drugs began to wear off, but she was determined."

Kate smiled sadly. "Her friend Lollie said she wanted to change her life."

Vera smiled. "Everyone here is supportive of each other. After a week or so, Tina had physically recovered from the symptoms of withdrawal and begun to get stronger. The girls all liked her. She found a particular friend in her roommate, Holly Jensen, who was also eighteen. Holly has been with us for several months, so she knows her way around. And Holly's pregnant, which gave them a special bond. Apparently your sister loved babies."

Kate's features clouded. "She collected dolls when she was a little girl. She liked the baby dolls best. Of course, I was so much older, we never really played together."

"Could we talk to Holly?" Jase asked.

Vera glanced over at her husband.

"I think in this case, that can be arranged," Jim said, rising from his chair. "I'll go get her." He walked out of the parlor, his footsteps receding down the hall.

"Have you talked to the police, Mrs. Lockwood?" Jase asked, wondering why Detective Benson hadn't mentioned the rehab center.

"Please, call me Vera, and no, we haven't. The police never came here asking questions. We didn't know anything useful even if they had. And the truth is, everything that happens here is private. We don't divulge information on the girls who live here, and we didn't even hear about the murder until several days later."

"When was the last time you saw Tina?" Jase asked.

"She had supper with us the night she was killed. We realized the next day she was gone, but we didn't know she had been killed until we read it in the *Morning News* a few days later."

"Do you know why she left?" Jase asked.

Vera gripped her hands in her lap. "It came as a complete surprise. Everything seemed to be fine at supper, then the next morning, she didn't come down for breakfast. Holly said Tina must have left the house while she was asleep."

Vera smiled sadly. "There are no bars on the windows or doors. No one forces the girls to come here and no one forces them to stay. Not all of them are strong enough to make it through the program."

"But my sister wanted to change so badly," Kate said. "Something must have happened to change her mind."

The sound of approaching footfalls ended the discussion and drew their attention to the door. A young woman with long dark hair and dark eyes followed Jim into the parlor. She was wearing a knee-length knit dress that curved over her baby bump.

"This is Holly Jensen," Jim said.

Jase rose to greet her and so did Kate. She smiled. "Hello, Holly. I'm Kate and this is Jason."

"It's nice to meet you." She didn't look like a prostitute. She looked healthy, her eyes bright and her skin clear, though Jase figured he'd find old needle marks under the long sleeves on her dress.

"You were a friend of my sister's," Kate said. "You knew her as Tina Galen, but her real name was Chrissy Gallagher."

Holly nodded. "Yes. Tina told me."

So Chrissy had decided she could trust Holly. Jase hoped that wasn't all Tina had revealed. He glanced over at Jim. "We'd like to talk to Holly in private…if that's possible."

Jim's attention swung to the girl. "Holly?"

"It's okay. Tina was my friend." She looked at Kate. "She talked about you all the time."

Vera rose from her chair, and she and her husband left the parlor, sliding the old-fashioned oak doors closed to give them privacy. Holly sat down in one of the overstuffed chairs, and Jase and Kate sat back down on the sofa across from her.

"Vera said you were sleeping when Tina left the house the night she was killed," Jase said.

Holly glanced away. "That's right." One of her hands moved down over the soft roundness of her baby in a protective gesture that was hard to miss. It didn't take a private detective to know she was lying.

"You can tell us the truth," Kate said, picking up on the gesture, as well. "You were my sister's friend.

I think she would want you to tell me what really happened."

Holly swallowed. Her lips trembled. "I can't. If…if I tell you, he'll kill me. He'll kill my baby."

Kate came off the sofa and crouched beside Holly's chair. She took hold of the young woman's hand. "We won't let that happen. We'll protect you. We won't let anyone come near you."

"You'll go to the police, and he'll find out it was me who told you. He'll kill me and my baby."

Jase rose from the sofa and stood in front of the girl. "No police, Holly. I give you my word." She looked him up and down, weighing his toughness and strength. In times like these, his size often worked in his favor.

"Tell us what happened that night," Kate pressed. "Please. Do it for Tina."

Tears welled in Holly's dark eyes and slipped down her cheeks. "It was Eli," she whispered. "Eli Zepeda." A sob caught in her throat.

"Just take your time," Jase said, sitting back down to give her some space.

Holly swallowed, her slender throat moving up and down. "Tina worked for Eli, but she wanted to quit. Eli knew she had come to the center for help. She was doing really great. She wanted to get her life back so badly."

Holly wiped tears from her cheeks. "That night, Eli broke into the house. Maybe he had been watching the place, I don't know, but he knew which room was ours. He told Tina she was his biggest moneymaker, and he wasn't letting her go. He had a gun. Neither of us doubted he would use it." Her voice shook. "I was so scared."

"What happened?" Kate gently prodded.

"Tina refused to leave. Eli was furious. He gave her

a choice. She could go with him—or he would take me instead. He could see I was pregnant, but he didn't care. Tina went with him to save me."

Holly started crying. "She died for me. Tina gave her life to save me and my baby." Her crying turned to great heaving sobs, and Kate drew her up from the chair into her arms. She wept on Kate's shoulder, cried as if her heart were breaking.

"It's all right, Holly," Kate soothed, her voice also choked with tears. "It wasn't your fault. Eli Zepeda is the man who killed my sister, and I promise you he's going to pay."

"She was my friend," Holly said tearfully. "No one has ever done anything like that for me before."

Watching the women, Jase clamped down on the rage burning through him. Elijah Zepeda was a murderer. They couldn't go to the police without evidence, and there was no way Jase was putting Holly and her baby in danger.

It didn't matter.

One way or another, Elijah Zepeda was going down.

CHAPTER FIFTEEN

"IF WE CALL the police, they'll want to talk to Holly," Kate said. "We gave her our word we'd protect her."

Maddox sliced her a glance. "No police," he said darkly.

A faint shiver moved down her spine. She should have known Jase wouldn't break his word.

The Yukon pulled away from the rehab center. The wind had picked up, rustling the leaves on the branches of the big live oaks in front of the house. It was early yet for a hurricane, but the weather bureau had mentioned the possibility.

Kate focused her attention on the road. "So what's our next move?"

"Next, I have a little talk with Eli Zepeda. But I don't go alone."

Kate stiffened. "That's right. You won't be alone because I'm going with you."

Jase shook his head. "Not this time, baby. You've seen this guy. He's bad news. If something goes wrong, you could get hurt—or worse."

She wanted to argue. She was going—whether he liked it or not. But she'd wait, pick the right time to have that discussion. "So who's going with you?" she asked instead.

Jase hit the hands-free button on his speakerphone, hit one of his contact numbers. When the call picked up on the other end of the line, Kate recognized Bran Garrett's voice.

"What's up?" Bran asked.

"You at the office?" Jase asked.

"At the moment, yeah. I'll be here awhile."

"Good, I'm on my way." Jase ended the call. Kate's attention swung back to the road, and she realized the route he was driving led to his office on Blackburn Street. A few minutes later, he pulled into the parking lot behind the brick building.

They went in through the back door and spotted Bran in the employee lounge, drinking a cup of coffee. In a T-shirt and jeans, with his dark hair, blue eyes and movie-star good-looks, the guy was seriously hot. But it was the heat of Maddox's big, hard body behind her, the memory of all those amazing muscles beneath her hands last night that had her pulse kicking up.

Jase walked over to the kitchen counter, poured coffee into foam cups and handed one to her.

"Thanks," she said, taking a sip, finding it surprisingly fresh and a lot better tasting than the stale brew she'd drunk that morning.

They sat down at the round, Formica-topped table with Bran. "So I'm guessing you got a break in the case," he said, sipping from his own foam cup.

"That's right. Looks like Eli Zepeda killed her. Broke into the rehab center where Tina was living and forced her to leave with him. She was dead the next morning."

Bran casually sipped his coffee, but his intense blue eyes said he was anything but calm. "You tell the cops?"

"Not an option," Jase said. "Tina's roommate tipped us. She's pregnant. We both know what'll happen to her if Zepeda finds out."

Bran leaned back in his chair. "It's time Zepeda paid

for some of the shit he's done. When are you going after him?"

"We need a location, someplace beside the motel, someplace we can isolate him from his crew. Soon as I figure that out, I'll be ready to go in."

"You're gonna need backup. I'll hang loose for a couple of days, give you some time. When you're ready, just let me know."

Jase nodded.

Kate leaned forward in her chair. "I might as well tell you both right now—I'm going with you. Nothing you can do or say is going to keep me away."

Jason's jaw went iron hard. "Bullshit. For once, you're going to do what I say."

"I'm going," she repeated. "You work for me, not the other way around."

"You can keep your damn money. This was never about money, and I'm pretty sure you know it." His eyes bored into her. "I need you safe. If you go with us to bring Zepeda down, you won't be."

Kate reached across the table and set her hand over his. She could feel the anger vibrating through him. "I know you think I'm being a fool, but I've seen you two in action. There's nobody I'd trust more to keep me safe than you and Bran."

Bran shifted, drawing her attention. His gaze locked with hers. "If we go after Zepeda, talking won't be all that happens. Things could get messy. You ready to deal with that?"

"Chrissy was my baby sister. Now she's dead. I'll deal."

Jase scrubbed a hand over his face and released a deep breath. "Lady, you are a definitely a pain in my ass." But the heat was gone, and there was something in his eyes that might have been respect.

Bran finished the last of his coffee, tossed the cup in the trash. "Looks like the lady is coming along." He shoved himself up from the table. "Keep me posted. I'll be ready when you are." As Bran strolled out of the lounge, Jase drilled Kate with a glare.

"You're pushing your luck. You know that, right?"

She felt the pull of a smile. It faded as she thought of what the men might do to Eli Zepeda. "I need to be there, Jase. The man murdered my sister. The fact I'm a woman doesn't matter."

His gaze slid over her, hot and intense. "It matters to me, Kate. You're a woman and I'm grateful for it." Jase downed the last of his coffee and rose from his chair. "Why don't I take you home and you can show me how much woman you really are."

Kate felt a rush of desire so strong it made her dizzy. The muscles in her legs felt weak just thinking about it.

She took a moment to collect herself, managed to rise unsteadily from the table. "Aren't you forgetting something?" she forced herself to ask. "We need to find a place where we can talk to Zepeda. How, by the way, do you plan to do that?"

Jase's burning gaze went from hot to shuttered. "Do a little hunting, tail him, figure out his movements. With any luck it won't take too long."

"Fine, let's get started." Walking ahead, she cast Jase a glance over her shoulder. "The sooner we get what we need, the sooner you can take me home."

Every muscle in Jase's big body tightened. The heat was back in his eyes as they headed out the door.

JASE MANAGED TO talk Kate into letting him do his job on his own—at least until he had the info they needed on Zepeda. No way was he going to be able to track the guy, follow his movements and find his lair, with a sexy blonde bombshell glued to his side.

He dropped Kate off with a vow not to go after Zepeda without her. He didn't want to take her into a dangerous situation, but he understood her need for justice—he had lost three friends in Afghanistan. He'd gotten justice for his brothers on the battlefield. It wasn't as personal as he would have liked, but at the time, it was the best he could do. And ending a bunch of terrorists in some way balanced the scales between right and wrong.

Jase spent the rest of the afternoon prowling the bars in Old East Dallas, talking to people without being too obvious. Amazing how many answers you could get with a few greenbacks scattered here and there.

Once it was dark, he was able to move around more freely. He spotted Zepeda outside the Sunshine Motel, but Eli didn't stay long. He was driving an older model cherry-red two-door Cadillac convertible, pretty much a pimp cliché, which made following him almost too easy. Jase wondered how many hours his women had spent on their backs to pay for it.

Jase tracked him to the low-rent apartment building where he lived a scumball's idea of the high life in a two-bedroom flat on the fourth floor. He discovered that Eli parked in the rear parking lot and went in through the back alley entrance with two other men. Jase was tempted to go in and just get it over with. But as much as he'd like to end the guy, he wasn't ready to commit murder—unless it was self-defense.

He ignored the rush that thought gave him.

Armed with the info he needed, he drove back to Kate's. It was way too late, nearly two in the morning. It was beyond rude to wake her at this hour, expect her to welcome him into her bed. He tried to convince himself to just go on home, get some sleep, call her in the morning.

Instead, here he was, standing in the lobby, probably making a fool of himself.

"You're Maddox?" the guard behind the front desk asked.

"That's right."

"Just go on up. Ms. Gallagher left word you'd be coming by late."

His pulse jumped. Kate was expecting him. He didn't know if that was good or bad. Sure he wanted to see her, but he didn't want her to think it meant more than it did. He wasn't a commitment kind of guy, never had been. Until Chase and Harper, he'd never really seen it work.

It's not a problem, he told himself as the elevator door slid closed and the car swept up to her tenth floor apartment. They were in lust, and both of them were okay with that. Besides, he had news. Tomorrow night, if they could formulate a workable plan, they would deal with Elijah Zepeda.

In the meantime, he would be spending the night in Kate Gallagher's bed. The simple truth was, Jase realized, there was no place he would rather be.

CHAPTER SIXTEEN

KATE'S STOMACH CONTRACTED when she heard the buzzer on her front door. Jase was here. Slipping out of bed, she grabbed her pink silk robe and slid it over the matching sheer nightgown she had put on just for him.

She tried to calm her nerves as she crossed the living room. As the night had lengthened, she'd figured he'd decided not to come.

She pulled open the door and stepped back to invite him inside. "I'm glad you're okay. I was worried."

"Were you?" His eyes ran over her sexy lingerie. "I'm fine. Didn't run into any problems." He moved closer, until their bodies were touching full length. One big hand slid into her hair, and he tipped her head back. "I'm glad you waited up." Then his mouth came down over hers.

No man had ever kissed her the way Jason did, as if he couldn't get enough, as if she were part of him, as if he could go on kissing her forever. She gripped his muscled shoulders and clung to him, kissed him back with the same hungry need.

The kiss changed, deepened, turned her insides to mush. She felt his lips on the side of her neck as he lifted her into his arms and strode down the hall to the bedroom, her nightgown draping over his arm like something out of *Gone with the Wind*.

"Jase…" His name whispered out as he set her on her

feet beside the bed and began to take off his clothes. She just stood there watching, mesmerized by the sight of all those glorious muscles, hypnotized by the way they flexed and moved. Naked and fully aroused, he turned to her, stripped off her robe, but left on her sheer pink nightgown.

His eyes ran over her, hot and a darker shade of blue. Hungry. "I love looking at you." He reached out and wrapped a thick blond curl around his finger. "All that golden hair, those long legs and that pretty little tattoo on your ass. I could just eat you up."

She whimpered. Jase eased her nightgown off her shoulders, and it pooled at her feet. His hand cupped her breast; he bent and took the fullness into his mouth. Her mind went blank while her body burned.

She didn't remember much after that, just the constant rush of heat, the need scorching through her, the feel of his mouth on her most sensitive places. Pleasure that seemed to have no end.

She moaned as he moved on top of her, drove deep, took and took and gave and gave. Hours later, relaxed and boneless, she fell asleep beside him. When she awoke the next morning, the bed was empty, just as before. She didn't like the way it made her feel.

Then she heard sounds in the kitchen and her heart leaped. Jason was still here.

Something warm unfurled inside her. She didn't want to think what it might be. Instead, she grabbed her terry-cloth robe—not the sexy one she had worn last night since they had work to do—made a quick bathroom stop, then hurried into the kitchen.

"Morning," Jase said. His short dark hair was slightly mussed, his jaw rough with a night's growth of beard. He looked amazing.

"Good morning." She glanced away, not sure what he would say about last night, what she might read in his face.

He caught her chin, lifted her mouth to his and pressed a soft kiss there. "Thanks again for waiting up," he said.

Her cheeks warmed. "I…ahh…wanted to hear what happened with Zepeda."

His smile was sexy and slightly arrogant. She'd wanted him—there was no point in denying it.

"I got the info we need," Jase said, pouring her a mug of coffee and setting it on the counter in front of her. "Zepeda lives in a low-rent apartment house not far from the motel. I'll get hold of Bran and the two of us will recon the place, figure the best way in and out. Once we settle on a plan, we'll fill you in. If we think it's safe, you can go with us."

She opened her mouth to tell him she was going no matter what, but he held up his hand and just shook his head.

"That's the only way this is going down, Kate. If it's safe for you to go in—or at least as safe as we can make it—you can come with us. Otherwise we go in by ourselves or this is over."

There would be no arguing this time. She could tell by the look on his face, the tone of his voice, that his mind was made up. And if he didn't go in after Zepeda, the bastard would get away with cold-blooded murder.

"All right, we do it your way, but I want you to know I understand the danger. Anything can happen with a guy like that. There's no way you can completely guarantee my safety."

"No, there isn't. But I plan to do my best."

Since that was all she could ask, she said nothing more.

Jase finished his coffee. "I've got things I need to do before tonight." He set his mug on the counter, and Kate walked him to the door. "I'll call you later." He leaned across and kissed her, then disappeared out into the hall.

The apartment fell silent. Kate felt as if the color in the room had suddenly faded. Hawk Maddox was such a powerful presence that without him, the energy seemed to have been sucked out of the air.

She thought of the butterfly tattoo that so captured his interest. She'd had it done after Andrew had ended things and she had begun to take her life back. Like the butterfly, she had come out of her cocoon, spread her wings and started to fly.

Maddox was exactly the opposite of Andrew. Instead of holding her back, trying to cage her in, everything she did with Jason made her feel stronger, more powerful.

Tonight they would confront Elijah Zepeda. They needed to find some kind of evidence that would prove his guilt without implicating Holly. Kate hoped they could find it. She refused to think what else could happen. She needed to stay positive.

Her phone rang just as she headed for the bathroom to shower and dress for the day. She grabbed it off the nightstand. "Good morning."

"Kate Gallagher?" a woman's voice asked.

"That's right."

"I'm calling from the Dallas County Medical Examiner's office. Your sister's body has been released. You can arrange for pickup whenever you're ready."

Her throat tightened. "Thank you for calling. I'll take care of it right away." She hung up the phone and sank down on the bed. Her sister was dead. The reality of it struck her again and her heart throbbed, an ache deep in her chest.

She took a steadying breath and dialed the number for the mortuary. It was Sunday. They would be getting ready for funeral services.

"Rockdale Mortuary," a woman said. "How may we help you?"

"This is Kate Gallagher. I talked to one of your people last week…a Mr. Bromley. He helped me make arrangements for my sister, Christina."

"Yes, Mr. Bromley gave me the details. I'm Mrs. Conroy. I have the information right here. Let me see…yes…here it is. Are you ready for us to pick up Christina and bring her home?"

Home. Rockdale hadn't been Chrissy's home for the last two years yet hearing the words felt right. "Yes, thank you."

"All right, we'll take care of it. You've done everything you need to do, Ms. Gallagher." Some of it she had handled over the internet. "I see you've chosen the flowers, the headstone. You just need to pick a date for the service."

Kate closed her eyes. The day didn't really matter. Not to Chrissy. Not anymore. "Would Wednesday work?"

"Let me check our calendar." Mrs. Conroy came back on the line. "I'm sorry, Wednesday is fully booked, but Friday would work. You'd requested a ten o'clock graveside service, is that correct?"

Her chest clamped down. She could barely force out the word. "Yes…"

"Reverend Wilcox is available that day, as well."

"Friday, then."

Mrs. Conroy's voice softened. "We'll take care of

everything, Ms. Gallagher. You don't need to worry about a thing."

Kate managed to swallow. "All right. Thank you. I'll see you Friday." She hung up the phone and just sat there with the phone in her hand.

She started to call her father, give him the day and time. Instead, she decided to text him. He said he wanted to come, but she wasn't really sure he would make it. She was even less sure she cared.

Kate walked into the bathroom, turned the shower on very hot, took off her robe and climbed under the scalding spray. She wished Jase were there. Jason could make her forget about Chrissy. Make all the sadness go away. He had a way of knowing exactly what she needed.

The thought occurred she was coming to depend on him way too much. After Andrew, the notion was frightening. The last thing she needed was another man. She had sacrificed her independence, become a completely different person to be with Andrew.

And it wasn't the first time.

After college graduation, she had fallen for the young, aggressive owner of a software development company. David had big plans for them as a couple. He expected her to charm his business associates, help him build his company. He expected her to be the woman of his dreams.

She had a knack for business, he had said. Which was probably the reason she had managed to get herself into the same situation with Andrew. Both times she had been sucked into a relationship that caged her in. Tried to change her in some fundamental way. She refused to let it happen again.

By the time she stepped out of the shower, Kate was feeling better. Being Sunday, the office was closed for the weekend, but she had talked to her assistant on Friday, and Laura had assured her everything was running smoothly.

Though she wasn't completely sure not being needed was a totally good thing.

With a long afternoon in front of her, Kate went into her home office and woke up her computer, clicked up Google, typed in *New Hope Rehabilitation Center* and started digging.

She'd been thinking about the rehab facility ever since talking to Holly and the Lockwoods. A dozen links popped up. She was surprised by the number of articles praising Reverend James Lockwood and his wife, Vera. The home had had tremendous success with the prostitutes who came there for help.

But the center relied on donations. Several organizations had held minor fund-raisers, but the home was at full capacity and the Lockwoods didn't have the money to open another facility.

If Eli Zepeda hadn't forced Chrissy to leave, would her sister have been able to conquer her addiction? Would she have left the dark world of prostitution and begun a new life?

Kate didn't know Tina Galen, but she knew Chrissy Gallagher. Her sister had been stubborn, difficult and spoiled, but she was also smart, hardworking and determined. Whatever Chrissy put her mind to, she would ultimately achieve.

Kate believed, with the help of the people at New Hope, her sister would have succeeded in making a new life for herself. And Kate would have been there to help her.

She leaned back in her chair. She hadn't been able

to help her sister, but maybe she could help girls like Holly and other women in the home.

Kate wasn't a psychologist or any sort of counselor, she was a businesswoman. Which meant the best way to contribute to the center was to help them raise money, possibly enough to open another home somewhere else.

An image arose in her mind of Eli Zepeda standing outside the Sunshine Motel, big and dark, hard-faced and mean, slapping the young prostitute, punishing her for some imaginary wrong.

Kate had to find justice for Chrissy's killer before she could move on, but with luck, that would happen tonight. They would deal with Eli Zepeda—and Chrissy's soul could finally find peace.

CHAPTER SEVENTEEN

THEY RENDEZVOUSED THAT night at Kate's. Jase still didn't like the glass-walled apartment, though the rational part of his brain told him that ten stories up they were safe.

The first time he'd been with Kate, the night he'd taken her on the sofa in the living room, he'd been too damned hot, too hungry for a taste of her to worry about it. He almost smiled. At least there were curtains in the bedroom.

At the moment, he sat across from her and Bran in the kitchen where at least there were actual walls. A diagram, a hand-drawn layout of the Hickam Apartments, showed the front entrance, where the elevator was located, rear exit into the alley, parking lot, and an outside fire escape that descended from the roof.

Jase had also drawn a map of the fourth floor, showing the location of Zepeda's apartment, which as near as they could figure included two bedrooms and a bath. The fire escape ran next to the living room window, providing an emergency exit. The kind of scum Zepeda ran with, he didn't stay alive by being stupid.

"The fire escape gives him a way out," Bran said. "But it'll work for us, too, if things go south."

Jase pointed to his drawing of the fourth floor, focusing Kate's attention there. "The inside stairwell is down at the end of the hall. An easy way to get in and out, unless for some reason we get trapped in the apartment."

"So what's our plan?" Kate asked. She wore black jeans, black sneakers and a black T-shirt, her long hair plaited into a single braid. She was ready, and after he and Bran had spent the afternoon reconning the building and the surrounding neighborhood, so was he.

"We wait and watch," Bran said.

"From what I could find out, Zepeda usually gets home at night a little after 2:00 a.m.," Jase said. "About the time the bars close. Sometimes he's alone, sometimes he's with a couple of his scumball friends. Once in a while, he brings in women to entertain them. He likes to keep his buddies happy and in his debt."

"If that happens tonight, we postpone," Bran said. "We don't have a deadline, and we don't want the women getting hurt."

"We can handle a couple of his drugged-up pals," Jase said. "But the less people involved the better."

Kate looked up at him. "What happens once we get inside the apartment?"

"The first thing that happens is you stay out of the way," Jase said. "We need to focus on Eli. It puts all of us in danger if we have to worry about protecting you."

Kate's chin shot up. "You won't have to worry about me."

Amusement slipped through him. She was so damned independent. He liked that about her...most of the time. "That's good. Just don't forget it."

"I can see the blood lust running hot in both of you," Bran said. "You want this guy and I don't blame you. But we need to be sure the bastard's guilty. I know it looks that way, but we need to be sure."

Jase nodded. "With any luck, he'll tell us something that'll connect him to the murder. Information we can give the police."

"What happens if he won't talk?" Kate asked.

Jase's gaze swung to Bran, and a silent communication passed between them. "That'll be up to Zepeda," Jase said.

Bran's hard smile looked completely ruthless. "Yeah. Maybe he'll confess."

Kate fell silent. Jase said nothing, either. There was no mistaking Bran's meaning.

"Let's start at the beginning," Jase suggested, focusing back on the maps. "We'll run through plan A a few more times and come up with a decent plan B." He checked his heavy stainless-steel watch. "We've got plenty of time, long as we're in place before Zepeda gets home."

Unfortunately, later that night as they waited in the darkness behind the apartment building, Eli showed up with three of his friends and three working girls to entertain them. The night was a bust.

The following night wasn't any better. Eli arrived with four guys and a woman. The only thing good was that after they left, Kate invited Jase up to her apartment as she had the night before, and he spent the hours before morning in her bed.

The third night they got lucky. At two thirty in the morning, Eli parked his Caddy in its usual spot in the lot behind the building and got out with just two members of his crew. One was short and stout, Latino, with thick arms and legs. Jase recognized him as Roberto "Berto" Valenzuela.

The other guy was African American, not as tall as Eli but lean and solid, his arms ropy with muscle. One of his eyebrows was scarred, his nose flattened. Delroy Peyton was a former middleweight boxer.

The men headed for the back door across the alley

that led into the building. It opened near the stairwell but also accessed the elevator in the entry.

"Stay out of the way till we've dealt with Eli's men," Jase said, crouching next to Kate behind a dumpster. Bran made himself invisible behind a thick shrub on the other side of the back door.

Kate nodded at the reminder. She looked more determined than frightened. All of them were dressed in black, and a heavy layer of clouds shuttered the moon, providing good cover.

Both men were armed to the teeth, Jase with his .40-caliber Kimber in a holster clipped to his belt, Bran with a Glock 9 mil beneath his black T-shirt, along with various and sundry smaller caliber pistols.

But using the guns to disarm Zepeda's men was a last resort. Gunfire in the middle of the night was the last thing they needed.

This late, the old brick building was quiet. As Eli approached, Jase caught the end of the dirty joke he was telling and the men's raucous laughter. Still chuckling, Eli slid his key into the lock on the back door. The lock clicked open, and Jase and Bran stepped out of the shadows.

Zepeda's men reacted but not fast enough. Bran's elbow jammed into Valenzuela's stomach, doubling him over. A sharp, side-hand blow to the back of the neck took him out. Bran wrapped a hand around Zepeda's nape and shoved him up against the brick wall, held him there while Jase dealt with the boxer.

Peyton swung a death blow, which Jase managed to duck. More than one jaw had been broken by that fast, hard right hand. Since punching it out with a former professional boxer was probably not the best idea, Jase looped an arm around Peyton's neck, dragged the guy back against his chest and squeezed. Peyton clawed and kicked, but Jase was bigger and stronger, and the guy finally went limp.

When Jase looked up, Bran had his Glock pressed beneath Zepeda's chin. "We just want to have a little chat," Bran said to him. "Alone."

Jase pulled a zip tie from his back pocket. "Hands behind your back," he said. With no other choice, Eli complied, and Jase slid the tie around his wrists. While Bran controlled Zepeda, Jase zip-tied Valenzuela and Peyton, both still unconscious. He also bound their ankles. Working beside him, Kate tore off strips of silver duct tape, slapped one over Valenzuela's mouth, then did the same to Peyton.

Jase dragged the unconscious men behind the dumpster. They wouldn't be making trouble for a while, long enough for them to finish with Zepeda.

"Let's go," Jase said to Kate, urging her through the back door, across the hall to where Bran waited with Eli by the elevator.

They rode up to the fourth floor, Eli quiet along the way. He was biding his time, hoping they would make a mistake. But with the barrel of Bran's Glock digging into the flesh beneath his chin, he was wise enough not to make any sudden moves.

Jase used Eli's key to open the apartment door, and they walked into the living room. Jase turned on the overhead light in the kitchen, whirled a chair around, and Bran slammed Zepeda down in the seat. Jase handed Kate a couple of zip ties, and she secured Eli to the chair. So far so good.

"The girl, Tina Galen," Jase said. "She worked for you?"

Eli grunted. "So what?"

"So she's dead. That's what. And you killed her."

Eli's big body tightened. "What the fuck you talkin' about? I didn't kill the bitch."

"No? Word is she was with you the night she was murdered. Someone beat her to death. That someone was you."

"Bullshit. She was alive and breathing when I left her."

Bran stepped close, grabbed the front of Zepeda's shirt and jerked him up from the seat as far as he could go with his ankles bound to the chair. "You like hitting women. Everyone on the street knows that. Keeps 'em in line, right? They know better than to fuck with you. That's what happened to Tina. You were teaching her a lesson, and you got carried away. You hit her too hard and killed her."

Eli shook his head. "That ain't right. That ain't what happened. No, sir."

"So what did happen?" Jase pressed, and Bran let Zepeda go.

Eli swallowed. "Okay, so I hit her a couple of times, slapped her around a little, gave her skinny ass a couple of kicks. Tina thought she could just up and quit. Bitch owed me. I give her a place to live, fed her. Got her the skag she needed. Bitch *owed* me."

Jase wrapped a hand around Eli's thick neck. "You hit her, all right—with a fucking bat! She was only eighteen years old!"

Kate stepped closer, set her hand gently on his arm. "Maybe it was an accident," she said, her voice soft, but her eyes were cold as ice.

Jase released his hold on Eli's neck and let her run with it. Maybe she could get something he couldn't.

Kate focused on Zepeda. "Is that what happened,

Eli? You didn't mean to do it. You were just trying to make her understand who was boss. But something went wrong and she died."

"Is that what happened?" Jase pressed. "You didn't mean to kill her. It was just an accident. Because if it was, that's understandable. Shit happens. Things get out of control."

Eli firmly shook his head. "I didn't do it. No way. Tina was alive when I left her."

"Where?" Kate asked, a damned good question, Jase thought. Where was the primary crime scene?

"Where did you leave her, Eli?" Kate pressed.

"In front of Reuben's Liquor Store. It was late. Place was closed. Nobody around. Somebody must have followed us, come along and killed her after I left."

Jase heard the slide ratchet back on Bran's semiauto. Bran caught Eli's jaw, forced his mouth open and stuck the barrel of the pistol down his throat. "You've got ten seconds. Admit you killed her or I pull the trigger."

The blood washed out of Kate's face.

Eli gagged and wildly shook his head. "Didn't do it," he said, trying desperately to talk around the barrel of the gun.

"Five seconds," Bran said.

Eli fought against his restraints and tried to shake his head, his teeth clicking against the metal. "I didn't do it…didn't do it…but…but I know who did."

Bran pulled the gun out of Eli's mouth. "Talk," he said.

Eli swallowed, managed to stop shaking. "I don't… don't know who exactly. She'd only worked for me a few weeks. Tina come to Dallas from someplace else, I don't know where. Back then, she belonged to somebody else."

"Another pimp?" Jase asked.

"Not exactly." Eli nervously shifted in the chair. "They find out I told, they gonna kill me."

Bran held up the pistol. "Or I could do it now. Up to you."

"Okay, okay." Eli huffed out a breath. "You know that mark she had on her neck? The kiss? That's their brand. They put it there so everybody on the street knows the woman is theirs. I shoulda turned her away, but she was young and still pretty and I wanted the money."

"Go on," Jase said.

"They must have found her, been keepin' track of her. They followed us that night. Soon as I was gone, they killed her. They was sending a message."

"Yeah, what message is that?" Jase asked.

"It was a warning. To me for taking her in. To the other women in their stable so they don't try to leave, and anyone who tries to interfere."

Silence fell. Jase flashed a look at Bran, who gave a faint nod. Both of them believed Eli was telling the truth.

"How do I find these people?" Jase asked.

"Don't know. You try, you gonna wind up dead as Tina."

Jase sliced another glance at Bran. They'd gotten the answers they had come for, though not exactly the ones they'd expected. "Looks like we're done here," Jase said.

Kate stepped in front of Eli. Jase's eyes widened when she drew back her fist and punched him in the face. "If you'd left Tina in the center, she'd still be alive."

Eli spit out a wad of blood. "You got that wrong. She was dead the minute she run away."

Jase pulled Kate back. "That's enough," he said,

though he couldn't blame her for wanting a little payback for her sister.

Bran moved close to Eli, into the harsh overhead light. "You know who I am?"

Zepeda wet his chafed lips. He nodded. Everyone in the hood knew Bran Garrett was former special ops. It was whispered on the street he could kill a man fifty different ways and never leave a trace. Nobody wanted any part of him.

"You and your men—all of you are still alive," Bran said. "If you don't want trouble you can't handle, this ends here."

A bead of sweat rolled down Zepeda's forehead. "No more trouble."

"Make sure your men understand," Bran said.

Zepeda flinched when Bran pulled a knife from his boot, but Bran just leaned over and cut the zip ties. "Ten minutes, then you can go down to the alley and cut your men loose."

Bran strode out of the kitchen, and Jase urged Kate out behind him. They moved into the hall and Jase closed the door.

"Thanks for the help," he said to Bran when they reached the alley.

"My pleasure," Bran said. He waved as he headed for his Jeep.

Since it was always better to have a second means of escape, Jase walked Kate back to the Yukon. He could feel her shaking as he helped her into the seat. Not nearly as calm as she'd seemed.

"You did good in there," he said as fired up the engine. "You handled yourself like a pro."

Kate swallowed. Beneath the passing streetlights, her face still looked pale. "Would Brandon really have done it? If Eli hadn't answered, would he actually have pulled the trigger?"

Hard to know for sure with Bran, but Jase didn't say that. "We wanted the truth. I'm pretty sure we got it."

"Who is he? I mean... I know he's one of the Garrett brothers and they're all filthy rich, but...who else is he? Zepeda was clearly afraid of him."

"Bran's former military. He was special ops."

"So were you, but there's something different about him."

"Yeah, well, Bran was a little more special than I was." Bran was Army Delta. Considering what Jase was capable of doing himself, he figured the street talk about Bran was true. Apparently, so did Eli Zepeda.

Kate settled back in her seat. At least she had finally stopped shaking. Guilt slipped through him. He shouldn't have taken her into such a dangerous situation. And yet as he thought of the way she had taken on Zepeda, he couldn't imagine leaving her behind. She'd been involved from the beginning. Until this was over, that wasn't going to change.

"So I guess that means there won't be any retribution," she said, bringing the conversation full circle.

"Eli's no fool. He'd rather make money than trouble, so we're probably okay." *At least for now.* What happened from here on out was a different story.

He glanced at Kate. She was still wound tight. In his line of work, he knew the feeling. Instead of pulling up in front of her building, he drove into the parking garage and pulled into a visitor space.

"Okay, if Zepeda didn't kill my sister, who did?" Kate asked.

Jase turned off the engine. "That's the question we need to answer."

She turned to face him, her long blond braid sliding over her shoulder. His groin tightened. After dealing with scum like Zepeda, he needed her tonight. Or maybe it was the fear for her he'd felt tonight.

"But how are we going to find the killer now?" she pressed. "It looks to me like we're back to square one."

"We're way further than square one. Tomorrow we'll go over everything we've learned and figure out where we go next."

Kate's eyes found his across the center console. "So...um...if we're going to be working together in the morning, it would probably be easier if you just stayed over."

Something relaxed inside him. He didn't try to hide the hunger in his eyes. He wanted her. He just wasn't sure he wanted her to know how much.

"Good idea," was all he said.

CHAPTER EIGHTEEN

KATE SAT NEXT to Jason at the kitchen table the following morning. Though she had tried to tell herself she needed to take a step back from him, she was glad he had spent the night.

After their confrontation with Zepeda and his men, she had been too wired to even think about sleep. Accompanying two former special ops warriors into danger, she'd been in way over her head. She'd had no idea how far the men would be willing to go to get the information they needed.

If she were being honest, she'd admit to being scared to death. Still, she'd managed to keep it together, do the job she'd been assigned and get through the mission.

By the time they got to her apartment, the adrenaline was wearing off, her knuckles were hurting from the punch she had thrown and her insides were shaking.

Jase seemed to understand. The minute the door was closed, he pulled her into his arms. "It's all right," he said, running a comforting hand up and down her back. "You're home. You're safe. Everything's okay."

A little sound slipped from her throat and she relaxed into his arms, absorbing his strength and heat. He just held her, making no demands, letting her settle and regain control of her emotions.

Eventually she began to feel something besides nerves and residual fear. She became aware of the roughness of the black jeans that clung to his powerful thighs, the hardness of his chest.

Tipping her head back, she pressed her mouth to his throat, felt the steady pulse beating there, kissed his jaw. The feel of his arousal sent heat sliding through her.

Jase kissed the bruised knuckles on her hand. "So brave tonight," he said, pressing a soft kiss on her lips. "I want you, baby. So damn much."

The gestured loosened something inside her. "I want you, too," she whispered, and Jase scooped her into his arms. She wasn't a small woman, but he made her feel that way, made her feel feminine and sexy and desirable.

They made love twice, releasing the pent-up energy both of them were feeling. Exactly what she needed, which Jase seemed to understand.

When morning came, she showered and dressed and went in search of him, found him sitting behind his laptop at the kitchen table. He always seemed more comfortable in there.

"What are you working on?" She poured herself a mug of coffee, carried the pot over and refilled his cup.

"Catching up on my email, taking care of a little personal business. I picked up some doughnuts." He nodded to the box on the counter, then glanced at her and smiled. "I borrowed your keys to let myself back in."

She returned his smile. The thought occurred that maybe she should just have a key made for him, but she quickly discarded the notion. She needed to tamp things down with Jase, not get involved any more deeply than she already was.

But she was definitely happy about the doughnuts. Grabbing a glazed, she sat down at the table next to him. "You said we'd figure out where we were."

"That's right. I made a few notes, things we've learned so far."

"Okay."

"We know Zepeda didn't kill her. Or at least, after last night, that's our working assumption. According to Eli, Tina was working for a group of people, not just one pimp, some sort of organized crime ring, something like that."

"A group located out of town."

"That's right."

"How do we find them?"

"I'm heading over to Reuben's liquors, see if I can find anything that'll confirm it as the primary murder scene. I want to have a look before I turn the info over to the police."

"It was raining that night. Do you think there's really a chance you'll find something?"

"You never know. Even if we don't, the CSIs might come up with something. Those guys are really good. You want to come with me?"

"Absolutely. I'm ready to go anytime. I just need to grab my purse."

As Jase closed down his laptop, Kate hurried back down the hall. Her purse sat on the dresser in her bedroom. As she walked into the bedroom, a memory arose of last night, and her body flushed with heat. The man was amazing in bed.

When she returned to the kitchen, Jase was waiting, his laptop tucked beneath the thick biceps stretching the sleeve of his T-shirt. He turned off the coffee maker, then waited for her to walk in front of him out the kitchen door.

Very courteous for a big alpha male, she thought. "Did you learn those pretty manners from your mom?"

she asked, curious about him as they crossed the living room to the door.

"My mom ran off with a traveling salesman when I was ten years old. Everything I know, I pretty much taught myself or learned in the marines."

She told herself his past was none of her business, but everything about Hawk Maddox intrigued her. "So your dad raised you?" she asked as they reached the garage and climbed into the Yukon.

"My dad was a no-good drunk," he said, and started the engine. "A mean one. Same answer, I pretty well raised myself."

He didn't tell her not to ask any more questions, but his eyes had gone flat and hard. She understood he'd had to take care of himself, but she wondered if anyone had ever loved him.

The way he looked, the guy was a total chic magnet, but lust wasn't the same as love. So the question lingered, who had loved him?

Just thinking about the *L* word in regard to Hawk Maddox made Kate uneasy. They were working together. At the moment they were sleeping together—friends with benefits—but that's all it was. Though she'd never been involved with a man in a purely physical relationship, that was all it ever could be. And exactly what both of them wanted, she reminded herself.

While her mind had been wandering, Jase had been driving toward Old East Dallas. As they'd left the apartment, she'd noticed he wore his gun on his belt beneath his T-shirt. It had to mean he was ready for some kind of threat. Though the temperature was climbing toward ninety-five degrees, Kate fought a shiver.

Jase pulled the Yukon up to the curb in front of Reuben's Liquor Store, a flat-roofed building with bars over the windows, a place she remembered passing the night they had gone to Mean Jack's.

A tall, thin man in a beat-up flat-brimmed straw hat left the store with a brown paper bag in his hand and strolled off down the sidewalk. A kid whizzed past on a bicycle, rolling along without using his handlebars. Other than the few cars passing on the street, there was no one else around.

"Take a look around," Jase said as they got out of the truck. "Take your time and be thorough. We might get lucky and find the murder weapon or a piece of it, a bit of fabric, could be anything. Look for any indication of blood, a rusty stain in a crack on the sidewalk, a dark smudge on the side of the building."

Kate nodded. "All right."

"If you find anything, don't touch it. We'll let the CSIs handle it. But I'd feel better calling the cops in if we could find some indication Eli was telling the truth."

They started prowling, looking for anything that might validate the story Eli had told. The rain that night would have washed a lot of the evidence away. Add to that, for days people had been walking on the sidewalk, going in and out of the liquor store, up and down the alley beside the building. If it was the original crime scene, it had already been contaminated.

Still, there might be something.

Kate kept her eyes on the ground, looking for the tiniest bit of something—she wasn't sure what. Twenty minutes into their search, she spotted a dark red pattern of spray on the wall that faced the alley.

Her mouth went dry as she moved closer. Could that really be her sister's blood? Her stomach heaved. "Jase! Over here!" She studied the red spatter and swallowed past the bile in her throat. "I think I found something."

Jase jogged up beside her. His gaze followed where her hand pointed. He crouched in front of the spray. "I think you're right. It's the right color, and a pattern like that could easily have come from a blow to the head."

He took out his cell and hit one of his contact buttons. "Benson? It's Maddox. I think we've found your primary crime scene on the Christina Gallagher murder."

She couldn't hear what the detective said, but Jase replied, "Heard a rumor on the street and decided to check it out. I think you're going to find blood spatter, and I think the DNA is going to match Christina Gallagher's."

CHAPTER NINETEEN

WITHIN THE HOUR, Detective Benson showed up with the Dallas PD crime scene unit. Jase had used the time to talk to the owner of the liquor store, Reuben Hernandez, but Reuben hadn't heard anything unusual going on outside before he'd locked up. Hadn't heard anything, hadn't seen anything, didn't know anything. *Yada yada yada.*

In this case, however, Jase believed him. Whoever had followed Zepeda the night he'd forced Tina Galen to leave the rehab center would have been careful not to kill her in front of witnesses.

Benson left the white-coveralled CSIs at work on the rusty spatter on the rough brick wall and walked over to where Jase stood.

"It's blood, all right," the detective said. "The lab will test it, see if it matches the victim's. If it does, they'll run DNA. You say you heard a rumor on the street? That's how you found it? You talk to someone who witnessed the murder?"

Jase shook his head. "Someone saw her in front of the liquor store that night. I came down to check it out. Kate found the blood." You didn't give up your sources. Unless, of course, Eli turned out to be the killer.

"I also heard the vic had only been working in Dallas a couple of weeks. Came to town from somewhere else. Word is, that tat on her neck is a brand. Signifies who she belongs to."

"You mean a pimp?"

"More like a group she worked for. Could be organized crime. Some kind of sex trafficking ring."

"I told you, we would have heard something about it."

"You just did," Jase said. The second time he had brought up the possibility.

Annoyance cut grooves into the detective's forehead. A light, humid breeze whipped strands of his thinning brown hair.

"You said the girl hadn't been in Dallas that long," Benson said. "She left Rockdale two years ago. Where's she been?"

"Good question. We figure that out, we're going to know a whole lot more than we do now."

Benson nodded. "If you come up with something else, let me know."

"Same goes," Jase said, but he didn't think the detective would go out of his way to keep Jase informed. As Benson walked away, Jase looked at Kate. She seemed transfixed, watching the crew at work in the alley, staring at the place her sister had likely been murdered.

Feeling a shot of pity, he set a hand at her waist. "Come on, darlin'. Let's get out of here."

She turned to him, the gold in her dark eyes glistening. She blinked away the moisture and nodded, let him lead her away. When they reached the Yukon, she stopped him with a hand on his chest, a simple touch that sent heat burning through him. It was crazy, the constant hunger he felt for her.

"We aren't very far from the rehab center," Kate said. "Would you mind if we stopped by and checked on Holly?"

"Not a problem. Might be good to talk to her again." He opened the passenger door and Kate climbed into the SUV.

It didn't take long to reach the center, a few blocks away. Standing next to Kate, Jase knocked on the front door.

Vera Lockwood answered, smiled when she saw them. "Kate and Jason. How nice to see you. Please come in." She was at least five inches shorter than Kate, small and fine-boned, yet with a presence that commanded respect.

They followed her into the parlor. "Would you like some iced tea or perhaps a cup of coffee?"

"Iced tea sounds good," Jase said.

Vera motioned to one of the girls who happened to be standing in the doorway, and she disappeared down the hall.

"We came by to check on Holly," Kate said. "How's she doing?"

"She's feeling a little tired, but that's natural so close to her due date. Aside from that, she's fine. But why don't you ask her yourself? I know she'd love to see you. After you left, she talked about how good it was to meet Tina's sister."

"We'd love to see her," Kate said.

Vera hurried out of the room and a few minutes later, Holly waddled into the parlor. Jase thought she looked five pounds heavier, all of it gained in one place.

Kate leaned over and hugged her, which wasn't that easy. "How are you?"

"Miserable." Holly smiled. "My whole body feels swollen and achy, but I guess that's normal." She'd pulled her long brown hair up in a messy ponytail. Her yellow sundress fit loosely, except where it curved around the lump in the middle of her body.

"I'm pretty sure it is," Kate said.

This time Jase sat down in the chair and let the women sit together on the sofa.

"Did Mrs. Lockwood tell you?" Holly said excitedly. "She arranged a place for me and the baby to live. A private home with an older Christian woman. Her name's Mrs. Slovenski. Mrs. Lockwood says she's lonely. She's really nice and she loves babies."

Kate smiled. "That's wonderful news, Holly." One of the young women returned with a tray carrying glasses and a pitcher of iced tea, which was great in the rising heat. Glasses were filled and passed around.

Jase tuned out as the women talked about babies and being pregnant—way too much information for him. But Kate was smiling, clearly enjoying the conversation. She'd probably want a family of her own someday.

The thought unsettled him, though he had no idea why. Kate was a woman. Of course she'd want babies. As for him, he'd never considered having kids. His lifestyle wasn't conducive to marriage and family. He'd made his peace with that a long time ago.

"We'd better get going," Kate said as the conversation wound to a close.

"Take care, Holly." Jase drained his iced tea and set the glass back down on the tray.

Holly's gaze swung in his direction, and uncertainty clouded her features. "Did you talk to Eli?"

"We did," Jase said. "Eli didn't kill Tina."

Surprise widened her eyes. "Are you sure?"

"Someone killed her after he left her. We think it was one of the men she was running away from when she came to Dallas. You know anything about that?"

Holly shook her head. "Tina wouldn't talk about her past. I figured something bad had happened to her, but then we've all had problems. She said she left it all behind when she came to Dallas. I think she was planning to keep moving, keep traveling till she found a place she felt safe. Then she found out about the rehab center and that gave her hope. She was planning to make a new life here in Dallas."

Too bad Tina never got the chance, Jase thought, hardening his resolve. They needed to find the truth of what had happened—before it happened to someone else.

"What about Eli?" Holly asked. "Did you…um… tell him about me?"

Kate reached down and gave Holly's hand a squeeze. "Eli doesn't know anything about you, and he's never going to. You don't have to worry."

Holly relaxed. "Okay."

They said their farewells. Holly left to continue her assigned duties, and Vera returned to the parlor. She walked them down the hall to the front door.

"Thanks for coming by," she said. "With the no-family restrictions, the girls get a little lonely. But we have to be careful who they interact with. They do better if they're away from whatever sent them spiraling into drugs in the first place."

Kate nodded. "I'll stop by the next chance I get. Tell Holly I can't wait to see her baby."

Vera smiled and waved as they walked down the front steps and climbed into the Yukon.

"I've been thinking about how I can help the center," she said as he pulled the vehicle into the street. "They're doing wonderful work. I'm not a counselor or anything like that, but I *am* a businesswoman. I think

I might be able to help them raise money to keep the center running."

"Sounds like a great idea. From what I've seen, seems like you can do just about anything you set your mind to."

Her expression softened an instant before she looked back at the road. "The thing is, I do consulting work for major corporations, which means I have contacts with top level people. Some of them might be willing to convince their companies to act as sponsors for the home."

Jase flicked her a glance. "Why don't you talk to Chase about it? Garrett Resources might be willing to make a sizable donation."

"I don't know him," Kate said. "I came to Maximum Security because of what I read about the company on the internet. Chase has a reputation as one of the best investigators in Dallas, but I've never met him."

For which Jase would be eternally grateful. "I can help with that. I need to stop by the office and check on a few things. If he's there, I'll introduce you."

Kate smiled brightly, and a ripple of heat moved through him. Since they still had work to do, he determinedly ignored it.

"I'll introduce you," he repeated. "Long as you keep in mind Chase is a happily married man."

Kate grinned. "That's okay. One hot cowboy is all I can handle."

Jase laughed and ignored a vague sense relief.

CHAPTER TWENTY

KATE HAD BEEN inside the Maximum Security offices before, the first time was when she'd come to hire Chase Garrett and wound up hiring Hawk Maddox instead.

Only a few people had been working in the office that day. Today the place was hopping. She recognized the petite dark-haired receptionist, Mindy—the name on the brass plate on her desk.

Mindy looked up, spotted Jase, remembered Kate and smiled. "Ms. Gallagher. It's nice to see you again." Her gaze slid down to the hand resting possessively at Kate's waist. "I hope Jason's taking good care of you."

Kate thought of what he had done to her in bed last night, and felt the heat creeping into her face. She had a feeling the receptionist didn't miss a thing. She inched away, putting some space between them.

"He's...ah...been working very hard on the case," she said.

"We both have," Jase added easily. "Is Chase in?"

"He's with Harper in his office."

"Great. Buzz him, will you? Tell him I'm headed his way."

His hand returned to her waist as he ushered her toward an office in the corner with the door standing open. Clearly Jase didn't intend to wait. Rapping lightly on the frame, he guided her inside without his boss's permission.

"Got a minute?" Jason asked.

"Sure." Chase Garrett rose from the leather sofa where he sat next to his wife, who also rose to greet them. She was lovely, fine featured, with a slender figure and sleek shoulder-length blond hair much lighter than her husband's dark gold.

The office was roomy. Like the rest of the building, it was decorated in a Western motif, with a wide oak desk and oak coffee tables in the seating area, where there was a brown leather sofa and chairs.

"This must be Kate," Chase said, closing the few steps between them. She was only a little surprised he knew who she was. She wondered how much Jason had told him about her.

Kate extended a hand. "Kate Gallagher. Nice to meet you."

"This is my wife, Harper."

"Hello." Kate shook Harper's hand. She'd seen pictures of Chase Garrett on the internet, a wealthy blond Adonis who, before he'd married, had women all over Dallas falling at his feet. From the warm looks passing between him and his wife, he was definitely off the market.

Garrett returned his attention to Jase. "What can I do for you?"

"I wanted Kate to meet you. I've been keeping you updated on the case so you know what happened to her sister and where we are in the investigation. We ran across a place that helps young women like Kate's sister, girls trying to turn their lives around, get off the street. The New Hope Rehabilitation Center. Kate wants to help the home raise money."

She managed a tentative smile. She wasn't expecting this, hated being put on the spot and not being prepared, but she wasn't willing to waste an important opportunity.

"It's a small private home," she said, "but they're doing a wonderful job. I'd like to help them raise enough to keep the center running and maybe even expand. I was hoping you might find time in your schedule to talk to me about it."

Chase turned to his wife. "Harper?"

She smiled. "I can put you in touch with the man who handles the Garrett Family Charitable Foundation. I like being involved, so I've been working with him on a fairly regular basis."

"Oh, that would be wonderful."

"Your timing is good," Harper said. "Charles is working on a benefit to raise money for a number of smaller projects. If you could put a proposal together, I could certainly get you a meeting."

Kate beamed. "That would be great. I really appreciate it, Harper."

"Why don't we get a cup of coffee or a Coke?" she suggested. "Give the guys a minute to talk."

"A Coke sounds great." Excitement coursed through her. Tossing a glance at Jason, she followed Harper out of the office. She could feel his eyes on her as she walked past, as blue and hot as a flame.

The air seemed cooler as they made their way through the office. She took a deep breath and continued behind Harper into the break room.

"Diet or regular?" Harper asked, pulling open the door to a refrigerator at the end of the kitchen counter.

"Diet for sure."

Harper grinned. "Definitely." She pulled out two ice-cold cans and handed one to Kate. Sitting down at the table, they popped the tops on the cans and each took a long, refreshing drink.

Like the rest of the office, the walls in the break room were adorned with antique farm tools, but in here there were also photos of the men and women who worked in the office. A picture of the Garrett brothers at the company Christmas party hung next to one of Chase standing beside a sleek twin-engine airplane.

"Your husband flies?"

Harper nodded. "It's Chase's plane but all the brothers fly. Whenever they get the chance, they go down to the family-owed ranch in the Hill Country. Jason has a smaller plane, a single engine Cessna he flies when he's hunting a bail skip."

Surprise filtered through her. She wished she knew more about him. She was beginning to realize he was far more than he seemed.

She took a drink of diet soda. She expected Harper to ask about the charity, but she didn't. Instead, she gave Kate a long, assessing glance. "So," she finally said, "what's going on with you and Jase?"

"BEAUTIFUL GIRL," CHASE COMMENTED. "Seems nice, too. I can see why you like her." He sat back down on the sofa, while Jase sat down in the heavy leather chair.

"Let me guess... Bran's been filling you in on my love life?"

Chase shrugged. "What are brothers for?"

"I like her," Jase said. "But I don't want to like her too much."

Chase lounged back on the sofa. "Why not? She's obviously intelligent. She owns her own company. And clearly you're more than a little attracted to her."

Jase just shook his head. "I don't do relationships. You know that."

"Maybe it's time you tried it."

Jase grunted. "Why is it married people are always trying to convince you to join the institution?"

"Could be because they're happy and they want you to be happy, too."

Seeing Chase with Harper, he could almost believe it. *Almost.* "It wouldn't work. I live hard, do a dangerous job. What kind of a life would that be for a woman?"

"Depends on the woman, I'd say."

Jase made no reply. It wasn't going to happen for him. It wouldn't be fair to a woman and especially not to Kate.

"So how's the case progressing?" Chase changed the subject.

"We've come up with some interesting intel. Better if I don't tell you how we got it."

"Good because I don't want to know."

Jase went on to relay the information he'd gotten from Eli Zepeda, the location of the primary crime scene, though not yet verified, and the people Tina had run away from, a criminal organization Jase believed could be involved in human trafficking.

It was a theory he had been working since he'd seen the photos in the medical examiner's office showing the ligature marks on Tina's ankles and wrists.

"Benson doesn't buy it," he said. "Thinks he'd have heard something about it by now. But my hunch says it's a possibility."

"Could be you're both right. A trafficking ring, but not necessarily located in Dallas."

"Yeah, that's what I'm starting to think. Word is, the

girl hadn't been in Dallas very long. Tina's roommate said she thought she was running from something."

"Have you talked to Kate about it?"

"No. This has been brutal enough without telling her there's a chance her sister had been caged like an animal for God knows how long, drugged against her will, forced to have sex with dozens of men."

"I see what you mean."

Jase glanced up as the women walked back into the office. Leather creaked as he stood up from his chair. "You ready?"

Kate smiled with excitement and he felt a little kick. It occurred to him how rarely he had seen her smile that brightly. Kate was a pretty woman. When she flashed that happy smile, she was downright gorgeous.

His body stirred. He took a slow breath and pulled his brain back from where it was traveling.

"Harper's going to schedule a meeting with Charles Stanton at the end of the week," Kate said. "She's offered to sit in. If she likes what she hears, she'll support the project."

Jase smiled. "Sounds great. I had a feeling you two would get along."

Kate looked at Harper and both of them grinned.

"You ready to go?" Jase asked. When Kate nodded, he joined her at the door.

Kate went up on her toes and kissed his cheek. "Thanks for this, Jason."

His face went warm. "They're my friends," he said a little gruffly. "I'm glad you got to meet them."

As he walked out of the office, he caught a last glimpse of Chase. His friend was smiling smugly. Jase was afraid of what that knowing smile meant.

The thought slid away as he followed Kate into the

main part of the office and spotted Jax Ryker and another PI, Jonah Wolfe.

"Got something for you," Jax said. The muscles in his barrel chest strained against the navy blue T-shirt he was wearing. The Maximum Security logo—a pair of old-fashioned iron handcuffs—rode above the name printed in white on the upper left side.

"Jax, meet Kate Gallagher," Jase said. "Kate, this is Jaxon Ryker and Jonah Wolfe. They're both PIs here at The Max." Wolfe was several inches taller than Jax, with a leaner, lankier build. His hair was a glossy black, his eyes dark brown and intense.

"Good to meet you," Kate said.

"Nice meeting you, Kate," Wolfe said. "I gotta go. I'll see you guys later." Wolfe strode off and Jase turned to Ryker.

"So what have you got for me?" he asked.

"I know you've been hunting Randy Harding. You mentioned you'd tracked him as far as Waco, but you didn't have an exact location."

"That's right. I need to get down there and find him."

"I've got an informant in the area," Jax said. "Called me on a case I'm working. I figured he might know something about Harding or be able to find out, so I asked him to look into it."

"Your guy knows where he is?"

"Got an address out in Bellmead. My guy says he's been jacking cars for an auto theft ring working out of Austin. Got a woman with him."

Jase nodded. "Rosa Diaz."

"Sounds right. Harding's been loaning her out to his friends. Apparently, she's scared to death of him. She wants out, but she's afraid to leave."

Tension settled in his shoulders. Looked like Rosa

had finally figured out Harding wasn't the good guy she'd believed. Jase softly cursed. He should have gone after Harding sooner. The man was violent and unpredictable. He'd already killed one woman in a fit of rage and wounded two cops.

"I gotta bring him in," Jase said. "I can't wait any longer." He hadn't tipped the police because he couldn't verify Harding's location, and if the cops started sniffing around, Randy would skip and Jase would have to track him all over again.

But things had changed for the worse for Rosa, and there was Tommy Dieter to consider. The kid wouldn't be safe until Harding was behind bars.

"I told him to stay on it," Jax said. "Get a location and whatever else he could find. Told him it would be worth his time."

"Definitely," Jase said. "I owe you one."

Ryker's hard mouth tilted into a smile. "I think we're probably even. You gonna need backup? I got a little time on my hands."

Bounty hunters often split fees. Jax was officially a PI, but he was licensed for bail enforcement, and he was a former navy SEAL. He was top-notch and Jase trusted him.

"This guy's bad news, so yeah. I'll call you as soon as I work out the details."

As Ryker sauntered away, Jase glanced over at Kate. "I know you don't want to hear this, but—"

"You have to go to Waco."

"I've got to go after Harding, Kate. I didn't call the cops because I didn't have enough info, and I didn't want the bastard to run. But I can't put it off any longer. The girl he's living with? I know her brother, Paulo. He's worried about his sister, and he has every reason to be. Rosa's in trouble and I can help her. If I pick up Harding and take him in, she'll be safe. I'm sorry for breaking my promise, but I can't just ignore this."

Kate looked up at him. "You have to help her. I wish someone had helped my little sister. Go to Waco. Do what you need to do."

He brushed a finger along her cheek. He wanted to kiss her, but Mindy was watching. Across the room, Lissa Blayne, another one of the office PIs, had shrewd eyes and loved to gossip.

"Let's go," he said softly, and led her outside to the parking lot. As soon as they'd loaded into the Yukon, he slid a hand behind her neck and pulled her in for the kiss he'd wanted to claim earlier. It was long, thorough and deep.

"Thanks for understanding," he said roughly when he pulled away. "I'll take Ryker with me and head on down. If Jax's info pans out, I'll be back in a day or two."

Her eyes remained on his face, her lips still moist from his kiss. Arousal stirred beneath the fly of his jeans. He wished it was dark outside.

"I have things I need to do anyway," she said. "I have to catch up on work at the office, and my sister's funeral is tomorrow morning."

"You never said anything."

"I know. I've been trying not to think about it. Besides, I didn't expect you to go."

Maybe not, but if he managed to get Harding locked up and Rosa out of danger tonight, he'd be there. "I'll take you home. I need to go by my place and grab my gear before we head out. The sooner I get to Waco, the sooner I can get back."

"Harper told me you owned a plane."

He nodded as he drove the Yukon out of the parking lot. "Cessna Turbo 210. It comes in handy sometimes. But Waco's only ninety-five miles away. If I drive, I won't need to rent a car when I get there."

And his extra gear, including a pair of tactical vests, was already loaded. Plus the restraints bolted into the sides in the back of the vehicle often came in handy, especially with a dickwad like Harding.

He needed the extra weapons from the safe in his apartment: short-barreled tactical shotgun, Browning 9 mil, his Ka-Bar knife in a thigh sheath and flash-bang grenades.

"I hope you find him," Kate said. "I hope they lock him up and throw away the key."

Amusement trickled through him. "I'll do my best not to disappoint you."

Kate's expression turned serious. "You've never disappointed me, Jason. The day I walked into your office and you agreed to help me was my lucky day."

He didn't know what to say, didn't know why his chest felt strangely tight. Glancing away from the softness in Kate's golden brown eyes, he hit the gas and pulled into traffic.

CHAPTER TWENTY-ONE

As KATE WATCHED the SUV drive away that afternoon, she felt an unexpected sense of loss.

She'd spent so much time with Jason she felt untethered without him. She tried to tell herself it was just the emotional stress she'd been under, but it was hard to convince herself.

Crossing to the elevator, she waved at the security guard behind the front desk, pushed the button and headed up to her apartment. The quiet struck her the moment she stepped inside. The big man who had filled so much of her life wasn't there. No hot glances, no possessive touches. It surprised her how quickly she missed him.

With a sigh, she tossed her purse on the sofa. She'd had boyfriends, had a live-in relationship after college, practically lived with Andrew, spent almost every night with him at his house or hers. But when the men were gone and she was alone, she had mostly felt a sense of relief.

Today, even the hours she had spent at her office later that afternoon hadn't helped. She was home again now. It was getting dark, and she just felt more and more lonely.

And worried. Jase would be in Waco by now, trying to track down a hardened criminal. A killer. She reminded herself that he was with Ryker, a former navy

SEAL. The two of them had worked together before. He trusted Jax. Together, they would bring in Randy Harding.

But Harding wouldn't be captured easily. He had murdered a woman, had shot two deputy sheriffs. If Jase brought him back to face justice, he would likely go to jail for years. He'd fight to stay free no matter what it took.

Nerves made her stomach queasy, reminding her she hadn't eaten anything since morning but a power bar at the office. A tired sigh escaped as she went into the kitchen, though she didn't really feel hungry. When her cell rang, she ran back into the living room and hurriedly dug it out of her purse, hoping it was Jason.

She felt a flicker of disappointment when Cece's name popped up on the screen. It was followed by a trickle of guilt, since Cece Jacobs was one of her closest friends.

"Hey, Cee, what's up?"

"I got your text about Chrissy's funeral. It's tomorrow morning?"

"That's right."

"You don't think we're going to let you go through it by yourself, do you?"

"Well, I—"

"Lani and I are coming with you. I'll drive so you don't have to worry about getting there or getting home."

Relief trickled through her. She'd been prepared to go alone. Knowing her two best friends would be standing next to her at her sister's graveside brought the sting of tears.

"Are you sure?"

"We're going with you. No discussion."

Her throat tightened. "Thanks. It means a lot."

"The service starts at ten, right?"

"That's right."

"It's almost a three-hour drive. We'll pick you up at six thirty. That way we'll miss the traffic."

Kate wiped moisture from her cheeks. "Okay."

"Listen, on a far more pleasant note, how's it going with your hot bounty hunter slash detective?"

Kate found herself smiling. "He's off to arrest some criminal. I'm kind of worried about him."

"Duh…bounty hunter? Hunting men is what they do."

"I know."

"So I guess that means you two are getting along."

"He works for me, remember? Plus, we're…um… friends." She tried not to think of the deep kiss in the parking lot. "We're making some real progress on the case."

"I was hoping by now you'd decided to let the police handle it."

"The police have done squat. I don't think they're that interested."

"Just be careful, okay?"

Like she'd been careful when she'd gone with two special ops guys to break into Eli Zepeda's apartment, like when she'd punched Zepeda in the face. "I will."

"So your bounty hunter… I guess you still haven't slept with him."

Her face heated. Silence fell as she tried to find the right words.

"Oh, my God! You *have* slept with him! I knew you couldn't hold out. Was he fantastic? What am I thinking? With a body like that, he had to be. You could just rub yourself all over him and it would be delicious."

Kate laughed. "I'm not talking about it."

"Better than great! I knew it!"

"Look, I gotta go." Not really, but she wasn't ready to have this conversation with Cece. "I've got some things I need to do."

"Okay, fine—for now. Just be careful, okay? With the murder case *and* with your hot alpha male."

She smiled. "I'll see you tomorrow." As Kate ended the call, her stomach growled again. She headed for the kitchen, actually hungry this time. It was good to have friends.

She remembered she'd said that about Jason, that he was a friend. As she rummaged through the fridge and took out lunch meat, light mayo and mustard, she decided it was true. They were friends. With a man like Maddox, that was all it ever could be. Jase wasn't a settled-down kind of guy, though he had been surprisingly monogamous while they had been together. She hadn't caught him even looking at another woman, not a hint that he was getting bored or interested in someone else.

Still, his life was catching criminals and bringing them to justice, and clearly he loved it. Which meant when the case was solved, he would be moving on and it would be over between them.

Her stomach twisted. Kate looked down at the food on the counter, but her appetite had disappeared.

JASE DROVE SOUTH on I-35 toward Waco. Ryker lounged in the passenger seat, the picture of toughness and strength. The lights from the dashboard illuminated his solid jaw and strong cheekbones.

Jase cast him a glance. "You got the meet set with your guy, right?"

"Eagles Club. It's off I-35 on Eighteenth Street. Dive

bar downtown. Guy calls himself Shifty. Says he's got fresh intel. Meet's set for midnight."

"If I recall, there's a Budget Inn in the area. We'll get a room, assemble our gear, maybe catch a nap before we head out. Could be a long night."

Ryker nodded.

When they reached the edge of town, Jase pulled into a Burger King just off the highway, went through the drive-thru for burgers and fries, then headed for the motel.

At two minutes till midnight, they crossed the sidewalk and pushed through the door into the Eagles Club, the interior dimly lit, illuminated mostly by red and purple lights behind the liquor bottles on the back bar. Red glass candleholders flickered on small round tables scattered across the room.

The place was only about two-thirds full, the customers talking among themselves, an occasional burst of laughter. Jase figured another half hour, the patrons would be well on their way to stupid, and drunks from nearby bars would wander in for a few more drinks before closing.

"Over there." Jax gestured to a guy at the far end of the bar. Late forties, dirty blond hair and a drooping mustache. He spotted them and stood up as they approached. Jase ordered a couple of Lone Stars and a fresh drink for his newfound friend, and they carried them over to a table against the far wall.

"This is Hawk Maddox," Jax said to him. "He's the guy I told you about. Give him whatever you've got."

Shifty looked him over, taking in his height and muscular build, probably figuring, even if he'd gotten cold feet about talking, it was too late to back out now.

"Harding's staying in an apartment out in Bellmead. I got the address."

Jase made a mental note of the street and number the guy rattled off.

"He's living with a woman and two other guys," Shifty said. "They're hard cases, kicked out of the military for dealing dope. Which is what they're mostly doing now, but they've managed to jack a few high-end cars and a couple of newer pickups. Always a good market for those."

Jase took a swallow of beer. "Got names?"

"Pike and Folsom. Pike's big and dark. Folsom's got a bad scar on his cheek. Cops are getting fed up. I don't think Harding will be sticking around much longer. Things are getting too hot."

"You think Harding will be there tonight?" Jase asked.

The guy shifted nervously and glanced around. Maybe that was how he got his name. "I don't know. Haven't heard of anything going down tonight, so he should be. Can't say for sure."

Jase took another long swallow of beer. "Anything else?"

"That's all I got."

Reaching into the pocket of his black T-shirt, Jase pulled out a folded hundred and slid it across the table. Shifty pocketed the money, stood up and hurriedly walked away.

Jase and Ryker both finished their beers. The Yukon was parked down the block. Jase plugged Harding's address into the nav system and drove the five-mile trip to Bellmead.

As their destination neared, the area grew more and

more run-down, seedy motels and apartments, the occasional liquor store.

"Up ahead on the left," Ryker said.

Jase slowed a little, not much. They rolled past a pair of two-story brick apartment buildings facing each other across an open area. Stairs accessed the second floor from the center of each structure, which was surrounded by patches of green too sparse to actually be called grass.

He drove around the block, checking out the dirt parking lot in the rear that served both dwellings.

"Number 18's in building A on the second floor," Ryker said. "That's the end closest to the parking lot."

"Close to his ride if he needs to run." Jase kept driving. A few blocks away, he pulled into a vacant lot. Access in and out from three directions, nobody around, just a few cars passing on the street.

It was a dark and humid night, flat-bottom clouds drifting past a thin sliver of moon. They got out, dropped the tailgate and started putting on their gear.

Jase strapped on his duty belt, which holstered his .40 cal. A nine-inch, push-button, telescoping baton hung from the belt, next to a can of Saber Red pepper spray, a Taser X26, a set of handcuffs and a high-powered flashlight. With the possibility of facing three armed assailants, they planned to go in hot, but using deadly force was always a last resort.

His pulled on his tactical vest. Extra magazines in the pocket and a spare set of cuffs—because two was one, and one was zero to a guy heading into danger.

Ryker wore black jeans. Jase wore black cargo pants. Both of them wore high-top black lace-up boots and black T-shirts. Their lightweight jackets read BAIL

BOND RECOVERY, printed in bold white letters on the back.

They headed toward the apartment building, staying in the shadows but covering ground as fast as they could.

Once they reached their destination, they separated to do more recon. Better to be prepared. Since they had no idea who was inside, they were going in balls-to-the-wall, surprise being their best asset.

It was late, most of the apartments dark, only one unit with lights on downstairs. Unit 18 had a dim light on in the bedroom, but from down below Jase couldn't tell what was going on inside.

Ryker came around the building and moved silently up beside him. "Didn't see anyone. Found another set of stairs leading up from the parking lot."

Jase nodded. "You take the back, I'll take the front." They moved off in different directions, making a sweep of the area, planning to converge on the second floor.

When Jase topped the landing, he reached up and unscrewed the bulb in the light fixture, the only one working on that side of the corridor, and kept moving. Ryker came up the stairs at the end of the passage next to unit 18, pulled his SIG P320 and took up a position.

Jase moved closer, pulled his Kimber and knocked on the door. He heard a man's voice, then a woman's, followed by the sound of heavy footsteps approaching. Jase stayed away from the peephole just in case, but with the light out, it was too dark to see.

"That you, Handley?"

Jase grunted, pretended to slur his words. "Come on…open the door."

The knob turned. The door cracked open enough

for Jase to get a glimpse of Harding in a pair of jeans, barefoot, no shirt, a big semiauto in his hand.

"Bail recovery!" Jase shouted. Harding tried to slam the door, but Jase kicked it open, sending the man crashing against the wall. His gun hand flew up, and the big semiauto fired into the ceiling, raining plaster down on their heads. Harding lunged, got in a punch before Jase shoved him back and pressed the barrel of the Kimber into the side of his neck.

Gun held two-handed, Ryker moved to clear the rest of the apartment. Only a few feet more to the bedroom when the door flew open.

"Gun!" Jase shouted. Ryker dove out of the way as shots exploded, and Jase dragged Harding down on the floor behind a chair.

Ryker pulled off two rounds, and Jase fired toward the men in the bedroom. When Harding tried to break free, Jase whacked him across the back of the head with the barrel of the Kimber, knocking him down, then turned and fired two more shots into the room, hitting one of the men.

The second man, scarred face, tall, broad and naked, stepped into the doorway and fired. Ryker took him out with a double tap to the chest.

Jase moved and so did Ryker. Jase went to the first man, the one still breathing. He was dark and burly, wearing only a pair of dirty white cotton briefs. He was alive and groaning, a bullet lodged in his right shoulder, his hairy chest covered in blood. Jase kicked his gun away, grabbed a pillow and pulled off the case, folded it into a square and pressed it against the bullet hole.

"Hold this. Keep pressure on it so you don't bleed to death." Not that he really gave a damn.

The guy groaned and pressed down on the square of cotton.

Jase felt a trickle of wetness on his face, reached up and wiped the blood off his cheek with the back of his hand. Somewhere in the fray, Harding had managed to land a punch. Jase wished he'd had time to throw a few punches of his own.

"We need to call the cops," he said to Jax. "Tell them we have Randall Harding in custody, along with two of his closest chums."

A shaky voice came from the bathroom doorway. "I have already called them." Rosa Diaz held up the cell phone she had managed to get her hands on. She was pretty, small and slender, with long, straight black hair nearly to her waist. She had bruises on her face and neck. Jase figured there were more under her ratty blue robe.

She walked into the living room, over to where Randy sat on the floor, his back propped against the chair, hands cuffed behind him.

Rosa leaned down and spit in his face. "You are scum," she said with a thick Spanish accent. "I hope they kill you!"

Harding growled low in his throat and leaped for her, but Jase stepped in and shoved him back down a little harder than necessary.

"Fucking whore!" Harding shouted.

"Leave her alone," Jase warned. "She's done with you."

Rosa got right in Randy's face. "You filthy pig. I should kill you myself!"

"Get her away from me, or I swear to fuck—"

Jase grabbed him by the throat. "You won't do jack shit, Harding. At the very least, you'll be spending the rest of your life in jail. You'll be lucky if they don't fry your sorry ass."

Harding fell silent. Sirens in the distance grew louder. Jase pulled out his cell and called 911, identified himself and told dispatch he and Jaxon Ryker were bounty hunters, legally armed. He told them about the firefight, who they had in custody, that one man was dead, the other wounded, explained the men had been holding a woman prisoner but that she was now safe.

Jase ended the call and looked over at Ryker, who casually held a gun on the men. "Good work," Jase said. "Thanks for the help."

"Nice when a plan comes together."

Jase almost smiled. It felt good to do good work, help someone, make people safer. He didn't like ending a job with casualties, but they had acted in self-defense. Still, the questions would be endless, the paperwork over the top. His plan to get home in time to go to Kate's sister's funeral looked like a bust.

When the first patrol car rolled up in front of the apartment building, Jase dropped the mag, emptied the weapon, and set it on the floor out of reach. With a last glance at Ryker, he pulled open the door, raised his hands in the air and walked out of the apartment.

CHAPTER TWENTY-TWO

THE DAY WAS DRAB, the sky sullen and dark, a damp drizzle clouding the air outside Kate's apartment windows. The weather matched her mood on the dismal day she would bury her sister.

She caught a glimpse of herself in the mirrored elevator wall, puffy eyes, her face too pale. She'd chosen a black skirt-suit, white cotton blouse and black pumps, her hair wound into a tight knot at the back of her head. The stark colors and severe hairstyle made her look even grimmer.

Though the outfit, like the weather, seemed fitting.

The elevator door dinged open and she stepped into the lobby to find her friend, Lani Renton, waiting. She was as tall as Kate, with short black hair and a slender build. She pulled Kate in for a hug.

"It's gonna be okay," Lani said. "Your sister's at peace now. When this is over, you will be, too."

Kate took a shaky breath and slowly released it. "It won't be over until I find whoever killed her. I won't stop until I do."

Lani reached down and caught her hand, gave it a gentle squeeze. "One day at a time. Come, on. Let's get going."

Kate spotted Cece behind the wheel of her Mazda compact SUV outside the front door. Lani opened the front passenger door, urged Kate into the seat, then got into the backseat behind her. They all clicked on their belts.

"How you holding up?" Cece asked as she put the car in gear and pulled into morning traffic.

"I'm okay...considering."

"You'll feel better once this is over," Cece said.

"I know," Kate agreed, though she wasn't really sure it was true.

"I can't even imagine what you've been through these past two years," Lani said. "Always worrying about your sister, wondering where she was, if she was safe."

"I wish she had come to me for help. She was right here in Dallas, and I didn't even know it." Kate explained how Chrissy had come to the city a few weeks before she was killed. How she was trying to get free of drugs and make a new life for herself.

She told her friends about the rehab center and how she hoped she could contribute in some way and help the women who lived there.

By the time they had reached the halfway point of the trip, Kate was starting to feel better. Talking to her friends really helped, she realized. The conversation turned to men, and she listened as her friends worked to cheer her up with their dating antics.

"So this guy, Jerry, finally convinces me to go to dinner with him," Cece said. "He was kind of cute, and I thought it might be fun. Then, when he comes to pick me up, he says he's got a surprise for me—he's going to cook me dinner at his house instead!"

Lani whooped. "You didn't fall for that old line. Tell me you didn't go."

"Stupidly, I went. We hadn't been there ten minutes when Jerry heads outside. He's got this hot tub, you see. The guy starts stripping off his clothes right in front of me. He's totally naked. I barely know him—and he doesn't even look that good! He climbs into the tub and says, 'Aren't you coming in with me?'"

"Is this guy still breathing?" Kate asked.

Cece rolled her eyes. "*Unfortunately.* I turned around and walked back into the house, grabbed my purse, ordered an Uber and left him sitting in the hot tub."

Everyone laughed. It felt really good. Kate knew the laughter would only last a little while longer, but she allowed herself to enjoy it.

"Okay," Cece said. "Your turn, Kate. You've got to tell us all about your hot alpha male. Give us a little vicarious thrill."

"No way." Kate closed her eyes, trying to block images of her and Jason in bed but not really succeeding.

"Come on, you've got to give us something," Lani pleaded. "Cece showed me his photo. The guy is totally juicy. He's got to be amazing. Just give us a hint."

"Come on," Cece whined.

Kate sighed in defeat. "Fine. I'll give you one word. That's it. Then we're done."

Cece bounced in the seat with excitement. "Okay, okay, one word," she conceded.

Kate couldn't stop a grin. "One word? Okay. *Stallion.*"

The car swerved then righted. "Oh, my God!" Cece fanned her face, and Lani whooped with laughter.

"*Stallion,*" Lani repeated, and they all started laughing again.

It wasn't until Cece turned off Highway 79 and headed for Oaklawn that the cheerful atmosphere faded. Cece drove through the tall brick pillars into the cemetery, and followed the narrow lane through the rows of headstones toward the green canopy set up in front of a fresh mound of dirt. The cemetery had been there since the 1930s so the trees were tall, the shrubbery dense.

It was the second time her friends had been to the old, historical cemetery. Lani and Cece had been with her the day she'd buried her mother. Now they were back for her baby sister.

Her throat closed up as the Mazda pulled in behind several cars that had arrived ahead of them. The engine went silent and Kate climbed out, her legs suddenly shaky.

Across the lawn, rows of white chairs sat beneath a dark green canopy. More flowers than she had hoped for sat in front of the grave: a wreath of pink carnations and pale pink roses, a spray of yellow and white chrysanthemums, a vase of lavender cremones and daisies. A blanket of baby white roses draped the casket.

Kate blinked to hold back tears, walked over and read some of the cards. Friends. A distant cousin. The gang at the office had sent the wreath of pink carnations and roses. Knowing it was her favorite color touched her. They had wanted to come, but she had asked them to stay in Dallas and take care of her business instead.

The funeral director, Mrs. Conroy, was there, speaking to the minister, Reverend Wilcox. Kate paused to talk to them briefly, thanked them for all they had done, then joined Cece and Lani to find seats in the row up front.

A tall slender man stepped into her path. Her father looked older, the lines in his face more pronounced. He wore a dark suit that set off the fine threads of silver in his hair.

"Katie…" The gentle way he said her name thickened the lump in her throat.

"Dad… I wasn't sure you'd come." He drew her close

and hugged her, held her a few seconds longer than she expected. They hadn't been close since he and her mother had divorced.

"Of course I would be here," he said. "Christina was my daughter."

She just nodded. She asked him about his wife and family, and he asked her about her job. She felt little connection. But he was still her dad and it was good to see him.

Then it was time for the service to begin. They took their seats, Kate next to Cece and Lani on one side, her dad on the other. She recognized a few of Chrissy's old friends in the chairs behind them, not many since Chrissy had been so much younger.

Kate settled back in the folding chair. It was time for the service to begin. Reverend Wilcox stood in front of the rose-draped coffin, a Bible open in his hand.

"We have gathered here today to praise God and to celebrate the life of Christina Gallagher, a young woman who died in the most blossoming years of her life. May God grant that in pain we find comfort, in sorrow, hope, in death, resurrection."

The rest of the service passed in a blur of words and prayers, the minister trying to bring comfort to family and friends. Distantly, Kate thought her only real comfort would come from finding justice for her sister.

The service finally came to a close, and all of them stood up. People walked over to pay their respects, then wandered back to their cars.

Kate was staring at her sister's grave when Cece gently nudged her. "Look who's here."

She followed Cece's gaze to see Jason striding toward her. Her heart squeezed. He was wearing a black blazer, black jeans and black cowboy boots. There was a night's growth of beard along his hard jaw. He looked tired and worried and amazing.

When he reached her, he simply opened his arms, and Kate stepped into them. All the tears she'd been holding back burst free as she turned her face into his thick neck and his hold tightened around her.

"It's all right, honey. I've got you."

In that moment, she realized he did. That he'd been there for her from the very beginning. That he had always looked out for her, always been there when she needed him. A soft pulse beat inside her, warning her that if she wasn't very careful, she would also find him there in her heart.

JASE HELD KATE while she cried, his brave Kate who never backed down from a challenge. Her tears didn't last long. She was strong and tough and determined. She took a shaky breath and eased away.

"I'm sorry. I didn't mean to do that." She wiped tears from her cheeks. "I can't believe you're here."

"I tried to get here sooner. It's a long story."

She reached up and touched the scab that had formed on his cheek, directly below the one on his eyebrow. "Did you get him?"

A muscle tightened in his jaw. "Yeah, we got him."

She turned to her father, who stood silently beside her. "Dad, this is Jason Maddox. We're…um…working together. Jase, this is my father."

"Frank." Her dad extended a hand that Jase shook. "Nice to meet you, Jason."

"You, too, sir." Frank Gallagher didn't look much like Kate, though she had probably gotten her height from him, as well as her gold-flecked brown eyes. Kate had barely mentioned him. Jase was a little surprised to see him at the funeral.

"And these are my friends, Cece Jacobs and Lani Renton. They drove me down."

Both of them were pretty. Cece had dark brown hair; Lani's hair was black and she was taller.

"Kate's talked a lot about you. It's nice to finally meet you. Thanks for looking out for her."

"We were glad to come," Cece said.

"It's nice meeting you, Jason," Lani said. "I know you and Kate have been working together. I hope you're making progress."

He could feel Frank Gallagher's dark eyes on him. Since he didn't know how much Kate had told him about the case, he kept his answer simple. "Some."

His gaze returned to Kate. He could see the stress in her face, the sadness. He was glad he had come.

"I'm afraid I have to go," Kate's father said. "It was good seeing you, sweetheart. I wish the circumstances had been better."

Kate swallowed. "Me, too."

Frank bent and kissed his daughter's cheek. "I'll call you, honey. I won't wait so long this time. I promise."

Kate nodded, but didn't look convinced. She watched her father walk away, then turned back to Jase. "I guess we should all get going."

"Since you didn't drive down," he said, "maybe you could fly back home with me."

Her head came up. "You flew down?"

"Drove Ryker back to Dallas early this morning. I called the funeral parlor, found out the time of the service. Flying was the only chance I had of getting here before it was over." He looked around. Most everyone was gone. "Almost didn't make it."

"I'm really glad you're here," she said softly.

"Go home with Jason," her friend Lani urged. "Your spirits could use a lift." She flashed an impish grin. "Pun intended."

Kate smiled faintly. "All right, I'd like that. I appreciate you both coming with me. It really means a lot."

Cece leaned over and hugged her. "Like we said, it wasn't open for discussion."

Lani hugged her. "We'll see you when you get home."

Kate watched her friends walk away. She looked back, studied the new cut on Jase's cheek. "Looks like Harding put up a fight."

"He didn't go down easy, that's for sure." Jase set a hand at her waist. "I'll tell you all about it on the way to the airport."

As he walked her across the grass, Jase told her about arresting Randy Harding, about wounding a man in the firefight in the apartment, about the man Jax Ryker had killed.

"It was self-defense, but the cops have to be sure. There's hours of questioning. They have to cross every *t* and dot every *i*."

"That's probably good."

"No doubt about it. It just gets frustrating, telling the same story over and over, answering the same questions a dozen different ways."

"What happened to Rosa?"

"There was obvious domestic abuse. Plus she agreed to testify against Harding and his buddy Yancy Pike. I spoke to her briefly, told her that her brother loved her and that he'd help her any way he could. She'll probably be okay."

"Pike's the one you shot?"

"Yeah."

Once Jase had her settled in his rental car, it didn't take long to reach the Coffield Airport, the small, regional airstrip where his Cessna was tied down. His flight that morning had been a little rough, but typical Texas weather, the clouds were mostly gone now and the sun was shining.

He parked in the return car lot, left the keys and they walked out to the plane. Jase helped Kate into the copilot's seat.

"This is nice," she said, running a hand over the sky blue leather interior that matched the stripe on the side of the airplane.

"You like to fly?"

"I'm not a big fan of commercial, but then who is?"

He smiled. "You'll like this better, I promise." He closed the door, walked around doing his visual inspection and unchocked the wheels. Satisfied, he climbed into the cabin and started the flight check, found everything to be in order, as he had expected.

He glanced over at Kate, saw her smiling for the first time that day.

He strapped into his seat. "Sit back and enjoy the ride." The engine fired, the propeller whirred to life and he finished the flight check. As the wheels started rolling and the Cessna taxied down the runway, he noticed the color was back in Kate's face, her golden brown eyes sparkling.

The plane lifted into the air and she grinned. "This is great." Her gaze went to the patchwork colors of the land spreading out below them. "I love it."

"After a night like the one I just had, it feels good to be up here where I can breathe."

"It really does. Thanks for bringing me."

"My pleasure." And it was. Her excitement had him

smiling. He laughed at something she said. The events of last night slowly faded, leaving him feeling clean and whole again.

She was good for him, he realized, buoyed by having her up there with him, enjoying the flight. But as the plane neared the city, his thoughts returned to the capture he'd made last night, to the scum he dealt with and the risks he took on a daily basis.

Kate was good for him.

Trouble was, he wasn't good for her.

CHAPTER TWENTY-THREE

KATE STARED AT the lights of Dallas through the floor-length glass windows in her living room. She'd tried to keep from falling back into the black mood she had been in that morning, but as the evening wore on, the sadness returned.

Jase had dropped her off and left to deal with some business he needed to handle. She figured some of it involved collecting the bounty on Randall Harding. He was back now, had returned with takeout from Luigi's, the family-owned Italian restaurant around the corner.

The man could really eat and he had been hungry. Kate had mostly pretended to eat, moving the pasta around on her plate, taking an occasional bite of green salad. The food didn't sit well in her unsettled stomach.

It was getting late. For the past couple of hours, Jase had been sitting at the kitchen table, working on his laptop. Kate had gone into her home office and answered some texts, tried to do her email, but it was hard to concentrate. Her mind kept spinning back to the cemetery, to the coffin in front of the mound of earth.

She walked back out to the living room, her eyes stinging at the memory as she stared through the glass. She blinked, and the lights of the city came back into focus. The sound of heavy footsteps reached her as Jase came up behind her. His blazer was gone, but he was wearing the same jeans and T-shirt he'd had on all day.

"It's getting late, honey. You ready for bed?"

The words didn't thrum through her the way they usually did. She felt none of the warm anticipation that usually stirred deep in her core. She turned and looked up at him. "You go on. I'll be there in a minute."

His gaze found hers, steady blue into her pain-filled brown. "You okay?"

"For a while, I was." She sighed. "I can't get her out of my head, Jase. I keep seeing her on that table in the morgue. I keep thinking of her in that satin-lined box." She swallowed and shook her head. "I'm sorry. Maybe you should go home. I'm not very good company tonight."

He studied her for several long moments, considering, as if making some sort of decision. "Let's go." He took her arm and urged her toward the bedroom. Maybe she could sleep, but she didn't think so. He wouldn't press her for sex, though. Not if she really wasn't interested. There was a sweet side to Jason Maddox that few people got to see.

Her thoughts returned to the moment, and weariness washed over her as he led her through the bedroom door into the room done in pink she usually found so comforting.

He reached up and loosened the now-drooping knot that still held up her hair, took the pins out and set them on the dresser. She didn't move as his fingers sifted through the heavy curls, spreading them around her shoulders.

"It's been a long, hard day," he said.

"Yes, it has."

Then he cupped the back of her head, leaned down

and kissed her. Slow and easy, not pushy but coaxing a reluctant response. Little by little, he shifted gears, took the kiss deeper, from gentle to hot, wet and wild.

Her body shot from cold to scorching. Kate gripped his heavily muscled shoulders as the kiss turned hard, rough and hungry. Heat crawled through her, prickled her skin, turned her mind to mush. Jason kissed her and kissed her. She felt like begging when he stopped.

A look of burning intent settled over his handsome face, a look she had never seen before. "Take off your clothes."

She stared, her mind fuzzy. "What?"

"You heard me. Do it, Kate."

Interest filtered through her, grew stronger when he peeled his T-shirt off over his head to reveal his sculpted chest. The eagle on his biceps promised to make her fly away.

"Do it, Kate."

Her mouth went dry while her insides turned hot and liquid. She reached for the buttons down the front of her blouse, opened them one by one, her eyes on his face. He looked different, harder, more in command. The change in him intrigued her.

"Lose the jeans," he said.

Heat slithered through her, settled in her core. She slipped off her sandals and unzipped the jeans she had changed into, pulled them down over her hips and stepped out of them.

"Get up on the bed."

There was something erotic about being naked while he still wore clothes. She moved toward the bed and started to pull back the covers, but Jase shook his head.

"Hands and knees," he said.

Her stomach contracted so hard she trembled. Dear God, had she really believed she wasn't in the mood?

He unzipped his jeans as she climbed up on the mattress, turned her head to watch him undress over her shoulder. Hard muscle rippled with every move, tightening the hot knot of anticipation coiling low in her belly.

In seconds his boots were gone, his jeans and briefs. Her mouth watered as he walked toward her. He was big and he was hard. This was Hawk Maddox and she wanted him. So bad a soft moan slipped from her throat.

Jase climbed up on the bed and moved behind her, lifted her hair aside and pressed his mouth against the nape of her neck. Soft bites and moist kisses trailed over her shoulders and down her spine. Big hands ran over her hips. He bent and kissed her butterfly tattoo.

Kate whimpered. When he stroked her, settled himself behind her and eased deep inside, pleasure scorched through her. There was no room for sadness, no room for anything but Jason and what he made her feel.

He started slowly, taking his time, heightening the pleasure. Some intuitive part of her knew this was for her, a respite from the terrible day she'd had, the awful grief and overwhelming despair.

She arched her back to take more of him and he increased the rhythm, gripping her hips to hold her in place, giving her what she needed. Heat erupted like lightning, burning over her skin, hurling her toward the peak. She cried out as a powerful climax struck, traveling from the base of her spine out through her limbs, gripping her and refusing to let go.

Jase didn't stop, just keep driving into her until she came again before he followed her to release.

Both of them collapsed on the bed, curled together spoon-fashion. Their hearts beat wildly, finally began to slow. Jase kissed the nape of her neck, then left to dispose of protection.

She was groggy, more than half asleep when he returned, curling her against him back to front. A big arm draped over her middle, keeping her close. She felt safe in a way she never had before, safe and protected.

Kate closed her eyes and drifted into a deep, untroubled sleep.

BRIGHT MORNING SUN beat through the windows. Yesterday had been sticky and hot, probably be the same today.

Jase sat at the kitchen table, his coffee now cold, a few crumbs of the pastry he'd picked up earlier left on his plate. His laptop sat open, his mind once more on the Gallagher case and finding Christina Gallagher's killer. Or possibly more than one.

He needed a lead. He phoned Detective Benson, but it was Saturday and Benson was off for the weekend. Jase asked if Heath Ford was there. Heath was a friend, the best homicide detective on the force, as far as Jase was concerned, and he always seemed to be working. Sure enough, Heath was there.

The line picked up. "Detective Ford."

"Heath, it's Maddox. I know you aren't working the Gallagher case, but I was hoping you could check, see if the liquor store has been verified as the primary crime scene."

"I don't have to check. I know it has. I heard Benson talking about it. Blood type found at the crime scene matched the dead girl's. Benson followed up, got a DNA match on her from the autopsy."

"Did they find any other DNA?"

"They found a splinter of wood from the murder

weapon, some kind of club, I gather. Skin DNA on the wood. Unfortunately, there was no match in the system."

So Eli had been telling the truth. Considering he'd had a pistol stuck in his mouth at the time, Jase wasn't really surprised. Zepeda had left Tina alive. If his DNA had been on the wood, his name would have popped. As many times as Eli had been arrested, he would definitely be in the system.

"Did Benson say if he's turned up anything else?"

"Not that I know of. He's got a lot of cases right now. We all do. Wish I could be more helpful."

"At least I know I'm on the right track. Thanks, Heath."

Jase looked up as Kate came into the kitchen. He should have gone home last night. He'd been spending way too much time with her. He needed some space. Figured she did, too.

Still, he didn't regret staying. She might not have known it, but she'd needed him last night. She'd had friends and sympathy all day. More of the same wouldn't have done her any good. She needed something else, something to challenge her, fire her blood, and he understood her well enough to know exactly what that was.

He'd done what he'd set out to do and given her a little peace. Kate had slept like a baby.

His body stirred just thinking about it. It took a real woman to handle a big man like him, and Kate Gallagher was up to the task.

She walked behind him, leaned down and kissed his cheek. "Thanks for last night. You were amazing."

His smile held a trace of arrogance. "You were pretty amazing yourself."

"I feel a lot better today. The funeral's over and my sister's at rest. I feel like I can move forward, get back to where we left off, concentrate on finding the killer."

"You've had some time to think. You've got a company to run. You could let me take over and get back to your life."

She just shook her head, moving the honey blond curls he admired so much. She was wearing tight brown leggings with a cute little blue-and-brown print top. Hauling her back to bed would be a lot more enjoyable than talking about murder.

"I'm not quitting." She headed over to the kitchen counter, poured herself a mug of coffee and took a sip.

"What about your job?" he asked.

"I haven't taken a vacation since I started the company."

"Hunting a killer doesn't exactly count as a vacation."

She just shrugged and took another sip of coffee. "I've been keeping up with things in the office. I worked part of the day on Wednesday, and I was on the phone with my people yesterday afternoon."

She walked back to the table and sat down, cradling the mug between her palms. "As far as work goes, everything seems to be under control."

Jase blew out a resigned breath. "In that case, here's where we stand. I made a few calls this morning." He told her about talking to Detective Ford, and that it appeared Zepeda had been telling the truth—the liquor store was the primary crime scene. He told her the CSIs had found skin DNA, but there was no match in the system.

"Which means it wasn't Zepeda," he finished.

"So where does that leave us? What do we do next?"

She took a sip of coffee. "We never talked to that guy Bandini. Maybe we should."

Jase shook his head. "We can, but at this point, I don't think it was Bandini. Both Zepeda and Holly said Tina was on the run. She was hiding from someone. She'd only been in Dallas a few weeks. Eli thinks whoever she was involved with tracked her to the rehab center, followed her that night and killed her."

"Why, though? It must have taken a lot of effort to find her. Why would someone from out of town go to that much trouble? Why did he want her dead?"

"Good question." One he might be able to answer. "Eli mentioned the tattoo on Tina's neck. He said it identified her as being one of *theirs*. A group, not a person."

"*Theirs*. I don't get it. What am I missing?"

He wished he didn't have to tell her. He'd tried to warn her off this case half a dozen times. "There's a possibility we haven't really discussed. There's…ah…a chance that when your sister left home, she somehow fell into the hands of a trafficking ring."

"Drug trafficking?"

"Sex trafficking, honey. Organized crime. Young girls are smuggled in from other countries or picked up off the street. They get them hooked on drugs, get them to service their customers in exchange for satisfying their drug habit."

The color washed out of her face. "You aren't saying these women are locked up somewhere and held against their will?"

He inwardly cursed. He hated this, hated having to tell her. "They can be. Mostly they stay because they're addicts. They need drugs, and they don't have anywhere else to get them."

Kate slumped back in her chair. "Oh, my God. I

didn't put it together. You're saying she could have been kidnapped right off the street. That it wasn't her choice."

"We don't know that's what happened. Not for sure."

"But it could be." A trembly breath whispered out. "Just when I think this can't get any worse, it does." She pushed her hair back from her face. "So you think she was being used in some sex trafficking ring, but since she came here from somewhere else, you don't think the ring is in Dallas."

"That's about it. Benson doesn't believe it's here, and Holly and Eli both said Tina came from out of town. She'd only been in Dallas a few weeks."

Kate closed her eyes. Jase could almost see her mind spinning through possibilities.

"She was being held prisoner," she said, working through the theory. "Forced to do sex acts for drugs. Somehow she managed to escape. She comes to Dallas because her older sister is here, but she wants to get clean before she makes contact."

He helped her spin out the thread. "She probably believed she was safe. As long as she didn't go to the police, she figured she'd be okay."

"But she was wrong," Kate said.

"She didn't talk—she was afraid to. But she knew too much so they couldn't let her live."

Kate shoved up from her chair, sending it scraping across the floor. "Oh, God, Jase."

He stood up, too, pulled her against him and felt her tremble. "Let me take over, baby. Let me handle things from here on out."

Kate jerked out of his arms. "No way in hell! I won't rest until we find them. I won't have a moment's peace until I see every one of those rotten bastards behind bars—or dead."

CHAPTER TWENTY-FOUR

KATE SAT BACK down at the kitchen table. After a couple of deep breaths, she managed to crush her emotions and bring her temper down from boiling to simmer. A thousand scenarios rolled through her head. None of them good.

When her sister had run away, their mother had never given up hope. But after the first year of searching, Kate had secretly begun to think her father was right and her sister was dead. Thousands of people were reported missing every year. Undoubtedly a number of them were killed in some sort of accident, others fell victim to murderers, particularly kids and young girls like Chrissy.

Eventually, the police had given up the search. Even the private detective her father had hired thought it was time to quit. Kate had continued to check Chrissy's social media, hoping something would turn up, but nothing was ever posted on any of her sites again. Kate had forced herself to move on.

Now she was faced with the possibility that her sister had been held prisoner, unable to get back home. Forced into a life of drugs and prostitution.

Kate was determined to find out. She wanted justice for Chrissy. Even more, she intended to do everything in her power to keep other women from suffering the same terrible fate.

She glanced up at the sound of Jason's cell ringing. He plucked it up off the table, checked the screen and pressed the phone against his ear.

"Hey, Tab. I've been hoping to hear from you." Jase nodded at something she said. "Hold on. I'm with Kate. She'll want to hear this. Let me put you on speaker." He set the phone down on the kitchen table.

"Hi, Tabby," Kate said.

"Hi, Kate. I haven't forgotten you two. I tried like crazy to track the place Tina's disposable phone was last used, working backward from the number on her website, but the phone pinged all over Eastern Europe. I haven't figured out how to get past the wall that's blocking the info, but I've got a couple of new ideas I want to try before I give up."

"Tell her what you found, Tab," Jase impatiently urged.

"After you guys were here, I set up an alert, anything related to a tattoo like the one on Tina's neck. I got a hit this morning. A young woman in San Antonio turned up dead."

Kate's stomach knotted.

"Where'd the info come from?" Jase asked.

"Got a gamer friend who works in the ME's office. He happened to notice the alert. When the body came in, he let me know."

"Same color, same location behind the left ear?"

"Yup."

"Tab, you're the best. I owe you."

"Yes, you do," Tabby said. "Don't worry. I'll figure a way to collect. Keep him out of trouble, Kate." Tabby ended the call.

"Another woman is dead," Kate said.

"That's right."

"You think San Antonio is where my sister was before she came here?"

"I don't know, but it's the best lead we've got. I know some people down there. I need to make some calls, get a few things lined up. Pack an overnight bag in case we need to stay. We can leave as soon as you're ready."

Jase didn't ask if she wanted to go. Maybe he had finally accepted that she was in this until it was over.

Kate hurried out of the kitchen, down the hall to her bedroom. They were on their way to San Antonio. Determination stirred inside her. She had no idea what they would find when they got there.

Except for another dead girl.

It DIDN'T TAKE long for Kate to shower and dress, then pack an overnight bag. She found Jason pacing impatiently in the living room. Though the view of the city was fantastic, he never stood in front of the windows. Fear of heights? She was pretty sure Hawk Maddox wasn't afraid of anything.

"I need to stop by my place to change and pick up some gear before we head out," he said. "We'll hit the drive-thru on the way, grab a breakfast sandwich or something. Then we'll head for the airport."

"We're flying?"

"Helluva lot faster."

They had almost reached the front door when the intercom buzzed. Kate recognized the lobby guard's voice, reached over and answered. "I was just leaving, Gordy. What is it?"

"Mr. Bradley's here to see you. Shall I send him up?"

She flicked a glance at Jase. His jaw was set, his features tight. He didn't like Andrew Bradley. Not for the first time, Kate wondered what she had ever seen in the man.

"I'm on my way out the door, Gordy. Tell him he'll have to call me later."

"Will do, Ms. Gallagher."

Jase pulled open the door and they made their way down to the parking garage.

Unfortunately, Andrew was waiting. He probably still had a parking pass. He smiled when she stepped out of the elevator, spotted Jason, and his smile melted away. "Still keeping bad company, I see."

Jase took a step toward him, but Kate set a hand on his chest. "Let it go, Jase. Give me a minute, will you? I'll be right there."

His jaw clenched. "If that's the way you want it." Grabbing her overnight bag, he strode off toward the Yukon.

Dammit. Men. Especially the macho variety. She turned to Andrew, who was staring daggers at Jason's broad back. In his usual expensively tailored three-piece suit, his hair freshly trimmed, Andrew looked good. Maybe it was his always-perfect looks that had fooled her.

Kate glanced up at him. "I'm sorry, Andrew, I don't have time to talk. I'm heading out of town for a couple of days."

"I came by to tell you how sorry I am for missing your sister's funeral. I didn't find out until it was over. You should have called me, Kate. I would have been there for you."

She hadn't wanted him there or anywhere near her. "We're over, Andrew. You don't seem to get that even though it was your idea."

He ignored the remark and glanced over to where

Jason leaned against the Yukon, his arms crossed over his chest.

Andrew cocked a dark eyebrow. "So that's the way it is. You're sleeping with him. I can't believe you're involved with a guy like that."

Irritation trickled through her. "A guy like what, Andrew? Jason's smart, he's interesting and he's always there when I need him. Unlike you, he's not a control freak." *Well, not exactly.* "And I don't have to pretend to be someone else when I'm with him—he likes me the way I am."

"I liked you the way you were. We enjoyed the same things. Had the same goals. We were perfect together."

"Then why did you end things?"

"Because I wanted to be sure it was right. Now that I've had time to figure it out, I realize what I gave up. Get rid of him, Kate. Give me a chance to make things right."

"Sorry, not interested. Find someone else." She started to walk away, but Andrew caught her arm.

"I've got a job for you. You've heard of Solerno Engineering? Stan Weiner, the CEO, happened to mention they're having some internal problems and need to hire a management consulting firm to help them figure things out. I told him you were the best in Dallas. Stan checked into it and he wants to hire you."

It was a major deal. It would make her company a lot of money, which Andrew surely knew. "At the moment, I'm involved in something, but I'll give him a call, see if we can work something out."

"He needs you now, Kate. He won't be willing to wait."

She studied his face, didn't miss the cunning she had overlooked before. How had she been so blind? "I think

I'm beginning to understand why you're so determined we should get back together. You think, with your help, Gallagher and Company can make some very serious bucks. Which, if we were married, would also make you some very serious bucks."

"There's nothing wrong with ambition, Kate. Not when it's good for both of us."

She looked up just then to see Jason striding toward her. Clearly he was tired of waiting.

"You coming with me or staying with him?"

She didn't have to think twice. "I'm coming with you. Let's go."

Some of the tension drained from his shoulders as she took his arm and let him lead her over to the Yukon. Jason opened the passenger door, and Kate settled herself inside. He didn't say anything as he drove out of the garage, but the set of his jaw said his temper was still running hot.

"Let's get something straight." His big hands gripped the wheel a little too tightly. "You're either with him— or you're with me. You can't have it both ways."

"Andrew had a business opportunity for me. It could be worth a lot of money."

"Yeah?" He flicked her a sideways glance. "And what's he expect from you in return?"

If he didn't look so serious, Kate might have smiled. "Nothing I'm willing to give." She couldn't remember the last time a man had been jealous of her. It felt kind of good.

"I don't like him sniffing after you," Jason grumbled.

"I'm surprised you care. You don't seem like the jealous type."

"I don't share, Kate."

She caught his gaze and held it. "Neither do I."

His shoulders relaxed. She figured that meant they had just struck a deal. Kate felt oddly relieved.

"I don't like him," Jase said. "You deserve a lot better than a dick like that."

She wondered what he'd say if she asked if he was interested in the position, but she had a feeling she knew the answer. Once the case was solved, Jason would be moving on. Since there was no point thinking about it, Kate settled back in her seat.

The atmosphere in the Yukon improved even more after they'd driven through the local McDonald's and picked up breakfast goodies. Both of them were hungry. They carried warm bags of sausage-and-egg biscuits into Jason's town house. The delicious aroma surrounded them as they sat down to eat.

Kate glanced around the sunny kitchen. She had liked his place before. Now she was struck by how cozy it was, somehow snug and warm, a contrast to her open, sparsely furnished, modern apartment, which had a tendency to feel slightly cold.

Jase had showered at her place earlier that morning. When they finished the meal, he went upstairs to change, came back down in crisp blue jeans and a short-sleeved white Western shirt with pearl snaps on the front. He was wearing his usual scuffed brown boots, instead of the shiny black lizard boots he'd worn to the funeral.

They headed back to the garage to load his gear into the Yukon.

"What's in the bag?" Kate asked as he stowed a heavy black canvas satchel in the back and slammed the lift gate.

"We don't know what we're heading into. Better to be prepared."

Weapons then. She wasn't surprised, yet worry filtered through her. She thought of the night she had gone with him and Bran Garrett to Eli Zepeda's, thought of the shooting in Waco. Danger could be waiting in San Antonio.

She was glad to be facing it with Hawk Maddox.

CHAPTER TWENTY-FIVE

JASE HAD A dark blue Mustang rental car waiting when he landed the Cessna at a small private airport not far from San Antonio International. Once he had the plane tied down, they drove to the northwest side of town for the meeting Dr. Jerry Maxwell had arranged at the Bexar County Medical Examiner's office.

Since you never burned a source, Jase didn't mention Tabby's friend in the ME's office, the guy who had called with the intel.

It took less than twenty minutes to drive from the airport via I-410 west to Louis Pasteur Drive, wind through the maze of buildings and make their way inside the multistoried structure.

As they approached the front desk, Jase flashed Kate a glance full of concern. Coming here had to be painful for her. He remembered the day she had gone to the medical examiner's office to identify her sister's body, ended up drunk at the Sagebrush Saloon and cried on his shoulder.

He opened his mouth to ask if she wanted to wait outside, but before a word came out, she just shook her head. "Don't even go there."

How the hell did she always seem to know what he was thinking? "Fine." Didn't really matter. He'd known what her answer would be. He needed to accept she wasn't backing down no matter what.

They stopped at the front desk to check in. Jase gave the blonde woman behind the counter his name.

The woman smiled. "Dr. Chow left word for you to come straight back."

Dr. Maryann Chow was waiting when they walked into her office. A thin woman with high cheekbones and glossy black hair pulled into a tight knot at the back of her neck greeted them.

"You're Jason Maddox?" she asked.

"That's right. This is Kate Gallagher."

"It's nice to meet you." The woman extended a smooth, long-fingered hand. "Dr. Maxwell gave me both your names and a little background on the case you're working. He also sent me the autopsy file of the first victim. Since the cases may be connected, I've been expecting to hear from the Dallas police."

"They're pretty busy right now," Jase said, giving the cops an excuse that also explained why the ME should cooperate with him. "That's the reason we're following up."

"Jerry said you would probably want to take a look at the victim."

Jase didn't glance at Kate. He was making an executive decision. He knew the pain she would suffer when she saw that dead girl and thought of her sister. He could protect her from that. If she didn't like it, too bad.

"I'd like to see her, yes. Ms. Gallagher is going to wait here."

Kate looked up at him but, amazingly, didn't argue. *Smart girl.* This was one argument she wasn't going to win.

"We'll go over the file after we're finished," Dr. Chow said kindly to Kate.

Jase followed the doctor out of the office, down to

the morgue. Inside the sterile, white-walled chamber, the woman walked over to a bank of stainless refrigerator doors, found the one she was looking for, and pulled it open.

Rolling out a stainless-steel table, she drew back a sterile white sheet to reveal a waxy, doll-like figure with plain brown, shoulder-length hair. There were bruises on her neck and torso.

"There was no DNA match," the doctor said. "At this point, we haven't been able to identify the victim. We're running facial recognition but nothing has popped so far."

"Cause of death?"

"Strangulation."

His gaze went to the bruises on her neck and the ligature marks on her hands and wrists. The doctor moved the head so he could see the lipstick tattoo.

"Same as the other victim?" Dr. Chow asked.

"The tat's the same, location's the same, behind her left ear. Ligature marks on both victims. Different cause of death."

She nodded. "Yes, I saw that in the file Dr. Maxwell sent." She pulled the sheet back up, covering the ghostly face and thin body, and rolled the drawer closed. It latched with a sharp click that sent chills down Jase's spine.

"We'll go over the details when we're back in my office."

He nodded. Kate would want to hear, and the cold, antiseptic room made his skin crawl.

When the doctor opened the door to her office, Kate stood up from the chair she perched on in front of the desk. "Was it…was she another victim?"

"Looks like it," Jase said, closing the door behind him. Dr. Chow sat down, and Jase sat down next to Kate.

The doctor studied the file on her computer screen. "Our Jane Doe was approximately nineteen years old. As I said, cause of death was strangulation, in this case by compression with an object, something like a metal rod or a length of wood pressed across the throat."

His interest stirred. "The cause of death in the first homicide was blunt force trauma, not strangulation, but the killer used a wooden bat of some kind."

Dr. Chow nodded. "Yes, it could have been some kind of bat or club."

"So there could be a connection between the cause of death of both victims," Kate said.

"It's possible. It's certainly something the police will be interested to know."

And so was Jase. Two dead women. Two bat-like weapons used to kill them. Or the same weapon used two different ways.

"From what I noted in the Dallas case file," the doctor continued, "there were ligature marks on the wrists and ankles of both victims and evidence of repeated sexual assault."

"You mean rape?" Kate asked.

"Those kinds of injuries, yes. Some were fairly old. I would say our victim was likely a prostitute."

Kate's fingers tightened on the leather purse in her lap, but she managed to keep any show of emotion off her face. "Jason thinks the women could be victims of a sex trafficking ring."

"I wouldn't know about that," Dr. Chow said. "You need to speak to Detective Edward McKenzie in the homicide division. He's in charge of the case."

Jase had met the guy once. McKenzie wasn't a fan

of bounty hunters in general, but he'd been grudgingly willing to exchange information when he thought there was some payback for him in return.

Jase stood and so did Kate. "We'll make that our next stop. Thanks for your help, Dr. Chow." They both shook the doctor's hand before they left the office.

It was late in the day by the time Detective Edward McKenzie managed to carve out some time for them. McKenzie agreed to meet them at a Mexican restaurant called the Thorny Cactus, downtown on the Riverwalk.

By five thirty, the after-work crowd was swelling inside the bar, patrons trickling in from the famous walkway that ran beside a winding channel off the San Antonio River. After the Alamo, it was the city's most famous landmark.

As they traveled the concrete walkway beside the channel, an endless stream of excursion boats filled and dumped passengers at various stops along the route. Even on a hot, sticky mid-May day like this one, the Riverwalk crawled with tourists.

They stepped inside out of the heat. Recognizing McKenzie, Jase set a hand at Kate's waist, guiding her through the crowd to a booth off to one side upholstered in a serape-style, striped, multicolored fabric. Bright pi-ñatas hung from the ceiling, and Mexican music played in the background.

McKenzie looked past the shot of whiskey in front of him, and spotted Jase walking toward him. He was off duty, the meeting unofficial. McKenzie was divorced and balding. He practically swallowed his tongue when he saw Kate.

The detective slid out of the booth and extended his hand to her. "I'm Detective Edward McKenzie."

"Kate Gallagher."

"I understand your sister was also a victim of murder. I'm sorry for your loss."

"Thank you." Kate slid into the opposite side of the booth.

"McKenzie." Jase slid in beside her.

The detective smiled sardonically. "Heard about your little fiasco with Randy Harding up in Waco. Another dead guy added to your body count, Maddox?"

"I guess you missed the part where I wasn't the guy who shot him. Not that he didn't deserve it. You might check with Rosa Diaz on that."

McKenzie just grunted.

A smiling Latina waitress arrived with a basket of tortilla chips and a couple of menus. Jase handed the menus back. "Maybe later." The server whirled away in a flurry of orange gathered skirts to take care of another customer.

McKenzie snagged a chip. "So you're investigating a murder in Dallas you think might be connected to the one we have here."

"That's right. Your ME more or less confirmed it. Same tattoo, same location behind the vic's left ear. Murder weapon either the same or similar."

"Are you thinking we might have a serial?"

"I guess it's possible. Considering the tats, I'm thinking it's more like trafficking. Some kind of brand that signifies ownership. Restraints used on the vic's hands and feet. Any evidence of anything like that going on in San Antone?"

McKenzie frowned. He took a sip of whiskey, then shook his head. "Nothing I've heard about. I'll make a point to look into it, though. You say the murder weapon was the same in both cases?"

"The same or similar. A bat or club of some kind,

wooden in the first case, unknown here, but used to kill in different ways. First vic died of blunt force trauma not strangulation."

"I need to take a look at the Dallas file. Who's the lead on the case?"

"Detective Benson."

"I know Roger. I'll get in touch. Anything else?"

"Where did they find the woman's body?" Kate asked softly.

"Couple of miles out of town, next to a dumpster behind a fleabag motel in Prospect Hill called The Padre. Lot of prostitutes hang out in the area. CSIs checked the place over, didn't come up with anything useful." He kept his gaze on Kate. "Anything else you'd like to know?"

"Yeah, there is," Jase said, drawing his attention. "I'd like to know if the girl was a local or if she came here recently from somewhere else."

"We knocked on doors, talked to folks in the neighborhood. She was known in the area as Darcy. No last name. One of the prostitutes said she hadn't been in the neighborhood long. No criminal record for soliciting, but she was clearly working the streets. I'd say she probably wandered in from somewhere else." McKenzie downed his whiskey and set the glass back down on the table. "That it?"

"Appreciate if you'd let me know if you turn up anything else."

McKenzie didn't look enthused. He slid out of the booth. "I suppose I can do that. Long as you do the same for me."

"Deal."

McKenzie reached for his check, but Jase plucked it off the table. "It's on me," he said.

McKenzie actually smiled. "Thanks." He sauntered across the room toward the exit, leaving them alone at the table.

Jase leaned back against the booth. "We've got two choices. We can head back to Dallas. Or we can have a couple of margaritas, spend the night and do a little more digging in the morning."

"You think we might come up with something more?"

"Probably not." He smiled. "But I don't fly after I've been drinking, and I could sure as hell use a margarita."

Kate laughed and the sound slipped right through him. He wished he could make her laugh more often.

"I vote for staying," she said. "We can't do anything more until tomorrow, anyway." She reached out and snagged a chip. "But instead of a margarita, I think I'll have a straight shot of tequila."

Jase laughed. Damn, he liked this woman.

CHAPTER TWENTY-SIX

THEY TOOK THE night off. Finished their drinks at the Thorny Cactus, then checked into an Embassy Suites just around the corner from the Riverwalk. Kate figured a big guy like Jason needed room to move around, which the suite provided, plus they could set up their laptops in the living room and do a little work before they drove out to The Padre Motel.

Once they were settled, they walked back downtown to a small country-western bar Kate had noticed earlier. A few more drinks, then the band started playing. Kate danced to half a dozen songs with Jason, who for a big guy was surprisingly good. She couldn't remember having a better time.

Made even better by the passionate lovemaking back at the hotel, followed by a deep, dreamless sleep.

It was scary, Kate thought the next morning, how well the two of them fit.

Not that Jason would see it that way. Maddox wasn't the kind of guy who'd be interested in any kind of ongoing relationship. Kate had known it from the moment she had seen him lounging against the wall of the saloon like a big handsome lion on the prowl.

Kate got up from her laptop as he ambled out of the bedroom, ready for their trip to the crime scene.

"Too bad you didn't bring your hooker outfit," he

teased, checking out her dark blue jeans and bright pink tank top.

"Guess regular clothes will just have to do," Kate said.

"Trust me, honey, as good as you look, you'll have half the johns in Prospect Hill trying to buy a night."

Kate grinned.

The Padre Motel could have been in Old East Dallas—same seedy neighborhood, same seedy clientele. She noticed Jase staying close to her as they knocked on doors, visited nearby businesses, and talked to people in the area.

Late in the morning, they got lucky. A heavyset black woman named Bessie who worked at a nearby minimart remembered the murdered girl.

"Darcy." Bessie propped a thick hand on her ample hip and took a drag on her cigarette. "That was her name. Used to buy smokes in here, come in 'bout every other day. She hadn't been 'round here long, just a couple of weeks. She was lonely so we talked some."

"You know where she came from?" Jase asked.

"You a cop?" the woman asked, squinting at him through a wandering tendril of smoke.

"Bounty hunter," Jase said.

"Uh-huh. You hunting her killer?"

"Yeah."

Bessie nodded her approval. "She said somethin' once 'bout Houston. Said she'd had a real bad time of it there. Said not to say nothin'. She's dead now, so I guess it don't matter."

"You tell the cops?"

"I don't like cops." She leaned back against the counter. "I hope you find that shit bird who killed her."

"Don't worry," Kate said. "We will."

JASE'S CELL PHONE rang just as they pulled into the rental-car lot at the airport. He grabbed it and checked the screen. "It's Tabby." He parked the Mustang and put the phone on speaker. "What's up, Tab?"

"I never got the location of Tina Galen's last call, but I figured you'd want to know the phone was purchased in Houston."

"Houston." Jase flicked a glance at Kate. "Looks like the second victim may also have a connection there. That's good work, Tab."

"Thanks. I'll let you know if I turn up anything else."

The line went dead, and Kate's gaze found his across the console. "Looks like we're going to Houston," she said.

"Looks like." Leaving the keys in the ignition, he cracked the car door and they climbed out into the afternoon heat.

"Are we leaving from here?" Kate asked as they walked toward the plane.

"If that works for you."

"I've got my carry-on. That's all I need. Where do we start looking once we get there?"

"I know a couple of people who might be able to help."

Kate smiled. "You always know a couple of people."

Jase grinned. "Comes in handy sometimes. I need to make some calls, get things rolling." Since it was hotter inside the plane than outside, he stood in the shadow cast by the wing and went to work, sending texts, calling informants, setting the wheels of information-gathering in motion.

By tonight, he hoped to locate someone who could give him a line on what was happening on the streets in the underbelly of the city.

While he worked, Kate phoned her office. Jase could hear her going over details with her team and answering questions. He phoned The Max to let Mindy know he wouldn't be in for a day or two and to give Chase an update on the case.

The good news was Garrett Resources, being an oil and gas company, had offices in a building on the Houston Energy Corridor. The company kept a couple of apartments there for staff and clients coming into the city to do business. Chase offered to let them use one.

"I'll find out which unit's available and call you back," Chase said. "The West Houston Airport's closest. If you land there, you can borrow one of the company cars."

"I'm liking this deal," Jase said, smiling. He ended the call and turned to Kate. "Looks like we've got a place to stay." He opened the door on the copilot's side and helped her climb into the seat. "Thanks to Chase, we've got the use of an apartment not far from the airport."

"Wow, that's great."

While Jase completed his visual inspection, Chase phoned back with the info. A little over an hour later, the plane landed at the West Houston Airport, where a pair of black Range Rovers sat side by side in the parking lot.

Jase matched the license plate number to the info Chase had given him and found a set of keys inside. From the airport, he drove to a three-story apartment building at an address on Briar Forest Drive. The furnished unit had hardwood floors, granite kitchen counters and lots of windows, which pleased Kate. Him? Not so much.

As soon as they were settled, they both set up their laptops and started digging for information. Beginning with the *Houston Chronicle*, Jase read crime reports, public arrest records, anything to do with murder, rape, gun crimes, assault and particularly prostitution.

He had picked up enough bail skips in the city over the years to be familiar with the high crime areas. Sunnyside was the roughest, with the sixth highest crime rate in the nation. The southwest side had a lot of gang-related activity, mostly at night. Areas in the Third Ward near the university could be very bad news.

A story about an undercover sting the cops called the Easter Bunny raid caught his eye. Twenty johns picked up in various locations over a period of a couple of weeks. The police were looking into the possibility that some of the women were trafficked.

He needed to follow up, talk to someone in the department, see what he could find out.

He was following a link to a drug bust when Paulo Diaz returned the call Jase had made to him earlier. Paulo owed him for getting his sister out of a jam. Jase wasn't shy about using whatever leverage he had to get the info he needed.

"I got a guy for you to talk to," Paulo said. "He knows what is happening in town, who is doing what, where to get whatever it is you need. His name is Hector Moran. Hector owes me money. I told him you would pay for information. You pay him and he pays me. Works for both of us."

"Sounds good."

"He's a little guy, skinny, with a tattoo of a skull on his cheek. He'll meet you at a cantina called El Lagarto at midnight. It's in the southwest on Acacia Street."

El Lagarto. The Lizard. Southwest Houston. Not good. "I'll find it. Thanks, Paulo."

"You saved my sister. I do not forget."

Jase scrubbed a hand over the roughness along his jaw. He hadn't shaved that morning. Where he was headed, the hard look it gave him worked in his favor.

He shoved back his chair from the kitchen table. "That was Rosa Diaz's brother, Paulo. He's got a meet set for midnight with a guy who knows his way around. Southwest side. That's a rough neighborhood. I don't suppose there's any way in hell I can keep you from going with me."

Kate just smiled. "No way in hell," she said.

Jase swore under his breath and left her sitting at the table.

El Lagarto sat in a run-down neighborhood that reminded Kate of Prospect Hill. Which reminded her of Old East Dallas. After a while, they all looked the same.

They were sad places and they were dangerous. She had known that, accepted it. Didn't matter. She still wasn't quitting.

Jase parked the borrowed Rover in a dark spot between a couple of beaters where it was less likely to be spotted. Kate had dressed down for the visit, in black jeans, black boots and a black T-shirt, no makeup, her hair in a single braid.

Jason—no, Kate mentally corrected—*Hawk* Maddox looked like a real badass. Also dressed in black, his jaw rough with a dark growth of beard, he wore a black leather vest over a black T-shirt, the eagle tat on his powerful biceps daring anyone to give him any flak.

He set a hand possessively at her waist as they walked up to the bar. They surveyed the interior, both of them looking for a skinny guy with a skull tattoo on his cheek.

"He's in the back left corner," Kate said, spotting the guy sitting in the darkest part of the cantina.

Jase urged her in that direction. Both of them pulled out chairs and sat down.

"You're Hector?" Jase asked, though there really wasn't much doubt.

"*Sí*, and you are Hawk. A bounty hunter."

"That's right."

His black eyes went to Kate in search of an introduction, but it never came.

A waitress appeared wearing too much makeup and a low-cut blouse. Jase ordered a couple of beers, and a shot of tequila for Hector, since his glass was empty. He paid for the drinks when they arrived.

"I need to know what's happening on the street," Jase said, his beer bottle untouched, just props so they wouldn't stand out. "I'm looking for men running whores, someone involved in prostitution on a large scale. You heard about anything like that going on?"

Hector shot back his tequila. With a hiss, he set the empty glass back down on the table, the sound disappearing in the noise and chatter around them. "You are dealing with fire, Senor Hawk. No one speaks of it. No one who wishes to live. Be very sure you wish to know the answer."

Kate ignored the chill that ran down her spine. Jase fanned three hundred-dollar bills out on the battered wooden table. Finding a killer was getting expensive, she thought, not that it changed anything.

Hector reached for the money, but Jase set his hand on the cash. "Tell me what you know."

Hector glanced nervously around the bar. "These people...they have no conscience. They will kill you like a fly on the wall."

"Some of the women have a tattoo behind their left ears," Jase continued. "A red lipstick kiss."

Hector's eyes darted left and right, searching for any threat. He nodded.

"Give me something," Jase pressed. "I need a place to start looking."

"What about your woman? You are willing to risk her life?"

Jason's jaw clenched. He shot Kate a look, as if he could will her to make the right choice.

"Those men killed my sister," Kate said. "I want them stopped."

Jase slid the bills closer. Hector eyed the money. "These people…they pick up women off the street, young, not so young. Some they take from homeless shelters. They smuggle women across the border. These are powerful men, senor. The whores are only a small part of their business."

Jase moved his hand away from the cash. "There's more money in drugs."

"Si." Hector picked up the bills, folded them and stuffed them into the pocket of his shirt.

"How do I find them?" When Hector didn't answer, Jase laid down another hundred, then another.

Hector swallowed. He wet his lips as if his mouth actually watered, eyeing the money, weighing the risk. "The women…they move them around. Their customers know the schedule, what day they will be in the area."

"How do they move them?"

Hector glanced around and Jase's gaze followed. The bar was full now, boisterous, the customers getting bolder with every drink. From the frown on Jason's face, he didn't like the looks of the crowd.

"Trucks," Hector said.

"Like vans or pickup trucks?"

"That is all I know." Hector reached out and picked up the money. "Do not trust the police." Rising to his feet, he slipped silently into the throng and disappeared out the front door.

Jase rose and so did Kate. She felt his warm hand at her waist, easing her closer to his side as they moved through the unruly crowd. Two men were arguing in Spanish, both lean-muscled and wiry, one with black hair shaved on the sides and combed into a peak, the other with a thin mustache and lip whiskers. They were both heavily tattooed, arms, necks, everywhere skin was exposed.

Jase kept moving. They had almost made it past the skirmish when the guy with the mustache pulled a gun and pointed it at the guy with the pointed hair. In a blink, the other guy had his weapon in hand. More guns appeared.

Jase seemed to have a sixth sense. He pushed Kate to the floor a second before the first shot rang out, and rolled on top of her. Kate bit back a scream at the barrage of gunfire that followed, shattering the mirror behind the bar, knocking chunks out of tables, drilling holes in the wooden floor.

Men yelled obscenities and bolted for the door, a stampede that would have run right over them if Jason hadn't managed to pull her behind an overturned table. His .380 was out of his jeans pocket, in his hand, but he didn't fire.

At the first break in the violence, he grabbed her arm and hauled her up, and they both raced for the door. Just outside, gunfire erupted again, loud blasts back and forth from both factions. Dirt kicked up around their feet as Jase gripped her arm and dragged her off the porch, and they ran together, trying to reach some kind of cover.

More shots blasted through the air. Jase grabbed the side of his neck as they ran, and fear slammed into Kate so hard for an instant, she froze. "Oh, my God, you're hit!" Jase tugged her forward, blood running between his fingers, soaking into his T-shirt.

"Get down!" He pushed her behind a battered pickup, and they ducked beside the front wheel.

"How…how bad is it?" She was shaking, her head spinning. Fear for him made her heart hurt as if someone had hit her in the chest with a fist.

Jason reached up and carefully probed the wound. Fresh blood covered his fingers. "It's only a graze. I'll be okay."

Okay? she thought. Jase had been shot and it was all her fault. It was not *okay.*

He checked their surroundings, then urged her toward the Rover, which thankfully was parked away from most of the gunfire.

They crouched next to a faded blue Toyota with the body lowered just inches from ground. The lot was almost empty, car engines firing, tires screeching as vehicles shot out of the parking lot and took off in different directions.

They made it to the Rover, which Jase had left unlocked, and now Kate understood why. Clicking the locks and flashing the lights could have been deadly. He opened her door, but no light went on—another precaution—and shoved her inside. Kate kept expecting to hear the scream of sirens, thought maybe she did, but they were a long way away.

Then Jason was behind the wheel and the engine roared to life. The Rover shot backward, jerked forward and screeched out into the street. Neither of them said a word all the way back to the apartment.

But something had changed for Kate tonight. Her sister was dead. Nothing Kate did was going to bring her back. It had never occurred to her that in trying to find Chrissy's killer she could lose someone else she cared about.

Someone else she loved.

She looked over at Jason. Blood still seeped from the long gash beneath his ear. It made her stomach roll to think what could have happened. She refused to risk getting him killed, maybe getting both of them killed in order to get revenge.

It was finished.

She was quitting.

An odd sense of relief filtered through her.

It vanished in a heartbeat. Because the minute she told Jason the hunt was over, it would also be over for them.

CHAPTER TWENTY-SEVEN

HE'D NEARLY GOTTEN *her killed.* Jase swore foully. It was still dark outside, but dawn wasn't far away. Lying beside him in bed, Kate slept soundly, curled trustingly against him. He had taken her hard tonight. Needed to reassure himself that she was alive, unhurt, okay. She seemed to feel the same pressing urgency.

He had nearly gotten her killed. The thought wouldn't leave him. He had known the neighborhood had a lot of gang-related crime. He hadn't expected a gunfight to break out between 18th Street and MS-13, or Surenos or the Latin Kings or whoever the hell they were.

He was lucky to get out of there with only a scratch.

It could have been worse, the voice in his head reminded him. The bullet could have been a little higher and he would be dead, leaving Kate to face a bunch of vicious gangbangers who would show her absolutely no mercy. Men who raped and killed as if it were no different from pulling into McDonald's and ordering a burger.

He'd worried about it the entire time she'd helped him clean and bandage the crease on the side of his neck with gauze and adhesive she found in the medicine cabinet, a butterfly bandage that would hold together but still leave a scar. Not that he gave a damn.

Then, by some miracle and the grace of God, she had told him she wanted to stop the search. She had told him she wasn't willing to risk either of their lives for revenge. It just wasn't worth it.

Jase had felt a sweeping sense of relief.

It was followed by a deep sense of loss. Because last night had reminded him that continuing their relationship wouldn't be fair to Kate.

For him, what had happened wasn't particularly unusual. It was the kind of situation that came with the job. It could happen at any time, in any place, and likely would again.

He'd seen the grief Kate had suffered over the death of her sister. If they were in a relationship and something happened to him, she would suffer again.

He didn't want that to happen. He cared too much for Kate.

Jase closed his eyes. With Kate snuggled against him, he finally managed to nod off for a while, wound up getting a couple of hours of sleep.

Kate was in the kitchen when he wandered in barechested in his jeans, scratching the roughness along his jaw, feeling the bandage she'd put on his neck last night, reminding him all over again the danger they'd been in. He poured himself a cup of coffee and eased down in one of the kitchen chairs across from her.

"Are you okay?" Kate asked, catching the look on his face but reading it incorrectly.

"Yeah, I'm okay. We'll fly back home as soon as you're ready." He took a sip of coffee, trying to steady himself.

Kate stared at him until he glanced away. "All right, what's going on?"

He rubbed a hand over his face. "I'm just tired, is all. Neither of us got much sleep."

"I did just fine—thanks to you. Why didn't you sleep?"

He sipped his coffee, his eyes meeting hers over the rim of the mug. He wished she wasn't so damned perceptive. "I could have gotten you killed last night."

"We both knew the risks when we went there. Nothing that happened was your fault."

He set the mug on the table, dreading what he had to do. "Maybe not. The thing is, once we get back home, I think we should cool things down a little. Take a break from each other." He didn't want to do it. He loved every minute of being with Kate. His chest tightened. *Loved every minute?* Dammit, had he actually thought the *L* word? Christ, he really was in deep.

"Take a break?" she repeated. "I can't believe you just said that. You sound exactly like Andrew."

Jase came out of the chair so fast it crashed over onto the floor. He gripped her shoulders and hauled her to her feet. "Don't say that. Don't ever compare me to that wormy bastard. I'm not good for you, Kate. After what happened last night, can't you see that?"

"Actually, I see just the opposite."

He refused to listen, didn't want to hear something that would justify doing what he wanted to do but knew would be wrong. He left her standing there and stormed back into the bedroom to get ready for the flight back to Dallas.

Couldn't Kate see he was trying to protect her?

Or maybe he was trying to protect himself.

GOD, SHE MISSED HIM. Kate couldn't believe how much. She was back at work, her apartment stripped of anything Jason had been keeping there, any reminder that he had ever been there. He had picked up his things as soon as they got back to Dallas.

The emptiness she felt without him ached like a hole in her heart.

His invisible presence was everywhere. He was so big and powerful, so much larger than life, it was impossible to forget him. She was more than half in love with him. Way more, if she were honest.

But she had known from the start this was how it would end, so she was at least somewhat prepared.

She immersed herself in work, made it a point to keep herself busy. She spent the days catching up and trying to drum up new business. She called Stan Weiner, CEO of Solerno Engineering, the potential client Andrew had mentioned. Weiner hadn't hired a consulting firm yet. She had an interview with him at three o'clock that afternoon.

Lani called a little before noon and suggested they meet for a quick lunch. She needed to eat so she said yes. The Blue Cottage café was just down the block. She and Lani arrived at the same time and sat down at a table in front of the window.

Lani grabbed a menu, ran a hand through her short black hair as she perused the contents. She glanced over at Kate and smiled. "Okay, no use wasting time. What's going on with Mr. Hot?"

Kate sighed and closed her menu. "We decided to stop the investigation. Well, actually, I decided. Mr. Hot decided that since his investigative services were no longer needed, neither were his services in the bedroom."

"Wow." Lani folded her menu, and set it on the table next to Kate's. "I didn't see that one coming."

"Fortunately, I did. Jason isn't a relationship kind

of guy. I knew that from the start. It doesn't make me feel any better."

"I liked him. And I could swear he was really into you."

The waitress, a plump, silver-haired woman whose name tag read Betty, came to take their orders.

"Cobb salad with blue cheese and a glass of iced tea," Kate said.

"Same for me," said Lani. Betty collected the menus and walked away.

"So what happened with the investigation?" Lani asked.

"It got too dangerous. I almost got Jason killed. I figured revenge wasn't worth it."

The iced tea arrived and Lani took a drink. "What happened?"

While they waited for their food, Kate filled her friend in on the flight down to Houston and the shoot-out that had convinced her to stop looking for Chrissy's killer. "I didn't really want to quit. I feel like I failed my sister again."

"You did the right thing," Lani insisted. "Your mom wouldn't want you getting killed, too."

The salads arrived, which gave Kate a chance to change the subject. She forced herself to eat. Lani made her laugh, then it was time to head back to work.

At one fifteen, she had a meeting scheduled with Jim and Vera Lockwood to review the package they were putting together. An outline of next year's budget for New Hope, as well as the cost of expansion. Kate had spoken to Harper about it, and, as promised, Harper had arranged a presentation with the head of the Garrett family charities.

Kate checked her watch. She needed to get on the

road if she was going to be on time. Her phone pinged as she rose from the chair behind her desk.

"Kate, it's Vera. I'm afraid I have to cancel. I'm at the hospital. Holly's in labor."

A rush of excitement poured through her. "That's great! Which hospital is she in?"

"Texas Presbyterian. She's been in labor nearly six hours. First babies can take a while, you know. But the doctor thinks she's going to deliver fairly soon."

"Good, I'm coming down."

"Really? Holly will be so thrilled. Jim's on his way, too. I'll have him bring the proposal so you can take a look at it while we're waiting."

"Perfect. I'll see you soon."

Holly's baby was born an hour after Kate arrived. While they waited, she drank too much coffee and went over the proposal Vera and Jim had put together, which looked very good. With a few tweaks here and there, it would be ready to present to the charitable foundation.

Excitement poured through her as she and the Lockwoods followed a young dark-haired nurse down the hall to see the baby. Through the plate-glass window, they oohed and ahhed over the pretty little baby girl, then the nurse led them down the hall to see Holly.

"You can all go in," Nurse Susan said with a smile. "Just don't stay too long."

Holly was beaming as they walked into her room. Vera and Jim both hugged her. A tired smile bloomed when she spotted Kate. "I can't believe you came," she said.

Kate returned the smile. "I wanted to be here. I saw your daughter through the nursery window. She's beautiful."

"Yes...and so sweet...like an angel. I named her Angela. I'm going to call her Angie." Holly's dark eyes suddenly glistened. "Angie wouldn't be here if it weren't for your sister."

Kate's throat tightened. Chrissy had sacrificed her life for her friend. Now her killer was going to get away with cold-blooded murder.

She managed another smile. "I know Chrissy's up there watching over you and Angie right now. She would be happy for you, Holly."

"I know." Holly was tiring, her eyes drifting closed. It was time to leave.

Kate said goodbye, and told the Lockwoods she would call them with the results of her presentation. She tried to keep her thoughts focused on business, but after seeing Holly, all she could think of was how, once again, she had failed her baby sister.

CHAPTER TWENTY-EIGHT

JASE SAT AT his desk at The Max, his laptop open in front of him. He had tried to convince himself to leave the Gallagher case alone. Kate had finally come to her senses, and he didn't take Hector's dire warning lightly.

Still, he found himself searching the Houston area online news for information. He didn't like the idea of a killer getting away with murder, but deep down, he knew he was doing it for Kate. Leaving her alone was the right thing to do. Kate deserved a stand-up guy who would make a good husband and father. Not a guy who would make her afraid every time he left the house that her man wouldn't be coming home.

Now that he'd made the decision, he wanted Kate to remember him. She wouldn't forget the guy who had found her sister's killer. Why it was so important, he couldn't say. He just wanted to make things right for her.

Earlier that morning, he had left a message for Tony Castillo, a friend in the Houston PD, a detective in the homicide division, guy he trusted, a former marine. Maybe Tony could give him something.

Jase checked his cell, returned a couple of text messages, then glanced up as Chase crossed the office in his direction.

"What's up?" Jase rose from his chair.

"I talked to Harper this morning. She was at a meeting with Kate and Charles Stanton in regard to that charity Kate's involved with, New Hope Rehab. I take it you two aren't seeing each other anymore."

Jase's chest tightened. It happened every time he thought about her. "She decided to drop the case. Since she doesn't need me anymore, I figured it was better for both of us if we ended things now, before it got complicated."

"So Kate didn't need you anymore. What about you, Hawk? Don't you need her anymore, either?"

Regret and something else sifted through him. He refused to call it despair. "I wasn't good for her, okay? Not long term. I'm a bounty hunter. Kate needs a settled-down kind of guy."

"You think so? Because I didn't see it that way. I don't know many women who would have gone with you to roust Eli Zepeda, but Kate did. She was with you on the case from the start."

Jase glared. "Yeah? Well, in Houston, I almost got her killed. It was a near thing, and I sure as hell don't want it to happen again. I'm not good for her. Surely you can see that. Now let it alone, okay?"

"Fine, whatever you want." Chase started walking away.

"How is she?" Jase couldn't resist asking. "Is she all right?"

Chase looked back. "Harper thinks she misses you. I have no idea why." Turning, he walked back to his office and closed the door.

Jase sat back down at his desk. He was doing the right thing. Kate was his to protect. He didn't have any other choice.

His cell rang. It was Paulo Diaz.

"Hey, Hawk, I got something to tell you, and it is not good."

"What is it, Paulo?"

"You remember Hector Moran?"

"Same Hector I met at El Lagarto?"

"That is the one. Hector is dead, amigo. Shot in the back last night."

Jase's trouble-instinct crawled up his spine. "Who did it?"

"I am not sure. Surenos, maybe. Or MS-13. It gets worse."

"Tell me."

"Word on the street is whoever went after Hector knows someone paid him for information. He died before he had time to talk, but they know someone was asking questions and they are determined to find out who. You and your woman are not safe. You are in very great danger, amigo."

His pulse was hammering. Kate was in danger. He had to get to her. Find a way to keep her safe.

"What about you? Will you and Rosa be okay?"

"No one knows I spoke to Hector. He can't tell anyone now, so we are safe."

"Thanks, Paulo, I owe you."

"Take care, amigo."

"You, too." As he packed up his laptop, Jase phoned Kate. When the call went to voice mail, he phoned her office.

"Kate had a meeting with a client," her assistant said. "But she planned to be back in the office before five."

"If she gets there before I do, tell her not to leave. Tell her it's important. Tell her I'm on my way." He ended the call and grabbed his laptop, spoke to Mindy and told her he was headed out but he'd be checking in. He rapped on the door to Chase's office and went in.

"What is it?" At the look on Jason's face, Chase came to his feet.

"Someone ordered a hit on an informant of mine in Houston. Word is, they know Hector was being paid for intel. Now they're gunning for whoever was asking questions. People saw us talking to him that night. They know what we look like. I'm a bounty hunter. I'm not hard to find. Add to that, we've been asking questions all over Texas. Sooner or later, someone's going to put things together, figure the connection and come after us. I've got to talk to Kate, find a way out of this. I'm heading over to her office now."

"You need help, you know where I am."

He nodded. "I'll keep you posted."

In minutes he was on his way down Blackburn Street. He couldn't stop a thread of eagerness mixed with the fear trying to cloud his brain. By the time he reached her office, his Kimber was in his holster covered by his T-shirt.

Kate was standing at the reception desk. She looked good. Beautiful. Better even than he remembered. He wanted to touch her so badly his mouth went dry.

He glanced around. Almost closing time. The receptionist was already gone. "We need to talk."

Kate gave him a phony smile. "Hi, Jason. It's nice to see you, too."

"No time." He grabbed her arm, ushered her into her office and closed the door.

"What is it?" she asked, picking up his anxious vibes. "What's going on?"

He didn't want to tell her. He had done his best to keep her out of danger, but he had failed. "We didn't quit soon enough, Kate. They killed Hector Moran last night and word is, they're looking for whoever paid him for info. I need to get you somewhere safe. We'll go by your condo, pick up whatever you need, then find a place to lay low till we can figure this out."

"Slow down. You're telling me the people who killed Chrissy are looking for us?"

"They killed Hector, so yeah. It won't take them long to figure out we were the ones talking to him at El Lagarto. Once they do, they'll come for us. Get what you need and let's go."

She looked as if she might argue, but in the end, she closed her laptop, grabbed it and her purse and they left the building.

Jase drove straight to her apartment. He felt a little better after talking to the guard behind the desk in the lobby, warning him to be on the lookout for trouble. But they needed to keep a low profile. Zepeda had warned them about the cops. Hector had warned them. The fewer people who knew, the better.

"No one comes up," Jase said. "No one. Got it?"

"Yes, sir. You can count on me."

"Thank you, Gordy," Kate said.

"Keep a sharp eye. These men mean business." They rode the elevator upstairs in silence. Kate didn't say anything until they were inside her apartment and Jase had checked to be sure the place was secure.

"All right," she said, propping a hand on her hip in a gesture he recognized. "Let's hear it. Start from the beginning."

Resigned, he started talking, beginning with the phone call from Paulo Diaz, Hector's murder and ending with Paulo's warning that they were now the ones being hunted.

Jase tried not to flinch as the color slowly drained from Kate's pretty face.

KATE REFUSED TO LEAVE. At least not without a plan. It had taken her a while to get over the shock of being told men were coming after them, but now that she had accepted the news, there was no way was she going into hiding.

"You aren't being realistic," she said. "We can't just disappear. We both have lives, businesses. We have to find these men and stop them."

"I'll find them. In case you've forgotten, it's what I do."

"Oh, I haven't forgotten. You're a big, bad, bounty hunter. But in case *you've* forgotten, Hawk Maddox, this is my life we're talking about. It's my life that's in danger, just like yours. I'm sure as hell not going to sit around waiting for these guys—whoever they are—to find me and put a bullet in my head."

"You need to trust me, Kate—just this one time."

Kate looked up at him, her heart squeezing with how much she had missed him. She rested a hand on his cheek, felt the familiar roughness of his unshaven jaw.

"I trust that you're the best at what you do, and that you'd to anything to protect me. Even give up your own life." The minute the words were out, she knew they were true, had known in some deep part of herself all along.

Jason captured her palm against his cheek and looked into her face, and she could feel the power of those blue, blue eyes. "I don't want you getting hurt. I couldn't live with that."

She forced herself to move away. "I can help you, Jason. Together we can find these men and put them away, put them somewhere they won't be able to hurt us or anyone else ever again."

He paced across the room and back, his muscled

shoulders rigid with tension. "Getting you more deeply involved in this is the last thing I want."

"I can't just go into hiding. It's not realistic and it isn't safe. We have to stop them. You know I'm right, Jason."

He fell silent for several heartbeats. Finally a re-signed sigh whispered out. "Unless we can find these guys and put them away, neither of us will ever be safe."

"We can do it if we work together," Kate said.

Jase paced away for several heartbeats, then walked back. "Since I'm not willing to leave your protection to someone else, we stay together—on one condition. After we get settled, I take you through some basic self-defense moves. And as soon as we get a chance, we practice your shooting."

"Fine."

He scrubbed a hand over his face. "We need to make a plan."

"Whatever plan we come up with, we're going to have to go back to Houston."

"Yeah," Jase said simply. "I know."

CHAPTER TWENTY-NINE

"FIND HER! ALL of you—spread out and keep looking! She can't have gotten that far. Whatever you do, don't let her get away!"

The men fanned out, at least five of them, running off in different directions. Two of them charged right past the entrance to the alley where she was hiding.

It was dark, the night so black Callie could only feel the rough brick walls as she crept along in the fetid, humid air. Carefully she picked a path through the rotten garbage strewn all over the pavement, past the overflowing metal dumpster, trying to ignore the disgusting smells, careful not to step on a beer bottle or nudge a tin can with her foot and give herself away.

Icy fear gripped her. Her heart pounded so hard she could feel the sharp thump in her ears. She had to find a place to hide before they caught her and dragged her back, before it was too late.

But her mind was fuzzy from the last drugs they had given her, pills so far, but she knew it was going to get worse. Especially now that she had run. She couldn't let them find her.

Her eyes burned as she thought about the last girl who had tried to run away. They had caught her in less than an hour, beaten her so badly she couldn't get out of bed for days.

But Callie had heard them talking about her, saying they were planning to sell her as a virgin. She was young, only thirteen, which made her worth a lot of money. She heard them mention some rich old man who liked young girls.

Tears slipped down her cheeks. She never should have run away from home. But things had gotten really bad, and she was desperate. She had left the day after her thirteenth birthday. She just couldn't take it anymore, the fighting, her stepfather slapping her mother, threatening Callie if she didn't do what he said.

Her mother worked as a waitress and didn't get home until late. After her stepdad lost his job as a dockworker at the port, he'd grown angry, had taken it out on both of them.

Then Steve started looking at her in a bad way, touching her when her mother wasn't around. She couldn't tell her mom about Steve. Her mother loved him. Even if Callie told her the truth, her mother wouldn't believe her. Callie didn't know what to do, and there was no one she could talk to about it.

Finally, she packed a small suitcase, headed for the nearest bus stop to home, got on a bus and left for Houston. Maybe if she went away for a while, she could figure things out.

The minute the bus doors opened, she was scared. She had known she was in trouble the minute she got off the bus and three men appeared out of nowhere and started following her down the street. Bad trouble. The worst trouble of her life.

A sound interrupted her thoughts. The men were heading back this way. She glanced frantically around, found a spot beneath a chunk of wet cardboard and huddled down in the mud and slime on the alley floor. She held her breath so she wouldn't make even the slightest sound as two of the men darted inside the entrance to look for her.

"See anything?" the tall skinny one asked. His name was Grady.

"I do not think she is here." Rico was the other guy's name, a Mexican with a short fat body and a thick accent. She eased in a slow breath as Rico turned and started back down the alley the opposite way.

Callie closed her eyes and said a silent prayer. As Rico passed the dumpster, she actually believed that God might be listening. Then the sound of a deep voice reached her and her eyes popped open.

"Well, look who I found," Grady said.

Callie's throat tightened into a scream.

IT WAS GETTING LATE. Kate hurriedly packed a bag, grabbed her laptop, and they took the elevator down to the lobby. They drove straight to Jason's to retrieve his gear, then headed south on I-45.

It was close to four hours to Houston, but Jase insisted on driving instead of flying. He needed his own ride, he said. He could count on the Yukon. Kate wondered if it had anything to do with the metal restraints welded into the back of the vehicle.

As they headed out of the city, Jase made several evasive turns and doubled back a couple of times to be sure they weren't being followed. On the road, they went to work making plans, Kate taking notes on her iPad.

"Let's start with what we know so far," Jason suggested.

Kate tried not to think how good it felt being with him again. Jase seemed to fill some part of her that felt empty without him. It wouldn't last long, she knew. And if she weren't careful, she could get hurt even worse than before.

"We need a working theory," he continued. "We can change whatever turns out to be wrong."

"Okay, we're pretty sure the group is working mainly out of Houston," Kate said. "Both murdered women came from there. Or at least we think they did."

"And Hector's info corroborates that assumption. He said the group picks women up off the street—they could be runaways, battered women, or girls who come to the city hoping to find a better life."

"Instead they wind up hooked on drugs," Kate said. "Feeding their habits by selling themselves."

"Hector also mentioned women in homeless shelters, and those being smuggled in from out of the country. Pretty typical for a trafficking ring."

Kate jotted down a few notes. "Hector talked about the women being moved around. That sounds like it could be important."

"It could be the key to finding them," Jase said. "I've got a call into an HPD detective named Tony Castillo. He hasn't called back, but sooner or later he will."

Worry filtered through her. "Hector said not to trust the police."

"He was warning us to watch out for dirty cops. I've worked with Tony before. Always been a straight-up guy. I trust him, but I won't take chances."

"So moving the women around. How would that work?"

"Could be they haul them to a specific location," Jason said. "A motel or a house on the outskirts of town, something like that. The women are waiting when the men arrive to take their pleasure."

"Pleasure." It made her stomach burn to think of

it. She loved sex with Jason, but it was consensual, a joy they both shared. She couldn't imagine having a stranger greedily using her body any way he wanted.

"If they move them from place to place, maybe there's no primary location," she said. "No single place they actually house and feed them."

"I'm betting they have a facility somewhere, a hub they work in and out of. Could be more than one. And if they're using pickups and vans to move the women from place to place, they've got to park them somewhere. Sooner or later, we'll figure out where."

They lapsed into silence after that. As tired and worried as she was, she slept for a while. When she awoke, they were pulling into the apartment Chase had loaned them before, out by the Energy Corridor near the Garrett Resources office. Since there was no record of their stay, no way to track them to that location, it was the safest place they could be.

Jason parked the car beneath the covered carport in the lot. They grabbed their bags and went up to the apartment.

Riding together for hours had heightened the sexual awareness that always seemed to spark between them. As Kate crossed the living room, she could feel the heat of Jase's body behind her. When she turned, the hunger in his blue eyes scorched right through her, heating her from the inside out.

Desire flared. She wanted him. She always seemed to want him. She replaced the feeling with a shot of anger.

"Not going to happen, big boy. You're the one who ended things, remember? I'm not going to be your booty call whenever you get an itch you need to scratch."

His jaw hardened. "That isn't the way it is, and you know it."

"Isn't it?"

"It was never like that. Not then, not now. I wanted you. No one else—just you. I still do." He stormed past her down the hall into the second bedroom and slammed the door.

Kate just stood there. She was the one he wanted? The only one he wanted? She couldn't believe he had actually said that. It wasn't true. Couldn't possibly be true.

As she had a dozen times, she went over the words he had said the day he had ended their affair. *I'm not good for you. After what happened, can't you see that?*

She'd thought it was just a line, the kind men used when they wanted to end a relationship they were tired of.

Now she wondered… Surely he didn't blame himself for what happened at El Lagarto? Perhaps even the brawl at Mean Jack's?

Even if he did, it didn't matter. Just like Andrew, he wasn't willing to take a chance on her, on them, and she was in too deep to settle for an occasional round of sex. The road to heartbreak was paved with sultry days and hot nights in the bedroom. Hawk Maddox wasn't leading her down that road again.

Kate stripped out of her clothes and headed for the shower. She dried her hair and went straight to bed. She could hear Jason in the other bedroom, then his heavy weight shifting on the mattress. Clearly he was having as much trouble falling asleep as she was.

Kate's resolve strengthened. Hawk Maddox was simply too much for her to handle. She wasn't willing to put her heart at risk again.

THE FOLLOWING MORNING, Jase was up first thing, rousing Kate, who was still half asleep, determined to begin their self-defense lessons.

"Are you sure about this?" she grumbled, yawning. "It's hard to believe self-defense lessons are going to be much good against a pack of vicious criminals."

Jase just smiled. "Always better to be prepared."

He had a couple of hours before the meeting he had set up when Castillo had returned his call. Jase showed Kate how to use an opponent's own weight against him, how to take a fall without getting hurt, demonstrated how to go after the most vulnerable places on a man's anatomy.

He didn't like the gleam in Kate's eyes when they practiced those particular moves.

They were both sweaty by the time they finished.

"Why don't you go get a shower?" he said. "We'll do some more work when we get back."

If it didn't kill him. Being that close to Kate, touching her, holding her. *Damn.* He had a set of blue balls that wouldn't quit.

Half an hour later, they loaded into the Yukon for his meeting with Castillo. Until this was over he wasn't letting Kate out of his sight.

"Where are we meeting him?" she asked as they rolled along the busy Houston streets.

Jase forced himself not to glance in her direction, to remember the way her skinny jeans hugged those long sexy legs and curved over her perfect ass. Remember how he'd felt wrapped around her when they had been practicing self-defense. The simple scoop-neck top she was wearing made him itch to cup her pretty breasts.

He forced his mind back on track. "Memorial Park," he said, his voice a little husky. "I didn't want anyone to see us or overhear our conversation. We have no idea where the threat might come from. And Tony's a cop. All the more reason to keep the contact on the down low."

Jase scrubbed a hand over the jaw he hadn't bothered to shave again that morning. He was tired from the long drive and lack of sleep, impossible with Kate lying in bed on the other side of the wall. He'd wanted her all night. Ached with wanting her.

He had never felt this way about a woman, never felt this driving need, this constant desire just to be with her. He had a feeling he never would again.

But Kate was right. He couldn't just sleep with her whenever it was convenient. It wouldn't be right. Or fair. And he couldn't offer her more than that. He lived a life of uncertainty. And even if Kate was seriously interested in a guy like him, which he doubted, sooner or later she would realize the mistake she had made.

He needed to keep his hands off her and his mind out of the gutter. Once this was over, he'd get out of her life for good.

In the meantime, they had work to do.

He turned into the park and wound his way along the lanes through the lush green landscape, tall pines and gnarled oaks. Dirt paths provided jogging trails, and there were ponds and creeks scattered around the park. When he reached the area where the meet was set, he kept driving just to be safe. He didn't see anything but a string of bicycle riders and a handful of joggers, working up a sweat along the road.

Circling around, he drove back to the parking area. A brown unmarked police car sat in one of the spaces not far from an old Chevy minivan. A caravan of kids climbed out as Jase pulled into one of the empty spaces. He spotted Castillo sitting at a picnic table on the grass.

"Thanks for meeting us," Jase said, shaking Castillo's nut-brown hand. He was a good-looking guy, about six feet, with an athletic build and glossy black hair. "Tony, this is Kate Gallagher."

"Good to meet you, Kate. Jase filled me in on what's been happening and told me about your sister. I'm sorry for your loss."

He had leveled with Castillo, taken a certain amount of risk, but they needed help. To get it, he had to trust someone.

"What can you tell us?" They sat side by side across from Castillo at a picnic table not far from the parking lot. A warm breeze rolled over the short green grass and rustled through the branches of the trees.

"You asked me about what they called the Easter Bunny raid. That was conducted by the sheriff's department over a period of a couple of weeks back in April. Picked up twenty johns from various locations. The deputies were mostly focused on the men and whether the prostitutes picked up in the sting were being trafficked."

"Were they?"

"Most of the women were older, been in the life for a while. A few young Mexican girls who'd crossed the border illegally. Nothing organized turned up. Nobody underage. Nobody being held against her will."

Kate shifted on the wooden bench. "Were any of the women marked with a red lipstick tattoo?"

"Jason mentioned that on the phone. I checked. There was nothing noted in the arrest records. But about a month ago, we got a report of a woman missing from a homeless shelter. Odds were she'd wandered off somewhere, so there wasn't much concern. Two weeks later, we found her body in a ditch. She'd been beaten to death. She had a lipstick tattoo on the side of her neck."

"Kate's sister had that mark, and there's a dead woman in San Antonio who also has it. Word is both of them lived in Houston before they were killed."

"So you think the homeless woman was being trafficked and escaped? They caught up with her and killed her?"

"I think that's what happened to Kate's sister, Christina."

Kate leaned forward, catching Castillo's attention. "Where was the woman's body found?" A question that had proved useful before.

"Field off Interstate 10 out near Brookshire. Not much around there. After I talked to Jason this morning, I made a few calls. There's a rumor on the street about an organization that's set up shop somewhere in the Houston area. First I've heard of it, but I have a hunch they been in business awhile."

"Trafficking?"

"Looks like it. They're running women, marking them as their property. The people who work for them call that lipstick tat *el beso de la muerte*. The kiss of death. The men who own them are known as Los Besos. They're bad hombres, Hawk."

"We figured that out when they murdered Kate's sister. The question is, how do we find them?"

Castillo looked at him hard. "A better question might be how do we stop them?"

CHAPTER THIRTY

THE CONVERSATION WENT from bad to worse.

"One other thing," Castillo said. "Last night, a call came in from the sheriff's office in Wharton, young girl reported missing. Apparently, she's been gone from home a couple of days. Stepdad convinced the mother she was just acting out. Sooner or later she'd come back on her own."

"But she hasn't."

"Not yet."

"How old is she?" Kate asked.

"Thirteen."

Kate glanced away.

"Her name is Callie Spencer," Castillo continued. "Only a child. As soon as I get back, I'll text you a photo."

"Do you...do you have any leads on what might have happened to her?" Kate asked.

"Her mother thinks she may have gone to Houston to see one of her girlfriends. Apparently, she and a girl named Penny Schweitzer were close when Penny's parents lived in Wharton. We checked it out. Callie never showed up at the Schweitzer girl's home. No phone call, nothing."

"They ping her cell?" Jase asked.

"Last call was made from a tower along Highway

69, which supports the mother's theory she was on her way to Houston."

"I'd appreciate if you'd send me anything else you've got on the girl," Jase said.

"I'll send you everything we've got and keep you posted on anything new."

From the park, Jase drove back to the apartment, making evasive maneuvers just to be sure no one followed—including Castillo. According to the detective, HPD hadn't heard a whisper about a human trafficking ring in the Houston area. Jase couldn't help wondering why.

Back at the apartment, he sat down in front of his laptop to do a little more digging.

"Hector said not to trust the police," Kate said, walking up behind him. "Maybe someone in the department's taking bribes to keep things quiet."

"Yeah, well, the more dead bodies pile up, the harder that's going to be."

"I can't stop thinking about that young girl, Callie Spencer. Do you think it's possible Los Besos kidnapped her?"

"She's a runaway headed for Houston, so I suppose there's a chance."

Kate sighed. "I hope we can stop them before any more women die."

Or anyone else, Jase thought, *especially not him and Kate*.

While Kate worked on her email and checked in with her office, Jase worked the internet. The file from Castillo showed up in his email, and Jase brought up the photo of the Spencer girl. Either the picture was old, or Callie looked even younger than her thirteen years. She was pretty, with the baby face of innocence, freckles across the bridge of her nose, long softly curling auburn hair and a fair complexion.

Callie Spencer was a pervert's wet dream. She'd be worth a bundle to some lowlife who was into young girls.

"Oh, Jason, she looks so young." Kate had returned to her place behind him. The scent of her soft perfume teased his senses and began to make him hard.

Inwardly he cursed. Damn, he wanted this case over and done, wanted Kate safe back home in Dallas. Safe from him and the temptation she posed.

Her cell phone chimed and she turned to answer it. At the smile on her face when the call ended, he came to his feet.

"What is it?"

"That was Holly. I went to see her at the hospital when her baby was born." Her smile widened. "A beautiful little girl she named Angie."

"Good for her," Jase said, trying to ignore Kate's wistful smile. There was a time he'd wanted kids, a family. Too late for him now. Just thinking about it made his chest feel tight.

"Holly called to ask if we were still looking for the men who killed Chrissy," Kate said excitedly. "She said she'd thought of something that might help us."

"We could sure use something."

"Chrissy told Holly the women were locked in the back of an eighteen-wheeler and driven out to truck stops on the interstate. That's where she was the night she escaped."

Jase felt a rush like a tip coming in on a skip he was hunting. "All right, Holly!"

"Not pickups or minivans, Jase. They're driving the

women around in big diesel trucks. That has to be a lot easier for us to track down."

"The only place you can hide an eighteen-wheeler is in plain sight. They're taking the women to places the drivers hang out."

"Like truck stops and rest areas. That's where they find their clientele."

"Yeah. Could also be places where a lot of deliveries are made."

"Like the port."

Jase nodded. "Port of Houston has trucks in and out all hours of the day and night."

"So how do we find out which trucks are hauling women?"

His mind replayed the conversation he'd had with Tony Castillo. "They found the homeless woman's body off I-10. Lot of truck stops along the interstate. We're going to have to do some basic detective work."

"Ask questions, you mean."

"That's right. If we get a lead, we'll stake the place out, see what turns up."

Kate grinned. "Just like in the movies."

Not quite, Jase thought. A stakeout was about as much fun as watching a mushroom grow. But he didn't say that. Maybe he could risk leaving Kate in the apartment. Might be the safest bet.

But what if it wasn't?

He'd cross that bridge later. In the meantime, they would keep digging.

IT WAS FULL dark when they arrived at the Flying J truck stop out I-10 near Brookshire, the closest fuel stop to where the homeless woman's body had been found. The diesel pumps were all full, the yard lined with eighteen-wheelers of every year, make and color.

Like all travel facilities on the interstate, trucks arrived and departed round the clock. Long-haul truckers often slept in the back of their rigs. Facilities were provided for the drivers: bathrooms, showers, and a place to purchase food. Kate figured the men, often far from home, were the perfect candidates for female companionship.

"I'll go in and wander around," she said. "If I buy something, it'll give me an excuse to ask a few questions."

"Keep it on the down low. We don't want word getting back to Los Besos."

Kate nodded. "What about you?"

"I'm a guy. I'm going to see if anyone in there can help me get laid."

Kate grinned. The way Jason looked—six foot four inches of solid male muscle, shadow of beard along his jaw, gorgeous blue eyes—half the female staff would likely volunteer.

They went inside separately. The main structure was a big stucco building with bathrooms for travelers in the back, and row after row of items up front to temp the unwary: packaged junk food, soft drinks and beer, coffee, hot dogs, even hot meals. Tourists, truckers and locals all wandered the aisles.

Kate meandered from row to row, finally stopped next to a clerk she spotted refilling shelves. "Is this place always this busy?"

The woman glanced up, older, dark brown hair, a little overweight. "It never stops. The people who own it must make a fortune."

Kate chuckled. She looked through the items on the

shelves as if she might be interested, picked up a souvenir stuffed Texas Ranger bear. "With this many people around, I imagine the place could be dangerous at night. I heard a woman's body was found not far from here."

"Yeah, I heard about that. Pretty uncommon for something like that to happen. Sheriff's department does a good job of keeping an eye on things around here."

Kate picked up the bear. "This is cute. I think I'll take it." Satisfied with the information she'd gotten, she went to pay for the bear, then headed back out to the Yukon. A few minutes later, Jase opened the door and slid in behind the wheel.

"Place looks legit. I don't think Los Besos is working out of here."

"I don't, either. The clerk mentioned a strong police presence. She said the woman who was killed was something out of the ordinary."

He cranked the engine. "Lot of truck stops along I-10."

The drove farther west to a Love's Travel Stop, which was also a bust. They stopped at a second Love's, hit a Travel Plaza, then started back toward the city. They went into a second Flying J, then a TexMart Travel Center.

The TexMart wasn't part of a big chain like the others, and something about it seemed a little off. There were just as many trucks parked in rows in the asphalt yard, but it wasn't as brightly lit. The inside of the building was less orderly, with empty spaces on the shelves, the bathrooms neglected.

Since Jason was deep in conversation with the guy refilling the beer cooler, Kate decided to give him some space. She bought a cup of coffee and went back out to the Yukon.

She watched several trucks pull in and a couple of them fuel up and pull out. Nothing looked suspicious. Jason still hadn't returned. She wished she could be a fly on the wall for the conversation he was having.

CHAPTER THIRTY-ONE

"Look, I'm not supposed to send anyone out there who wasn't referred by a regular customer," the clerk said.

"Dude, I got an old lady and three kids," Jase said. "Only time I get any is when I'm on the road. One of the drivers mentioned this place. Said if I wanted some action, this is where I could find it."

"But you said you don't remember the guy's name."

"Joe something. Drives for one of the big moving companies." Jase reached into his pocket and took out his wallet, pulled out a fifty-dollar bill. "Man, my old lady's pregnant again. It's been so long my balls are turning blue. Cut me a break, will you?"

The clerk was a slim guy in his late twenties with wheat blond hair and an unassuming face. He studied the fifty, reached over and plucked it out of Jase's hand. "Truck's in tomorrow night around eleven. You need to know the password to get in."

"What is it?"

"Firebird."

Jase grinned. "Thanks, bro." He looked down at the name tag pinned to the guy's shirt. "I won't forget this, Wally."

The clerk just grunted. As Jase walked away, the smile slid from his face.

He climbed into the Yukon. "Truck'll be here tomorrow night." He clicked on his belt and pulled out onto the interstate.

"Are we going to call the police?"

The question he'd been considering. "It's a risk. I trust Castillo, but he can't make the bust alone. He's got to bring in his superiors, and if one of them's dirty, word will get back to Los Besos. If that happens, we'll be in more danger than we are now."

Kate sat back in her seat. "So what are we going to do?"

Jase rubbed a hand over his unshaven jaw. "If we don't bust these guys tomorrow night, we might not get another chance." There really was no decision to make. "I'll call Castillo as soon as we get back to the apartment."

Jase phoned the detective the minute he walked into the living room. "You need to leave Kate out of this," he said. "Can you do that?"

"I'll do my best," Castillo said.

The detective called back the following morning. "The bust is set, but you need to be there. You're the guy who was given the info. The arrests will go smoother if you're there to play your part."

"Don't worry. I'll be there." Jase ended the call.

Convincing Kate to let him go without her was going to be the tricky part. He probably should have told her sooner, but he waited, hoping to avoid an argument. He knew he was in trouble when she walked out of the bedroom that night dressed completely in black, her thick blond curls pulled into a low ponytail.

"It's going to take a while to drive to the TexMart," she said. "If the truck is supposed to be there at eleven, shouldn't we get going?"

"The cops will get there early enough to set up a

perimeter. They'll stay out of sight until the truck is in position and working the johns who show up."

"How much longer do we wait?"

He sighed. "Look, Kate. The cops are handling this, but things could go south. You're just another person for them to worry about. Be better if you stayed here."

"Maybe. Maybe not. Either way, you're going and so am I. We're so close, Jase. I quit before and it didn't do any good. I'm not quitting again."

"Christ, you're a pain in my ass."

Kate had the audacity to grin. She leaned up and gave him a kiss on the cheek. "But in a good way, right?"

Jase hauled her into his arms and kissed her the way he'd been wanting to, long, hot and deep. Kate moaned. She was trembling when he let her go.

"If…if you think that's going to persuade me to stay home, you're wrong."

Amusement slipped through him. "Actually, I just wanted to kiss you." Stupid as it was. "But you have to promise to stay in the car, out of the way."

"I will, I promise."

He nodded. "Get your gear and let's go."

Forty-five minutes later, they pulled up at the rendezvous point, parked in a spot a short distance from a line of patrol cars. The plan was for Jase to gain access to the truck using the password he'd acquired last night. It wasn't a good idea to risk an unfamiliar guy, and if he could get the door open, the cops could swoop in and take control of the situation with less chance of the women getting hurt.

At least that was the plan.

Jase and Kate both got out of the Yukon. Castillo left his men to walk back and speak to them. The detective was heavily armed and wearing tactical gear, as were the rest of the men. "I didn't expect to see Kate here."

"Yeah, well, you ever try to stop a woman whose mind is made up?"

Castillo didn't see the humor. "You need to stay out of the way, Kate."

"She isn't officially here," Jase said. "I'd like to keep her out of this if we can."

Castillo turned a hard look on Kate. "Stay in the car until this is over. We have no idea how this is going to go down. We don't want civilians getting hurt."

"I won't interfere," she said.

Castillo just nodded and returned to his men. Jase took an armored vest out of his gear bag and swung it on over his T-shirt, then shrugged into a blue denim shirt to cover it and the gun holstered in the belt at his waist. Then they settled in to wait.

And wait. And wait. And wait.

At 2:00 a.m., a crusty old sergeant named Mackessey, the man in charge, called off the bust. The truck never showed. Jase was pissed.

He tossed his vest into the back of the Yukon and strode up to Castillo. "This is exactly what I was afraid of. You got a dirty cop on the job. Maybe more than one. By now Los Besos knows exactly who's been tracking them. Thanks for the help." He turned to leave, but Castillo caught his arm.

"I had to go through proper channels. You know how it works. If there's a dirty cop, it isn't me. I'll find someone I can trust and we'll figure it out. You can still count on me. I swear it, Hawk."

Some of Jase's anger deflated. Castillo had always been a straight shooter. On the other hand, he couldn't afford to take chances. "Fine. If I come up with anything, I'll let you know." Like hell he would. "I expect you to do the same."

"You got it."

But after tonight, Jase's plans had changed. He might still trust Castillo, but not the cops the detective was working with. Someone was dirty, and a dirty cop could be deadly.

He returned to where Kate stood next to the Yukon. The bad news was, just as he'd feared, they were in deeper trouble than before.

"Take the battery and sim card out of your phone," he said, once they were inside. "They know who we are now. We don't want them tracking us."

Panic flashed in her eyes. "You think they can do that?"

"No idea, but I'd rather play it safe. From now on, we're using burners. I keep a couple in my gear bag in the back."

The headlights of half a dozen patrol cars went on as the cops pulled out and headed back to Houston. Jase drove off, but instead of pulling onto the interstate, he circled around and returned to the truck stop.

Drawing his .38 revolver out of his ankle holster, he handed the gun to Kate. "Wait here. Lock the doors."

She accepted the pistol without a word and settled it in her lap. She'd told him she knew how to fire a weapon. He wished they'd had time to practice, but looking at her, he had a feeling she knew what she was doing. The way things were going, the knowledge might come in handy.

Jase walked into the truck stop and glanced around for Wally, but didn't see him. A dark-skinned woman worked behind the counter. "You seen Wally?" Jase asked.

"He's not here. Wally called in sick."

Jase pulled a twenty out of his wallet. "You know where he lives?"

The woman eyed the twenty. It wasn't a lot but it beat minimum wage. "There's a trailer park just down the road. He's in space 14."

"Thanks." Jase handed the woman the money.

"Did you find him?" Kate asked as he settled himself behind the wheel.

"Wally called in sick. He lives in a trailer park down the street." About a mile away, the Countryside Trailer Park sat off to the left. Jase pulled in, his headlights illuminating a row of single-wide trailers, grass and weeds growing up under the wheels.

Bumping along the rutted dirt lane, he pulled up in front of space 14 and turned off the engine. A dim light burned inside the trailer.

"I'll be right back."

Exiting the Yukon, he knocked on the door to a battered old Airstream about the size of a bedroom on wheels. He could hear shuffling, then the door slowly opened.

Wally looked like he'd been run through a meat grinder. Black eyes, split lip, bruises all over. The bags under his eyes said he hadn't been sleeping. Probably hurting too much.

"What the hell...?" Wally blinked, recognized Jason. "You! Get the hell away from me!" He tried to close the door, but Jase shoved it open and pushed his way inside.

"Take it easy, okay? I'm not here to hurt you."

"What are you? A cop? Are the cops out there right now?"

"I'm not a cop, and the police don't know anything

about you." He didn't burn an informant. Wally was just a guy trying to get by.

The kid sat down on the sofa, which also served as a pullout bed. He fingered his swollen nose. "Did you tell the police about the truck? You must have. There was never any trouble till you came around."

"I'm a bounty hunter. I'm looking for someone. The guy I'm after is part of Los Besos."

The color leached out of Wally's thin face. "They thought I'd snitched to the cops, but I didn't. I think they believed me, but they beat me up anyway. Said this was a sample of what would happen if I opened my mouth."

"I don't think they'll come back to the TexMart. Too risky. You should be okay."

Wally picked at the dried blood on the corner of his mouth. "I never wanted their dirty money, but they didn't give me a choice. Those guys are bad dudes."

"Real bad. What they do to those women is even worse."

Wally knuckle-rubbed his head, making his pale hair stand up. He sighed. "I know. I feel bad about that."

"Give me something I can use and I'll find them, put them out of business. I won't involve you or the cops. I'll handle it on my own."

Wally looked down at the bulge of the semiauto in the belt beneath Jason's shirt. He shook his head. "They'll kill me."

"They won't know. I give you my word. I just need a name, something to go on."

Wally bit his lip.

"There's a girl…" Jase said. "She's only thirteen. Ran away from home a couple of days ago. I think Los Besos picked her up."

Wally squeezed his eyes shut.

"She's just a kid, Wally. You know what they'll do to her."

"Jesus."

"You can stop it. You can save her. I just need a name."

A shudder rippled through his slim body. "All right, but you better keep your word."

"Count on it," Jase said.

"I heard a couple of them talking. There's this guy... name is Harlan Burke. Works at a place on Bissonnet over off the Southwest freeway. Paradise Massage. He's connected, not sure how. Keeps the women in line, I think, but I'm not sure. That's all I know."

"Thanks, Wally. You did a good thing." Jase left him sitting on the sofa, his head between his knees.

"We caught a break," he said as he slid in behind the wheel of the Yukon. "Got the name of a guy in Houston who works for Los Besos. Name's Harlan Burke."

"You know where to find him?"

Jase nodded. "With any luck, I'll find Burke—and get a nice relaxing massage while I'm at it."

KATE WALKED INTO the apartment feeling edgy and unsettled. It was after three in the morning. Both of them were frustrated and strung tight. Their plan had failed, and it looked as if someone on the police force had given them up to Los Besos. Or at least given them Jason's name.

According to Detective Castillo, he had kept her name out of it. If they could actually trust his word.

She dropped her purse on the sofa, renewed anxiety prickling her nerves. She glanced over at Jase standing in the center of the living room staring toward the window, his hands propped on his hips. The denim shirt was gone, leaving him in his white T-shirt, his big semiautomatic pistol riding on the heavy leather belt around his waist.

His arms bulged with muscle. The bandage was gone from the side of his thick neck, but the gash from the bullet remained. He looked like exactly what he was. A hard, tough man. A bounty hunter. Hawk Maddox.

Kate wanted to eat him up.

She took a steadying breath. What difference would one more night make? One more night in bed with him? She knew he needed her tonight, could see it every time those fierce blue eyes swung in her direction. The danger they faced was real. No one could know the outcome. There was a chance they could both end up as dead as her sister.

What difference would one more night with Jason make?

She toed off her black sneakers and started toward him, saw his chest expand as she pulled off the rubber band holding back her hair and tossed her head, sending her long curls swirling around her shoulders. She could have sworn his nostrils flared.

His breath came faster as she stopped to peel off her black top and strip off her jeans. At the hunger in his eyes, her stomach contracted and her breathing quickened to the rhythm of his.

She was a foot away when she stopped again. There was still time to change her mind.

Jase straightened, seemed to grow even bigger, more powerful. "Kate…"

She met his gaze and didn't back away from the challenge she read there. Reaching for his belt buckle, she unfastened it and slid off his leather belt, set his weapon down on the end table.

She was in his arms before she saw him move, his mouth crushing down over hers, his arms tight around her. Her fingers slipped into his thick brown hair, and she kissed him the way he was kissing her, hot and deep and amazing. She clung to his neck as he walked her backward till her shoulders came up against the wall.

Jase unhooked her bra and tossed it away, filled his hands with her breasts. "Kate..."

A soft sound escaped her throat. Every part of her throbbed and burned. Bending his head, Jase took the heavy weight of her breast into his mouth, suckled and tasted until she moaned.

The next thing she knew her panties were gone and she was naked. Jase pulled his T-shirt off over his head and she ran her hands over his sculpted chest, felt heat surge into her core as hard muscle bunched beneath her fingers.

Unzipping his jeans, he freed himself, lifted her and wrapped her legs around his waist. She was shaking, desire nearly tangible, need a force she couldn't fight any longer. She wanted him so badly she went light-headed when he drove himself inside.

"Kate..." he whispered again. No man had ever said her name the way he did, like a prayer or a vow.

He kissed her again, kissed her and kissed her, all the while, driving himself inside her, pushing her toward the brink.

When she tipped into climax, she cried out his name and the world spun away. Sweet euphoria spilled through her, a hot rush of dense, saturating pleasure. Seconds later, Jase followed her to release.

For long moments, he just held her, her head on his shoulder, her arms around his neck. It felt so right, so perfect. Her heart constricted. She was in love with him.

She knew it. Could no longer deny it. It was stupid. Insane. Loving him would only bring her heartache. But it was already too late.

She told herself it didn't matter. For now he was hers. She was going to take everything he could give her.

"Let's go to bed," she said, pressing a soft kiss to the corner of his mouth.

Jason just nodded. She thought that he was feeling the same hopelessness that weighed her down, but she couldn't be sure. She felt like crying. She felt like making love with him again.

Jase carried her into the bedroom and settled her on the mattress, dealt with the condom she hadn't remembered him putting on. Stripping off the rest of his clothes, he joined her in bed and began to kiss her all over again.

Kate gave herself up to the pleasure and told herself that it would be enough.

CHAPTER THIRTY-TWO

CALLIE HUDDLED ON the mattress on the floor of the small, airless room. A sealed window let in thin rays of sunlight, but the bars blocked any chance of escape.

The first time she had managed to slip away unnoticed, but her freedom hadn't lasted long. After they had dragged her back to the place they kept the other women, she had been sure they would beat her. Instead, they had simply locked her in different room, one she couldn't get out of.

She'd been fed and bathed. The woman in charge brought her a pill to make her sleep, and refused to leave until she swallowed it. The day they had kidnapped her, the same woman had ordered two other girls to hold her down while she checked to be sure Callie was still intact...down there.

She had cried for hours afterward.

They had their proof that she was a virgin. Now they were grooming her for the man who would buy her—like a prize cat or a show dog, she thought miserably. They wanted the highest price they could get for her. The better she looked, the prettier, the more money she was worth.

She wondered if her mother had called the police when she'd discovered Callie was gone. Her mom loved her. Surely she would be worried about her. Maybe the cops were looking for her right now.

She held on to that hope every time they forced her to swallow another pill. Whatever drug it was took away her will to fight, and she just sat on the mattress like a lump.

She wondered how much longer she had until the man who wanted her came to claim her.

Please God, let the police find me first. Please, please, please. But God hadn't helped her before. She didn't really think He would help her now.

A fresh wave of grogginess closed down her mind, and Callie curled up on the mattress. She tried to keep her eyes open, but it was no use. When she gave in to sleep, she dreamed she was back in the grassy field behind her house in Wharton where she and her friend Penny used to play. She dreamed that she was safe, but she knew it was only a dream.

BOTH OF THEM were wary the following morning, speaking to each other with exaggerated politeness, pretending the hot sex last night never happened.

It shouldn't have. Jase knew it and so did Kate. She should have stayed as far away from him as she could get. Jase should have beaten down his lust and refused her offer of comfort.

He told himself that's all it was. He was uptight and worried. Kate gave him ease with her beautiful body. He should have refused, but he had never been much of a martyr, and he had greedily taken the gift she offered.

Worse yet, he wanted it to happen again.

He'd been quiet all morning, feeling guilty and not feeling guilty at the same time.

"Okay, enough of this." Kate marched into the kitchen where he was working on his computer. "I wanted you. You wanted me. We're both adults. We can forgive each other for being human, okay?"

Relief swept through him, and he couldn't stop a smile. "Honey, you are amazing." One of his eyebrows kicked up along with the corner of his mouth. "Any chance we can be human again right now?"

Her laughter broke the tension. "Sorry, big guy, we have too much work to do."

He looked into her smiling face and something tightened in his chest. Every day his feelings for Kate grew deeper. It was dangerous for both of them.

"We need to practice some moves," he said gruffly. His gaze ran over her sexy, feminine curves, and his groin tightened. He wanted to practice some moves, all right, but they had nothing to do with self-defense.

Inwardly he groaned.

"Too bad we don't have a mat of some kind," Kate said.

"Yeah." He went over to his gear bag, pulled out a six-inch fixed-blade knife. "We'll do some knife work today. I'll show you the right way to attack and ways to defend."

Her eyes gleamed. She seemed to be liking this stuff a little too much.

"I'm ready whenever you are," she said, smiling.

Jase steeled himself, and they went to work.

Two hours later, he headed in to take another shower—this one cold—then he sat back down in front of his laptop. Finally able to concentrate, he pulled up Google and keyed in Paradise Massage.

The website popped right up, a three-story building on Bissonnet, which, in the webpage photo, looked slightly run-down. Jase remembered hunting a skip in the neighborhood a couple of years back. It was an area known for prostitutes.

He started working ownership files, but it looked like the building was leased from a corporation. He needed to know the names of the owners. He dug out the disposable he was using and phoned Tabby's number.

"Hey, hot stuff," he said. "You got time to give me some help?"

"Sure, stud muffin. Whatcha need?"

He laughed. "Okay, I deserved that. I need to know the ownership of a building on Bissonnet off the Southwest Freeway in Houston. The lessee is Paradise Massage. I think whoever is running the business may be involved in sex trafficking. Can you get me some info?"

"I'll call you right back."

"Be sure to use this number."

"Okay, will do." The line went dead.

Kate wandered over and stood looking down at the photo of the building on the website. "I wonder if they keep the women there."

"Could be. Area's known for prostitutes."

"We're getting close, Jase. It feels like it's all starting to come together."

"Unfortunately, the closer we get, the more dangerous it is."

"I know."

He continued to dig around on the net while Kate checked in with her office, and the day slipped past. "I could sure use something to eat," he said.

"I noticed a coffee shop down the road. Why don't I go get us a sandwich and bring it back?"

He couldn't stay with her every minute, he told himself. Still, he didn't like leaving her alone. "Why don't we both go?" he said.

They ended up eating there, a nice little café with great pastrami sandwiches. On the way back, they stopped at a grocery store to pick up some food: bread and lunch meat, some pastry and a fresh bag of coffee. Long as they had leads to follow, they wouldn't be leaving Houston.

The disposable rang as Jase walked back into the apartment. It was Tabby. He put the phone on speaker. "Hey, Tab, what have you got?"

"Building's owned by the Atrias Corporation. Which is owned by the Winman Company, which is owned by Briton, Inc."

"I'm guessing these guys don't want to be found."

"Wait a minute," Kate said. "Briton. I know that name. Briton has offices in Dallas. They're on our potential client list. One of my employees, Robin Murdock, had a meeting with the VP of Mergers and Acquisitions a few months back. They were thinking of going public, wanted to be sure they had all their ducks in a row."

"What happened?" Jase asked.

"They postponed the offering. They never ended up hiring a consulting firm, as far as I know."

Tabby spoke up. "I'll see what I can find out about that. Also, I figured you'd need names, so I cross-checked some other info and dug a little deeper. Two names popped up, connected to all of this in some way. Maximillian Schram and Arthur Wiedel. I'll send you their bios. That's it for now."

"You're the best, Tab. Thanks." Jase ended the call and looked up at Kate. "Your connection to Briton might come in handy."

"I'll call Robin, see if she knows anything useful." While Kate used the burner phone he'd given her, Jase brought Paradise Massage back up on the screen and found their phone number. He dialed it and waited while the call rang through.

"Paradise Massage," a female voice answered.

"My name's Tom Wilford. I saw your website on the internet. My back's killing me. Any chance you could fit me in sometime today?"

"Just a minute, let me check." The receptionist came back on the line. "We only have one opening today. You can have it if you can be here in thirty minutes."

"I can make it. I'll see you then."

Kate caught the back end of his phone call. "You're going there today?"

"I've got an appointment at four o'clock. If they've got Callie Spencer, the sooner we figure this out, the better."

Striding into the bedroom, he stuffed his little .380 into his jeans pocket. Digging the .38 out of his gear bag, he carried the revolver back to the kitchen and set it on the table.

"I've got to get going if I'm going make it in time. Lock the doors and don't let anyone in but me."

She nodded, for once didn't give him any flak. He couldn't resist leaning down and kissing her. "Last night shouldn't have happened, but I'm not sorry it did."

Kate looked up at him, her gaze steady on his face. "Neither am I," she said softly.

Jase forced himself to turn away and head out the door.

JASE WAS GONE. She prayed he'd be okay. Her mind went back to the self-defense lessons he was giving her. She hadn't thought she would enjoy them, but she had. It gave her a feeling of confidence unlike she'd known before. It felt good to know you at least had a fighting chance against someone trying to hurt you. When this was over, she might just take some professional courses. Though it wouldn't be nearly as much fun without Jase.

A thought that brought down her mood.

Needing to focus, Kate phoned Robin Murdock's direct line again. She hadn't picked up the first time. Robin wouldn't have recognized the number, probably thought it was some kind of telemarketer.

This time she answered.

"Robin, it's Kate. Have you got a minute?"

"Hey, Kate. You get a new phone?"

"No, this is a friend's. I called to ask you about a company you talked to a few months back in regard to a consulting job. Briton, Inc. Do you remember?"

"I remember making a sales call, but the VP I talked to said they'd decided to postpone going public. He kept my card, though. I'm hoping he'll call me back when the time comes."

"Do you remember his name?"

"I talked to Victor Markum. He's VP of Mergers and Acquisitions."

"Did they say when they'd be ready to move forward?"

"Let me take a look at my notes." A drawer opened and closed, papers rustled. Digital had its benefits but also its drawbacks. "Looks like they may be ready to move ahead soon. Maybe I should follow up, see if they need our services. It could be a very big job."

"I'd appreciate if you'd hold off a few days, Robin. If it looks like it could turn into something, the project is yours."

"All right. Thanks, Kate. Just let me know." Robin hung up and Kate paced the apartment. She had no idea how a company as reputable as Briton could be involved in human trafficking, but in the world today, you never knew what could happen.

She glanced at the kitchen clock. Jase should be at Paradise Massage by now. A smile touched her lips. She envied the woman who would be running her hands over that magnificent body.

CHAPTER THIRTY-THREE

"RIGHT THIS WAY, TOM."

Jase followed the masseuse down the hall, a woman in her late thirties with short dark brown hair and slightly plump curves. She was wearing a black skirt and a long-sleeved white blouse cut low enough to show plenty of cleavage. She wore makeup, enough to cover the dark circles beneath her eyes, false eyelashes and red lipstick.

She might have been pretty once, but Jase figured if he pulled up her sleeves, he's see the track marks of a user.

He let her lead him into a narrow room on the first floor. A massage table sat in the middle. There was no window, just a single fluorescent casting dull white light. The room smelled of cheap perfume and rubbing alcohol. The sheet on the table was more gray than white. He could hear people moving around overhead, and wondered if they were servicing customers upstairs.

The woman smiled. "I'm Rena. I'm going to take care of you today. Why don't you take off your clothes and get comfortable? When you're ready, just wrap that towel around your hips and lie down on your stomach on the table."

Not unless he absolutely had to. Jase surveyed the confining space that made him feel like he needed a shower.

"You know, Rena, the truth is I came here for more than just a massage. A friend of mine told me one of you ladies took real good care of him when he came here the last time he was in town."

Rena flashed her impression of a seductive smile. "We're all qualified massage therapists. Some of our customers require more specialized treatment, and of course we like to keep them happy." She moved closer, ran her palms over this chest and down his arms. "You're in real good shape, honey. You aren't a cop, are you? I don't need any trouble."

"Ex-military. Same needs as every other guy."

"All right. How much would you like to spend? Everything here is billed separately."

He pulled out a fifty-dollar bill and Rena frowned. "A massage is sixty, hun. There's a sign right on the front desk. Anything more is another hundred."

He hadn't missed the sign. "This is all I brought with me. Anyway, we can make some kind of deal?"

Rena shook her head. "Sorry. Management has very strict rules."

Jase stuffed the bill back into his pocket. "I didn't think it would cost so much. I'll have to get some more cash and come back later."

Her hand slid over the fly of his jeans and cupped him through the heavy fabric. "I'll tell you what. I'm just filling in down here for a friend—I usually work upstairs. If you can come up with a couple of hundred, you can join our little party tonight. I can make you feel real good, Tom. Or if you prefer, you can choose one of the other girls."

Exactly what he had been hoping. He knew how a brothel worked. He'd been stationed in Okinawa when he was a young marine. "That sounds good, Rena. What time?"

"Any time after ten, honey." She handed him a plastic key card. "That'll get you in the front door."

"Thanks." Jase flashed her a smile and walked out of the dingy room. As he stepped into the hall, he took note of an elevator up to the second and third floors, a set of stairs at the far end of the hall, then went back the way he had come.

The receptionist looked up as he passed. "That didn't take long," she said with a knowing smile.

"Been a while." Jase winked. As soon as he got outside, he inhaled deeply, grateful to be breathing fresh air. Unfortunately, he would have to come back. Looked like his hunch could be right, and they were keeping women in the rooms upstairs.

Before he headed for the car, he circled the perimeter of the building, locating ways in and out, best place to park for an easy getaway. When he reached the parking lot of the Briar Forest apartment, he pulled out his burner phone and punched in the number for The Max.

Mindy answered. "Hi, Jason. Chase has been looking for you. Your phone doesn't seem to be working."

He rattled off the number of the disposable as he got out of the car. "I've got some trouble. Be careful who gets that number."

"Okay, I'll be careful. I'll put you through to Chase."

"Thanks."

Chase picked up on the second ring. "Hawk. I've been trying to call you. What's going on?"

"Had to switch to a burner. Don't want them tracking me." He explained to Chase about his conversation with Detective Castillo and Los Besos, about the truck stops and the raid that went south.

"Somebody tipped them, Chase. We got at least one dirty cop, which means they know my name."

"Not good."

"I got a lead on a brothel Los Besos runs, got an invite to sample some of the merchandise tonight. It could be the break we need, but I hate leaving Kate alone. The apartment feels safe, but I still don't like it."

"Listen, Jase, Reese is in Houston on business. He keeps an apartment just down the hall from the one you're staying in. My brother has skills. He may not be ex-military, but he learned plenty during his black-sheep years before he wound up in juvy. He'll have a weapon and he knows how to use it. I'll call him, bring him up to speed."

Jase knew the brothers' story, knew that after their parents divorced, Chase and Brandon had been raised by their mother and her Irish cop family, while Reese had been raised by their megarich dad. Bass Garrett had spoiled his middle son rotten. Expensive cars and too much cash had been the formula for disaster. Reese had started running with a very bad crowd and wound up in trouble with the law. Even Bass's millions couldn't get him out of a year in juvenile detention.

Afterward, he had moved in with his mother, grandparents and brothers. His juvenile record had been sealed, and his family had helped him turn his life around.

"You've got Reese's cell," Chase continued. "He'll be glad to help."

Jase figured he would. Since the end of his marriage, Reese had been at loose ends. Plus, like Bran and Chase, Reese was a friend.

"Thanks. I'll talk to him."

Jase rode the elevator up to the third floor apartment.

He found Kate anxiously pacing back and forth in the living room. The worry on her face reminded him why a relationship would never work.

"Thank God you're okay," she said. "I was so worried."

"I'm fine. Everything went according to plan." He closed the door. "They're definitely running women there. I'll find out more when I go back tonight."

She frowned. "You're going back?"

"No choice. We've got to figure out what's going on. The longer it takes, the more likely they are to find us first."

A knock sounded at the door. Jase pulled the .380 out of his pocket and checked the peephole. He smiled as he repocketed the weapon, opened the door and welcomed Reese Garrett into the apartment.

"That didn't take long," he said to Reese.

"Chase called. Sounds like you got trouble."

"Big trouble. Reese, this is Kate Gallagher. Kate, Reese Garrett."

"Nice to meet you." She extended a hand and Reese shook it. With his wavy black hair, blue eyes and Garrett good looks, Reese had females sighing all over Dallas, worse since his divorce. But the Garretts respected another man's territory. Jase didn't have to worry about Reese poaching his woman.

He clamped down on the thought. Once this was over, he and Kate would be going their separate ways. Sooner or later, she would find someone else. He looked down, surprised to see his hand balled into a fist.

"My brother gave me the basics," Reese said. "What can I do to help?"

KATE HAD SEEN Reese Garrett's photo in the *Dallas Morning News* more than once. The Garrett family was worth millions and known for their philanthropy. Articles were always being written about them. Reese was CEO of Garrett Resources, smart and talented, and according to the media, doing an excellent job of running the company.

He was even better looking in person, tall, just a few inches shorter than Jase, built more like Brandon, with a lean, athletic frame.

Jase filled in any holes Chase had left in the story he'd told his brother, and Reese volunteered to stay with Kate while Jase went back to the brothel.

"Wait a minute," Kate said. "I don't need a babysitter. I've got a .38 revolver and I know how to pull the trigger. Somebody tries to get in here, they're going to be very sorry. You're the one who needs help."

"Reese can't go with me," Jase said. "Hardly fitting for the CEO of Garrett Resources to be caught in a whorehouse."

Kate looked at Reese. He wore confidence like an expensive shirt. The man was over-the-top good-looking, but it was Jason's tough good looks, amazing body and protective nature she was drawn to.

"You need backup, Jason," she said. "Let me go with you. I'll wait in the car. If you aren't back by whatever time we set, I'll call the police."

"No. Besides, we can't trust the police."

"If it's an anonymous phone call, the cops will show up to see what's wrong. If you're in danger, they'll help."

"Yeah, and probably take me to jail."

"Better jail than dead," Kate said.

"Kate's right about backup, Hawk. It's a twenty-minute drive to Bissonnet. Twenty there, twenty back. You could be dead before we even know something's wrong. I'll drive the Rover, wait for you outside. You aren't back, I'll call 911 and leave before the cops get there. The distraction alone might be enough for you to get out."

"That's a good idea," Kate said. "I'll go with Reese. You don't want me here alone, right? I won't be alone. I'll be with Reese."

A deep breath seeped from Jason's throat. Kate could tell he didn't like it, but he didn't have much choice. He looked at Reese. "You sure about this, bro?"

Reese just smiled. "Why not? My life's been a little dull lately."

Jase scratched his jaw. "Looks like I'm outnumbered."

They used the time to work out details. No matter what happened, it was always better to be prepared.

Kate and Reese sat next to Jason in front of the laptop as Jase used Google Maps to familiarize them with the area on Bissonnet near Paradise Massage, and went over observations he had made when he was there earlier. Entrance, exit in the rear, second set of stairs to the upper two floors.

It seemed as if it took forever for ten o'clock to finally arrive. At the same time, it seemed like a snap of the fingers. Since Jase was leaving ten minutes ahead of them, Kate walked him to the door.

"Be careful," she said.

"Always." His beautiful blue eyes locked on her face.

When Kate leaned up and pressed a soft kiss on his mouth, Jase hauled her into his arms and very thoroughly kissed her. "Stay safe," he said a little gruffly.

Jase walked out the door, and Kate turned to see Reese watching her.

"He's a good man," Reese said.

"I know."

Reese checked his Rolex. "We'll give him enough time to get inside and settled before we arrive." He had changed out of his business clothes, navy slacks and a blue Oxford shirt, into black cargo pants and a black T-shirt that hugged his body. Like Bran, he had a lean, broad-shouldered build. A semiautomatic pistol rode in a holster clipped to his waist.

He looked nothing like the important businessman he had been that afternoon. This man was tougher, edgier, not a guy you would want to mess with.

"You ready to go?" Reese asked.

Kate had also changed and was dressed in black. She had one last thing to do. Reese's eyes widened when she walked out of the bedroom with the revolver holstered and clipped to the belt around her waist. She was getting the hang of this detective work. She wasn't legal yet, but she planned to change that soon, and considering the circumstances, she wasn't going in unprepared.

She pulled her T-shirt out to cover the weapon. "I'm ready."

A smile touched the corner of Reese's mouth. "So I see."

The two of them walked out of the apartment.

CHAPTER THIRTY-FOUR

HUMID DARKNESS ENCLOSED the land around the building that housed Paradise Massage. Dim light oozed through the windows on the second and third floors. Jase walked straight to the front and used the key card to open the door.

There was no one in the reception area when he walked in, just a small lamp on an end table, burning into the shadows. The hallway leading to the massage rooms was dark. It was quiet except for the sounds of voices and people moving around upstairs.

He headed for the elevator. The plan was for Reese to follow, then park where he could see the Yukon, stay long enough to make sure Jase got out all right.

Jase didn't like the idea that Kate would be with him, but he didn't much like the notion of leaving her alone, either. Besides, he knew her well enough to know she was going one way or another. The good news was, he trusted Reese to keep her safe. And Reese was right—Jase needed the backup.

He rode the slow-moving car up to the second floor, and the doors opened into another dark hallway. He walked toward the light and music spilling out of an open doorway just down the hall, and paused in the entrance. The room was furnished with dark green velvet overstuffed sofas and chairs. Hors d'oeuvres trays loaded with meat and cheese covered a table next to a makeshift bar against the wall. Men of mixed nationalities and various employments occupied the furniture, some with scantily clad women perched on their laps.

Naked breasts bounced as the women laughed and strutted their wares. A woman in her forties approached him, silver-streaked dark hair, busty, with a slender figure. She wore more clothes than the others, black leggings and a low-cut black blouse belted with a gold sash and dangling gold earrings. The proverbial madam of the house.

Two large men stood against the wall, one at each end of the room, watching the customers. The woman was the mediator. The men were enforcers.

"Hello, handsome." She smiled up at him. "I'm Veronica. You must be Tom."

"That's right."

"Rena mentioned you might be joining us tonight. I'm glad you could make it." Nineties music played. He recognized some of the old songs.

He let his gaze move around the room, taking in the selection of available females. Blondes, redheads, tall, short, buxom, slender, skin tones of every color. Some wore short nightgowns, others wore push-up bras and thong panties.

No thirteen-year-old who looked like the photo he'd received of Callie Spencer. He wasn't sure if that was good or bad.

"Looks like you've got something for everyone," he said.

One of Veronica's dark eyebrows arched up. "Two-hundred-dollar cover. The rest you can negotiate with the girl of your choice."

"Sounds fair enough." He pulled out his wallet and took out two hundred-dollar bills, made sure Veronica saw he only had an extra couple of fifties. Not good to come to a whorehouse loaded with cash or he might get his head bashed in.

Of course, if they figured out who he was, that was still a distinct possibility—and the reason there was no ID in his wallet.

"How about a drink?" Veronica asked.

He nodded. "Jack rocks sounds good."

He followed her to the bar and she fixed him a drink. Jase sipped as he turned to survey the room once more. He was there for information, not sex. Which made choosing the right girl imperative. Veronica drank from a stemmed martini glass, her shrewd gaze going from him to the women in the silent game of chance she seemed to be mentally playing.

Which woman will he choose?

She beckoned a petite blonde in her thirties. "Come over here, Terri, and meet Tom." The blonde, who looked as if she had plenty of experience, crossed the room in a silver thong and silver pasties. If you liked ample curves and a double D bosom, Terri was for you.

"Nice to meet you, Terri," he said. Her hair was short enough he could see she didn't have the lipstick tattoo. Maybe none of them did, but Terri wasn't the woman he needed so he'd get another try.

"Who's the redhead?" he asked as Terri wandered off. The girl was young, early twenties, big blue eyes and a vacant expression, like she wished she were anywhere but there.

"That's Eve." When Veronica motioned for her to approach, Eve pushed away from the wall and walked toward him on towering platform heels. Jase noticed her legs were a little shaky. "Eve, meet Tom," Veronica said.

Her eyes shifted to the floor. "Hello, Tom." She was new at this game, exactly what he was looking for.

Jase smiled. "Hello, honey. So are you up for a little fun?"

She swallowed, looked up at him. "Sure," she said, but her fake smile wobbled.

Veronica seemed pleased with the exchange, her eyes wandering over his chest. "Looks like your lucky night, Eve." She waved over her shoulder as she walked away. "Have fun, you two."

Eve took his hand, her fingers icy cold, and led him out the door, passing a couple of young guys, seventeen or eighteen, on the way into the party room.

Jase followed Eve down the hall into one of the bedrooms and closed the door.

"You'll have to wash up first," she said. "And wear a condom. That's the rule." There was a sink and toilet in a minuscule bathroom, condoms stacked next to the faucet handles.

Eve gasped as he reached over and moved aside her long red hair. Surprise hit him at the sight of the lipstick tattoo.

Eve stepped away.

"Take it easy, honey. This really is your lucky night. I'm not here for sex. I just want to talk."

Panic filtered through her. "If...if you can't get it up, I can help you. That's part of my job."

"Let's just talk, okay? Why don't you sit down and get comfortable?"

Eve eased down on the bed, her eyes on his face, looking for any sign he wanted more from her than words.

"How did you get the tattoo?" he asked.

Unconsciously, she reached up and touched her neck,

then clasped her hands between her knees. "I—I can't talk about it. Let's just do this and get it over with." She stood up and started to pull down her red satin thong, but Jase caught her arm.

"Easy. All I want is a little conversation. It'll mean an extra fifty for you."

She wet her lips. They were painted a pretty rose, not bright red. "Do you know Harlan Burke?" he asked, giving her the name Wally had supplied.

Eve swallowed and glanced toward the door. "He's the guy in the party room. The one with the slitty eyes and thinning blond hair. The big one's Marvin Duff."

"All right, good. That's good. How did you start working here?"

Her gaze went back to the door. "Why do you want to know?"

"I'm a...ah...a writer. I'm doing an article on how women wind up in the life."

She eyed him with suspicion. "You don't look like a writer."

That was for sure. "Okay, let's start with something easier. How long have you been working here?"

She shrugged. "A little over a month."

"How did you get here?" He sat down in the chair across from the bed.

Eve looked at him and her big blue eyes filled with tears. She had a small pointed chin and a kind of fragile sensuality that matched her willowy frame. "I shouldn't tell you."

"Why not? We have to fill up some time or you're going to get in trouble for not doing your job."

She nodded. "Okay." She took a shaky breath. "I was living with this guy out in Prairie View. He was a real prick, you know? He'd get drunk and start hitting me.

I wanted to leave but I never did. I started taking pills and pretty soon I was hooked. One night he beat me real bad, and I just couldn't take it anymore."

"So you left."

She nodded, wiped away the wetness on her cheeks. "I packed a bag and hitched a ride to Houston. It was only a couple of days before I ran out of money. I needed food, drugs. I was living on the street when a couple of men picked me up and brought me here. I've been here ever since."

"You haven't tried to leave?"

She tipped her head toward the door. "You saw those two guys out there. The first week I was here, they drugged me, knocked me out cold. While I was unconscious, someone put the tattoo on my neck. I belong to them now. That's another rule."

"Are there other places like this one?"

She nodded. "A couple, I think."

"What if I prefer a younger girl? Someone under-age?"

"They keep the young girls somewhere else, and they cost a lot more."

A loud banging sounded on the door the instant before it crashed open. Harlan Burke and Marvin Duff rushed into the room. The stun gun in Duff's hand hit Jase in the middle of the chest as he shot to his feet. He wavered, tried to push through it. Duff hit him again and he went down like a sack of cement, his head hitting the corner of the dresser. Blood ran down the side of his face, but he couldn't really feel it.

Eve shot to her feet. "We were only talking!" Fear laced her voice. Another jolt shot through him, zipping along his nerves with agonizing force, and his teeth clenched together.

"That's the problem, sweetheart," Duff said calmly. "Your job ain't to talk—it's to get the guy's nuts off."

She was shaking. She looked at Jase with pity but there was nothing she could do. "How...how did you know what we were doing?"

"You stupid bitch." Burke laughed. "You see that mirror on the wall? We got customers who like to watch. Plus it's a good way for us to keep an eye on things."

Eve made a little sound in her throat. Jase struggled to move, but every muscle was frozen, his whole body locked up tight. His head pounded and his vision blurred. He'd have to wait, find an opportunity.

Burke shoved Eve toward the door. "Get your ass back in there and get to work. And keep your mouth shut."

"What...what about him?"

"I'll take care of him," Duff said.

"Get going!" Burke shoved Eve forward. When she didn't move fast enough, he grabbed her arm, hauled her around and slapped her, then he pushed her out the door and walked out behind her.

Duff moved closer. The stun gun hit Jase again, and he silently groaned. As he lay on his side on the floor, Duff kicked him in the ribs a couple of times, kicked him in the head, and his brain finally went dark.

He wasn't sure how long he was out, but he woke up groggy and bleeding and tied to a chair in a storeroom. He hoped like hell Reese wouldn't wait too long before he called the police.

CHAPTER THIRTY-FIVE

"I'M NOT WAITING any longer," Kate said. "He should have been back fifteen minutes ago."

Reese shifted in the seat behind the wheel of the Rover. "He's on the job, Kate. Things happen. You'll make it worse if you blow his cover."

"Something's wrong. I know it. He's in trouble. I'm not waiting." Kate cracked the door and stepped out of the Rover. At the same time, Reese got out and strode around to her side of the car.

"I believe in following your gut. Let's go."

"Should we call the police?"

"Could make things worse. Let's take a look around first, call if we have to." Reese started for the building, Kate right beside him, keeping up with the man's long strides. Sticking to the plan they had formulated on the drive over just in case, they went to the rear entrance. According to Jason, there was a stairwell just inside, easy access to the second floor where he figured the men were being entertained.

They paused at the locked door, and Kate bit her lip as Reese reached into the pocket of his cargo pants, pulled out a pair of expensive leather driving gloves and pulled them on. A set of lock picks appeared out of another pocket, and Reese went to work.

It was only a matter of seconds before the lock turned, Reese opened the door and they stepped inside.

So the millionaire businessman was skilled at B&E. The man was full of surprises.

They quietly climbed the back stairs, the sound of laughter and voices getting louder as they neared the second floor. Up ahead, one of the doors began to swing open and they flattened themselves against the wall. A man walked out smiling, zipping his fly as he continued along the hall back toward the elevator at the opposite end.

"How are we going to find him?" Kate whispered.

"We'll just have to look." Figuring Jase wasn't in the room the man had just left, Reese stared opening doors on one side of the hall while Kate opened doors on the other. Just a quick peek to see if Jason was in there.

The occupants were so busy they didn't seem to notice the brief interruption. Kate wished she could block the images of naked men and women in every conceivable position, but it wasn't likely.

The din of voices and music was coming from a room not far from the elevator, probably where the men were being entertained. Halfway down the hall, Reese paused to listen, then pulled his pistol. Kate drew her revolver and hurried over to join him.

"Someone's throwing punches. Let's take a look."

Kate eased close enough to hear what was happening on the other side of the door.

"Who the hell are you?" a man's deep voice demanded. "You can make this easy or hard. Either way, you're gonna talk."

Kate's heart jerked at the sound of a fist driving into flesh. Reese looked at her and mouthed, *Three, two, one*, turned the knob and shoved open the door.

Reese and Kate both rushed inside what appeared

to be a supply room, their pistols pointed at the big, brawny, dark-haired man with his fist drawn back.

"Hands in the air," Reese commanded without raising his voice. "Move. Now. Over against the wall." Eyeing the heavy weapon, the man moved cautiously in that direction.

Kate's gaze locked on Jason, slumped forward in the chair he was tied to. His jaw was bruised, blood trickling from a cut on the side of his head.

Reese handed her his Swiss Army knife. Kate steadied her grip and cut the plastic zip ties binding his wrists and ankles. His head came up. His eyes found hers, and they swam with some unreadable emotion. He seemed to collect himself and took a shuddering breath. His shoulders straightened as he pushed to his feet.

"Damned glad to see you two," he said weakly. He shook his head, trying to clear it. "You call the cops?"

"Not yet," Reese said.

"Anyone see you come in?"

"I don't think so."

"Good. Let's get some answers before we leave." He staggered, straightened, walked to the beefy man and pulled something out of the guy's pocket.

"Let's see if we've got any juice left." It was a stun gun, Kate saw, the way they must have taken Jase down.

He jammed it into the side of the beefy man's neck. A strangled scream turned into a series of jerky muscle spasms that sent the man sprawling on the floor, gasping for breath like a fish on dry land.

"Still works just fine, eh, Marvin?" Jase walked over to a stack of linens in the storeroom where Reese had tossed the weapons he had taken. Jase picked up his little .380.

While Marvin was still half dazed, Jase dragged him

into the same chair he had been tied to and pressed the gun against the side of the man's head.

"Where are they keeping the rest of the women?" he asked.

"Fuck you."

Jase ratcheted back the slide on the pistol and returned it to the side of Marvin's head. A few feet away, Reese casually aimed his gun at the man in the chair. "Where are they?"

"Go ahead and shoot me. I ain't talking."

"You've got three seconds. Three… Two…" The gun pressed more solidly into flesh and bone.

"Okay, okay, take it easy. It's just business, you know? They got a couple more parlors like this one. Men got needs, and everybody's gotta make a living."

"Give me the names."

Marvin ground his jaw. "I don't know. They keep everything separate. I just work here, do what they tell me and collect my pay."

"What about the trucks?"

He seemed surprised Jase knew. "A couple of times a week, they load the women into the back of a big rig and haul them out to service their customers. Older women, druggies, girls what don't behave. Got it divided into cribs in the back. Everybody wins."

Not everybody, Kate thought. Not girls like Chrissy or the dead girl in San Antonio. She prayed Callie Spencer wasn't a victim.

"Who runs the operation?"

"How the hell would I know? You think they'd tell me? I just keep the women in line."

"What about Burke? Who's his boss?"

When he didn't answer, Jase cuffed the back of his head with the pistol.

"All I know is Burke makes a cash run to Dallas every Tuesday. That's it." He tipped up his chin. "You can go ahead and pull the trigger—but if you do, you're as dead as I am."

For an instant, Jase's fingers tightened around the pistol grip, then he stepped away.

"What about calling the police?" Kate asked.

Jase looked at Marvin. "What do you think, Marv? Maybe we can make a deal. We let you go, you tell them I got away and keep your mouth shut about what you told me. That way your employers don't kill you, and we don't have to deal with the cops."

Marvin warily lifted his head, pondering the notion.

"It's your choice," Jase said. "But odds are you're dead if they find out you talked."

Recognizing the truth in his words, Marvin slowly nodded.

To make it look good, Reese holstered his gun and pulled out a pair of zip ties like the ones Marvin had used on Jase. He pulled the guy's hands behind the chair and used the zip ties to keep him there, also bound his ankles. Kate stuffed a washrag into his mouth and tied it with a strip torn off a terry-cloth hand towel.

"Let's go," Jase said. He checked the door to be sure no one was in the hall, and they moved quickly out of the room toward the back stairs, then outside to the vehicles.

"She's with me," Jase said to Reese when they reached the Yukon. As if Kate would have let him drive away without her. The man had been stunned, beaten and suffered a head injury. She had no idea how badly he was hurt.

Reese nodded. "I'll see you back at the apartment." He strode off toward the Rover.

When Jase reached the driver's side, Kate moved in front of him. "Not happening, big guy. I'm driving."

She thought he would argue, but instead, he went around and slowly climbed into the passenger seat. Kate slid into the driver's seat and started the engine. Her tension didn't ease till they were home.

Kate returned from the bathroom with a cool cloth for Jase's head. He sat on the sofa in the living room, his head resting against the back. Reese had come by to make sure he was okay, then left for his apartment at the other end of the hall.

"How are you feeling?" Kate asked as she gently placed the cloth on his forehead.

His eyes cracked open. "I'll be damned glad when those ibuprofens kick in. Other than that, I'm okay."

"I'm sorry we didn't get there sooner."

He sat up on the sofa, the cloth falling into his lap. "You did exactly right. The stun gun threw me. I wasn't expecting that. Even after they dragged me into the storeroom, I figured I could find a way to take them down. I wasn't really worried because…"

"Because…?"

"Because I knew you had my back."

"You mean Reese."

His expression darkened, turned almost fierce. "I mean you."

Warmth spread through her. She thought of the decision she had made and that she had been right to go in. "I did what I thought was best."

"Reese said your instincts were spot-on."

She shrugged. "I guess I'm starting to know how you think. I knew you would have found a way to get word to us if you could have."

"I couldn't ask for a better partner, Kate."

Her heart squeezed. They were good together in a lot of different ways. She wished Jason could see that.

"We didn't call the cops. Are you feeling up to telling me why not?"

He leaned back and closed his eyes, replaced the cold cloth on his forehead. "Because if we had, they would have raided Paradise Massage, but the other locations would just close up shop and move somewhere else. The only way we're going to stop these guys is to find the men at the top."

"What about the girls?"

He sat up again, set the cloth on the end table. "From what I saw, most of them were lifers. Probably been arrested for soliciting half a dozen times. A girl named Eve was marked with the lipstick tattoo. She was definitely a victim. With any luck, we'll get her out of there soon."

Kate hoped so. She couldn't help thinking of her sister and what she had suffered.

"The thing is, Eve said they sold young girls," Jase continued. "They're high-end product, and they keep them at a different location. If they've got Callie Spencer, that's where she'll be. We find the men at the top, we get those girls out, too. And once the men are locked up, we don't have to keep looking over our shoulders for someone trying to shoot us."

He was right. Waiting was their best chance of success and their only real option if they wanted to stay alive. "So how do we find them?"

"Duff said Harlan Burke makes a cash run to Dallas every Tuesday. We follow Burke and he'll lead us to the guys up the ladder. One more rung closer to the top."

"You think Duff will actually keep quiet?"

"Los Besos plays for keeps. Duff knows that. Good

ol' Marv is going to convince them I was just some guy, not a cop and not any kind of threat to them. He's got no choice—if he wants to live."

"So you think Burke will make the cash run."

"Why not? The cops aren't going to show up because we didn't call them. I think Burke will keep doing his job. If he makes a run to Dallas, we'll follow him, get the info we need."

CHAPTER THIRTY-SIX

"YOU DUMB FUCK. I give you a simple task and you botch it." Harlan Burke sat across from Marvin Duff in the downstairs office at Paradise Massage the following morning.

"I told you—the guy got hold of my stun gun. You saw what a big bastard he was. He zapped me, left me half dazed, tied me up and got away."

"You said he wasn't a cop."

"That's what he said. Cops never showed up, so he must have been telling the truth."

"So what the hell was he doing here?"

"Said he just wanted some company. Said he got his rocks off just talking to a hooker. We get guys like that once in a while, just want some female attention."

"Not guys who look like that," Harlan said. "Hard to believe that guy has a problem with women. What the hell was Eve telling him?"

"She said he just wanted to know how she wound up being a prostitute, so she told him about her no-good boyfriend. Could be the guy was just lonely."

Harlan stood up behind the desk. "We'll keep an eye out, but unless something happens, we're better off ignoring the whole damn thing."

"What about Veronica? You gonna tell her what happened?"

Harlan grunted. "Not likely. You never know which side that bitch is gonna to take."

"Whatever side does her the most good," Marvin said darkly.

"Like I said, we'll keep an eye out. Aside from that, I've got work to do and so do you."

Marvin just nodded. He couldn't remember feeling so relieved.

JASE SPENT MONDAY setting up surveillance he hoped would lead to Harlan Burke's run to Dallas, which was supposed to happen the next day. The strip mall across the street from the massage parlor provided a place to park the Yukon, just one of more than a dozen vehicles mostly hidden by a row of trees.

If the run went down, they would follow Burke's car the first 150 miles of the 240-mile route back to Dallas. Jax Ryker would be waiting in Fairfield to take over and follow the car to its final destination.

Since Burke had never seen Kate or the Yukon, she would be driving while Jase kept a low profile in the passenger seat.

They were packed, loaded and waiting Tuesday morning, hoping like hell Burke didn't change his schedule. The massage parlor opened at ten. Jase had taken a risk that Burke wouldn't leave much earlier than that, but they couldn't afford to be spotted, and he figured a whorehouse was a late-night business. Not likely Burke would be an early riser.

It turned out to be a long day of waiting. Hot and sticky the first half of the day, the wind kicking up in the afternoon. Jase was grateful for the breeze.

All day long, men and women streamed in and out of the massage parlor, some actually there for the low-cost massages the business offered, others, he figured, heading upstairs for women to service their needs.

As the afternoon heated up and the car got hotter inside, Kate napped for a while, then went into the deli and bought sandwiches and Cokes. Then Jase napped while Kate kept watch.

It was late afternoon when he focused his binoculars on a white four-door Audi driving out of the alley behind the building in the direction that led to the interstate.

"It's him," Jase said, sliding low in the seat. "Give him a minute to get on the road."

The Audi pulled into traffic and Kate started the engine.

"Stay as far back as you can. Odds are he's heading up I-45. That's the fastest route."

The Audi disappeared around a corner, and Kate kept her distance but maintained the same speed. "What if he's watching for a tail?"

"If he is, he won't be expecting a woman."

She eased back on the gas, giving Burke a chance to pull even farther ahead. The Audi drove onto the Sam Houston Tollway and they followed a safe distance behind, giving Burke as much room as they could without the risk of losing him.

Once the Audi merged onto I-45, Jase began to relax. "It's a long way to Dallas. Stay back as far as you can and just keep pace with him. There's plenty of traffic on the road heading north. If we're lucky and Marvin Duff kept his mouth shut, Burke won't be expecting anyone on his tail."

The trip progressed exactly as Jase hoped. He phoned Jax Ryker, and let him know they were on their way and should be in Fairfield in a couple of hours.

"Keep me posted," Jax said. "I'll be there before you get there."

When they reached Fairfield, Burke pulled into a service station on the edge of town. Kate drove past, took the next off-ramp while Jase phoned Ryker. When the Audi drove back onto I-45, Ryker picked up the tail and followed the car toward the city.

Jase traded places with Kate and drove the rest of the way to Dallas well out of Burke's sight, receiving updates from Jax along the way. Then the call came in Jase had been waiting for.

"Burke just pulled up in the parking lot of a place called the Blue Bayou. It's an upscale nightclub on Elm Street." Several minutes passed. "Burke just went inside carrying a briefcase," Jax said. "Looks like you got what you needed."

"Looks like. Thanks, bro, I owe you."

"We aren't going in tonight, are we?" Kate asked.

"No. We'll drive by, get a feel for it, go in tomorrow night."

"Good. I definitely need a shower and a change of clothes."

"Yeah, me, too. In the meantime, I need to talk to Tabby, see who owns the place, get as much info as we can."

Jase set the nav system for the address Jax had given him. The club was jumping as he cruised past, a line of patrons out the door and halfway down the block. The customers were expensively dressed, a crowd of twenty- and thirtysomethings with plenty of money to spend.

Tomorrow night he'd pay the club a visit, see what he could find out. He was sure Kate would demand to go with him. Which in this case would be good. A couple would blend in better than him going by himself.

Jase sighed into the quiet inside the Yukon. At least the club wasn't in Old East Dallas—and it was a whole lot classier than Mean Jack's.

CHAPTER THIRTY-SEVEN

By NIGHTFALL, THEY WERE back in Dallas—but still on Los Besos' hit list. Which meant returning to their homes wasn't an option. Of course they couldn't stay in hiding forever, but they were making progress—or at least Jase believed they were.

Fortunately, Reese planned to be in Houston for another week and had volunteered the use of his recently purchased penthouse condominium. His ex-wife had gotten his fancy Bluffview home as part of the divorce settlement, which Reese didn't seem to mind.

Jase didn't think their marriage had ever been a passionate love match, more a practical financial arrangement, since Sandra Montgomery Garrett's family was Dallas elite, same as Reese's.

"Wow, this is some place," Kate said as they carried their bags out of the private elevator and set them down in the entry. Lots of glass and polished dark wood floors, a sleekly modern high-ceilinged interior done in cream with gold and aqua accents. "It was really nice of Reese to let us use it."

"He's a great guy."

Kate flicked him a glance. "Funny, he said the same about you."

Good to know Reese was trying to help him out. He wondered if his friend actually believed there could be some kind of future for him and Kate.

Instead of a reply, Jase grabbed Kate's rolling carry-on, tossed his heavy gear bag over his shoulder and led her down the hall toward the bedrooms in the guest wing. He went into one of the bedrooms, tossed his bag up on the king-size bed.

They'd been sleeping together since the night of the failed stakeout at the truck stop. He knew it wasn't smart, that it would only make things harder on both of them when it was over, but being the selfish bastard he was, he wasn't giving her up until he had to.

"This work for you?" he asked.

Her chin tipped up. "I like sleeping with you, Jason. I like the way you make me feel. So yes. If it works for you, it works for me."

Something squeezed hard in his chest. He wanted to tell her that having her in his bed definitely worked for him, that he liked sleeping beside her, liked everything about her. He wanted to say that if things were different, he wouldn't let her go.

Kate went to work unpacking the few belongings she had brought with her, setting her toiletries in the bathroom while Jase phoned Tabby.

She picked up on the second ring. "Hey, Hawk, I was about to text you. Did you get those bios I sent on Schram and Wiedel?"

"Things have been a little hectic, Tab. I'll take a look at them as soon as we get off the phone."

"On the surface, they both look clean. I can go deeper if you want."

"There's something I need more. According to my latest info, there are at least two more massage parlors in the Houston area linked to the Paradise that are running women. At least one of them may be selling underage girls. I need the names and addresses."

"I'll take a look, see if I can connect the dots."

"Great. Also, I got a lead on a nightclub here in Dallas called the Blue Bayou. Upscale nightclub on Elm Street. It's also connected in some way. I'm not sure how. Kate and I are heading over there tomorrow night. Anything you can come up with before we go in would really help."

"I'll get back to you." Tabby ended the call.

Jase went into the kitchen, which was a gourmet chef's dream. He set up his laptop on the modern dark wood kitchen table and brought up his email, checked out the bios Tabby had sent on Schram and Wiedel, who apparently were big real estate developers. One of their corporate entities owned the building that housed Paradise Massage, but real estate was real estate—didn't mean they were involved in human trafficking.

In the meantime, he went online to check out the Blue Bayou, which appeared to be one of the hottest, most lavish clubs in town. Under different circumstances, he would have enjoyed taking Kate.

The way things were now, he'd be worried about keeping her alive.

THE FOLLOWING DAY, with big plans for the evening, Kate needed clothes. Instead of taking a chance on their residences being monitored and someone from Los Besos following them back to Reese's, Jason drove her out to the Galleria, careful to be sure they weren't being tailed on the way.

"No reason to worry at the moment," Jase said. "We've been keeping a low profile. Even my office doesn't know where we are."

"Mine, either."

He nodded, trusting her to make that decision. Kate realized Jase trusted her more every day.

Once inside the huge shopping mall just off the Dallas Parkway, he checked their surroundings, then left Kate in a small boutique next to two more women's apparel shops.

"Don't go anywhere else," he said. "I'll be back to get you in thirty minutes."

Typical male. How did a woman shop for a night at a ritzy club in thirty minutes? He could just wait, she decided, until she was finished.

She bought expensive French lingerie in the first boutique, hit the jackpot at the second store with a sexy black cocktail dress. The dress was super short and fitted; narrow straps on the bodice sparkled with glittering black sequins. The outfit desperately called for a pair of black high heels, which she found at the third shop: strappy, sky-high Jimmy Choos she couldn't afford and couldn't resist.

At the third shop, she also found a dress on the sale rack in case they had to go back a second night. This one was pink, with a flirty little skirt trimmed in black that she could wear with the same high heels. She bought a pair of dangly rhinestone earrings, and she was set.

She was just grabbing her shopping bags to go back to the boutique when Jason appeared in the doorway. "You ready?"

"What, you aren't going to yell at me for leaving the first store?"

His mouth edged into a grin. "You're a woman. Women love to shop. I figured you were smart enough to stay close, and you were."

She laughed. She glanced down at the bags he was carrying. "You going to show me what you bought?"

"Tonight," he said. "If you're finished, let's go get something to eat."

They headed for the Grand Lux Café to enjoy what so far had been, aside from a series of updates from Tabby and business calls from Kate's office, a surprisingly normal day.

Kate ordered a delicious Asian chicken salad while Jase ordered a prime rib sandwich and fries. She wondered how a man could eat the way he did and never gain weight. But she knew he did serious workouts and kept himself in extremely good physical condition.

Which reminded her of the shower they had shared last night, and the feel of that incredible body pressing her against the wet tile walls. Her face heated up and so did other parts of her anatomy. It took a supreme effort to drag her mind back to sanity and stab a bite of lettuce.

"Have you heard from your father?" Jase asked casually, taking a drink of iced tea.

Thank God he couldn't read her thoughts. "Just this morning, actually. When he couldn't reach my cell, he called my office. I phoned him back before we left the apartment."

"Everything all right?"

"He said he just wanted to say hello."

"That's great, Kate. It means he cares."

"I guess. It's hard with our lives so different."

"Maybe you can carve out some time to go see him, meet the rest of your family."

She'd never really thought of it that way, that she had a half sister and brother, and a stepmom, a family she had never met. Her dad had extended an invitation at the cemetery and also this morning on the phone.

"Maybe I will," she said, taking another forkful of salad. It would give her something to do after Jason was gone. Something that would help her forget him. The salad stuck in her throat.

Jason paid the bill and they slid out of the booth, wove their way through the crowded restaurant back outside and drove back to Reese's lavish apartment.

"This is place is really nice," Jase said as they stepped out of the private elevator. "But it isn't for me."

"Too cold, right?"

He smiled. "Yeah."

"Reese probably had it professionally decorated. I wonder what kind of place he would choose for himself."

"Hard to tell with Reese."

Later in the afternoon, Tabby called with information on the nightclub, which was owned by a man named Rafael De Santos. Kate looked him up on the internet, a hot-looking Hispanic man with short black hair and intense dark eyes. In an expensive suit, he looked like a male cover model.

There were several news articles about him and the club he had opened, with photos that showed the wildly extravagant interior. Even under the tenuous circumstances, Kate was looking forward to the evening.

It was after 10:00 p.m. Jase had gotten dressed in one of the other guest suites, giving her space. Now he was pacing the living room, anxious to leave.

Kate checked her makeup in the mirror above the black granite counter in the bathroom and fluffed her long blond curls. Straightening the sequined bodice of the black silk dress, she tugged down the very short, very snug skirt and headed for the living room.

Jase turned and she stopped dead in her tracks. She could almost feel her jaw unhinging. Dressed in an expensive, perfectly tailored black suit over a purple designer T-shirt, his hair shaved on the sides and moussed into a peak on top, Hawk looked amazing, as if he'd stepped out of *GQ*.

Kate barely recognized him as the tough man in the black jeans and leather vest he had been at Mean Jack's.

His gaze slid over her head to foot, and the heat in his eyes had desire pulsing low in her belly.

"Beautiful," he said.

She swallowed, her stomach quivering. "You…um…too." She set her palms on the lapels of his black jacket, noticed a small tattoo above his right ear, a pair of arrows, one above the other, pointing in opposite directions. "Is that real?"

He chuckled. "I drew it on with a Sharpie. It'll be there awhile."

"What's it mean?"

"Two opposing arrows mean war or conflict. It's just part of the image."

"What about the tattoo on your calf?" Which was definitely real. "You never said."

"Friends in Afghanistan, marines in my unit who died while I lived."

Her heart ached for him. She had read about survivor's guilt, knew that when you lost close friends it was even more difficult. "I'm glad you made it out okay."

Jason glanced away, the subject clearly painful.

"You look…really different," Kate said, bringing him back to the moment.

"Tricks of the trade." He adjusted the heavy gold rings on his fingers. "A bounty hunter has to be a chameleon."

He looked so good she couldn't resist going up on her toes and pressing a kiss on his lips. An instant later, she was in his arms, his mouth crushing down over hers. Heat scorched through her—the instant before he let her go.

"Remember where we left off when we get home," he said a little gruffly. "In the meantime, we've got work to do."

Kate simply nodded. Heat still throbbed in all her womanly places. Remembering would not be a problem.

"Leave your ID here. Tonight you're Kitty Cordell, high-class call girl."

She glanced down at her black silk dress and heels. She hadn't been going for cheap.

"Two thousand a night," Jason said as if he read her mind, and Kate grinned.

"So who are you?" she asked.

"Brock Devlin, in from Atlanta, plenty of money to burn and looking for a good time."

Brock Devlin. *Oh, yeah.*

Jase took her arm and led her out of the apartment. Instead of the Yukon, a sleek silver Mercedes AMG S coupe waited in the circular drive in front of the building.

"We're taking that?"

"That's right. You got enough money, you can rent anything you want." He smiled as he settled her in the passenger seat. "No expense spared while I'm in Dallas."

"We're spending a lot of money," Kate said as he slid into the driver's seat.

"Don't worry, it's dirty money, part of the stash I keep for expenses. I got it picking up a drug lord, came out of a huge pile of bills sitting in the middle of the dealer's bed. This is just a prop. I don't spend it on anything but work."

"Why not?"

"I'm not a thief. Like I said, it's just for show. Undercover cops do the same thing."

She didn't say more. She trusted Jason to do the right thing, the way he always did. She settled back to enjoy the evening.

This was fun, she realized. She hadn't expected that. But now that she knew the game, she was determined to play her part.

She flicked a glance at Jason. "You look good behind the wheel of a Benz."

He laughed. "Pretty much anybody looks good behind the wheel of a hundred-sixty-thousand-dollar Mercedes."

She smiled and settled back in the seat. She didn't stop smiling until the Mercedes pulled up to valet parking in front of the Blue Bayou nightclub. Then the possibilities of what could go wrong had her smile slipping away.

CHAPTER THIRTY-EIGHT

AFTER PASSING A hefty tip to one of the bouncers to get them in the front door, Jase set a hand on the small of Kate's back and escorted her into the nightclub. It was first class all the way, the interior three-stories high, ringed with open balconies that looked down on a dance floor crisscrossed with tiny blue LED lights.

Blue neon light illuminated the bar and the booths along the walls. A strobe light beat over the dance floor while a DJ inside a glass-enclosed booth played a throbbing tune that had the place jumping.

"Let's get a drink," Jase suggested, steering Kate toward the bar. He tried not to notice the sexy little black dress she was wearing, cut just low enough to make him sweat. Thick blond curls tumbled around her shoulders, and those long legs went on forever.

He wished it didn't feel so good to be spending his nights in her bed, wished she didn't mean more to him than just a hot piece of ass.

Truth was, he was in deep with Kate Gallagher. Kate was smart and strong and determined. She was everything he admired in a woman. He was in a place he had never been before—though now was hardly the time to be thinking about it.

He helped her up on a bar stool and took the one beside her, pulled out a wad of cash in a flashy gold money clip. The way he was dressed, the car he was driving and the cash he'd been tossing around sent a message to the management. He figured it wouldn't take long to hear from someone.

"I'll have a vodka lemon drop martini," Kate said, getting into her role. She seemed to have a knack, which made his job a whole lot easier.

"What kind of vodka?" the bartender asked.

"Grey Goose is all right."

Jase surveyed the back bar. "She'll have Beluga Gold."

The bartender eyed the money clip in Jase's hand. "What about you?"

"I'll have a single malt. What have you got?"

The bartender mopped the counter in front of them. "Got a sixteen-year-old Lagavulin. That do?"

"That's fine."

The bartender, average height and build, blond and good-looking, went to work. A few minutes later, he returned with a stemmed martini glass and a heavy low ball glass filled with a shot of amber liquid. Setting the drinks on top of the bar, he cruised off to wait on other customers, more than enough to keep him busy.

Jase took a sip of the expensive scotch and turned to survey the room. The music was loud, but the crowd seemed to be enjoying it. His gaze went to the second floor, where he spotted a second bar, one that looked quieter.

"Come on, beautiful, let's go upstairs."

Kate's eyes flashed to his. It was simple truth, not flattery, and had been the first time he'd said it. She took a couple of sips of her drink, bringing the level down so she could carry it, and they wove their way through the throng of moving bodies. Though an elevator wasn't far away, the stairs gave him a chance to check out their surroundings.

Jase wasn't sure what he expected to find tonight—maybe nothing that would do them any good. But according to Tabby, the building was also owned by a corporation connected to Schram and Wiedel. Tab was still trying to locate the other two massage parlors in Houston.

At the top of the stairs, he urged Kate toward the second bar, more of a lounge, with comfortable dark blue leather couches set around low, black glass tables.

A maître d' approached, silver-haired and oddly dignified for a crowd like this. "Good evening. My name is Arnold. I understand this is your first visit to the Blue Bayou."

"That's right." Information Jase had dropped to the bouncers at the front on his way in.

"The owner, Mr. De Santos, would like to extend a personal invitation for you and your companion to join him." Arnold stepped back and indicated a lean, black-haired man on the sofa in the far corner of the bar. A sexy blonde sat on one side of him, a dynamite redhead on the other.

"Lead the way," Jase said. "Kitty?" She fell in behind the maître d' and Jase followed.

Rafael De Santos rose to greet them, extending a slender manicured hand. Jase accepted the handshake, his own nails carefully trimmed and buffed. He knew how to play the game. Under the right circumstances, it was how he got paid.

"Welcome to the Blue Bayou, Mr.…?"

"Devlin. Brock Devlin."

"Rafael De Santos. I own this place." He reached out to Kate, who extended her hand, but instead of shaking it, De Santos brought Kate's hand to his lips and kissed the back. "Rafael De Santos at your service, lovely lady."

"Kathryn Cordell," Kate said, nicely adjusting to the moment. "My friends call me Kitty."

De Santos smiled. "My friends call me Rafi. Welcome to the Blue Bayou."

The guy had two female companions of his own, but he was clearly interested in Kate. Had to give De Santos credit for balls. He had shit for brains or he'd know Jase was thinking about stomping those balls into grease spots on the carpet.

"Please…" De Santos said, stretching a hand toward the opposite sofa. "Won't you join me?"

Jase nodded. "All right, thanks." He took a seat across from De Santos, and Kate sat down beside him. Jase made a point of toying with her wrist, linking their fingers together, staking his claim, which De Santos seemed to ignore.

"Your drinks need refreshing." De Santos snapped his fingers at a passing waiter, and the guy turned around so fast his head nearly spun off his shoulders.

"Lagavulin single malt, I understand," De Santos said.

Jase nodded.

De Santos looked at Kate. "And yours, Beluga Gold lemon drop."

Kate smiled and held up her empty glass. The waiter set it on his tray and took off at a run toward the bar, and Jase's gaze followed, snagged on the man in the short white jacket working behind the counter. Black hair a little too long, olive complexion, high cheekbones. The guy looked familiar.

Jesus. Mark Kingsley, special agent FBI. They'd met

a couple years back when Jase was hunting a skip and Kingsley was working undercover—which apparently he was now. They'd formed a wary partnership that had become stronger over time. Kingsley and the feds arrested a well-known drug dealer and Jase brought in his skip, worth 15 percent of a three-million-dollar bond.

For an instant, his gaze locked with Kingsley's. Recognition was instant, the message clear. *You keep quiet and I will too.*

"I would like you to meet my friends, Dolores and Bunny," De Santos said, regaining Jase's attention.

"Pleasure," he said, thinking the buxom blonde looked more like a *Bunny* than the redhead.

"Nice to meet you both," Kate said.

Their drinks arrived. "So, Mr. Devlin, you are here on business?"

"Of a sort," Jase said, taking a sip of his drink.

"Where do you come from?" De Santos asked.

"Atlanta."

"I see. And what sort of work is it you do in Atlanta?" De Santos pressed.

Jase took a sip of his drink. "I work strictly for myself." Code for *I do anything that makes me money.* Which De Santos clearly understood.

De Santos swirled the the liquor in his glass, making the ice cubes clink together. "And you, Ms. Cordell? You are also from Atlanta?"

Kate smiled. "Actually, I live right here in Dallas. Brock and I only met this evening."

De Santos picked up on the implication. A woman who looked like Kate didn't waste her time on blind dates. "Well, then, perhaps you will come and see us again."

She gave him a sophisticated smile. "Perhaps I will."

De Santos's gaze returned to Jase. "How long will you be in Dallas, Mr. Devlin?"

"I plan to be here at least a few more days."

"If there is anything you need, please let me know. We like to keep our customers happy."

Jase lifted a dark eyebrow. "Is that so?"

De Santos smiled, his gaze narrowing on Jase like a raptor swooping down on its prey. "Perhaps, if time permits, tomorrow evening you would care to attend a small party upstairs in my personal quarters. Very private, you understand. Ms. Cordell, of course you are invited, as well."

Jase sipped his drink and slowly nodded. "That sounds good. What time?"

"Any time after ten."

"We'll be there." Jase set his unfinished scotch on the table and stood up from the sofa. "Time to go, babe. You've got a long evening ahead."

She stood up beside him, leaned in close, went up and kissed him full on the mouth. "I'm ready whenever you are, honey," she breathed.

De Santos rose, too. "It's been a pleasure, Mr. Devlin. Ms. Cordell."

Jase nodded. "Thanks for the drink. We'll see you tomorrow night."

They left the club and headed back to Reese's penthouse, Jase making sure they didn't pick up a tail on the way.

"What do you think he's involved in?" Kate asked once they were safely inside.

"Aside from drugs and prostitution? Probably the usual array of illegal gaming, extortion and money laundering—anything that makes a buck."

"What do you think he wants from us?"

"I know what he wants from you and he isn't going to get it. What he wants from me—probably a connection in Atlanta. Between now and tomorrow night, he'll be finding out everything he can about Brock Devlin. Fortunately, it's a cover I've used before and it goes deep."

"Tabby?"

"That's right. De Santos will discover I'm exactly what he's hoping I'll be—a shady character who lives high and hard and is always interested in making more money."

"Tomorrow night could be dangerous."

"No question. The good news is there's an FBI friend of mine working undercover behind the bar. His name is Mark Kingsley. We've worked together before."

Her eyes widened. "FBI! Seriously?"

He chuckled. "Dead serious, honey. I figure Kingsley will try to track me down either tonight or sometime tomorrow. Mindy has the number of my burner. I'll phone the office in the morning, make sure she gives it to him when he calls."

"I don't suppose we could just hand this whole thing over to the FBI and forget it."

"I wish we could. I've got a hunch we may know things they don't, which means they may need our help. Plus, if we don't show up tomorrow night, De Santos might get suspicious and pull the plug."

"You mean go underground and move the women somewhere else."

"Exactly—assuming he's got the juice to make that happen. Whatever's going on, we have to see this through." Finding Chrissy Gallagher's killer was no longer enough. The hunters were being hunted. He had to put an end to Los Besos before both of them wound up dead.

Music throbbed somewhere in the rooms below. It was late, dark outside the window. The men had moved Callie that morning, blindfolded her, tied her hands in front of her and shoved her into the back of a van.

The ride had been long, hot and exhausting. When the van doors finally slid open, she felt weak and disoriented, her stomach rolling with nausea as they half dragged, half carried her across the alley into a freight elevator and took her to a room up several floors.

She was in a bedroom, nicer than where she was being kept before, with plush dark blue carpet, a queen-size bed and a private bathroom.

But the door was locked, and though there was a window, it was three stories to the ground, too far to jump. She thought about doing it, though. Maybe dying would be better than what they had planned for her.

Curled up against the headboard, her legs tucked beneath her, Callie shivered in the air-conditioning. She was wearing a thin white cotton nightgown, no panties. Her small breasts protruded like tiny buttons against the fabric. She felt vulnerable in a way she never had before. She had never been more afraid, not even when they had first taken her.

So far the men had left her alone, but she knew that was going to change. She had heard them talking. The man who had bought her would come for her tomorrow night. Whoever he was, he was rich. They spoke about him like he was a god. He would be guest of honor at a lavish party, one of the men said.

Afterward, he would take her away with him, take her anywhere he wanted, do anything to her he wanted.

Her throat tightened and tears burned her eyes. The police hadn't found her, and now she wasn't even in

Houston anymore. Did her mother miss her? Was she frightened for her daughter?

A shudder rippled through her. She would almost be glad when it was over. When the man had come and taken her away. At least she would know what she was facing. Maybe she could find a way to fight him. Maybe she could even find a way to escape.

Callie wished she could make herself believe it.

She felt like crying but no tears came. Crying wouldn't save her. It was too late for tears.

CHAPTER THIRTY-NINE

JASE'S BURNER PHONE rang at ten the next morning as he sat at the breakfast table. Reese's housekeeper kept the kitchen well stocked, so Kate had volunteered to make breakfast: scrambled eggs, bacon and toast. The delicious smells made his mouth water.

"Maddox," he answered as he pressed the phone against his ear.

"What the fuck, Hawk? Tell me you aren't hunting Rafael De Santos."

Jason smiled at FBI Special Agent Mark Kingsley's greeting. "I'm not hunting De Santos. I'm hunting Los Besos and about half a dozen other entities I haven't got a handle on yet. De Santos is somehow involved."

"Los Besos? You think Dc Santos is connected to Los Besos?"

"I'm surprised you don't know. The guy's in it up to his ears. We just need to prove it."

"Dammit, man. You've got to stay out of this. We've been working this operation for months. We're just beginning to make progress. You get in the middle, you're liable to blow the whole damn thing."

"Just hear me out, all right? That's all I ask."

Kingsley sighed into the phone. "Fine. Where do you want to meet?"

"How about the Mesquite Diner? Where we met before."

"Not good. I don't want anything connecting back to that operation. How about the Dolphin Café next to the aquarium?"

"All right, that'll work." Not too far from Reese's fancy new condo in the Design District and the Blue Bayou on Elm, the area where Kingsley was probably renting a temporary apartment. "What time?"

"I can be there at noon."

"I'll be there."

"What about the woman you were with last night? She in this, too?"

"Her name's Kate Gallagher and unfortunately, yes. She's in it till it's over. Kate comes with me."

"I'm sticking my neck out on this, Maddox. I hope you know that."

"Yeah, well, so am I. See you at noon."

When the call ended, Kate set his breakfast in front of him, and his stomach growled. The aroma of bacon and eggs drifted up as she set the other plate on the table across from him and sat down.

"FBI?" she asked, picking up her fork.

He nodded. "Kingsley, yeah. We're meeting him at noon."

"I can't wait to hear what he has to say."

Jase dug into his eggs, which tasted delicious. "I'm pretty sure Kingsley's thinking the same damn thing."

SPECIAL AGENT MARK KINGSLEY was lean, hard and handsome. With his shoulder-length black hair, olive complexion and carved features, Kate thought he looked more like a drug dealer than an FBI agent. Which was probably the point.

He slid into the booth across from them and ordered a cup of coffee, same as she and Jase had already done.

He didn't speak until the aging waitress delivered it a few minutes later.

"You want to go first or shall I?" Jase asked.

Kingsley stretched his long legs out in front of him and leaned back in the booth. "Definitely you first."

"Fine. But I expect the same courtesy."

Kingsley just nodded. Kate sat quietly as Jase filled the agent in on the case they had been working since her sister's murder, which took a considerable amount of time.

Kingsley turned his attention to Kate. "So you hired Maddox to help you find your sister's killer."

"That's right. Since then we've been working together. We found a second victim in San Antonio, both women marked with the same lipstick tattoo."

"Los Besos," Jase said.

"The kiss of death," Kingsley added.

"One of the victims was bludgeoned to death," Jase said. "The other strangled. Both where killed with a baton or club of some kind, possibly the same weapon utilized in two different ways."

Kingsley's gaze sharpened. He took a sip of coffee, giving himself some time. "Go on."

"There are three massage parlors in Houston where the women are being held. Paradise Massage is one of them. We're hoping to come up with the names of the other two fairly soon."

Kingsley straightened in his seat, beginning to look impressed. "What's Los Besos got to do with Rafael De Santos?"

"He's taking payoffs from them, a cash delivery every week. We're trying to find out who he's working for."

"If he's involved with Los Besos, he's top of the

pecking order," Kingsley said. "The guy running the show. But we think he's trying to move even higher, get into the big leagues."

"You wouldn't be talking about Maximillian Schram and Arthur Wiedel? Their names keep popping up, wealthy real estate developers."

Kingsley groaned. "Briton, Inc. That's our target. We know Schram and Wiedel are heavily involved in drugs and organized crime. Haven't run across a connection to trafficking."

"My sister, Christina, was a sixteen-year-old runaway when she was picked up two years ago and taken somewhere in Houston. We believe she was drugged, beaten and prostituted against her will until she finally escaped. One of them tracked her down in Dallas and murdered her. I want that man brought to justice." She felt Jase's hand settle on her thigh, comforting her with his touch.

He looked over at Kingsley. "All right, your turn."

"I've got a couple of things you might be interested in. First, something big is going down at the club tonight. I'm not sure what it is, but De Santos is pulling out all the stops. Private party in his quarters, sparing no expense."

"Lucky for us, we're invited."

"Christ," Kingsley grumbled. "I should have known."

"What else?" Jase asked.

"There's this guy. They call him Batman. He's mean, enjoys his work. He's De Santos's top enforcer. He'll be there tonight."

Kate's shoulders tensed. "What's his name?"

"Emanuel Vargas."

"I want him dead."

"Easy, darlin'. You can't just go in there and kill the guy," Jase said.

"He murdered my sister. At the very least, he needs to spend the rest of his life in prison."

Kingsley's dark eyes pinned her. "Listen to me, Kate. This is FBI business. You need to leave justice to the law."

"My sister is dead."

"I know what that feels like." Kingsley looked at Jason. "Hawk does, too. Let the FBI handle it."

Kate made no comment.

"We have to show at the party tonight or De Santos might get suspicious," Jase said. "He's likely hoping to build a business relationship, probably looking for a way to expand into Atlanta. I told him we'd be there."

"I don't like it," Kingsley said.

"Yeah, well, neither do I, but it's too late now."

Kingsley swore softly. Defeated, he blew out a deep breath. "All right, I guess that's how it's going to be." He pulled a slip of paper out of his pocket and slid it over to Jason. "I'd appreciate if you'd pass any info to Agent Troy Wister. That's his number."

Calling Agent Kingsley while he was undercover would put his life in danger. Even so, Jase slid the paper back to him.

"No can do," Jase said. "I guess I forgot to mention we got a dirty cop in Houston. I'm not sure how far it reaches. Now that I think about it, I also didn't mention that whoever's running Los Besos put a hit out on Kate and me."

"Jesus." Kingsley sat back in the booth. He rubbed a hand over his face, his gaze going from Jason to Kate. "So I guess we'd better end this before one of you gets hurt."

"I'd appreciate it," Jase said.

Kingsley reached for the folded slip of paper, turned it over and wrote another name and number on the back. "You know this guy. He's heading up the investigation. He worked with one of the detectives in your office a while back when he was head of the terrorism task force. You got a problem, call him."

Jase took the paper and showed it to Kate. *Special Agent in Charge, Quinn Taggart.* Jase nodded. "Taggart's a good man."

"That's his private number." Kingsley stood up. "Let's see what happens tonight and I'll call you tomorrow." He tossed money down for their check and his own. "Be careful."

"You, too," Jase said.

Turning, the agent walked out of the café.

It was late afternoon when Kate heard the ring of Jase's disposable.

"It's Tabby." He put the call on speaker. "What have you got, Tab?"

Kate hurried across the living room so she could hear.

"I got the name and location of the other two massage parlors in Houston. One's in a building owned by Atrias Corp. The other property is leased from Winman. Both of those entities are connected in some form or another to Briton."

Jase flashed a look at Kate. "What are the names?" he asked.

"One's the Garden of Eden. The other is the Pleasure Dome…you know, like Mad Max?"

"Yeah, I get it," Jase said. "Text me the addresses."

"Will do."

"Thank you, Tabby," Kate said.

"Give 'em hell, Kate." Tabby hung up the phone.

Kate's heart was beating a little faster when the addresses came through a few minutes later, both on the outskirts of Houston, along with phone numbers and websites. Kate pulled up the websites on her laptop. Daytime operation 10-6 p.m. Evenings by appointment.

She checked Google Maps to see what the exterior of the massage parlors looked like, found both buildings were low-rises. One was in a seedy neighborhood, a run-down structure in need of repair. The other was well maintained, even nicely landscaped, but there were iron bars on the second-and third-floor windows.

Thinking of the women inside, pity welled in Kate's heart.

Jase pointed to the website that looked like a jail. "Garden of Eden. That's got to be where they keep their prime, high-grade merchandise—the underage girls."

"We have to get them out of there," Kate said, trying not to imagine what the girls were suffering.

"We can call Agent Taggart and give him the info, but it's going to set everything in motion. There won't be any turning back. I want this over as much as you do, but we can't afford to strike too soon."

"You're right," Kate said. "If we do that, we could end up being the ones who pay—maybe the girls, too. I think we should wait and see what happens tonight."

Jase nodded. "De Santos has something special planned. Let's find out what it is."

CHAPTER FORTY

KATE WORE THE black-trimmed pink crepe dress with the short flirty skirt. The halter top left her back bare, and of course she wore her black, super-high, Jimmy Choo heels.

Jason wore the black suit he'd had on last night with a collared, sapphire-blue silk shirt open at the throat. The color accented his eyes. The man could rock a suit, that was for sure.

The club was booming by the time they got there. A big dark-skinned bouncer whose name tag read Axel recognized them from the night before. "Names?"

"Devlin and Cordell."

He checked them off the guest list. "Follow me." Axel led them through the crowd to the back of the club where Dc Santo's private elevator waited.

"No firearms." Axel didn't bother to ask if Jase had a gun with him, just lifted the lid of the inlaid wooden box next to the elevator. "You can pick up your piece when you leave."

Jase flicked open his jacket and pulled his Kimber out of the holster clipped to his belt. He was Brock Devlin tonight, brash enough to carry whatever weapon he wanted. He set the pistol inside the box, and the bouncer closed the lid, turned and pushed the elevator button. Axel ushered them into a mirrored car that swept them up to De Santo's third floor residence.

Kate stepped out of the elevator into an elegant, sophisticated living room with gray-and-white marble floors, and contemporary crystal chandeliers suspended from twelve-foot white molded ceilings. Huge silver-framed mirrors hung on the walls, reflecting the white silk furnishings and draperies, even a marble fountain.

De Santos had spent some major bucks on his extravagant apartment. Their host appeared to greet them in a designer tuxedo with black satin lapels. He walked gracefully toward them. "Mr. Devlin and Ms. Cordell. Welcome to my home."

Jason smiled. "Brock and Kitty will do."

"Of course. And I am Rafi."

"Your home is beautiful, Rafi," Kate said. "You have excellent taste in interior design."

"Thank you. Perhaps later you will allow me to show you around."

Kate smiled. She didn't look at Jason. She knew the exact set of his jaw, the tight frown she would see marring his forehead. "I would enjoy that very much."

"Looks like you went all out," Jase said, managing to be polite. "What's the occasion, Rafi?"

"A few special friends are in town. I wanted to make certain they had a good time."

A waiter in a short white jacket offered a silver tray filled with champagne flutes. Kate took one of the long-stemmed glasses.

"It's a '98 Dom Perignon," De Santos said. "A favorite of mine."

Kate took a sip and smiled. "Wonderful. Nothing better than good French champagne."

De Santos turned to Jason. "Single malt, if I recall."

"That's right."

"I keep something special for my friends." De Santos led them over to the bar and walked around behind it, selected a particular bottle of scotch and poured a hefty portion into a Baccarat crystal snifter. "Eighteen-year-old Dalmore. I think you'll like it."

Jase took the snifter, swirled and inhaled. He took a sip and nodded. "Very nice."

"I'll be busy this evening with my guests, but I thought perhaps we could speak sometime tomorrow about a business proposition I have in mind."

Jase nodded. "I'm intrigued. Late afternoon would work."

"Three o'clock, then. In my office." He turned to Kate. "If I can find a moment to break free, I'll give you that tour."

"I'll look forward to it," Kate said.

De Santos made a slight bow and melted into the crowd.

Kate linked her arm with Jason's. "Let's wander a little." She hadn't been to an extravagant cocktail party since she and Andrew had broken up, but she hadn't forgotten the rituals. She was in her element here, which Jase seemed to understand.

"Lead the way," he said.

They ambled from room to room, each one equally extravagant, done in variations of the white-and-silver theme in the huge, high-ceilinged living room. The residence, which mirrored the footprint of the first floor, had to be at least ten thousand square feet.

They stopped at one of the several buffet tables to sample the gourmet dishes: lobster en croute, blackened shrimp, oysters on the half shell, filet mignon, stuffed capon, endless salads and luscious desserts.

Not all of the apartment was open to the party, Kate noticed. A bearded security guard in a black tuxedo stood in the middle of the corridor to an extensive wing, legs splayed, arms behind his back in a parade-rest position. *No Admittance* seemed to be stamped on his forehead.

"Wonder what goes on in there." Kate's gaze went down the long hallway.

"Be interesting to know."

"Whatever it is, I don't think we're invited."

Jase eyed the guard. "Maybe not. I guess we'll have to wait and see."

We'll have to wait and see? Unease swirled in her stomach. Surely Jason wouldn't break into De Santos's private quarters? On the other hand, they needed information. Maybe they could find it.

They wove their way through the elegantly dressed throng, spotted a couple of famous rappers; a woman Kate recognized as currently starring in the Dallas Broadway production of *Phantom of the Opera* at the Music Hall at Fair Park. There were fashion models and even a movie star, though Kate couldn't remember the woman's name.

All evening, she had been watching for Special Agent Kingsley, but she didn't notice him until they went out to the terrace, where Kingsley was making drinks behind one of the portable bars.

Jason urged her in that direction, stopped right in front of him. "How about a refill?" he asked the agent, pointing to his heavy crystal snifter.

Kingsley's dark gaze zeroed in on him. "That the scotch the boss keeps for special guests?"

"That's the one," Jase said. They barely made eye contact. Kate thought it was more than possible De Santos had cameras all over the residence, watching his guests' every move.

Kingsley refilled her champagne flute. "Enjoy your evening," he said as he moved on to another guest. They stayed on the terrace awhile, soaking up the warm night air, then headed back inside.

"Apparently De Santos is the man of the hour," Jase said, noticing the *Morning News* press badge on a woman snapping photos of celebrities for the society page.

"Look over there." Kate took a sip of champagne. "The guy with the bodyguards? That's Denny Reyburg, the social media magnate."

"In the flesh," Jase said.

And there was plenty of it. Denny was at least sixty pounds overweight. Not quite six feet tall, dark hair pulled back in a man bun, Denny had a pudgy face and a bad case of acne.

He'd invented a new social media platform called Grouper. Instead of a bird, the symbol was a giant fish whose mouth opened and closed. It had made Denny Reyburg a household name and a billionaire at least two times over.

"The tabloids aren't kind to him," Kate said. "They say he's a spoiled brat who's never grown up. Supposedly, he throws tantrums when he doesn't get his way, has a brutal temper and treats his employees like dirt."

"I guess if you have enough money, you can do whatever you want."

Kate watched De Santos walk up to Reyburg, and the two of them spoke briefly. A third man joined them, dark suit, hard-faced, short black hair combed straight back. He said something to De Santos, and the two of them walked away.

Reyburg, followed by his two powerful bodyguards, one with a shaved head, the other with earrings in both ears, headed for the wing that had been blocked off to the rest of the guests. The guard let them pass, and the men disappeared down the corridor.

"I wonder what's going on?" Kate murmured.

Jase took a drink of his scotch, his eyes on the corridor where the guard was back in position. "I don't know, but I've never liked being left out."

Kate's eyes widened. "You aren't thinking we should crash their private party?"

"Probably ought to at least check it out."

Check it out? This was getting worse by the minute.

Kate took a steadying breath as Jason lead her back outside, into the warm night air. The apartment wrapped in a U-shape around the terrace. Glass doors led into the residence on both sides—including the side that was forbidden.

They wandered casually among the guests. Jase led her out of sight behind a row of tall, potted cypress not far from the bar. From there, they could reach one of the glass doors without being seen.

She hoped.

Her heart was pounding, hammering away as he went to work with a tiny multipurpose pocketknife, and a few seconds later, the glass door swung open.

"After you, darlin'." Pleased with himself, Jase hauled her back inside the apartment.

IT WAS HAPPENING TONIGHT! Callie had heard them talking. Tonight the man was coming for her!

Earlier Mrs. Barclay, the older woman who had been in charge of her since she had been brought to this place, had come to her room to get her ready.

Callie had protested and tried to fight, but another woman had come to help, and she and Mrs. Barclay had held her down and forced her to swallow a mouthful of pills. Callie had been stripped, bathed and dressed in a clean white cotton nightgown, her auburn hair parted in the middle and tied with pink ribbons on each side of her face. She looked like a little girl.

Callie's throat ached with unshed tears. She felt light-headed and dizzy, her mouth cotton-dry. *I want to go home*, she thought. *I just want to go home*.

Footsteps sounded in the hall. The lock turned, the door swung open. It was Mrs. Barclay standing next to a man in a black suit.

"Time to go," Mrs. Barclay said.

"No…please… I want to go home." But the words came out slurred, and her legs wobbled.

"Do as you're told," the woman said. "The man you belong to now isn't going to put up with your nonsense. You understand me? You will do exactly what he tells you." Mrs. Barclay nodded to the man in the suit, and he moved forward.

He took hold of Callie's arm and started pulling her toward the door. When she struggled and tried to get away, Mrs. Barclay slapped her across the face.

"Stop that right this minute. If you don't, I'm going to give you a shot of something a lot stronger than the pills. Either way, you're going to do what I tell you. It's up to you."

Her head was already spinning, her muscles as limp as noodles. She didn't want any more drugs. When the man drew her forward, this time she didn't resist. What was the use, anyway?

With a sob in her throat, Callie let them lead her out of the room.

CHAPTER FORTY-ONE

"Looks like we're in one of the guest rooms in this wing of the residence," Jase said as he glanced at their surroundings. He hadn't planned to take things this far, hated putting Kate in even worse danger, but they had to find a way to stop Los Besos and time was running out. "Come on."

Leading Kate toward the door on the opposite side of the room, he cracked it open and checked to see what was happening out in the hall.

A flash of movement coming in their direction caught his eye, and he eased the door almost completely closed. He could hear the sound of footsteps, waited until the group passed, then cracked the door enough to see three figures disappearing down the hall.

An older woman with silver-streaked black hair, a guy in a suit and a young girl in a nightgown. The man had a solid grip on the girl's arm as he tugged her along.

No way, Jase thought as recognition struck. But Detective Castillo had sent photos of Callie Spencer, the teenage girl who had disappeared in Houston. With her long, fiery auburn hair and fine features, there could be no mistake.

"What's going on?" Kate whispered, coming up beside him.

"You remember the missing girl in Houston, Callie Spencer?"

"Of course."

"She's here. Looks like they've got her drugged up pretty good. She was having trouble walking."

"Oh, my God. Where did they take her?"

He checked the door again, saw the group disappear around a corner out of sight. "Let's find out."

Stepping into the passage, he waited for Kate and quietly closed the door. Kate took off her high heels and carried them as they made their way along the hall. When they reached the corner, Jase stopped and they flattened themselves against the wall.

He waited several seconds, then glanced around the corner, saw a door swing open to what appeared to be a library lined with shelves of books. Denny Reyburg lounged in an overstuffed chair, Callie Spencer standing right beside him. Another man was there, the man with the black, slicked-back hair who'd been talking to De Santos.

The older woman and the man who had brought the girl turned and started to leave the library, and Jase urged Kate back the way they had come. Disappearing behind the first door, they waited in another of the guest rooms as the man and woman retreated down the hall.

"That was close," Kate breathed.

"Too close," Jase agreed.

"What about Callie? We can't just leave her."

Jase pulled out his cell phone and hit the contact number he'd plugged in for FBI Special Agent in Charge Quinn Taggart.

The agent, sounding half asleep, finally answered the phone. "Taggart."

"Taggart, it's Jason Maddox. Kingsley gave me your number."

"Yeah, Mark said you'd managed to get yourself involved in FBI business. It's late. What's going on?"

"I'm with Kate Gallagher at the Blue Bayou. Callie Spencer, the girl who recently went missing in Houston, she's here—in De Santo's private apartment. She's in trouble."

Taggart took a moment to refresh his memory. "I remember the case. You sure it's her?"

"It's her."

"Kingsley brought me up to speed on De Santos's connection to Los Besos. I was hoping we wouldn't have to show our hand so soon, but I guess this leaves us no choice. I'll call in local resources. Stand down and we'll take it from here."

"I'll do my best," Jase said, and ended the call. But he wasn't letting that little girl disappear into the hands of Los Besos or Rafael De Santos or anyone else.

He heard movement in the hallway, cracked the door and saw Denny Reyburg coming out of the library, tugging Callie along in his wake. She was barely able to put one foot in front of the other. Both Reyburg's bodyguards were with him, one in front, one behind, guiding him and the girl toward an elevator at the far end of the hall.

"He's taking her downstairs," Kate said. "That elevator must open into the alley."

"He'll have a car waiting. They'll be gone before the FBI can get here."

Kate started forward, but Jase caught her arm. "Let me handle this, Kate, please."

"I can help. We don't have time to argue. Let's go."

Since she was right, he bit back a curse and both of them ran for the exit stairs next to the elevator.

Jase jerked open the door, which set off the alarm and

pissed him off. He hit the stairs at a run, Kate's heels flew out of her hand, and she pounded down the stairs right beside him. The alarm went silent when the door closed behind them, but the damage was done.

They didn't slow down until they reached the exit to the alley, where both of them slid to a halt. Jase cracked open the door to see a big white stretch limousine idling in front of a black Cadillac Escalade whose engine was also running. A chauffeur in a bill cap sat behind the wheel of the limo. The privacy partition was up, and all three-hundred-plus pounds of Denny Reyburg sprawled in the rear seat of the car.

The passenger door stood open. The bodyguard with the shaved head leaned in, trying to load the girl inside while the guy with the earrings waited a few feet away.

"Hurry up and get her in here," Reyburg demanded. "I have plans for her tonight."

"Callie!" Kate pushed past Jase and bolted into the alley. He swore as she launched herself at the bald-headed bodyguard. Jase grabbed the guy with the earrings, spun him around, slammed a fist into his face and drove another into his stomach.

The guy fell back a couple of steps and yanked a big semiauto out of the shoulder holster beneath his black jacket. Jase kicked the gun out of his hand and sent it flying, threw a series of left-right combos that knocked the guard staggering backward.

Trying to wrestle Callie free, Kate fought like a tiger, but the bodyguard knocked her down and Reyburg pulled the girl into the back of the limo. He managed to slam the door and the vehicle lurched forward. Gravel spun beneath the tires as the limo roared off down the alley.

Jase dodged a blow, linked his hands behind his opponent's neck and pulled his head down, jerked a knee up into his face. Bone crunched, the guy went down hard, and Jase ran for Kate.

She was on the ground, the bodyguard's gun pointed dead center in the middle of her forehead. Jase's insides did a slow, tight roll, and he charged, slamming into the bodyguard, taking both of them down, the pistol sliding a few feet out of reach.

The bodyguard ended up on top, got in a couple of solid punches. Jase looked up to see Kate pressing the guy's own pistol against the side of his head.

"Get off him!" she demanded, holding the gun in a two-handed grip.

"Take it easy, lady. I was just doing my job."

"Bullshit! She's only a little girl!"

Jase rolled to his feet and picked up the other guy's pistol, a Browning 9 mil. Taillights flashed as the limo pulled around a corner and disappeared out of sight.

"We gotta go!" He tucked the pistol into the waistband of his slacks, but Kate was already running for the black Escalade idling in the alley, jumping into the passenger seat and pulling on her seat belt.

Jase slid in behind the wheel and slammed his foot down hard on the accelerator. Tires spun and the Escalade leaped ahead in pursuit. He buckled his seat belt, pulled out his cell phone and tossed it to Kate as the SUV slid around a corner and picked up speed.

"Taggart's number's in my contacts. Fill him in and give him our location." He prayed the taillights he was following were the right ones and just kept driving, slowly gaining on the other vehicle.

Kate made the call and Jase heard sirens behind him, but he didn't let off the gas. If the limo got away, the girl could end up dead—or worse. A guy with Reyburg's money rarely went to jail.

"There!" Kate pointed at the entrance to an underground garage, and Jase saw the limo taillights disappear into its depths. Kate spoke to Taggart while Jase made the turn, slowing to follow the limo, which had stopped in the garage up ahead.

The SUV slid to a halt, and Jase and Kate both shot out of the car. They rushed to the limo, and Jase pulled open the rear passenger door.

The limousine was empty.

KATE FRANTICALLY SCANNED the garage, but there was no sign of Denny Reyburg or Callie Spencer.

Jase grabbed the limo driver by the back of the neck and hauled him out of the car. "Where are they?"

"I don't… I don't know."

Jase squeezed the driver's neck and shoved him down on his knees. "Where. Are. They?"

"She's just a little girl," Kate pleaded. "Tell us where he took her."

"I—I don't know, I swear. He's…he's got a place somewhere in the building, but I don't know where it is."

Jase squeezed the driver's neck until he started wheezing. "Try again."

"Okay…okay! Reyburg's got a place in the basement. He takes the girls down there. That's all I know."

Jase shoved the driver away, and he and Kate both ran for the elevator. Kate pushed the button for the lower floor, then spotted the stairs. "There!" She grabbed Jase's arm and they raced in that direction.

They came out in an area filled with equipment: pipes and furnaces, water lines, air-conditioning ducts, refrigeration units.

Kate looked at Jason. "Surely he wouldn't bring girls down here...would he?"

"If he does, he's got a lair, someplace he feels safe."

She nodded. "Then let's find it."

"Keep your gun handy," Jase said, and her fingers tightened on the big semiauto she had picked up in the alley.

Jase took off one way while Kate took off the other. Circling around, she made her way between rows of equipment, the noise made by the machines concealing the sound of her footsteps. Her bare feet were raw, the bottoms cut and bleeding. No time to worry about it now.

Fifteen minutes later, she was still searching.

"Nothing," Jase said when they came back together.

"We can't give up."

He nodded, and they took off again in two new directions. The basement of the high-rise was huge. If Reyburg had a place down there, it could be anywhere.

Kate began to move deeper into the center of the building. As she ducked behind an air duct, she spotted what looked like a big white storage tank with a door cut into one side, and remembered reading Denny's father had been in the underground storage tank business.

Reyburg was standing in front of it and so was Callie Spencer. The hard-faced man from the party stood behind the girl, a wooden club across Callie's throat, held in both hands, prepared to deliver a crushing blow—the way he had used the weapon to kill before.

Emanuel Vargas.

"The boss sent me here to solve your problem," Vargas said. "You need to leave—now. You can't be found with an underage girl. I'm going to take care of this for you."

"Get away from her," Denny demanded. "She's mine!"

"You want to go to prison, Mr. Reyburg? When things settle down, De Santos will get you another girl. Get out of here. Let me handle this."

Callie whimpered. Her eyes were huge, her face bone white.

"I don't want another girl," Denny argued. "I want this one. She's pure. I've never been the first before."

"You're a fool, Reyburg. Get out before it's too late."

Kate glanced around. No Jason. No police. She was Callie's only chance. Her heart felt close to exploding in her chest. It was now or never. She took a calming breath and stepped out from behind the air-conditioning duct, the gun gripped in both hands.

"It's already too late." She sighted down the barrel and fired, aiming the shot as close to Vargas as she dared without hitting Callie. The bat dropped out of his hands as he dove for cover, and the girl collapsed to the ground.

Reyburg started running, lumbering down the path he used to access his lair. Kate fired at Vargas again, determined to keep him away from the girl, knowing Jase would hear the shots and come running.

"You killed my sister," Kate said, firing off another round. "Now I'm going to kill you!" She ducked out of sight and kept shooting, pinning him behind a piece of heavy equipment. Vargas returned fire, blasting a stream of bullets that pinged off the steel machinery.

Glancing around, Kate spotted a chunk of concrete, picked it up and tossed it one way, then ran toward Vargas from the opposite direction.

The distraction worked. Vargas fired a series of shots toward where the concrete had landed. Combined with the noise made by all the equipment, Kate slipped right up next to him and pressed the gun against his head.

"Move and you're dead."

Vargas froze.

"Toss the gun. Do it slowly."

When Vargas hesitated, Kate pressed harder and he tossed the pistol away. Fury nearly blinded her. She wanted to pull the trigger so badly her hand shook. "You killed Chrissy. She never had a chance."

Jase stepped out of the shadows. "Don't do it, Kate. He isn't worth it." Jase's pistol pointed at Vargas. "The cops are on their way down. Let them have him."

"I want him dead."

"I know, honey. But that's not the way it works. Put the gun down and back away."

Over the din of machinery, the sounds of shouting and footsteps reached her. The police were in the basement.

"Put down the gun, honey."

Kate looked over at Jason. She wasn't a killer. Her hand trembled. Very slowly, she bent and set the pistol on the ground. The next instant Vargas moved and a second gun appeared in his hand. Gunfire echoed, and Kate screamed as a barrage of bullets slammed into his body, knocking him backward, sending him sliding across the concrete floor.

The cops rushed toward her, but Jason reached her first, pulling her hard against him, enfolding her in his arms.

"It's over, baby. It's over."

She buried her face in his chest. "Is he dead?"

"He's dead. The cops got Reyburg, and there's an ambulance on the way for Callie."

She glanced around in search of the girl, saw a policewoman leading her away.

"It's over," she said.

Jason didn't let go. "That's right, honey. We'll have to give the cops our statements. Then we can go home."

CHAPTER FORTY-TWO

DENNY REYBURG'S UNDERGROUND lair was a treasure trove of evidence for the Dallas police. Besides the king-size bed and lavish furnishings that provided all sorts of DNA, the converted storage tank held proof of Reyburg's pedophilia in the form of photos and souvenirs from his encounters.

He was charged with committing forced sexual assault with a minor, kidnapping, attempted murder and a mile-long list of other offenses. His bodyguards and his driver were arrested as accomplices.

Special Agent in Charge Quinn Taggart showed up at the crime scene, a big blond man with a buzz cut. Jase filled him in and gave him the names of the massage parlors Tabby had uncovered. A few feet away, an EMT cleaned and bandaged Kate's feet and gave her some paper slippers to wear till she got home.

Callie Spencer was taken to the hospital, where her mother was on her way from Houston to meet her.

"We'll be winding this up as quickly as possible," Agent Taggart said. "De Santos is being arrested as we speak. Kingsley's handling that. We've got enough on him for racketeering, human trafficking and half dozen other charges. By morning, those three massage parlors will have been raided and arrests made."

"What about Briton, Inc.?" Jase asked.

"Sorry, that's FBI business."

"Schram and Wiedel are both connected to all of this," Kate argued. "Surely you must have something."

"Like I said—"

"So I'm guessing you don't have enough to charge them," Jase said.

Taggart ignored him. "Go home and get some sleep. If we need you, I've got your number. Will I be able to find both of you there?"

Jase looked at Kate and pain sliced through his chest. As soon as Los Besos was dealt with, it would be time for them to go their separate ways. "For the time being," he said.

One of the FBI agents took their statements. When they were finished, they went through it all over again with a Dallas PD detective. Finally, they were allowed to leave. Since the rented Mercedes was still parked at the club, a police car drove them back to Reese's penthouse.

"I guess there's no way I can go into the Blue Bayou and pick up my Jimmy Choos," Kate grumbled as Jase carried her down the hall.

"Probably not." Unlocking the door, he carried her inside and settled her on the sofa.

"How much longer do you think before we can go back to our own places?"

"Let's see what happens tomorrow. If Kingsley's right and De Santos is top dog in Los Besos, with him in jail, we should be safe. With any luck, Mark'll call and bring us up to speed, or Taggart will. Worst case, we can read about it on the internet and Tabby can run some of it down for us."

"I hope Callie's going to be okay."

"Maybe you'll get the chance to talk to her, see for yourself."

Kate smiled. "I'd like that." She yawned. "I'm really tired, Jase."

"So am I, honey." Lifting her back into his arms, he carried her down the hall to the room they'd been sharing and settled her on the bed. "You were really something tonight." He leaned down and very softly kissed her. "You were amazing."

Kate slid her arms around his neck. "So were you, big guy. Why don't you take off your clothes and come to bed, and we'll show each other just how amazing we really were."

Jase laughed and started stripping off his clothes.

THE SUN WAS shining the next morning when the call came in from Mark Kingsley. According to the FBI agent, all three massage parlors in the Houston area were raided just before dawn. Dozens of arrests were made, guys ready to spill information.

Twenty-five members of Los Besos were rounded up, and the underage girls in the Garden of Eden were taken into protective custody.

"Wow, that's great news," Kate said as Jase relayed the call. "I feel like my sister is finally getting justice."

"It's a good feeling," Jase said.

While Kate was in the shower, his phone rang again, Detective Tony Castillo with more good news.

"I guess you heard about the raid," Castillo said.

"Sounds like it went down without a hitch," Jase said.

"I'm not crazy about the feds getting involved, but in this case they didn't have much choice. But that's not the reason I called."

"What's going on?"

"After the truck stop debacle, I went to my lieutenant, Adam Gray. He's a good guy and a good police officer. Lieutenant Gray doesn't like dirty cops. When I told him what went down, he got Internal Affairs involved. Two police officers and a lieutenant from one of the precincts on the southwest side have been charged with aiding and abetting, taking bribes—you name it. Gray runs a tight ship and with these guys off the force, he plans to make sure it stays that way."

"That's good news, Tony," Jase said. "I appreciate your help with this."

"Not as much as we appreciate yours and Kate's," Castillo said. "Gray said to tell you HPD owes you."

Jase smiled. "I'll remember that."

He had a lot to tell Kate, and she was as relieved to hear the news as he had been. The bad guys were in jail. They were safe. They could finally get their lives back.

They reassembled their cell phones and moved out of Reese's condo, back into their own homes—though Jase still spent almost every night at Kate's.

He had tried to convince himself to end things, but after everything that had happened, he was beginning to think maybe it could work out between them. Beginning to believe it would be all right if he stayed.

Kate wanted him there and he wanted to be there. What was wrong with that? He was happy in a way he had never been before. Coming home to a woman who cared about him filled him with a quiet joy, a feeling that all was right with the world.

Deep down, he knew he was being selfish. Kate deserved a helluva lot better than he could give her. She deserved a stable guy who wanted to settle down, give her kids and be a good dad.

But even as the thought occurred, he began to imagine that maybe he could be that guy. Maybe he could have a family of his own, something he had never dared consider.

He liked kids. Maybe it could work. The idea filled him with a fierce desire for the kind of life other people had. Why couldn't he and Kate have that life together?

He was in the kitchen helping her make dinner, smiling and laughing, trying to keep his hands to himself, when her cell phone rang.

"Darn, I left my phone in the living room." She reached for a towel to dry her hands.

"I'll get it." Jase started in that direction.

"It's on the table in front of the window," Kate called after him.

"No problem." He crossed the room and leaned down to grab it. Everything happened in an instant. Glass shattered as gunfire erupted and pain exploded in his chest.

"Jason!"

A gurgling sound came from his throat. Kate's voice was the last thing he heard as his knees buckled, and everything went black.

CHAPTER FORTY-THREE

SHE HAD BELIEVED they were safe. Dear God, they'd both believed it.

Kate sat in the waiting area outside the emergency room of Baylor University Medical Center. The halls were frantic with people, doctors, nurses and technicians. Gurneys rattled past, white soles squeaked on linoleum floors. All the noise and commotion moved past her in a blur.

An ache swelled in her throat. A sniper's bullet had smashed through her living room window. It was Jase's secret fear, she had finally figured out. Now he was clinging to life after a bullet had torn into his chest.

Fresh tears welled, spilled over and ran down her cheeks. She wiped them away with her fingers, but more tears surfaced. Who had done it?

Whoever it was had been lying in wait for hours, perhaps even days. A patient killer. It had to be Los Besos. Why had Jase been so sure they were no longer a threat?

She didn't know what to do. She just wanted Jason to live.

"Kate…?"

It took a moment for the familiar voice to register. She looked up to see Harper standing next to Chase, the golden-haired couple, two of Jason's closest friends.

Kate rose shakily to her feet.

She felt Harper's fingers link with hers. "He's going

to be all right," Harper said. "He has to be. The world needs men like Jason."

A sob escaped from her throat, and the next thing she knew Harper had pulled her into a hug. "He hated those windows," she cried. "We should have stayed at his house."

"It's not your fault," Chase said, drawing Kate's attention, giving her a chance to bring herself under control. "Whoever did it would have found a way to get to him sooner or later."

She sank back down in the chair, and Harper sat down beside her. "Who did it?" Kate asked. "Was it Los Besos?"

"The police are working on it," Chase said. "So is Bran. He's working the crime scene now. I talked to him a little while ago. He says the shots came from a vacant apartment in the building across the way."

Kate swallowed past the lump in her throat. "Jason's really bad, Chase. I rode in the ambulance with him. They didn't think he was going to make it to the hospital."

A muscle clenched in Chase's jaw. "Jason's a fighter. And he has you on his side. That gives him something to live for."

Her heart squeezed. She loved him so much. She hadn't said it out loud, had barely said it to herself. The thought of him dying tore everything loose inside her.

"Until they catch whoever shot him," Chase said, "one of us is going to be with you at all times. We aren't taking any chances."

She hadn't considered the danger to herself. Now she realized that whoever shot Jason might be coming after her. At the moment, it didn't seem to matter. "Thank you." She looked up to see the emergency room doctor walking toward her, a man with dark red hair, very fair skin and a freckled forehead.

"Mrs. Maddox?"

"I'm Kate Gallagher."

"Jason's fiancée," Chase added with a glance warning her to silence. Sometimes only family members could get information. She was grateful for his quick thinking, even if it gave her heart a pang.

"H-how is he?" Kate asked.

"We've got him stabilized. They're taking him into surgery now. The bullet went through his chest and exited his back. It missed his spine, but a fragment of metal lodged in the left ventricle of his heart. I won't lie to you, Kate, this is a very difficult surgery. It's going to take some time."

Her throat constricted. She couldn't manage to form a word so she just nodded.

"There's a waiting room on the surgical ward. Someone will bring word to you there."

"Thank you."

They took the elevator up to the waiting room outside surgery, and settled in for whatever time it might take. Over the course of the evening, Jax Ryker showed up, Jonah Wolfe, Mindy Stewart and Tabitha Love. They all hugged her and kept her company while they waited for news. Other people showed up and stayed for a while, all of them worried and praying for Jason's recovery.

He didn't have a biological family. Kate wondered if he knew how many friends he had who loved him.

She took a deep breath, realizing she needed her own friends there. She wasn't sure why she hadn't called Lani and Cece. Maybe because they were always there for her when something really bad happened. Maybe calling them made the possibility of losing Jason all the more real.

"I'll call Lani," Cece said to her when she phoned. "We'll be there as soon as we can."

When they arrived half an hour later, Kate stood to greet them, and both women hurried over to give her a hug.

"I'm sorry I didn't call you sooner," Kate said, wiping away fresh tears. "I should have... I can't seem to think."

Cece hugged her. "We're here now. You don't have to be sorry for anything."

Kate introduced her friends to the group in the waiting room. Another hour passed before the doctor pulled open the waiting room door.

He walked toward them, a small man in a set of baggy green scrubs wearing round, wire-rimmed glasses. At the grim look on his face, everyone stood up.

"I'm Dr. Crossman. Jason is out of surgery. He's in the ICU recovering. We expect him to be there at least several days."

"Is he...is he going to be all right?" Kate asked.

"I'm afraid it's a waiting game now. He's strong and healthy. He's in top physical condition. He's got a good chance. As time goes on, we'll know more."

Kate sank back down, her legs too shaky to hold her up. "Thank you, Doctor."

"If anything changes, I'll let you know."

She pushed herself back to her feet. "When can I see him?"

"Not for a while, I'm afraid. I'd suggest you go home and get some sleep. You can come back and check on him in the morning."

"I'm staying here," Kate said.

Dr. Crossman gave her a sympathetic glance but didn't try to dissuade her. He had probably dealt with determined family members before. Not that she was actually a relative.

Then Reese Garrett showed up, and it occurred to her that the Garrett brothers wielded a lot of power in Dallas, their charitable contributions well-known. Watching Reese speak to the doctors and nurses, it was obvious the hospital would do whatever the brothers wanted in order to please them.

Reese spoke to Chase, then sat down next to Kate and took hold of her hand. "He made it through surgery," he said. "Jason's tough, Kate. He'll get through this and come out all right."

Kate had no idea what would happen, but she wanted to believe it so she nodded. "Thank you for everything you did to help us."

He made a brief acknowledgment, but his jaw looked tight. "Do the police know who shot him?"

The door to the waiting room opened again, and Kate glanced up to see Bran Garrett striding toward them. "Not yet," Bran said. "I can't tell you who did it—not so far—but I know who didn't do it." Bran looked as tired as Kate felt. "It wasn't Los Besos."

"How do you know?"

"Because whoever did it, the guy was a soldier. Everything he left behind in that empty apartment screamed military sniper. I'm going to find him, Kate, and deal with him. You don't have to worry about that."

She didn't tell him to leave it to the police. She was beginning to think the way the men did, the way Jason did. Sometimes you had to find your own justice.

Bran didn't stay long. When he left to do more digging, the others followed, all but Lani and Cece.

Chase remained too, her protection until they found the shooter.

She trusted these men the way she trusted Jason. She prayed he would survive to return to the family who loved him.

CHAPTER FORTY-FOUR

PAIN SEEMED TO weigh him down. There was a thin layer of numbness, but the pain was there, burning deep in his chest. His eyelids felt too heavy to lift. He could hear the steady beeping of a heart monitor next to the bed. He could breathe, but there was a tube down his throat, making it hard to swallow.

He had no idea what had happened. Something pretty damn bad. Something that had left him close to death. He wasn't sure how long he had been this way, could be days, maybe a week.

Once a nurse had disturbed him enough he had managed to open his eyes for an instant before exhaustion sucked him back under. In those few moments, he had seen Kate sleeping in a chair next to his bed. He didn't think it was an illusion, and it filled him with relief.

He couldn't handle the thought that if he had been hurt this badly, Kate might have been injured, too. Or worse.

He slept again. It felt like an eternity and at the same time merely seconds. When his eyes slit open, the block in his throat was gone. Clear liquid dripped from a plastic tube into his arm and patches stuck to his chest, feeding the heart monitor beeping the endless hours away.

Kate was still there. Asleep once more in the chair beside him. He wondered how long she had been there, wondered how long she meant to stay.

The third time he opened his eyes, he managed to stay awake long enough to get a real look at her. She was thinner, paler, dark circles beneath her eyes.

"Jason..." She shot forward in her chair, reached out and gently took hold of his hand. He could feel hers trembling. "Thank God."

"Kate..."

She leaned over and kissed his cheek, then rushed out of the room shouting for the nurse. He must have faded again. When he came to, she was there waiting. Just as she'd been before.

She was exhausted and worried, yet hope shined in her eyes. Seeing her that way, knowing the long hours she had endured for his sake, everything she had sacrificed for him, cut him to the core.

She held a cup of water to his dry lips. "Just take it easy, okay?"

He took a sip of water, managed to swallow. "How long...have I...been here?"

"Five days." She gave him a wobbly smile. "You really had us worried."

"What...happened?"

Her brown eyes filled with tears. "Oh God, Jason, you were right about the windows. I'm so sorry. A sniper shot you. The police are looking for him. So is Bran."

"Los... Besos?"

"Bran doesn't think so. He and Jax are trying to find the guy who did it."

Now that he knew what had happened, fear for her filtered through the pain. "Who's protecting...you?"

"One of the guys from The Max has been with me every minute. They want to make sure I'm safe."

Relief slipped through him. "Good...guys."

"They love you." She started to say something more, but stopped herself. "We all do."

His eyelids began to droop. He needed to sleep, and since he trusted his friends to keep Kate safe, he let himself drift away.

The next time he awoke, it was dark outside the windows. Then it was morning. Eventually, he began to feel better. Stronger. Each day Kate was there, and as he progressed, his mind began to clear. He began to accept the truth he had known for some time.

He was in love with Kate Gallagher. Deeply in love. Kate was everything he had ever wanted in a woman. Everything he needed.

Everything a guy like him could not have.

He would never forget the pain in her face as she sat next to his bed for hours on end, the worry, the agonizing fear. No woman should have to go through that. Certainly not the woman he loved.

He'd get better, he vowed. No matter what it took. He'd get out of the hospital and go after whoever had shot him. But he wouldn't put Kate through that. He was in love with her, the kind of love that wouldn't happen to him again.

Because he loved her so deeply, he wanted what was best for her. And the best thing for Kate was for him to give her up.

IT HADN'T TAKEN Bran long to figure out Los Besos wasn't behind the shooting that had nearly ended his friend's life. Not after he'd discovered the sniper's lair in the empty apartment in the building across from Kate's.

It was easy enough to piece together what had happened if you knew what to look for. The lock on the door had been jimmied to gain entrance and a pane broken out of the living room window. The trajectory of the bullet fit the location, and empty food wrappers scattered around the apartment said the guy had been lying in wait for days.

Once Bran had talked to Ryker, things began to move even more quickly.

"After you figured out the guy was ex-military," Jax had told him as they sat at Bran's desk at The Max, "I got to thinking about the skip Jase and I went after down in Waco a few weeks back. We were there to bring in a killer named Randall Harding, but there were two other men with him that night, a hard case named Folsom and a guy by the name of Yancy Pike. Folsom made the mistake of running into one of my bullets. Jase put a bullet in Pike's shoulder, but the wound wasn't fatal."

"I've got a bad feeling I know where this is headed."

"Pike was ex-army, Bran. A sniper. He was arrested in Waco, but I figured it was worth a phone call to make sure he was still in jail. Sure enough, ten days ago, Yancy Pike was released on bail."

"*Son of a bitch.* We need to find him."

Jax smiled. "I got a call yesterday from one of Maddox's snitches, kid named Tommy Dieter. He heard about the shooting, said he owed Hawk for helping him out of a jam. Said he'd been snooping around asking questions."

"He know where Pike is?"

"Guy's staying in a scumbag apartment out off Webb Chapel Extension. Dieter says he's doped up and laying low."

Bran clenched his jaw. "There's no place low enough for that bastard to hide. You get an apartment number?"

"I got it. Let's go."

Bran pulled open the bottom drawer of his desk and

took out his Glock. They left the office in his black Jeep Wrangler and drove out Lemmon Avenue to the apartment building where Pike was staying.

When they reached the front of the unit, Bran pulled his weapon and so did Jax. They took up spots on each side of the door, and Bran banged hard on the paint-chipped wood.

"You got one chance to come out of this alive, Pike. Give yourself up!"

"Fuck you!" Pike punctuated his curse by a blaze of gunfire that blasted through the front door. Bran returned fire, stepped back and kicked the door open. He spun aside as Pike fired again, then sent a deadly double tap into Pike's chest.

Yancy Pike went down in a pool of blood, exactly the death he deserved.

Bran holstered his weapon.

"Nice work," Jax said.

Bran just nodded, his adrenaline still pumping. He sighed as he waited for the police to arrive. He and Ryker would be facing a barrage of questions. But there was no doubt he had fired in self-defense, and it was worth it to see justice done.

His first phone call went to Kate.

JASE WAS OUT of the hospital and back in his apartment. He had phoned Chase the morning of his release and asked him for a ride back to his town house.

"I'm surprised Kate didn't insist on taking you home and babying you till you're feeling better," Chase said as he drove away from the hospital.

"Yeah, well, I don't need babying. I never did." He sliced Chase a sideways glance. "What I had with Kate was great—while it lasted—but now it's over and done."

Chase frowned. "Kate know that?"

His chest hurt just thinking about it. "I'll talk to her, make her understand. I'm not the kind of guy to settle down. You know it and so does Kate."

Chase made no comment.

He helped Jason into the town house and got him settled on the sofa in the living room. "One of us will come by every day to check on you, bring you something to eat."

"There's plenty of food in the kitchen. I always keep the place stocked. I just need to rest a little and I'll be fine."

"I'm sure you will. Be smart and don't push yourself too hard." Chase headed for the door. "See you in the morning."

He was sleeping when Kate phoned later that afternoon. Just hearing her voice made his heart hurt.

"I didn't think they were letting you out until tomorrow," Kate said, sounding hurt. "I can't believe you didn't call me."

"Reese pulled some strings. He's good at that kind of thing."

"Are you hungry? I'll pick something up and bring it over."

"I'm okay. Listen, Kate. I didn't plan to do this on the phone, but maybe it's better this way."

"Better? What's better? What are you talking about?"

"The bad guys are in jail. Your sister's killer is dead. We both knew from the start this was a temporary thing. It's time you got on with your life and I got on with mine."

Silence fell on the other end of the line. "Why don't we talk about this when you're feeling better?"

But it would only make things harder. "There's no use putting it off. What we had was great, but it's done."

She took a deep breath and slowly released it, the soft sound whispering over the phone. "If that's the way you want it, then I guess that's it."

His chest clamped down. Giving Kate up was the last thing he wanted. He wished he could tell her the truth, but it wouldn't be fair to either one of them. "That's the way it's got to be."

"I'm glad you're okay, Jason. Even if things didn't work out between us, you were a great friend. Thank you for everything you did."

His eyes burned. He rubbed the sting away with the heel of his hand. "If you ever need anything just call me, okay? Just call and I'll be there."

"Goodbye, Jason."

"Bye, Kate." The line went dead. He didn't expect to feel the same empty deadness inside.

You did the right thing, he told himself.

But he hadn't known it was going to hurt so much. Hell, how could he? He had never been in love.

THREE DAYS PASSED. Kate buried herself in her work, but it didn't really help. She felt sick with grief, as if someone she loved had died, felt as if some part of herself had been cut away. She hadn't realized how much she had come to count on Jason, how much he had become a part of her life, her happiness.

That he had ended things shouldn't have surprised her. From the start, she had known he would leave. Accepting that didn't make her feel any better. Every night when she got home, she found herself searching for him, waiting for his phone call, then crying herself to sleep.

The fourth day, she began to pull herself together.

During the agonizing hours she'd sat next to Jason's hospital bed, she had made some life-altering decisions. After Andrew, she had realized she wasn't the person she had believed herself to be.

Jason had shown her the person she was inside, the person she was meant to be. That person needed challenge and adventure in her life, something more than examining books and ledgers and filing reports.

The first thing she did was apply for her private investigator's license. There were courses she needed to complete. After some research on which weapon to purchase, she chose a Glock 19. There was a background check before the purchase could be completed, then she took the pistol out to the shooting range to improve her skills, and applied for a concealed carry permit.

She never heard from Jason. Not once. But her course was set. It was time to talk to Robin Murdock, put her plan in motion. Robin had often expressed a desire to own her own consulting firm. Kate had a business proposition for her.

They set a time to meet at the office, went into the conference room and sat down across from each other at the rectangular walnut table. Robin was two years older, attractive, single, a high achiever and very good at her job.

"So what's this about, Kate?" Robin took a drink from her can of Diet Coke out of the vending machine down the hall.

"I want to expand the business, Robin. To do that I need your help."

"Are you're thinking of hiring more employees? We'll need to bring in someone for business development if you do."

"I'm going to need marketing help, but not to grow

the consulting business. I want to take the company in a new direction. I want to expand into small-business and corporate security. Embezzling, stealing corporate secrets, identity theft, forgery, that kind of thing."

Robin sat back in her chair. "Wow, I had no idea you were interested in something like that. It sounds intriguing, but I don't see how I fit in."

"You'd be in charge of the consulting side of the business, the work we do now. I'd specialize in the security aspect. I've applied for my private investigator's license. After the work Jason and I did to find my sister's killer, I knew what I wanted to do."

"Isn't that sort of work dangerous, Kate?"

"It can be. But if I keep learning, keep developing my skills, I think I can be really good at it. It's challenging and interesting, and I think we can make money at it. But it's more than a job to me, Robin. It's something I really want to do. What do you say? Are you willing to try it?"

Robin grinned. "I've been itching to take on more responsibility. To tell you the truth, I don't see where I have much to lose. You're the person taking all the risk."

Kate smiled. "I guess I am." She thought about Jason and the risk she had taken in loving him. It hadn't worked out, and the pain of losing him still made her ache inside, but she treasured every day she had spent with him. If she had it all to do over, she would do it again.

"That's something I discovered about myself," she said. "I'm willing to take a risk."

She wished Jason had been.

In a strange way, she felt sorry for him.

JASE SAT AT his desk at The Max. The investigation business was brisk, Ryker on a murder case, Wolfe working undercover for some big corporation, Bran working a personal security detail for some Hollywood movie star.

Everyone was busy but him. He hadn't been able to motivate himself since he'd ended his relationship with Kate. Instead of looking ahead, setting new goals, getting things done, all he thought about was Kate.

Had he actually believed he'd be over her by now? He had foolishly believed time and distance would numb his feelings for her. Instead, he missed her more every day.

He looked up as Harper and Chase walked through the front door, laughing and holding hands, felt a pang at how happy they looked. He knew Harper had been in contact with Kate. They were working on the black-tie charity benefit that would donate a portion of its proceedings to New Hope Rehab.

It was all Jase could do not to ask about her, find out what Kate was doing. Make sure she was okay. Did she miss him? Or was she already over him and seeing someone else?

The thought made his stomach burn. In the end, he stayed at his desk. If he asked about Kate, it would only make him feel worse. He reminded himself he was doing the right thing.

By now, Kate would probably agree.

CHAPTER FORTY-FIVE

"GALLAGHER AND COMPANY CONSULTING." At the front desk, Laura Delgado adjusted the phone earbud in her ear. "Please hold while I see if Ms. Murdock is available." She pressed the intercom button. "Robin, you've got a call from Victor Markum, VP of Briton, Inc. Are you available to take the call?"

Kate sat next to Robin in her office, where they were working on their expansion plans.

"It's Victor Markum," Robin said to her excitedly. "It's such a big firm I didn't really think he'd call."

Kate gripped Robin's arm. "We need to talk. It's important. You have to call him back."

"Are you sure, Kate? This could make us a lot of money."

"She'll have to call him back, Laura," Kate said through the intercom. She turned to Robin. "I'm going to tell you something but it can't leave this office."

"Of course."

"The FBI is investigating Briton, Inc. The company has big-time criminal connections. So far the Bureau hasn't been able to get the evidence they need. This might be a way we can help."

"You aren't serious."

"Think about it, Robin. Why would a corporation of that size choose a company as small as we are? Because we have a first-rate reputation, and they think they can control what we write in our report."

Robin sat back dejectedly. "I was afraid it was too good to be true."

"I'll call Markum back. If it looks like this could be a way to get inside information, I'll call the FBI." When Robin nodded, Kate hurried into her office and closed the door. She returned Markum's phone call and prayed he hadn't already contacted another company.

Victor took the call.

"Mr. Markum, this is Kathryn Gallagher at Gallagher and Company Consulting. I'm returning your earlier phone call. What can we do for you?"

"I spoke to Ms. Murdock at an earlier date about our intention to take Briton public. We'd like someone to take a professional look at the business, make management recommendations, that kind of thing. It would just be our main office there in Dallas, of course. But we'd like you to give us a written report, something we can use as we move forward."

"We can do that. I can oversee the project myself."

"We'd need it done as quickly as possible. A week would be good, ten days at most."

"I'll have to make some adjustments to my schedule, but I think I can make that work."

"Great. When can we meet?"

"How about this afternoon?"

"All right, say two o'clock in my office?"

"I'll be there." Her hand trembled as she ended the call and made the next one. She still had the private number Special Agent in Charge Quinn Taggart had given her the night of Denny Reyburg's arrest. She punched it into the phone and waited impatiently for him to pick up. "Come on...come on."

"Taggart."

"Agent Taggart, this is Kate Gallagher."

"Kate. This is a surprise. I hope everything's all right?"

"Everything's fine. I'm calling because I may be able to help you get the information you're looking for on Briton, Inc."

"That's FBI business, Kate. I told you that before."

"Yes, you did. Are you any closer to bringing charges against them than you were then?"

Silence fell. "All right, I'm listening."

"As you probably know, Schram and Wiedel are getting ready take the company public. Victor Markum just phoned my office. He wants to hire Gallagher and Company for a management consulting job. He wants us to write a report they can use in their prospectus. That gives us an in. It means I might be able to find information that will help you."

"You're getting yourself involved in what could be a dangerous situation, Kate."

She thought of her sister and Emanuel Vargas, of Los Besos, and the sniper who'd shot Jason. She'd learned a lot about danger. "I'm well aware of the risks."

"We need to talk, Kate."

"Is that a yes?"

"The FBI can't have any official involvement."

"So it is a yes."

"It's an unofficial maybe."

"I'm meeting Markum today at two."

A sigh whispered over the phone. "I'm checking the location of your office on Google Maps as we speak. Looks like there's a Starbucks just down the block. I can be there in twenty minutes."

"I'll see you there." Kate hung up the phone. She

had lost Jason, but she was a survivor. She had a different life ahead of her now.

ANOTHER WEEK SLID PAST. Jase had just taken a contract with A-1 Bail Bonds to locate a skip named Porter Emerson. The guy had dodged a hit-and-run charge. He was no hardened criminal, so it should be an easy retrieval—which was the reason he'd taken the job. He was still only 90 percent. Mostly he just needed something to do.

It was after four, getting close to the end of the day, at least for some of them. He was in his office tracking down leads on his laptop when Harper walked in. Chase was still there, but instead of heading for her husband's office, she spotted Jason and started walking toward him.

He stood up to greet her. "Hey, Harper, what's up?"

"I know Chase isn't going to like me sticking my nose into your business, but I think this is something you should know."

His chest tightened. "Is it Kate?" Harper sat down in the chair beside his desk, and Jase sat back down beside her.

"I have a hunch you've been dying to ask me about her. Maybe I'm crazy, but I think you're in love with her."

Jase glanced away.

"What, no denial?"

"It doesn't matter."

"I think it does. So I'm going to tell you what's going on."

Worry trickled through him. "Is she all right? Tell me."

"Kate has decided to become a private investigator."

He stiffened. "No way."

"She's taking PI classes. She bought a pistol, applied for a concealed carry permit. She's expanding her company to include business security investigation, which she will personally handle."

He just shook his head. "I've got to talk to her, make her understand."

"There's more."

His head came up. "More? What do you mean there's more? What else could there possibly be?"

"Kate's working undercover for the FBI. Special Agent in Charge Quinn Taggart."

Jase shot up from his chair. "Son of a bitch! I've got to find her. Get her to see reason. She'll be heading home soon. Unless…is she…ah…seeing someone?"

"No, Jason. I think after you, she decided she'd had enough of men for a while."

He closed down his laptop and yanked it off the desk. "I've got to go. Thanks, Harper. I really appreciate it."

Harper just sighed. Jase took off for the parking lot. He still had a key to Kate's apartment. He'd meant to give it back. Now he was glad he hadn't. If he was already inside waiting for her, she'd at least have to hear him out.

Knowing how stubborn she could be, it wasn't going to be an easy conversation.

So why the hell was he so damned eager to get there?

IT HAD BEEN a long but fruitful day. The main office of Briton Incorporated Real Estate Group was located in a six-story, historical brick building in the 900 block of Jackson Street.

Kate had been given carte blanche to move freely inside the building, even given after-hours access. Amazingly, it had never crossed anyone's mind that she might be there for anything other than to review their existing systems, give management advice on how to improve efficiency, and increase corporate profits. *Her job.*

The VPs believed she would write a report suggesting a few simple changes, which they would implement. She would write the report, and Briton would have a solid sales tool to use in their public offering prospectus.

Instead, Kate was going to find a way to nail the bastards. It couldn't be more perfect.

She was tired as she rode the elevator up to her apartment. The broken window had been repaired, but the place no longer held any appeal. Memories of the time she'd spent with Jason seemed to linger in every room, along with the sharp memory of the shooting and how close he had come to dying.

In what little spare time she had, she'd been looking for a new place to live. Anything to get rid of the aching loss she still felt whenever she thought of him.

She turned her key in the lock and walked into the living room, gasped and dropped her purse when she spotted the large figure on her sofa.

Everything inside her melted into a puddle of yearning when Jason rose and started walking her. God, he looked so dear and she had missed him so much. Kate steeled herself against the pain that welled in her heart, straightened her spine and lifted her chin.

"Jason. What are you doing here?"

I T WAS EXACTLY the greeting he had expected, and yet it made his heart ache. He held up her apartment key. "I brought your key back."

Kate walked over and snatched it out of his hand. "You could have mailed it."

"I wanted to talk to you."

She didn't budge. "What about?"

"About your new career."

Her lips thinned. "I can't believe Harper told you."

"You don't think it's any of my business?"

"No."

He took a step closer, then wished he hadn't when he inhaled her soft perfume. "I spent weeks protecting you, trying to keep you safe. Now you're out there putting your life in danger."

"What do you care, Jason? You didn't want me. You wanted your own life, and I wasn't part of it."

His chest clamped down. "You think I didn't want you? That's what you think?"

"Of course that's what I think. We aren't together. That's the choice you made."

His eyes found hers, and he saw the pain hiding just beneath the surface. He'd told himself he had done the right thing, that it was the best thing for Kate. Now he wondered… What if he had been wrong?

"You don't understand," he said. "I saw the way your sister's death affected you. I saw the way you looked when you sat next to me in that hospital room, the pain in your face, the worry and fear. I didn't want to risk making you suffer that way again."

"I see. By ending things, you were just looking out for me."

"Dammit, Kate! Can't you see? I was trying to protect you!"

Kate looked up at him. "Protect me? From what, Jason? Life? Well, I don't want to be protected from life. I could have had that with Andrew. I want to live my life—every single minute of it. And that's what I'm going to do."

The words hit him like a blow. She was going to go ahead without him. And he wouldn't even be there to protect her. "I wanted you, Kate. I've never wanted anything more than I wanted you." He couldn't hold back the words. "I still do."

Tears sprang into her eyes. "Is that the truth, Jason? You really thought you were protecting me?"

"I'd never hurt you, Kate. I'd do anything to keep that from happening. What if something happened to me? I could have died that night. The kind of work I do, there would never be any guarantees."

The tears in her eyes rolled down her cheeks. "Haven't you figured it out yet, Jason? I love you. I would rather be with you for a few years, a few months, even a few days than never be with you again."

Something tore open inside him, something deep and fierce. He pulled her into his arms, drawing her so close he could feel the beating of her heart. "I want you, honey. So damn much. Being without you is killing me. I love you, Kate Gallagher. I've never said those words to another woman. I've never felt the things I feel for you. I'd do anything for you, baby. Anything. Even give you up."

Her arms went around his neck and a sob caught in her throat. "You don't have to give me up, Jason. Not ever."

His throat swelled and he held her even tighter. She loved him. And God knew he loved her. "This is your last chance. If you stay with me now, I'll never let you go."

Kate tipped her head back and smiled up at him through her tears. "I'm yours forever if that's what you want."

Relief made his whole body lighter, as if the awful burden he had been carrying had been lifted off his shoulders. "I love you, Kate. I feel like my heart can start beating again."

And as the words spilled out, Jase realized it was the truth.

CHAPTER FORTY-SIX

KATE YAWNED AS she padded into the kitchen the following morning. They had spent the night together, and it had been perfect. She was crazy in love with Jason, and now she knew he loved her, too. Deep down she had always believed that, but she had never imagined he would actually do something about it.

There were still obstacles ahead of them. First she had to convince him that working with the FBI was the right thing for her to do. She wasn't backing down, but she believed this time they would find a way to work things out.

"Smells great," she said, inhaling the delicious aroma of bacon and eggs. Pouring a mug of coffee, she carried it over and sat down at the table.

"I figured it was my turn." Jase turned off the stove and started dishing up the food.

Kate sipped her coffee. "A guy as hot as you who also knows how to cook? I am one lucky woman."

He chuckled as he set the plates on the table, leaned down and kissed her. "I'm the one who's lucky." He took a seat beside her.

"Okay, do we eat first and fight later, or fight while we eat?"

He laughed. "How about I just agree with you now and we enjoy the meal."

She picked up her fork. "You mean it?"

"You're worried about your career. Now that I've had time to think about it, I realize you're right. Just because we're together shouldn't mean you have to change what you want to do with your life."

She leaned over and kissed him. "Hawk Maddox, you're even smarter than I thought."

He smiled. "In fact, I was thinking, maybe, under the right circumstances, there might be times we could work together. We made a good team before. No reason we couldn't do it again."

Kate slathered grape jelly on her toast. "Actually, I was thinking the same thing."

Jase set his knife on the edge of the plate. "So tell me about Briton and what you're doing for the FBI."

Kate laughed. "I knew you had an ulterior motive for cooking me breakfast."

Jase chuckled but didn't deny it. The man would definitely be a handful. Still, she liked that he challenged her. She also liked that he would be supportive, plus he was good at his job and she could use the help.

For the next half hour, she filled him in on the consulting job she had taken, a job that allowed her to move freely though the offices of the Briton Real Estate Group.

The company handled buyers, sellers, landlords, did asset management and mortgages. They were the principal investors in their own projects, including new home construction and apartment complexes. One of their divisions acquired distressed real estate, things like strip malls and shopping centers.

Realistically, the job was far too big for one person. To do it right, she needed to bring in an entire consulting team. But Markum just wanted a superficial study and a glowing report on how well the company was being operated.

A one-man job suited Kate just fine, since her goals were the exact the opposite of his.

"So what have you got so far?" Jase asked.

She took a sip of coffee. "I can't say for sure, but what I think I'm looking at is a giant money laundering scheme. For example, their apartment rental records show a ninety-nine percent occupancy rate for a dozen big complexes. Hundreds of apartments, all the money accounted for, deposited in various banks. But when I drove by the units, I could see they were less than half full. They're run-down and in undesirable locations. My guess is they're banking drug money and paying the taxes on it."

"Whitewashing dirty money," Jase said.

"Exactly. I bet they're using all sorts of businesses—strip malls, shopping centers, motels. There has to be at least a second set of books, maybe more. If I can get my hands on those records—"

His big hand slammed down on the table. "No *f*-ing way!"

"Jason!"

"Dammit, Kate, think this through. We know these guys were involved with Los Besos. According to the FBI, Schram and Wiedel are into drugs and organized crime. That means fraud, racketeering, and God knows what else. If they even get a whiff you're trying to bring them down, they'll end you."

"I can do it without getting caught."

"Oh, yeah? How?"

"I've been watching their routine. That's what I get paid to do. Watch their systems at work and suggest improvements. While I was looking over their management operations, I noticed they've got two CPAs working separately in the accounting department. I have computer access to one set of bookkeeping records, but not the other." She grinned. "But I know which computer they're using to store that other set of records."

"Yeah, how do you plan to get them?"

"My preliminary report's due a week from Monday. I wait till Friday, stay a little late that night so not many people are around. I go into the accounting department and get into the second computer, download the files and I'm out of there."

Jason's sigh whispered out. "That sounds good when you say it fast, but unless you're a computer expert, odds are you won't get past the password."

She sagged back in her chair. "I know. I'm still working on that. I'm no computer whiz. If I'm going to do this full-time, I'm going to need to find someone. In this case, I'm thinking maybe someone in the FBI might be willing to recommend someone who'll help."

"The FBI can't do jack without a warrant. I know someone who can help. She can do a remote connection and get everything you need."

Her eyes flashed to his. "Tabby."

Jason just smiled.

HE HATED IT. Hated that Kate was putting herself in danger. But now he understood. Should have figured it out in the first place. Kate was who she was—the woman he had fallen for at the Sagebrush Saloon. She craved challenge and adventure, same as he did. And she wanted to make a difference. Her thirst for life was one of the things he loved about her.

It was Saturday. They met with Tabby at her house later that morning.

"You're going to have to do some legwork," Tabby said as she finished a Monster energy drink. "It'll be after hours. The computer will probably be turned off, so you'll need to turn it on. If you wear an earbud, I can help you get in and get us hooked up."

"That'd be great, Tabby."

"It'll take too long to remotely download everything that's on the hard drive, so you'll have to look at the files, pick what you want. We'll work together, get it done as fast as we can, then you can shut the computer back down and get out of there."

"Okay, that sounds good," Kate said.

Jase wasn't so sure. One thing he'd learned—nothing ever went the way you planned.

"If it works, it'll be great for the feds," he said. "Not so great for you. Unless you want to end up testifying—which would make you a walking target—you need to cut some kind of deal before you turn over the evidence. The FBI gets the files, but you're out of it."

She looked at him with so much admiration he felt a fresh tug of love for her. Kate was the best thing that had ever happened to him. He'd been a fool to ever let her go.

THE WEEK SLID PAST. Kate continued working at Briton. After hours, they continued to smooth out their plans. The inner office door was kept locked after closing, Kate had discovered, so Jase bought her a set of lock picks. He gave her lessons on how to use them, then badgered her relentlessly until she was good enough to satisfy his demanding standards.

Victor Markum had been helpful all week, making introductions, giving her whatever information she asked for—within reason. He was an attractive man in his fifties with a toned, athletic build. Smooth, she would call him.

Unfortunately, he was a little too attentive. She had a feeling he was going to expect something from her in repayment for getting her the job. So far she had been able to dodge his attentions without offending him.

She had also met Arthur Wiedel, slightly older than Victor, black hair and harsh features. "Aggressive, hard-edged and unforgiving," his employees said behind his back. Wiedel ran the company with an iron hand. Kate had no trouble believing he could be involved in criminal activities, even murder.

His partner, Maximillian Schram, a man in his early seventies, was the top money man. He had started the business and run it for years before turning it over to Wiedel, who had brought in Victor Markum.

She was learning a lot about the company, enough to write a credible report. By Thursday, everything was set. The only fly in the ointment came when Jason insisted on being inside the building while she completed the job.

"How are you going to get in?" she asked, not happy he didn't trust her to do it alone.

"Walk in. It's a real estate company. There's a residential sales office on the bottom floor, a commercial division on the second floor. Lots of people in and out."

"You went into the building to check it out?"

He shook his head. "Tabby emailed me a set of plans. I've already found a place I can stay out of sight while I wait for you. You can text me when you're finished. You don't text, I'll know you're in trouble."

"I don't like it. You're not exactly the kind of guy who blends into the wallpaper. People will notice you."

"Doesn't matter. No way I'm letting you go in there

without backup. If things go sideways, you're going to need some help. You worked with me as a PI. You know how important that is."

She thought of Bran and Reese, Jax Ryker and Detective Castillo, people who had helped them. "I'm sorry. You're right."

He leaned over and kissed her. The pact was sealed. They'd bring it home together.

Friday night arrived. Jase dressed in a navy three-piece, pin-striped suit with a red power tie, a successful real estate broker there to make a deal. He drove the Yukon and parked in the lot across the street at fifteen minutes before closing.

Realtors were in and out of the sales offices at all hours, though on Friday people tended to take off early for the weekend, the reason Kate had chosen that time.

Jase passed a few people leaving as he walked into the lobby, took the stairs instead of the elevator up to the third floor without encountering anyone else. He managed to use up enough time that the offices were officially closed by the time he reached his destination. A few people were still working, but they were concentrating on their tasks, eager to finish and leave.

At the end of the hall, he checked the glass window in the mail room door, found the room empty, went into the package room at the back and settled in to wait.

As he checked his watch for the hundredth time, he thought of Kate and said a sinner's prayer that she would be all right.

CHAPTER FORTY-SEVEN

KATE HAD BEEN working in the building all afternoon, moving from one location to another, as the employees were used to her doing. Just before closing, she carried her laptop into the accounting department and opened it on one of the empty desks. A few minutes after five, the last employee in the department walked out the door, leaving her alone.

Kate headed for Solomon Daniels's office, the CPA she believed kept the second set of books. The door was locked, but the lock was nothing out of the ordinary, just there for privacy.

Pulling on a pair of latex gloves, she made short work of the mechanism, her hours of practice paying off. She opened the door, slipped inside, sat down at the computer and stuck in her earbuds. As soon as the computer booted up, she checked in with Tabby.

"It's asking for the password," Kate said. Inside her gloves her palms were sweating.

"I'm going to give you a code. Type it in, then sit back and wait."

Kate typed in the code and the computer went to work. "I'm in." Blocking thoughts of the penalty for hacking, she focused on Tabby's instructions.

"Go to menu, then to the folder you want to access."

Kate clicked the menu tab and a list of folders popped up.

"Click on the one you want."

She recognized the company names Atrias and Winman, clicked the first one up.

"Highlight the files you want," Tabby said. "Pick the ones that seem most important. The more time it takes, the more likely you are to get caught."

A chill slipped through her. Kate took a steadying breath and studied the list. With no idea what to choose, she picked files that connected to something she and Jason had learned during their investigation. Half a dozen with the word *Houston* in the title, two files that referenced *Forrester Trucking*. Three with *Blue Bayou*. The files started downloading.

In the Winman folder, she found a list of residential apartment buildings in Dallas and Houston, motels in both locations, and also two big shopping malls. The computer was running hard.

She was almost done when she heard someone in the outer office. Her heart lurched in fear, and adrenaline shot into her blood. The computer kept running. Only one of the files she had chosen remained. She ducked behind the desk, and prayed whoever was outside wouldn't come into the office.

Instead, a key slid into the lock, the door swung open. It was Solomon Daniels's assistant, Tobias Reeves, a young man with high ambitions. One of the commercial real estate salesmen from the second floor was with him, Dapper Don she had jokingly called the slender blond man whose last name she couldn't recall.

"Looks like Mr. Daniels forgot to turn off his computer," the salesman said.

"I'll turn it off for him." Tobias started forward and Kate held her breath. The machine had stopped running, but the screen was still lit. As Toby rounded the desk on one end, Kate quietly slid around the desk on the opposite end, keeping low and out of sight.

"Maybe he left it on for a reason," the Realtor said. "I do that sometimes."

The assistant paused. "You might be right. I'd better leave it alone." Turning, he walked back around the way he had come, grabbed the file he needed, and the men left the office.

Kate's heart was still racing, pounding in her chest, when her earbud crackled to life. "Got it, Kate," Tabby said. "Time to go home."

Relief poured through her. "Thanks, Tabby." Shutting down the computer, she pulled off her gloves and stuffed them and the earbuds into her pocket, walked out and closed the door. Shutting down her laptop, she grabbed the handle and hurried across the room.

Her heart was still beating a thousand miles an hour with the remnants of fear and exhilaration. She was smiling as she texted Jason, opened the door and stepped out into the hall. Her smile slid away when she came face-to-face with Victor Markum and Arthur Wiedel.

JASE GOT THE TEXT, but he couldn't breathe easy till he met up with Kate on the bottom floor. It wasn't part of the plan. She was supposed to leave the building and head directly for her car. He was supposed to leave separately and meet her in the parking lot.

But the back of his neck was tingling, a sure sign that something was wrong. He wasn't a guy to leave loose ends, and if he left the office and Kate didn't show up outside, he might not be able to get back in—or at least not in time.

He was standing in the lobby, watching the elevator

descend, the weight of his Kimber comforting where it rode in its holster beneath his pin-striped coat.

The doors dinged open and Kate walked out, but she wasn't alone. Jase recognized the men from their photos—one polished and sophisticated, the other rough-and-tumble, like a dockworker in a borrowed suit. Victor Markum and Arthur Wiedel.

"This way, Ms. Gallagher."

Jase pasted on a smile as he strode toward her. "Kate! There you are. What happened? You're late. We've got to hurry. Turtle Creek won't hold our dinner reservations." He took her arm and started leading her away.

"Just a minute!" Markum caught up with them. "I'm afraid Ms. Gallagher is going to have to cancel. She has some work to do before she can leave for the weekend."

Jasc looked at Kate, saw that her face was pale. "That doesn't seem fair. How about if Kathryn makes up for it by coming in early on Monday?"

Kate turned to the men. "It's a special evening. I'll have your report on Monday, just as I promised. I hope you don't mind."

Markum looked disappointed. He smoothed back the sides of his sandy brown hair, clearly hoping for a little more from Kate than just a report.

"All right, fine," he said. "I'll see you Monday, Kathryn." Markum and Wiedel left the building together. Jase gave them time to reach their cars and drive away, then he and Kate walked out to the parking lot.

"Thank God," she said as he opened her Camaro door. "I thought I was going to faint when I walked out of the office and they were standing in the hall."

"I had a feeling something wasn't quite right."

"Victor insisted Arthur and I come up to his penthouse apartment and go over some recent information. It was a ruse. Wiedel would have left me alone with him."

Jase lifted an eyebrow. "You sure you don't want to rethink this private investigator business?"

Kate just grinned. "Not a chance. I'll just have to make sure I've always got good backup."

Jase chuckled, leaned over and kissed her.

THE FOLLOWING DAY, Jase picked up the flash drive Tabby had remotely downloaded. Back at Kate's apartment, they reviewed the files together and both of them felt sure they were exactly what the FBI was looking for.

A deal was struck and a meeting set. The flash drive with the evidence against Briton was handed over to Special Agent in Charge Quinn Taggart at a small café not far from The Max. In return, Jase and Kate were out of it. No longer connected to the investigation in any way.

With any luck the FBI would find enough on the flash drive for warrants, undercover surveillance, whatever they needed to complete their investigation. Taggart believed the files would ultimately lead to the arrest and conviction of the entire criminal organization.

Kate turned in her management consulting report Monday morning, as promised. She made it clear to Victor Markum that if he expected anything more, he was out of luck.

Jase figured *he* was the lucky man. He was the guy who ended up with Kate.

EPILOGUE

OVER THE NEXT few weeks, the FBI arrested Victor Markum, Maximillian Schram and Arthur Wiedel. The men were charged with a list of criminal activities that would keep their attorneys fat and happy for years.

All three were currently out on bail, but Agent Taggart was sure they would eventually be convicted and spend a good portion of their lives in federal prison.

Then Kate got a thank-you call from Callie Spencer. Which resulted in Jason flying her down to Houston to visit the teen and her mom.

"You saved my life," Callie said tearfully. "I'll never forget what both of you did for me."

"We were just glad we were there when you needed us," Kate said, fighting tears of her own.

"I told my mom the truth about why I ran away," Callie said. "But she had already figured it out. When we got back to Houston, my stepdad was already gone."

"We're glad to hear it, Callie," Jason said.

"Mom made me promise never to hide things from her again. She said she would always believe me—no matter what."

Kate thought of her own mother and how much she missed her. "Moms are good that way."

The evening of the charity benefit finally arrived. Kate wore an off-the-shoulder white chiffon gown while Jason looked amazing in a perfectly tailored black tuxedo. A sight she couldn't have imagined when she had met him that night at the Sagebrush Saloon.

Kate sat at a table with Jason, Chase and Harper, and Reese and his sophisticated, fashion-model date. Filling out the seating—to Kate's amazement—were her dad and his wife, Jennifer.

Jase and her father had put the trip together as a surprise, and Kate was touched by the gesture. She was thrilled to discover how well she liked her stepmother. Jen was kind and smart, and she worshiped Frank Gallagher. Kate was happy for both of them and looking forward to spending time with them and the siblings she had never met.

Priced at an outrageous sum, tickets to the benefit sold out completely, which meant a great deal of money was raised for the New Hope Rehabilitation Center.

It was a wonderful night, topped only by the next night when Jase took her country-western dancing at the Sagebrush Saloon.

A slow song was playing. They were dancing cheek to cheek, their bodies snuggled together. Jase did a graceful turn and pulled her back. He smiled. "I knew you were the one for me when I saw you dancing with that scrawny biker."

"You did not."

"I did. I tried to tell myself it wasn't true, but deep down I knew. I went back to the bar the next day, but your car was already gone. I went back on Friday night, but you never showed up."

"You didn't tell me."

"I never told you I loved you, either. But I do. More now than ever."

That first night he had been a cowgirl's fantasy.

As far as Kate was concerned, he still was. Her heart swelled with love for him.

They two-stepped the next song, then Jase led her over to the bar and lifted her up on a stool.

"I was going to wait till next Wednesday, same night we first met, but I couldn't take the pressure any longer." He nodded at the bartender, who set a shot of tequila down in front of her.

"What's going on?" Kate asked.

"There's something in the bottom of your glass. I'm hoping like hell you like it."

She slid the shot glass over, reached in and pulled a beautiful diamond solitaire out of the clear liquid. Her throat closed up. "Hawk."

"I love you, Kate. So damn much."

Her eyes stung as she looked down at the ring. "It's beautiful."

"I fell a little in love with you that first night. I'm crazy in love with you now. You're it for me, Kate. Everything I've ever wanted and more. Will you marry me?"

She looked up at him with tears in her eyes. "I love you, Jason. So much." Her hand trembled as she slid the ring on her finger. She grinned and threw her arms around his neck. "I'll marry you, cowboy. Anytime you say."

Jason laughed with relief and kissed her.

She agreed to marry Hawk Maddox at the Sagebrush Saloon. Her life had taken another unexpected turn. And nothing had ever felt so good.

* * * * *

AUTHOR'S NOTE

I hope you enjoyed Kate Gallagher and Hawk Maddox in *The Deception*, book two in the Maximum Security series. In my next novel, Brandon Garrett meets Jessica Kegan. Jessie's brother, killed in Afghanistan, once saved Bran's life. When the search for her father's killer puts her in grave danger, Jessie comes to Bran, a man who owes her family a debt he can never repay.

I hope you'll watch for Bran and Jessie in my next Maximum Security novel. Till then, all best wishes and happy reading.

Kat

SHADOWS AT DAWN

CHAPTER ONE

LAST WEEK IT was murder. This week it's stolen diamonds. Mindy Stewart loved working at The Max. Her job was never dull.

Seated behind her desk in the reception area, Mindy reached over to answer the phone, then directed the call to Jonah Wolfe, one of the agency's detectives.

Mindy had only been working at Maximum Security a couple of months. Originally hired as a temp to fill in for the receptionist who had retired, and do some bookkeeping. She managed to impress Chase Garrett, the owner, who had offered her a full-time job.

In the weeks since then, the private investigators, bodyguards, and bounty hunters who worked out of the office had accepted her as a member of the team. It felt really good to be part of such an interesting crew.

She checked the time on her computer. It was well past five o'clock, but everyone worked their own schedules, so people were in and out at all hours of the day and night. Mindy got overtime pay, and she didn't mind working late. Part of her job was reorganizing office ledgers and updating Chase's QuickBooks, so there was plenty for her to do.

As she grabbed her purse, she glanced across the office at the men still working. The open area was decorated in a Western motif, a tufted dark red leather sofa and chairs up front in the reception area, with antique farming tools on the walls.

Jonah Wolfe was a former police detective, incredibly handsome with his too-long black hair and dark eyes. He was involved in a serious relationship, but even if he weren't, the man was too intense and brooding to appeal to her.

Jason "Hawk" Maddox was a big, good-looking man, but he was somehow overwhelming to her. Like Wolfe and Chase and the other guys in the office, Maddox was protective of the women who worked there, even the female detectives. He waved at Mindy as he and Wolfe headed out the door, and she waved back.

Along with a female PI, there were a number of single men in the office, guys who worked part-time. It seemed like all of them were attractive, but it was Jaxon Ryker who made her adrenaline spike and her pulse speed up whenever he glanced in her direction.

Which, fortunately, wasn't that often. Jax probably went for tall, svelte blondes, not petite, curvy brunettes. Even if he were interested in her—which clearly he wasn't—a disastrous affair with the former Navy SEAL-turned-PI would ruin everything.

Mindy loved her job. She wanted to keep it.

Still, she couldn't deny the man pushed her buttons. Six feet of wide-shouldered, solid male muscle, military short dark hair and deep brown eyes, Ryker was handsome as sin yet seemingly unaware of his masculine charms.

And he was nice. Always polite, always considerate. He never flirted, never teased, and constantly kept a respectful distance.

Sometimes it drove her crazy.

Finally satisfied with her progress for the day, Mindy

shoved her round tortoiseshell glasses up on her nose, slung the strap of her purse over her shoulder, and headed for the door to the parking lot behind the office. She managed not to glance at Jax as she left, but it wasn't easy.

The early April weather was humid, warm but not hot, the last of a pink-gold sky fading to darkness. She spotted her little red Volkswagen Beetle, one of the few vehicles left in the lot, and started in that direction.

If she hadn't been working for a security firm, listening to crime stories on a daily basis, she might not have noticed the white Chevy van whose motor sparked to life and began idling in the shadows not far from her car.

When her steps unconsciously slowed, she told herself she was being ridiculous, a paranoid response to the guys' sometimes gruesome, often frightening tales.

Pausing to dig her car keys out of her purse, she took a deep breath and tried to calm her racing heart. When the effort failed, she forced her feet to move, closing the distance between her and her vehicle. She had almost reached her destination when the van doors slid open. Three men dressed head-to-foot in black, wearing black ski masks, jumped out and started running toward her.

Terror struck. Mindy let out a terrified, high-pitched scream, dropped her purse, whirled and started running.

JAX'S LONG DAY wasn't over yet. Before he picked up a pizza and headed home for a couple of beers, he had a meeting with a client on the other side of Dallas, a cold case he had been working where the mother of a murder victim had discovered new evidence she believed would help find her daughter's killer. The police weren't convinced, but Mrs. Donahue had hired Jax to prove it. Or at least find out the truth.

He checked his heavy black wristwatch. If he wanted to make his appointment on time, he needed to get on the road. Grabbing his laptop off the desk, he headed for his dark blue Dodge Ram pickup, parked in the lot behind the office, his mind on the case he figured would earn him a nice fat fee—and maybe help bring a killer to justice.

He had just stepped out the back door when a blood-curdling scream cut through the sticky evening air. A petite young woman with long dark hair and glasses struggled with three masked men.

Adrenaline shot into his blood. *Mindy!* Even as he bolted into a run, Jax registered the men's appearances: one tall and lean, one average height and weight, one big and beefy, thick-shouldered and muscular. He was flat-out running by the time Mindy spotted him and started screaming his name.

"Jax, help me! Jax!" Kicking and biting, she fought like a wild thing, but she was no match for the men. As they hauled her toward the open van doors, Jax grabbed the taller man and pulled him off her, pounded a fist into his face and slammed another into his stomach, doubling him over. A hard right hook sent the guy careening backward, hitting the ground on his back and sliding across the asphalt.

The second man, Mr. Average, stepped in and swung a punch Jax ducked. He shot out a kick, knocking the assailant into the side of the van, then heard the sound of a switchblade snapping open behind him.

"Jax, watch out!"

As the second guy ran for the van, Jax whirled toward the new threat, dodged the flashing blade of the big beefy man and shoved Mindy toward safety, then went back in for the kill. Rage burned through his usual calm. She worked with him; as far as he was concerned, she was under his protection. More than that, she was kind and sweet, and he cared about her far more than he should. Jax wanted to end the bastards who were trying to hurt her.

"Run!" he shouted. "Go back to the office and lock the door! Call 9-1-1!" A knife flashed. Jax dodged the sweep of gleaming silver wielded by a big, thick-fingered, extremely capable hand and jumped back, out of the way of another slashing attack as he and the beefy man crouched and circled each other. From the corner of his eye, he saw the tall, thin man back on his feet and rushing toward him.

Jax looked up to see Mindy swinging her purse like a ball and chain, smashing the bag into the side of the tall man's head, sending him staggering, grunting as he landed on his hands and knees.

"Bitch!" the guy screamed, shaking his head to clear it, drawing the big man's attention and providing the distraction Jax needed. He kicked the knife out of the beefy man's hand and threw a punch that sent him reeling. The second man had already climbed into the van and shoved the vehicle into gear.

"Come on!" the guy shouted from where he sat behind the wheel. "Let's go!"

The tall guy got up off his knees and ran to the open van doors, and the beefy, muscular man shot in behind him. Tires burned and smoke rolled up from the wheels as the vehicle screeched away.

Every instinct urged Jax to jump in his pickup and follow, but concern for Mindy won out. Turning, he strode toward her.

"Jax!" Mindy hurled herself into his arms. "Jax..." she breathed.

Relief had him tightening his hold. "It's all right, honey. It's over." She was shaking so hard her teeth chattered. She clung to him, and he couldn't resist smoothing a hand over her pretty dark hair.

"It's all right," he softly repeated. "You're safe. I'm here. Everything's okay."

Mindy looked up at him. Behind her glasses, her big blue eyes glistened with tears. "You saved me."

His chest clamped down. What if he hadn't walked out of the office when he did? What would have happened to her? Why had she been targeted? Was it a random abduction attempt, or something more?

"Come on. Let's get you back inside. We need to call the police."

She nodded, released her death grip, pulled out of his arms and started walking. When her knees buckled, and she nearly went down, Jax scooped her into his arms.

"Adrenaline rush," he said. "It'll be over in a minute."

She didn't argue, just rested her head on his shoulder and let him carry her into the office. After pausing to lock the back door behind them, he carted her into the break room and set her down on the brown vinyl sofa.

Jax smoothed long dark hair out of her face with his finger. A faint bruise was beginning to form on her cheek, and a fresh rush of anger rolled through him. "You gonna be okay?"

Mindy swallowed and looked up at him. "Those men were...they were trying to kidnap me. I don't...don't understand. Why would they be after me? What could they possibly want?"

His jaw hardened. "Don't worry. We'll figure it out."

Pulling out his cell, he hit 9-1-1 and reported the attempted kidnapping to police dispatch. He had tried to get a license number, but conveniently the plate was smeared with mud except for what looked like an *H* on the letter side and maybe a 3.

Since he had only a partial, and minimal physical descriptions of the assailants, he wasn't sure how much good reporting the incident would do.

He was just glad Mindy was safe.

As they waited for the police to arrive, he walked out of the break room to phone Chase Garrett. His boss wouldn't be happy to learn one of his employees had been attacked in the parking lot. They were all like family to him.

"I'm on my way," Chase said when Jax finished the story.

"No need for that," he said. "I'll take care of Mindy and talk to the police. You don't have to worry. We can talk things out in the morning, work up a plan."

"So you'll stay with her tonight?" Chase pressed, just to be sure she was safe, though he had to know Jax wasn't about to leave her.

"Absolutely. These guys knew what they were doing, Chase. If the attack wasn't just random and Mindy was the target, they'll be back. They won't give up that easy."

"All right, but call me if you have any more trouble. If I don't hear from you, I'll see you in the morning." Chase hung up the phone.

Next Jax called to reschedule his now-overdue meeting with Eleanor Donahue, the mother of the murdered girl. He might have to ask Wolfe to take over. For now, it looked like he had another case that was going to take precedence.

In his new case, the victim was still alive. Jax intended to keep her that way.

CHAPTER TWO

MINDY SIPPED FROM the bottle of water Jax had retrieved from the fridge in the break room. She wondered if he had noticed that water was her go-to drink of choice. Surely not. He rarely glanced in her direction.

He was looking at her now, with so much concern in his thick-lashed dark eyes it made her chest feel tight.

She remembered the way he had rushed to help her. "You were amazing," she said.

"Yeah? Well, you were pretty amazing yourself. If you hadn't fought those men the way you did, I wouldn't have had time to get to you. You did great, honey, but next time you're in trouble and I tell you to run, you need to do what I say."

Her eyebrows went up. "Three to one is not exactly fair odds. I couldn't just leave you."

Amusement touched his lips. "Most people would have."

"Not me."

A slow smile broke over his face. "In that case, thanks."

It occurred to her that he was a former navy SEAL. He could probably handle three men as easily as one. It didn't matter. No way was she running away when it was her fault he was in danger.

"Sounds like the cops have arrived," he said at the

sound of sirens screeching out in front. "I'll be right back."

The air seemed to deflate as he left the room. She heard the police talking to Jax in the main part of the office. When they came back into the break room, she recognized two of the officers who patrolled the area, the same ones who had shown up the night Chase's wife, Harper, had gotten in trouble. Officer Alvarez was a tall man with thick black hair. The other man, Officer Simmons, was older, heavier, with short hair laced with silver.

"Why don't you start at the beginning," Officer Simmons said, pulling out his notepad and flipping it open.

Since she didn't really know where the problem had actually begun, she just jumped in. "It was getting late. I work after hours quite a bit."

For the next few minutes, she filled the officers in on the kidnapping attempt and Jax's amazing rescue, but she couldn't tell them much about the men who were responsible. Officer Simmons wrote down the basic information, including vehicle and physical descriptions of the attackers, then he and his partner checked out the area outside where the attack had occurred.

As the officers finished and were preparing to leave, Detective Lieutenant Walter Gunderson arrived.

"Ryker," the detective said, clearly acquainted with Jax. With his thinning light brown hair and tired eyes, he looked older than the early forties Mindy guessed him to be.

"Gunderson," Jax said.

"You're the guy who stopped the attack?"

"That's right."

"She's lucky you were here."

Jax made no reply, but the hard set of his jaw said he knew it was true. Mindy certainly agreed.

"I'm afraid I'll need you to start over, Ms. Stewart," Detective Gunderson said as the two police officers left.

Mindy looked at Jax. "This is probably going to take a while, and it's getting really late. Now that Detective Gunderson is here, there's no reason for you to stay. I can drive myself home when we're done."

Jax's powerful shoulders tightened. He shook his head. "Not gonna happen, sweetheart. You just tell the detective what he needs to know."

"But—"

Jax's stony expression said there was no use arguing, and secretly she was glad. Just thinking about what had happened—what could have been so much worse—made her feel light-headed.

As she ran through the details of the kidnap attempt a second time, Jax added the partial plate information, as well as basic descriptions of the three men.

He mentioned little things she hadn't noticed, like a scar on the back of the big man's right hand, which Jax believed was probably made by a knife—the man's weapon of choice. The eye color of the guy Jax called Mr. Average—a pale shade of blue—and the tall man's sneakers, expensive Giuseppe Zanotti high-tops, black with red leather trim.

"He had a rough voice, probably a smoker," Jax added. Mindy shivered at the memory of him calling her a bitch. Then the detective started asking questions that might lead to the reason for the attack.

"So, no boyfriends, current or otherwise, who might be upset with you?" Gunderson asked.

"I haven't been seeing anyone. Not for more than six months." She glanced at Jax, then away. "I've been too busy to date." Not quite true. She just hadn't found anyone interesting. After she'd met Jax, no other man seemed to compare. But she'd die of embarrassment if he found out.

"What about friends or family members?" the detective asked. "Anyone who might be angry with you, someone who might be holding a grudge?"

"I don't have a lot of family. My mom's in a long-term care facility. She was mentally impaired in the same car accident that killed my dad and brother."

Jax's jaw subtly tightened.

Gunderson asked about her finances, loans she might owe that hadn't been repaid, gambling debts, anything and everything that might account for the kidnapping attempt, but nothing seemed to point to an answer.

Finally finished, the detective rose from his chair. "Kidnapping is a serious offense, Ms. Stewart. You need to keep your eyes open. Call us if you think of anything that might help us find the men behind the attack." He turned to Jax. "I take it you're on the case?"

"That's right."

The detective just nodded, clearly seeing something in Jax's expression Mindy didn't. Jax let him out the front door and locked up behind him.

"So you're going to follow me home?" she asked as they headed for the parking lot.

"Oh, I'm not just following you home. If you don't want me sleeping on your sofa tonight, I'll be in my truck out in front."

Her eyes widened. "What?"

"Those men were deadly serious, honey. The way it looks, you weren't a random choice. Which means there's a chance they'll try again. No way am I leaving you alone. Until we know what the hell is going on, you've got round the clock protection."

"But I can't pay for something like that!"

"Don't insult me."

Color washed into her cheeks. They were colleagues, friends of a sort. "I'm sorry. Thank you. And you aren't sleeping out in your car. My sofa folds into a bed, so you won't be that uncomfortable."

He looked like he wanted to say something about their sleeping arrangements but didn't.

"I do have a…um…cat. Her name is Muffin. She usually sleeps with me so unless you're allergic or something—"

"I'm not allergic to cats. I'm more a dog person, but cats are okay."

Mindy smiled. "She's very sweet. I promise she won't bother you."

He just nodded. "I've got a couple of calls to make, then we can go."

BEFORE IT GOT any later, Jax wanted to phone Jason Maddox. Though Maddox worked mostly as a bounty hunter, he was also a licensed PI. Jax held the same licenses, and the two men often worked together. Add to that, they were close friends.

Maddox answered on the second ring, still clearly awake. Not unusual for the guy they called the Hawk. "Ryker, what's up?"

"We had some trouble at the office tonight. Three guys in a white van went after Mindy."

"What the hell? Went after her? What happened? Is she okay?"

"She's pretty shook up, but she's all right. I'm just glad I was still here when it went down." He filled

Maddox in on the abduction attempt on the cute little receptionist who brought out the protective instincts of every man in the office, and his plan to spend the night at her house.

"I can come over if you think those dickwads might show up at her place."

"I think they'll take a step back and regroup," Jax said. "They had the attack well planned. If I hadn't stayed late and happened to walk out when I did, it would have gone down like clockwork." He thought of Mindy fighting off three hardened men, and a fresh wave of fury rolled through him. "But I have to say, our girl gave them bloody hell."

Maddox grunted. "Good for her."

Jax sobered. "She couldn't have held them off much longer, Hawk. They weren't pros, but they weren't amateurs, either."

"We need to figure out what's going on," Maddox said.

"Chase is meeting us tomorrow morning at the office."

"I'll be there."

"Maybe we can come up with something that makes sense."

"You'll take care of her tonight?"

"You know I will."

"Yeah…" Hawk said. "I do."

Jax ignored the subtle innuendo. He had gone out of his way to make sure no one guessed the attraction he felt to Mindy, but Maddox was his closest friend.

"Call if you need me," Hawk said.

"Will do." Jax hung up the phone. Pulling open the bottom drawer of his desk, he punched in the code for his gun safe, drew out his .38 Colt revolver and strapped it to his ankle. He took out his holstered HK45 Compact Tactical semiautomatic pistol, the same weapon he had used as a SEAL, and set it on the desk. From now on, he planned to be armed.

As he rose from the chair, Mindy looked at him with big, worried eyes. She still wasn't completely used to working around men and women in the security business, but she was learning.

"You ready?" he asked as he clipped the pistol to his belt.

Mindy eyed the gun, looked up at him and nodded.

He had already retrieved his laptop from where he had dropped it in the parking lot. Fortunately, the padded case had protected it. He grabbed the handle and they started for the door.

Mindy was also carrying her laptop. "I have some work to do in the morning so I planned to leave my computer here overnight, but the way things are going, I think I better take it with me."

"Good idea." There was a chance the laptop contained information that might help them figure out what the kidnappers wanted. He planned to take a hard look at it once he got Mindy home.

She slung the strap of the computer over her shoulder and grabbed the battered purse she had retrieved from the parking lot. As they walked outside, she started toward the little red Volkswagen Beetle that seemed to fit her just right, but Jax caught her arm.

"It's after midnight. You might as well leave your car here, and I'll drive you back to work in the morning."

She hesitated. He could tell she was still trying to come to grips with the notion he would be spending the night. "I…um…hate to waste gas so, okay, I guess that works."

He walked her over to his pickup and opened the passenger door, glad he had installed running boards along both sides of the extended cab. Then again, if she'd needed his help to get in, he would have an excuse to put his hands on her again.

Until tonight he had never touched her. Now he'd fantasize about the soft fullness of her breasts against his chest, the long, silky strands of her hair teasing his cheek as he'd carried her into the office.

Jax swore a silent curse. He'd be sleeping on Mindy's sofa tonight, a task made nearly impossible with her asleep in a bed down the hall—*with her cat.* He hated to admit he was glad it was a cat curled up with her and not some other guy.

He sighed as he rounded his truck to the driver's side. For weeks, he'd steered clear of her. She was Chase's employee, the receptionist at The Max. That made her completely off-limits. The attraction he'd felt from the first time he had seen her had no place in his life or hers. But little by little, her sweet smile and vivacious, always cheerful attitude began to melt his iron resolve.

He'd begun to wonder about her, think about her even when he wasn't in the office. He hadn't realized how much he'd come to care for her until he had walked out into the parking lot and seen three masked men attacking her.

A fresh shot of fury burned through him as the scene flashed back into his head, and his hand unconsciously fisted. He took a deep breath and forced himself to relax.

He needed to table whatever feelings he had for Mindy, bury his fantasies and do his job. Keeping her safe was all that mattered and to do that he needed to remain objective.

Strapping himself in behind the wheel, Jax made a final scan of the parking lot, saw nothing out of the ordinary and started the engine.

"Put on your seat belt," he said. He didn't call her sweetheart or honey, which he shouldn't have done in the first place. Instead, he focused on the address she had given him, which was not far away. He'd be watching for a tail, taking evasive measures until he was sure they weren't being followed.

From now on, he was on the job. Mindy Stewart was a client, nothing more. Jax planned to do whatever it took to keep it that way.

CHAPTER THREE

MINDY LAY IN bed staring up at the ceiling. It was late, quiet and dark, Muffin, her little black-and-white short-haired cat, curled up at her feet.

Her bedroom was decorated in rose and cream, a feminine room she had designed herself. She usually found it comforting. Tonight her nerves remained on a jagged edge, and even having Jax Ryker, armed and staying in her apartment, didn't put her worries to rest.

She kept thinking of him in her living room, stretched out on the foldout sofa that was far from comfortable but better than outside in his car.

She still couldn't wrap her mind around it. Jax had saved her from being abducted. He had come to her rescue just like in her fantasies. He had fought for her, held her in his arms, and even called her honey. If the circumstances were different, it could have been the best night of her life.

Unfortunately, reality intruded. Men had tried to kidnap her. She had no idea why or what would have happened if Jax hadn't been there to stop them.

A chill washed through her just thinking about it. Were they rapists? Murderers? Did they want her to drive to an ATM and clear out her bank account? She had heard of that happening. But she didn't have much in her checking account and only a rainy-day amount in her savings.

Surely it wasn't enough for the kind of risk the three men were taking in a kidnapping attempt. For God's sake, it was potentially a death penalty offense!

Mindy closed her eyes, but she couldn't fall asleep. Would the men try again? What could they possibly want? Jax couldn't protect her forever. What if they just waited until he was gone?

She listened for sounds of him. She had left her door cracked open so Muffin could reach her food and water in the laundry area off the kitchen. Every once in a while, she could hear Jax moving around in the living room or turning on the tap at the kitchen sink. Eventually the knowledge that he was there and not leaving lulled her enough to fall asleep.

The sun was up when she awoke the next morning. She was halfway to the bathroom when she remembered she wasn't alone. Jax had spent the night in her living room!

Being up so late, she had managed to oversleep. Was he still there? But she knew deep down he wouldn't leave her. Not while he thought she still might be in danger. He just wasn't that kind of man.

It was Saturday. Mindy showered and brushed her hair, dressed in dark blue skinny jeans and a loose-fitting lavender print blouse, shoved her feet into low-heeled sandals, put on her glasses and opened the bedroom door.

The aroma of freshly brewed coffee made her smile. She hurried down the hall to her sunny yellow galley kitchen, and saw Jax sitting at the round white table next to the window, a steaming mug next to a big, powerful hand.

"Good morning," he said, sensing her presence without turning his head. When he did, her lungs seemed incapable of filling with air. His short dark hair was uncharacteristically mussed and he hadn't shaved, leaving him with a day's growth of beard along his hard jaw.

There were words for a guy who looked as good as Jaxon Ryker, but they all seemed to have escaped her head. Only the basics formed. Hot. Sexy. Incredible. Thank God he was wearing a T-shirt over that massive chest. Although…

"Good morning," she finally managed to say as she poured coffee into a mug for herself and loaded it with sugar and cream. "Did you sleep okay?"

"I wasn't here to sleep. I was here to make sure no one bothered you. But I managed to catch a few hours off and on."

"Oh. I'm sorry. I didn't expect you to stay awake all night for me."

Something flashed in his eyes; then it was gone. "I need to look at your laptop. I didn't want to do that without your permission."

"Of course. That's not a problem. I'll get it." She hurried into the living room to retrieve her computer from where she had left it on the coffee table last night.

Her apartment wasn't large. She preferred a smaller, cozier place to live, where she felt safe, more in control of her environment. Her decorative tastes ran to the traditional: a moss green carpet, a rose-and-moss-green-flowered sofa and wingback chair with matching throw pillows. Brass lamps sat on delicate mahogany Duncan Phyfe tables.

She had lots of antiques and family heirlooms: crocheted doilies that had belonged to her grandmother, Hummel figurines her mom had collected, some Blue Willow porcelain dishes. The items made her feel closer

to her to her mother, and family she had lost in the accident.

She grabbed her laptop and carried it into the kitchen.
Jax set it on the table and opened it. When he sat back
in the chair, Muffin jumped up in his lap.

"Muffin!"

"She's all right." A big hand stroked gently over the
cat's soft black fur. When Jax rubbed beneath her chin,
Muffin started to purr.

"I hope she didn't bother you last night."

"She paid me a visit, didn't stay long."

"She…um…doesn't usually get along with men."

He smiled. "Maybe she's just choosy."

Mindy smiled back. "Maybe she is."

Jax set the cat on the floor. Muffin ambled away, and
Jax returned his attention to the computer.

"My password is c-o-u-r-a-g-e," Mindy said, spell-
ing out the letters.

He typed it in and looked up at her. "Courage?"

"It's from the Stewart clan motto. 'Courage Grows
Stronger at the Wound.'" She glanced away. She didn't
tell him how much courage it had taken to survive the
loss of her dad and brother, the mental impairment of
her mother, which still hurt every week when she went
to visit her.

But when she looked back at him, Jax seemed to
understand.

"I'm sorry about what happened to your family,"
he said.

She swallowed. "Visiting my mom is tough. It's
worse because she doesn't know who I am." She managed to smile. "Mom seems happy, though, in whatever
world she lives in now. And the facility does a great job
of taking care of her."

He nodded. "I guess that's something. How old were you when it happened?"

"Seventeen. I was visiting my grandmother on the night of the accident. We were always close. Gran raised me after that. She passed a few years ago."

"I never had much of a family. My dad took off when I was ten, and my mom suffered from depression. They're both gone now. I'm still tight with a couple of my cousins, some of my SEAL buddies."

She felt a pang. She knew what it was like to be without family. "You and Jason seem close."

He smiled and took a sip of his coffee. "Maddox is a good guy. Which reminds me, we need to get going. I'm meeting him and Chase at the office this morning. Since I'm not leaving you alone, you're coming with me."

"All right. I planned to go in anyway."

He checked his watch. "We've got a few minutes before we have to leave. Let me take a look at your laptop first."

Mindy looked over his thick-muscled shoulder to her computer screen. "So what are you looking for?"

"Not sure. What kind of records do you store in here?"

"Nothing much. I do my personal banking online at Wells Fargo, but there isn't much in my account."

Jax perused the files on her desktop, apparently saw nothing out of the ordinary, then went to her email.

He glanced up. "Anything personal in these? You said you hadn't been dating for a while." His eyes found hers, looking at her as if the answer were important.

"I don't have a significant other, if that's what you're asking."

"I'm asking if anyone's been pushing you to go out,

following you, sending you unwanted emails, anything like that."

She shook her head. "No." She smiled. "The pizza delivery boy flirts with me when he shows up at my door, but that's about it."

The corner of his mouth edged up. "We'll let him slide for the moment."

She grinned. "Since he's still in high school, he probably isn't much of a threat."

Jax chuckled and went back to work. He got her Facebook password and took a look around. She didn't go on very often, so there wasn't much there. Twitter wasn't really her thing. Too time-consuming. She used Instagram, but he didn't find anything there.

Jax went back to her email, looked in her inbox, regular emails from some of her friends, ads from Amazon, Target, L.L. Bean, places where she purchased products online. He returned to the emails.

There were messages from people she kept in touch with. Shelley Bachman was an acquaintance from high school. Kayla Hildebrand was one of the other temps at DeMarco Staffing, the agency she had been working for when she got the job at The Max.

Jax went to the sent items folder and glanced through old emails from three or four months back she hadn't bothered to delete.

"When I worked for DeMarco, I did some bookkeeping on the side, mostly friends, people I knew. Susan DeMarco referred me to a couple of her acquaintances. A college student named Ricky Malone needed help getting his taxes done, and a guy named Ryan Shipman, whose company was barely making it financially. It saved them money and helped me make a little extra."

Jax moved through the rest of her trash mail, then

went back to her inbox when a new message pinged. Her face warmed when she read the email from her best friend, Nicki Carson. Nicki wanted her to go out on a blind date with a guy named Thomas Koenig.

Thomas has a PhD in psychology. He's gorgeous and believe it or not, he's got a super-hot body. Guys like him are usually wimps, but Thomas is an exception. I really think you'd like him. Say you'll come out with Ben and me.

Jax's dark eyes swiveled in her direction. There was something in them, not disapproval, but something else she couldn't read. "Not a good time for you to be out dating right now."

"Don't worry, I'm not going on a blind date with some shrink that Nicki thinks I'll fall all over. We have totally different taste in men."

"Is that right…?" Jax drawled, his mouth edging up.

"That's right." Mindy's tastes agreed more with Muffin's, but she couldn't say that. Not even jokingly.

"Care to elaborate?"

She couldn't believe he had even asked. "No."

He turned back to her laptop. "There's a notice here from the Texas State Bank. Your monthly statement is ready. I thought you banked at Wells Fargo."

"I'm authorized to write checks to pay mom's bills."

"Paying for a health care facility like that must be expensive."

"It is. The only good thing that came out of the accident was the settlement my mother received. The other driver was completely at fault. He was young, and his parents were extremely wealthy. The money my mother got is what pays for her medical care."

Jax's head turned in her direction. "How much?"

"After attorney's fees, her portion was five million dollars."

His dark gaze sharpened on her face. "That's a lot of money. How's it handled?"

"A trust fund was set up at the time of the settlement. A monthly check is deposited into the bill-pay account I manage at Texas State Bank."

"Who's in charge of the fund?"

"A lawyer who did work for my father, a man named Marcus Handley. He's with Gibbons, Eckstein, and Riggs, Attorneys at Law."

"Like I said, five million is a lot of cash. Even if some of it was spent on your mother's care, there's probably still a lot left."

"Around three million according to the latest quarterly statement from Handley's accountant."

"We need to follow up on this, Mindy. Someone tried to kidnap you. They didn't want you dead, or they would have just shot you. That means they want something from you. Maybe access to three million dollars."

"It's not my money. It's my mother's."

"If you were kidnapped, would Handley pay the ransom?"

Mindy sucked in a breath. "Oh my God."

"Exactly."

CHAPTER FOUR

JAX SILENTLY CURSED as Mindy's pretty face drained of color.

"It never occurred to me that the men in the van might believe they could ransom me for money from the trust fund."

"How many people are aware of the money?"

She shook her head, shifting long mahogany curls around her shoulders. The scent of lavender teased his senses, and his groin tightened. Jax bit back another curse.

"I never even think about it," Mindy said. "It's there to take care of my mother. Paying her bills is just something I do to help."

"So no one you can think of would know you have access to three million dollars."

"I don't really have access. Mr. Handley controls the funds."

"We need to talk to him, see if he can tell us something that will help us figure this out."

"It's Saturday. His office is closed. I'll call him first thing Monday morning."

"You have his home number?"

"Yes, for emergencies."

"Sweetheart, the attempted kidnapping of one of his clients is definitely an emergency."

Her cheeks pinkened. He wasn't sure if it was from

the realization of just how serious this was or him slipping up and calling her sweetheart again.

"I'll phone him right now." As she pulled out her cell, a text message appeared on her screen. "It's from Nicki. I haven't answered her email, so she's texting me about tonight."

"The pretty boy shrink, right?"

Her color deepened. "I told you I'm not going."

"You might want to tell that to your friend—unless you want a bodyguard along on your date."

Her chin went up. She started to argue, but Mindy was smart. At the moment, she needed his protection and she knew it.

"Fine, I'll tell her," she said.

"Not about the kidnapping attempt. The fewer people who know about that the better. At least for the time being."

She nodded, texted her friend that she wouldn't be going out with Thomas Koenig, the pretty boy with the PhD. Jax wished he didn't feel so relieved.

"I'll call Mr. Handley and see if he can see us this morning."

"You can call him from the office when we get there. I'm going to go get cleaned up. I won't be long. Don't open the door for anyone."

He headed for the guest bathroom at the end of the hall, took a quick shower, and was ready to leave in less than five minutes. As he drove to the office, he made a quick pass through Burger King for a couple of breakfast burritos for him, and an egg-and-cheese biscuit for Mindy, which they ate on the way.

When he pulled the Dodge into the parking lot, Chase's silver Mercedes sat next to Maddox's big black SUV. When they walked through the back door, Lissa

Blayne, one of the female PIs, was on the phone. Wolfe was just leaving.

"Heard what happened last night," Jonah said to Mindy. "You okay?"

The bruise had darkened on her cheek, which Wolfe didn't miss. "Jax was there," she said. "He took on three men. Because of him, I'm okay."

Wolfe's obsidian eyes swung in Jax's direction. "Nice work," he said. "Let me know if you need my help."

"Will do. Thanks."

"Chase and Maddox are waiting for you in the conference room," Wolfe said.

Jax nodded. He tipped his head in that direction and Mindy led the way. Chase and Jason stood up as they walked in. Both men were in their thirties—Maddox tall and brawny, taking up too much space, Chase dark blond, lean and hard-muscled.

"You all right?" Chase asked. He noticed the bruise on Mindy's cheek and his jaw clenched.

Behind the lenses of her glasses, Mindy's big blue eyes shot toward Jax. "I'm okay. But if Jax hadn't been there…"

Jax cleared his throat. He didn't need any more reminders of what would have happened if he hadn't walked out of the office when he had. "We need to figure this out," he said, rolling out a chair at the long oak conference table for Mindy, then one for himself.

"Where are we so far?" Chase asked as Jax and Mindy sat down.

Jax didn't miss the *we*. Mindy was important to all of them. She was part of The Max crew, a member of the family. They wouldn't let anyone hurt her.

"Best guess so far, it may have been a ransom attempt." Jax went on to explain about the accident that had killed Mindy's father and brother and left her mother mentally impaired. He told them about the three million dollars being held in trust for her mother's care, and that Mindy handled the monthly disbursements.

"I just get a check once a month I use to pay Mom's bills," Mindy said. "Mr. Handley controls the money."

"The kidnappers may not know that," Maddox said.

"That's right," Chase said. "We need to figure out who knew about the trust fund money."

Jax swiveled his chair to face them. "We're hoping to speak to the attorney who manages the trust sometime today." He turned to Mindy. "Why don't you go ahead and call him."

"From here?"

Jax nodded. He wanted to make sure the guy didn't try to put her off.

Mindy pulled out her cell and hit Handley's contact number. The phone rang several times before it was answered.

"Marcus? Hi, it's Mindy Stewart. I know you're busy and it's the weekend. I'm really sorry to bother you—"

Jax took the phone out of her hand. "Mr. Handley, this is Jaxon Ryker. I'm a private investigator with Maximum Security. Last night a kidnapping attempt was made on Ms. Stewart after she left the office."

"What?"

"Fortunately, the effort failed. I need to speak to you. I'm hoping you have information that can help me find the men behind the attack and keep Ms. Stewart safe."

"Is Mindy all right?"

"She managed to escape unharmed, but until these men are stopped, she's in danger."

"I see. I'm not sure how I can help you, but I'm more than willing to try."

"Thank you so much, Marcus," Mindy chimed in.

Jax set up a meeting at Handley's house that morning and ended the call.

"You brought your laptop," he said to her. "I want you to make a list of anyone who might know about the trust fund money. Girlfriends, old boyfriends, people you worked with before you came here. I need addresses and phone numbers if you have them."

Maddox spoke up. "If there's anyone at your mother's health facility who's shown more than a passing interest in how her bills are being paid, you need to list them, too."

"Good idea," Jax said.

Mindy took her laptop out of its case, set it on the conference table and went to work.

Jax tipped his head toward the door and the men left her to her task.

Chase paused outside the conference room door. "What about the van? Any way to track it?"

"I'll phone Detective Gunderson, see if any sign of it's shown up. Maybe the parking lot or street cams caught something useful."

"We need to set up a protection detail," Maddox said. "You don't have to do this by yourself."

"It's not a problem," Jax said. "I'll stay at her place at night. During the day, she'll be here working. As long as one of us is with her in the office, she should be safe. While she's here, I'll have time to do some digging, follow up on whatever we come up with."

"Looks like you're taking the lead on this," Chase said.

"I was there when those bastards went after her. I've got a personal stake in bringing them down. So yeah, I'm taking the lead."

Chase nodded. "Good enough. Just keep us in the loop and let us know if you need more help."

"Will do." As Chase walked away, Jax started to head back to the conference room, but Jason caught his arm.

"You gonna be able to stay objective on this? Like you said, you've got a personal stake—and I'm not talking about the men in the van."

Jax eased out a slow breath. There was no point in lying, not to Hawk. "I want her. You know it, but no one else does, including her. She needs my protection. I won't let my feelings get in the way."

Jason nodded. "Good enough." He grinned. "Can't be easy sleeping on the sofa with the woman you want in a bed down the hall."

Jax just grunted. It wasn't easy. It was damned hard—for about half the night. Inwardly cursing at the pun, he walked back into the conference room just as Mindy finished typing up her list.

"I sent the names to your phone. I'll print us a hard copy."

He took out his cell and studied the list. There weren't that many people. He knew who Nicki Carson was, the friend who wanted to set up her up with the shrink. Marcus Handley's name was there. "Who's Blake Davis?"

"The CPA Mr. Handley uses. He does the quarterly reports."

"What about Curt Wyman?"

She glanced away. "He's a guy I dated for a while before I started working here."

"He knew about your mother's trust fund?"

She shrugged. "We were pretty serious for a while. So, yes, Curt knew. Then he started drinking too much and using drugs. We started arguing, and then he got arrested, and I broke up with him."

Jax's senses perked up. "Arrested? What was he charged with?"

"Burglary. He…um…broke into a bunch of rich people's houses and stole jewelry and things."

"Bingo," Jax said.

CHAPTER FIVE

THEY WERE ON their way to Marcus Handley's house. Mindy brought up the subject of Curt Wyman again. "I know you think Curt is the guy who tried to kidnap me, but I would have recognized him even in a mask, and besides, he's still in jail."

As the pickup rolled along, Jax flicked her a sideways glance. "Actually, he's out. He cut a deal with the DA's office to testify against the jewelry fence he was working with, a guy the cops had been after for a while."

She mulled that over. "I'm not really surprised. Curt was a stockbroker when he lost all his money. He's a decent guy or at least he was."

"I take it you haven't heard from him since his release."

"No, and I don't expect to. He accepted the breakup when it happened."

"How did you feel about it?"

She glanced over to where he sat behind the wheel. It seemed an odd question. "What does that have to do with anything?"

"Nothing. Forget it."

She didn't like to talk about Curt. She should have left him sooner, when things first went downhill, but she'd felt sorry for him. She hoped he didn't screw up his second chance. "The truth is I was glad when we finally broke up. I was ready to end things way before it actually happened."

Jax nodded. She would have sworn he seemed relieved.

"Even if Curt's out of jail, he definitely wasn't one of the men in the parking lot."

"Maybe not, but I looked into his case. The guy was no dummy. If he hadn't gotten careless, he might still be lining his pockets with money from stolen goods. No doubt he's smart enough to come up with a kidnapping scheme if he thought the payoff would be big enough."

"I don't think Curt would do anything to hurt me. He just liked living the high life—expensive cars, Armani suits. We had fun at first. But I didn't really care about the money, and Curt did. When he ran out, he went a little crazy."

"Crazy enough to kidnap you for ransom?"

She sighed and leaned back in the passenger seat. "I don't think so, but I don't know for sure. I didn't think he would burglarize people's homes, but he did." She said nothing more as Jax pulled up in front of the address she had given him for Marcus Handley's house, an impressive two-story red brick Georgian with white shuttered windows and doors.

Marcus personally greeted them, a thin, silver-haired man dressed in khaki chinos and a yellow button-down shirt. He leaned over and hugged her in a rare show of emotion.

"I'm glad you're all right," he said.

"Thank you." She made the introductions, and Marcus led them into a private study lined with bookshelves loaded with heavy leather-bound volumes. Marcus sat down behind a wide mahogany desk, and she and Jax sat in dark brown leather chairs across from him.

"Would you like some refreshment? Coffee or a soda, perhaps?"

"We're fine," Jax said.

"All right, then." Marcus focused on Jax. "Tell me what I can do to help you find the men who tried to abduct Mindy last night."

"First I need to know what you would have done if you had received a ransom demand from the kidnappers. Would you have paid the money for Mindy's release out of her mother's trust fund?"

Marcus didn't hesitate. "No." He looked at Mindy. "I'm sorry, my dear, my power only extends as far as the distribution of funds for your mother's care and personal welfare. I could have gone to court and tried to obtain permission to release the funds to the kidnappers, but it would have taken time, and I'm not sure the judge would have granted my petition."

Mindy shifted in her chair. "Can you think of anyone who might have thought you'd pay the ransom?"

"Very few people know about the trust fund. The settlement wasn't highly publicized at the time, and it was almost twelve years ago. Whoever tried to kidnap you must be someone you've met or dealt with recently. At least that would be my guess."

"How about you?" Jax asked. "Any new hires, people who recently gained access to the fund?"

"We have a few new employees at the firm but none who have any connection to the trust fund or would have any knowledge of it. Mindy handles the day-to-day business of her mother's care. She submits a monthly request for the money, and I grant it."

Interest moved across Jax's hard features. His stare remained on Marcus. "What if Mindy submitted a request for a few million dollars? Would you be obliged to grant that request?"

Awareness dawned in Marcus's pale blue eyes. His narrow shoulders straightened beneath his yellow shirt. "As Mindy was a minor at the time of the accident, the terms of the settlement aren't something we've discussed. It simply never came up." His gaze swung to Mindy. "The fact is, once you reached the age of twenty-one, my dear, you've had overriding control of your mother's funds."

Surprise rolled through her. "I didn't know that, but it doesn't change anything. It's still Mom's money."

"That's right," Marcus said.

But Jax's worried gaze fixed on her face. "You understand what this means?"

"I would never take my mother's money."

His features softened. "Under normal circumstances, I know you wouldn't. But to put it bluntly, those men could have used any means necessary to force you to sign over the money in the trust."

A FAINT STORM blew across the city, stirring up leaves and trash on the street. All the way back to the office, Mindy rode in silence. Jax was worried about her.

"Nothing is going to happen to you," he said as he pulled into the parking lot behind the building. "I won't let it. You know that, right?"

She turned toward him in the passenger seat. "I know," she said softly.

He wasn't sure she believed him. He didn't like the thought that she might not trust him to take care of her.

He sighed as they walked back into the office. The afternoon was slipping away. Since a fast-food breakfast wasn't much of a meal, he suggested they head down to Clancy's, the Irish pub down the block, The Max crew's favorite hangout.

The wind had died down to a mild, pleasant breeze by the time they arrived. The restaurant wasn't busy this hour of the day. The lunch crowd was already gone, the after-work, supper and drinking crowds not in until later. The smell of hops and lemon oil greeted them as they walked into an interior that was all dark wood paneling and lots of Irish green. A long bar lined with stools and an old-fashioned carved back bar dominated the room.

Jax led her to one of the wooden booths, and they sat down across from each other. Mindy ordered a bowl of beef barley soup and Jax ordered a corned beef sandwich, but passed on his usual Guinness. Until he knew what was going on, he needed to be at the top of his game. Mindy was his to protect. He'd do everything in his power to keep her safe.

"How's your lunch?" he asked when he'd finished his sandwich, though Mindy was still eating—or pretending to. The small bowl of soup she'd ordered sat mostly untouched.

"It's great. I'm just not very hungry."

He reached across the table and set his hand over hers, felt the smooth warmth of her skin. His attraction to Mindy had always been strong, but knowing what could have happened to her, his protective feelings made the attraction even stronger. Everything about her turned him on—her pretty, girl-next-door face and gorgeous mahogany hair, her sweet smile and always optimistic personality, her petite but womanly figure.

His gaze went to the full swells beneath her silky blouse and his body stirred. He reminded himself she was out of his reach and let go of her hand.

"We're going to figure this out," he said. "Until we do, I won't let anyone hurt you."

Mindy looked up at him with those big blue eyes, and he felt it like a kick in the stomach. "You and the other guys in the office…you've all been great to accept me the way you have. It's just…it isn't really your job to take care of me. I mean, I work for The Max, but that doesn't make me your responsibility. It's too much to ask."

He wanted to tell her that she meant more to him than just an office employee and friend, but it was the wrong thing to say. He wasn't the right guy for Mindy. She was too sweet to handle a hard guy like him. He wanted her, but he didn't want to take advantage, and if he wasn't careful he would. She deserved better than a few nights in his bed, the length of his usual relationships with women. If she was even interested.

The thought she might not feel the same fierce attraction to him that he felt for her did not sit well.

"We're friends," he said. "Friends help each other. I've got the skills you need right now to keep you safe. Okay?"

She studied him for several long seconds, but he couldn't read her thoughts.

"Okay…" she said reluctantly.

Jax paid the bill and they headed back to the office.

"I need to call Gunderson, see if the cops have turned up anything on the van. Then I'm going to pay a visit to Curt Wyman."

"What?"

"I want to talk to him, see what he has to say. You don't think he's involved, but we need to be sure. I'll call Maddox, have him come over and stay at your place while I'm gone."

"If you're going to talk to Curt, I'm coming with you."

"If Wyman's behind the attempt, he might not be alone. Anything could happen. I want you somewhere safe."

She turned on the sidewalk and propped a hand on her hip. "I'm going, Jax. I realize you know a lot more about this kind of thing than I do, but I know Curt and he isn't going to open up to you. Not the way he will with me."

He didn't miss the determined set of her features. The look in her eyes said she was not backing down. He was impressed. He was a former navy SEAL. Most women did what he said without question. This was the second time Mindy had stood up to him. He was learning something new about her. Mindy Stewart was a lot tougher than she looked.

Plus he had a hunch she was right.

"Well?"

"All right, fine, you can go. Let me make that call to Gunderson, then we'll go."

He opened the door to the office, and she walked past him into the waiting area. "You know where Curt lives?" she asked.

"I'm a detective, remember? I know where he lives."

Mindy flicked him an impertinent glance that had him biting back a grin. She walked over to her desk, drawing his attention to the stretch jeans curving over her sweet little ass, and inwardly he groaned.

Forcing his thoughts back to the job, he sat down at his desk and phoned Walt Gunderson. "It's Ryker," he said. "Anything new on the Stewart case?"

"Not much. We picked up the van on some street cam video. Lost it in the warehouse district, but it gives us a place to look. Too bad they disabled the cameras in your parking lot." Both cameras had been taken out with a single shot each. These guys had been prepared.

"By now Chase probably has them back online," he said. "But that doesn't help us."

"No, it doesn't. I'll let you know if we come up with something new."

"Thanks." Jax didn't mention the possible ransom motive. If the lead proved false, information about Mindy's connection to three million dollars' worth of trust fund money wasn't something he wanted floating around.

He hung up the phone and headed for the front desk. "You ready?"

Jax wasn't looking forward to a visit with Mindy's old boyfriend. But he had to admit he was curious.

CHAPTER SIX

WITH THE WEATHER improved from the day before and the Saturday traffic fairly light, it wasn't a bad drive to Curt Wyman's expensive condo in Uptown Dallas. The guard recognized her and let them pass without comment. Mindy rode in silence next to Jax as the glass elevator whisked them up from the slick, futuristic lobby to the fourteenth floor.

"He might not be home," she said as they reached the front door. "He liked to play golf with some of his clients on the weekends."

But Curt answered the bell, his eyes widening at the unexpected sight of her standing out in the corridor. "Mindy!" He was an inch taller than Jax, with an athletic build and glossy blond hair neatly combed. When he leaned down and hugged her, Jax's body went tense.

"I can't believe you're really here," Curt said.

Mindy pulled away from him, embarrassed at the unexpectedly warm greeting. "Curt, this is Jaxon Ryker. He's a private detective. We need to talk to you."

Curt's gaze went to Jax, slid over the powerful, heavily muscled body outlined by his snug, dark blue T-shirt and jeans. The faint outline of a semiautomatic pistol bulged beneath the fabric at his waist.

Curt stared at Jax, whose features looked hard. One of his big biceps flexed, and Mindy could almost smell the testosterone in the air.

"May we come in?" She eased between the two men. "It's really important, Curt."

"Of course. You know you're always welcome." Tossing Jax a dark glance, he stepped back to let them pass, and she walked into a living room stacked with cardboard boxes.

"You're moving?"

"Things happen. I'm out of jail, which you obviously know. I'm starting over so I need to make some changes."

"Or maybe not," Jax drawled. "Maybe you could keep your fancy lifestyle—if you could get your hands on Mindy's mother's money. Isn't that right, Wyman?"

Curt frowned and shook his head. "What are you talking about?"

"Three men tried to kidnap me Friday night," Mindy said. "Jax thinks they were planning to torture me until I signed over my mother's trust fund money."

The color washed out of Curt's face. "I don't understand." He was a good-looking guy, and yet he no longer held the slightest appeal for her.

"You knew about the trust," Jax said. "Your burglary scheme failed, and you needed money, so you went after Mindy."

Curt turned toward her, his gaze pleading. "I'd never hurt you, Mindy. I—I loved you. I know I didn't show it when we were together, but it's true. I know I don't deserve you, but I'd do anything if I could have you back."

"You're right, Wyman. You don't deserve her. Where were you last night?"

Curt's gaze swung to Jax. "I went on a date with a girl I just met. I've been trying to put my life back together, but the evening was a complete and total bust. She wasn't Mindy. It didn't take me long to figure that out. Her name's Margaret Aimes. You can call her, verify I was with her until after midnight."

He was telling the truth. Mindy could always tell when he was lying.

Jax's stare didn't waver. "Give me her name and number."

Curt nodded, left to retrieve a pen and paper, and wrote down the phone number. He walked over and handed it to Jax, but his attention returned to Mindy. "If I could do things over, I would. I'm really sorry, Mindy."

A flicker of sadness moved through her. There was a time when she had hoped they would have a future together. "I'm glad you got a second chance. I hope you make it work."

They left the condo and took the elevator back down to the underground lot.

"You believe him," Jax said as he helped her into the pickup.

Mindy nodded. "I could always tell when Curt was lying. He didn't do it often, and he was never any good at it."

Jax rounded the Dodge and climbed in behind the wheel. "You know he's still in love with you."

She glanced out the window as he started the engine. Was it possible? She had no idea, but it really didn't matter. "I meant what I said. I hope he makes his second chance work."

She could feel Jax's dark eyes on her. "If he straightens himself out, you interested in going back to him?"

Curt compared to Jaxon Ryker? No contest. "I'm over him. I was never really in love with him. I just wanted to be. I enjoyed his company and I liked having a man in my life. I miss that." She had always wanted a home and family. She still did. Just not with Curt Wyman.

Jax looked like he wanted to say something, but instead he focused on backing up and pulling the truck out onto the street.

"I should have taken something out of the freezer for dinner," she said as the pickup rolled back toward her apartment. "With everything that's been happening, I forgot."

"You cook?" He seemed surprised.

She shoved her glasses up on her nose and hooked her hair back over her ear. "My grandmother grew up on a farm outside Dallas. She was a fantastic cook. She raised me, so yes, I like to cook." She smiled. "I'm really good at it."

A low groan slipped from Jax's throat. "What if we stop at the store and pick up whatever you need?"

She laughed. "We don't have to do that. I keep a lot of stuff in the pantry. I can make pasta or something. Do you like Italian?"

"Hell, yes."

She smiled. "I'll make a salad to go with it and we'll be fine."

Except that when they got to her home and Mindy found her front door pried open, thoughts of supper shot right out the window. The entire apartment looked as if an earthquake or a tornado had totaled the place.

"Oh my God!"

Jax's HK45 slid easily out of its holster. "Stay here." He started forward, the gun gripped in both hands, panning the living room for any sign the intruders might still be there.

"Oh no, Muffin!" Mindy bolted forward, but Jax's arm shot out, blocking her way.

"I said stay here!" he said sharply, but softened his tone when she shrank back from him. "Let me check things out first, make sure it's safe, okay? I'll be right back."

Her color returned, and she nodded. He made a sweep of the apartment, checking the bathrooms, under the bed, the closets, but whoever had been there was gone.

The apartment was in complete disarray, sofa and chairs overturned, drawers left open, the books on the shelves knocked onto the floor. The place was a mess, but it wasn't vandalized. The apartment had been methodically and thoroughly searched.

He found Muffin beneath an overturned chair next to the kitchen table, holstered his weapon, knelt and extended a hand. "It's all right, sweetie. You're okay."

The cat meowed and crept slowly toward him. Jax stroked a hand over her fur, then scooped her against his chest. When he looked up, Mindy was standing in the kitchen doorway.

Unlike his SEAL teammates, clearly she wasn't afraid to disobey his orders. He almost smiled.

"She's okay." He handed her the cat, which she cuddled against her full breasts. He had never been jealous of a cat before. He sighed. There was a first time for everything.

Her hand shook as she stroked the cat. "She's all I really care about." She sniffed and dragged in a shaky breath, but didn't cry. "The rest is just stuff."

Her positive attitude was one of the things he liked best about her. "That's exactly right."

"Do you…do you think the break-in is just a coincidence? Teenagers, maybe, who did this for fun?"

The front door had been jimmied open, probably with a crowbar. "I don't believe in coincidence," he said. "And teenagers might vandalize your place for some warped idea of fun, but this place was searched. Whoever did it was looking for something."

"What?"

"No idea."

"Should we call the police?"

It was definitely a crime scene, and probably linked to the abduction attempt. They needed to phone Lieutenant Gunderson. Maybe the CSIs could come up with some prints or something. He'd get to it, but he preferred to stay one step ahead.

"First I want you to take a look around, see what's missing. Try to touch things as little as possible."

She nodded, started walking around the apartment, surveying the damage. Things were moved and overturned, the medicine chest emptied into the bathroom sink, the kitchen canisters dumped out on the counter. The desk in her bedroom had been thoroughly searched.

She sighed as she walked back into the living room. "Good thing I had my laptop with me."

"Yeah."

She glanced at the destruction in the apartment. "They made a terrible mess, but they didn't go out of their way to destroy things for no reason. Most of it can be put back the way it was."

"They were definitely searching for something."

"Some of my flash drives are missing. That's the only thing I noticed. The only information on them was my personal QuickBooks accounts, my tax records, stuff like that. I had photos on one of the drives, but they're also on my laptop so I didn't really lose them."

"What about the trust account info?"

"The backup for my mom's checking account was on one of the drives, but it's just her monthly bills and personal expenses. There's nothing about the trust fund, no mention of how much is in it, and nothing that would give them any way to access the money. That was always handled by Mr. Handley."

"Must have been hoping to find something they could use."

She glanced around and her shoulders sagged. "I guess."

Jax mentally ran through possibilities, didn't immediately come up with anything. "Call the bank and put a hold on your checking accounts, just in case. I'll call Gunderson. As soon as the cops take our statements, we'll head over to my place, spend the night there." He'd call Chase and Hawk as soon as he got home. Maybe they could come up with a workable theory.

Mindy surveyed the mess around her. "What about my apartment?"

"We'll come back in the morning, feed Muffin and clean the place up."

Her eyes gleamed, and seeing her so close to tears made his chest ache. "I always go see my mother on Sunday mornings."

"Not a problem. We'll make it work." He forced himself not to reach out and touch her. "Go ahead and make that call, then go pack an overnight bag."

She walked a few steps away, pulled out her cell and phoned the bank, then started picking her way through the debris to her bedroom.

Jax sighed. As soon as they were finished talking to

the police, he was taking her home with him. He had fantasized about Mindy Stewart spending the night in his bed.

He'd never dreamed if that night actually came, he'd be sleeping on the sofa in his living room.

CHAPTER SEVEN

MINDY WALKED THROUGH the door of Jax's apartment. He followed close behind her, a bag of groceries in his left hand, his right free to reach his weapon. She had never imagined having a bodyguard, but she was glad Jax had volunteered for the job.

On the way to his house, he had suggested they order pizza or Chinese takeout, but she figured as a bachelor he ate that a lot. He'd been disappointed that he didn't get the home-cooked meal, so she'd persuaded him to stop at the market. They were having spaghetti and meatballs, French bread and a salad with herb vinaigrette.

Not that she was all that hungry.

Still, she needed to stay healthy and to keep up her spirits. She believed in Jax. He was working with Hawk, Chase and the Dallas police. They would figure out what was going on. In the meantime, Jax would keep her safe.

His one bedroom apartment was Spartan, with a dark brown tweed sofa and chairs in the living room, a coffee table made from the crosscut slab of a redwood tree varnished to a glossy sheen, and a huge flat-screen TV.

The place was masculine in the extreme and suited him perfectly. It was also immaculately clean. Jax was former military. The lessons he had learned had obviously stayed with him.

The kitchen was larger than her own. As Mindy started cooking dinner, water boiled in a pot on the stove, steaming up the room and the lenses of her glasses. She took them off and set them on the windowsill. She could see without them, just not that well, but certainly enough to cook. She returned to stirring the spaghetti sauce, simmering in the skillet, and looked up to see Jax walking in.

Her breath hitched. He was the hottest, sexiest man she had ever seen.

"Smells great," he said.

Mindy looked down and stirred the sauce. "I hope you like it."

"You cook for Wyman?" Jax asked.

"Sometimes. He preferred going out most nights."

"If you were my woman, I'd have a hard time letting you out of the house." He smiled. "And you can cook, too. How much better does it get?"

A flush stole over her. *If she was his woman?* She refused to let herself imagine it.

He grabbed the wooden spoon off the counter, reached around her to scoop up a bite and swore under his breath when he burned his tongue.

"Be careful," she said.

He just smiled. "It's delicious." He was standing so close she could feel the muscles across his chest moving against her back. The front of his jeans rubbed against hers where they curved over her behind.

She almost moaned.

Jax eased away. "So…you and Wyman, you were pretty serious for a while, before he started drinking and doing drugs."

She nodded. "Smoking pot mostly, but still…"

The pasta and sauce were done. She turned off the

stove and turned to face him. "That wasn't the only reason we broke up. There were...other issues."

"Yeah, like what?"

Oh, boy. She wished she hadn't opened this particular Pandora's box. "We were...um...incompatible in other ways." She could feel the color rising in her cheeks. Jax noticed, and his dark eyes sharpened.

"You mean physical ways? You two weren't compatible in bed?"

She moistened her lips, barely able to force out the words. "That's right."

Jax's gaze held hers. "Why not?" He seemed to be demanding an answer. Her breathing went shallow. Her heart beat too fast. Did she have the courage to tell him?

"Curt was pretty much...um...a beta kind of guy. He liked me to...um...take the lead in the bedroom. But that's just not my thing."

She had barely seen him move, but suddenly he was closer, just inches away. "So you like a man who takes charge."

She swallowed. She could see the heat in his eyes, feel the hunger in every muscle in his body. He wanted her. This was her chance to fulfill every fantasy she'd ever had about Jaxon Ryker.

She looked into his hard, handsome face. "Yes."

One step and he was pressed full-length against her. A big hand slid into her hair to cup the back of her head and hold her in place as his mouth came down over hers. Her eyes closed and her lips parted. Jax was kissing her, deeply and thoroughly, the way she had always imagined.

She moaned and he deepened the kiss, ravaging her mouth, sending delicious shivers through her body, and still it wasn't enough.

"You want this?" he asked as he pressed his lips against the side of her neck. "You want me?"

Her breath hitched. "Jax… I've wanted you for so long."

A low groan escaped. "Mindy, baby…" He kissed her again, and then he was lifting her into his arms and carrying her out of the kitchen and down the hall to his bedroom.

He kissed her as he set her down beside his king-size bed and began to strip off her clothes. His big hands were everywhere, unbuttoning her blouse and tossing it away, unfastening her bra and sliding it off her shoulders.

He cupped her breasts, lifted and caressed them with a reverence she had never imagined, then he lowered his head to take the fullness into his mouth. A soft moan escaped as he explored and tasted and drove her insane. Desire rolled through her, thick and hot. Her head fell back, shifting her long hair across her back.

Jax returned to kissing her, and for a few precious moments, her passion-fogged brain functioned enough to shove up his T-shirt, urging him to strip it off over his head. Jax complied.

Hard muscle surrounded her, deep sculpted valleys, six-pack abs, toned pecs, the perfect fan of curly dark chest hair, narrowing down in a single line that disappeared into the top of his jeans. She loved that he didn't have Curt's pale, hairless chest. Jax was all man and proud of it.

She pressed her mouth against a flat copper nipple, and a shudder rolled through his powerful body.

"I've got to have you, baby. I know I shouldn't. I know it isn't right, but I need you. Tell me I'm what you want, too."

"Yes… Oh, yes, Jax. Please…"

"Jesus, honey…" The next thing she knew she was naked and he was lifting her, settling her in his big bed. He left her long enough to strip off his clothes, then he joined her on the mattress and started kissing her again.

"I want everything from you," he said, his hands moving over her breasts, skimming lower, sliding hotly, expertly down her body, touching, stroking, making her burn. "I want everything you're willing to give. But I promise I won't rush you."

She whimpered. She wasn't that experienced with men, as apparently Jax could tell. Mindy pulled his head down and rained kisses all over his face, kissed the corners of his mouth.

Jax framed her face between his palms and kissed her deeply again. She wanted more—wanted all of him.

"I need you," she said. "Please, Jax…"

A growl came from low in his throat. He stroked and teased, didn't stop until she was pleading, begging him to take her. His heavy weight pressed her down in the mattress, skin to skin, hard muscle to feminine softness.

Pleasure rolled through her, sweet and thrilling as he finally claimed her, his movements sure and deep. Even with the difference in their size, somehow her body meshed perfectly with his. She picked up the rhythm he set and heard his low growl of passion.

He increased the pace, took her and took her. A shattering climax struck, sending her over the edge, but Jax didn't slow. Instead, he drove her up to a second towering peak before his muscles tightened and he followed her to release.

Mindy clung to him, her skin damp, soft pleasure pulsing through her as, little by little, they began to spiral down. She could feel the thudding of his heart, felt the brush of his lips in a last soft kiss, before he left to dispose of protection. When he returned, he cuddled her against him spoon-fashion and just held her.

"That was amazing," she said.

Jax chuckled. "I'd take you again, but you've had one helluva day."

She flushed, pleased to know he wanted her again so soon. She loved the way he felt wrapped around her, loved that he made her feel so safe. She was drowsy but not really sleepy. She wasn't used to having sex more than once, but with Jax the idea shot a surge of heat right to her core.

"Maybe having some dinner would help you regain your strength," she said with a smile, surprised she felt comfortable enough to tease him.

Faint laughter rumbled through him. "That sounds like a challenge." He kissed the side of her neck, lightly nipped an earlobe. "Dinner's done. Why don't we wait, heat it up a little later?"

Mindy smiled, rolled onto her back and laced her fingers in his short dark hair. "Why don't we heat things up right now?"

Jax laughed and kissed her.

The second round of lovemaking was as good as the first. Everything would have been perfect, except that someone might be trying to kidnap—or maybe even kill—her.

CHAPTER EIGHT

"I WANT TO know what you're doing to find that flash drive." Susan DeMarco sat across from Elliot Russo in the living room of an elegant suite at the Houston St. Regis Hotel. She had flown down in the company jet ostensibly on business, but in reality it was purely an excuse to get away from her overbearing husband and relieve some of her own sexual tension.

"If that joker from her office hadn't interfered, the girl would have handed the drive over—I can guarantee you that."

"That *joker* is Jaxon Ryker. He's a navy SEAL. Your men should have been smart enough not to take him on."

Elliot clenched his jaw but made no reply.

"Apparently, you didn't have any better luck at her apartment," she said.

"The men looked hard. They took every drive they could find, but I checked them out and none of them was the right one."

"That only makes things worse. Do you know what will happen if the information on that flash drive gets out? Jonathan will divorce me, and I'll lose everything."

"Maybe she doesn't know she has it. If she knew, she could have blackmailed you months ago."

"I can't take that chance. Ryan swore he only made one copy of the video, and she was the only person besides him who had access. She has to be the one who has it."

"Why don't you try offering her money? She's a fucking receptionist. She can't exactly be rolling in dough. She took the side job with Shipman to make some extra cash. Offer her ten thousand. For someone in her position, that's a lot of money."

"It's common knowledge how much Jonathan is worth. If I offer her ten thousand, she'll want a hundred at the very least. And whatever I give her will never be enough. There's no way to know if we have all the copies. We need to finish what we started. Force her to give us the drive, then get rid of her. With her and Ryan both out of the way, it's over and done."

Elliot's sensuous lips thinned. She figured he was silently berating her for being stupid enough to let Ryan make a video of them having sex in the first place. But it had been such a lark at the time, and he had destroyed the evidence right in front of her. At least he'd pretended he had.

She sighed. Elliot was tough and clever, dark and good-looking. He knew people who could handle things, people who would do just about anything for money. As long as she kept him in plenty of cash and sexually satisfied, he was happy to do her bidding.

Susan ran a manicured nail down his cheek. "You took care of it before. I trust you to handle it again."

Elliot's expression filled with dark intent. "I'm the one you could always count on. You know that…even if you forgot for a while."

He was right. Her brief affair with Ryan had led to disaster. He was dead now, but she still wasn't safe.

She gave Elliot a seductive smile. He was five years

younger, but at forty-two, she was still a beautiful woman. And her ruthlessness appealed to him.

"If you bring me the drive," she said, "take care of the girl, and don't leave any loose ends, we'll take a trip together. Go off somewhere for a couple of weeks where no one will find us."

Five-star luxury appealed to both of them; the Bahamas, perhaps, or Turks and Caicos. Elliot would keep her satisfied. She would play to his sexual kinks, and he would stay firmly at the end of her leash.

"I'll need to do some planning," he said. "We can't have any more mistakes."

"Fine, but you need to finish this as soon as possible."

Elliot's hooded gaze slid over her, undressing her with his eyes. He expected a reward, and she was willing to give him one. She could trust Elliot to handle the problem, and things would get back to normal.

She just needed to get the flash drive and get rid of the girl.

HE SHOULDN'T HAVE *done it.* Mindy worked for Chase. She was a valuable member of the crew, part of the family. She was a friend.

Scratch that. Jax had never been able to think of Mindy Stewart as just a friend, not from the first time he had seen her. Certainly not after he'd gotten to know her.

Definitely not after she had spent the night in his bed.

He didn't want to be Mindy's friend. As she lay sleeping curled against him, he asked himself what *did* he want from Mindy?

The answer came swiftly. More of her sweet little

body, no doubt of that. He was fairly sure they didn't have any sexual compatibility issues.

But as he was getting to know her, he realized he wanted more than just physical gratification. From the start, he'd been attracted to Mindy's sweet, feminine nature, had known she was smart. Now he knew she wasn't afraid to stand up to him, knew she was strong in a way he respected and brave in a way he admired.

He liked everything about Mindy Stewart, believed she was someone special. He wanted to see where the relationship might go, see if the incredible attraction he felt for her, and what Mindy seemed to feel for him, could become something deeper.

Something he had been searching for but never allowed himself to actually consider. The odds of finding that special someone, the forever kind who made your life complete, were simply too great. Now he was beginning to believe there was a chance that special someone was right in front of him.

She stirred beside him, shoved heavy dark hair out of her face, looked up at him and smiled.

He reached over and looped a thick curl behind her ear. "Good morning."

"Is it? Morning, I mean?"

"Almost."

Her expression turned troubled, and her soft smile faded. "I have to go see my mom, and then I have to go home and clean up the mess in my apartment."

"Don't worry. We'll get everything done."

"And we still have to figure out what's going on."

"Yeah, we do." He'd been about to get up, let her sleep a little longer, but the sadness in her pretty eyes drew him.

He kissed her, felt her arms slide around his neck and

her heightened breathing. He spent the next half hour distracting her with another round of mind-blowing sex, then left her drowsing while he went to make coffee.

Jax sighed. He was in deep with this sweet, beautiful girl. Deeper than he'd ever been with a woman before. For once, Jax didn't care.

SHE SHOULDN'T HAVE *done it.* As she showered and dressed for the day, Mindy had no doubt sleeping with Jaxon Ryker was a stupid, reckless thing to do. True, it had been wonderful, better than she'd ever imagined.

But it was a fantasy.

Jax wasn't the kind of guy for her. He was too male, too rugged, his life too dangerous and unstable. She needed a guy who was nice and safe, with a good-paying job and a retirement account. The kind of guy who would give her kids and make a good father.

This morning, the notion held little appeal. What man could compete with Jax Ryker? None she had ever met.

They finished their coffee and prepared to head out when a knock sounded at the front door. Jax's hand went to the pistol holstered at his waist—exactly the kind of thing that made him completely unsuitable. He checked the peephole, cast her a glance, and she stepped back out of the way.

Jax pulled open the door.

"Hey, lover! I was hoping you'd be home." A beautiful blonde with long legs and a stunning figure stood outside on the porch.

Every warning Mindy had just given herself flashed through her mind with shocking clarity. Through the crack in the door she could watch the exchange, and it made her insides churn.

"It's not a good time, Candace," Jax said. "I've got company. I asked you not to show up unannounced."

The woman's full lips curved into a pout. She tried to see inside, see who Jax was entertaining, but he blocked her view.

"All right, fine," she said, "if that's the way you want it." She smiled. "Call me when you get a chance. You've got my number. I'm in town for a couple of days."

"I'm busy, Candace."

The woman turned and started walking, her high heels tapping, her round behind swaying seductively. "Think about it, honey," she called over her shoulder. "Remember the fun we had."

Jax closed the door and turned to Mindy. "Sorry about that."

She tried not to feel hurt, tried to ignore the sharp ache stabbing beneath her ribs. "It's none of my business," she said softly, trying to brush past him.

"Wait a minute." Jax caught her shoulders. "It *is* your business. I'm not interested in Candace. I haven't seen her in weeks. The only woman I'm interested in is you."

Her eyes burned. She swallowed past the lump in her throat. "It would never work, Jax. You know it as well as I do. We're just too different."

"It could work. Crazier things have happened, right? Why don't we just concentrate on finding the people who are after you and then we'll see where we are, okay?"

She didn't answer. Her throat was too tight to speak. It was ridiculous. She had known from the start Jax wasn't for her.

The hands on her shoulders tightened, his hold gentle but firm. "Give me a chance," he said. "That's all I'm asking. I know it's a lot, but—"

She set her trembling fingers over his lips to stop the words. Her heart was beating, thudding against her ribs. Jax wanted a chance to be with her? She'd never suspected he was the least bit interested in something permanent, but the look in his eyes was fierce.

It didn't matter. What she'd told him was the truth. "Let's…let's do what you said and figure out what's going on. That has to come first."

He scrubbed a hand over his face. He hadn't shaved that morning, leaving a sexy dark shadow along his jaw. "You're right. Jesus, I'm sorry. I don't know what's the matter with me."

Mindy closed her eyes, refusing to think about it. Jax would regain his senses. Deep down he had to know she was right. It was only a momentary lapse because having sex with her was new to him. He was tired of Candace. Sooner or later, he'd be tired of her, too.

She ignored the pang of sadness that came with the thought.

He led her out to his pickup, and they set off down the road. As he drove toward the Avondale Rehabilitation and Skilled Care Center, Mindy blocked memories of what had happened between them last night. She didn't dare think about it. Couldn't allow herself to imagine it happening again. If she did, heaven help her, she would want him just as much as she had before.

The care center was always busy on Sundays, family members stopping by to see loved ones. The nurse, an auburn-haired woman named Mary, didn't have her mother quite ready for the visit, so Mindy and Jax sat in the lobby to wait.

A folded copy of the *Dallas Morning News* rested on a maple end table next to the mint green vinyl sofa.

Mindy picked it up and began leafing through it. A story at the top of the second page caught her eye.

Murder Victim Identified

The body of Ryan Shipman, reported missing five days ago, was found in a shallow grave east of Ferris. It's believed wild animals uncovered the remains. Though the coroner has not yet confirmed the cause of death, early reports speculate it is the result of a shooting.

MINDY GRIPPED JAX'S ARM.

He looked down at her. "What is it?"

"I know this man. Ryan's the guy I mentioned, the man I did some bookkeeping for a few months back. I can't believe he was murdered."

Jax took the paper out of her hand and skimmed the article, his dark brows drawing together. "It looks like this just happened. He was only missing five days before they found his body." He glanced at her. "First men try to abduct you. Then your apartment is trashed. Now a guy you worked for turns up dead. I don't like it."

A chill swept through her. Mindy didn't like it, either.

The nurse walked up just then. "Your mother is ready for you. She's sitting out in the garden."

They rose, and Jax walked her to the glass door that opened into the shady courtyard in the center of the complex.

"You want me to come with you?" he asked.

"My mother wouldn't know if you were there or not. I won't be long. I'll meet you back in the lobby." She left him there and followed Mary out into the sunshine. It was slightly breezy, the wind shifting through the branches of the trees.

"She's had her breakfast," Mary said, rolling the

chair a little deeper into the shade beneath the tree. "Maybe you could finish the book you've been reading to her."

Mindy nodded. Mary had set the book on the wrought-iron bench at the base of the tree, a Jane Austen novel, *Emma*. Mindy felt a pang. Her mother used to love romance novels. Sitting silently in the wheelchair, Ellen Stewart had aged far beyond her fifty years, her hair now white as snow, her skin deeply lined and nearly translucent.

"Hello, Mom."

Her mother didn't look up, didn't even move, just stared straight out into the garden. A never-changing smile curved her lips. For an instant, Mindy's eyes misted. It never got easier. Seeing the person her mother had become, trying not to think of the vibrant woman she had been before the accident ten years ago. Mindy had been a senior in high school at the time.

She took a deep breath and tried to focus on something more pleasant, the warm day, the soft breeze, the rustle of leaves on the branches overhead. Thoughts of Jax crept in. He was waiting for her in the lobby, there to keep her safe.

A calmness settled over her. Jax was there. She'd be okay. She took a deep breath, sat down on the wrought-iron bench, opened the book and started to read.

CHAPTER NINE

JAX WATCHED MINDY through the glass door leading into the courtyard. He could see her lips moving as she read to her mother, occasionally reaching over and very gently touching the white-haired woman's hand.

It made his chest feel tight. He'd never had a family; his dad left when he was ten, and his mom suffered from depression, and was hooked on alcohol and prescription drugs. He tried not to think what it might be like to have someone as caring as Mindy in his life.

He sighed as he waited for her to finish, pulled out his cell and phoned Detective Gunderson. "It's Ryker. I need you to bring me up to speed on the Ryan Shipman murder."

"What's Shipman got to do with you?"

"Probably nothing, but I need to make sure. I'll let you know if it amounts to anything."

Gunderson filled him in on what the cops had so far. "ME's report's not final, but Shipman took three shots from a .45 caliber, two in the chest and one in the head. He was severely beaten before he was killed, and they cut off his little finger."

"Looks like they wanted something more than just making him dead. Information, maybe?"

"Could be," Gunderson said. "Shipman had a gambling habit. Word is, he'd recently run up a big debt, and his bank accounts were low."

"So whoever he owed likely killed him."

"I don't know. Hard to get money from a dead guy. There's something about it that doesn't feel right. CSIs are still working on the scene. I'll let you know what we come up with."

"I'd appreciate it, Walt."

"By the way, we found the van. It was parked in a vacant warehouse. Interior was set on fire, but the van wasn't completely destroyed. We might find something useful. I'll let you know."

"Thanks."

"You keeping an eye on the girl?"

"You can bet on it."

He hung up the phone when Mindy walked out, a little surprised he was standing by the door, close enough to watch over her, not waiting in the lobby. She'd get used to it. He planned to keep her safe no matter what it took.

His gaze ran over her face. He didn't like how fragile she looked. "You okay?"

She nodded. "It always takes me a while to get past it. I'll be all right in a few minutes."

He set a hand at her waist, letting her know he was there for her, walked her out to his Dodge. He'd made a fool of himself this morning. He was supposed to be doing his job, nothing more.

But he'd broken that code by sleeping with her. Then when Candace had shown up, the look on Mindy's face had reached inside and caught him right around the heart. He was back in control—thank Christ for that. Especially after the Shipman murder.

"Are we going to my apartment next?" she asked as he started the engine.

He glanced over at her and smiled. "Good news on

that front. Chase called. He drove Harper and Lissa over there this morning. Chase talked the manager out of a key and the three of them cleaned the place up. Muffin got fed. She's doing just fine."

Mindy's eyes glistened behind the lenses of her glasses, making them look even bigger and bluer. "They didn't have to do that."

Jax reached across the center console and caught her hand. "They're your friends. They wanted to help. That's what friends do. Everything's okay at your place. We're heading down to the office, meeting Chase, Hawk and Lissa. I talked to Gunderson. I want to run the Shipman murder past them, see what they think."

The two men and Lissa Blayne, the only female detective currently working in the office, a pretty blond former detective in the Dallas PD vice division, were sitting in the conference room drinking coffee from the thermal pot sitting on the side table.

Jax grabbed a bottle of water and handed it to Mindy, filled a foam cup with coffee for himself. They carried the drinks over and sat down at the table.

"How are you holding up?" Chase asked Mindy.

"I'm all right, I guess. Considering…" Mindy's gaze went from Chase to Lissa. "I want to thank you both for what you did this morning. I can't believe you cleaned up my apartment."

Lissa reached over and squeezed her hand. "With all of us working, it wasn't that bad." She smiled. "If my house gets vandalized, you can come over and clean it up, and we'll call it even."

Mindy relaxed and smiled. "Deal."

Jax took a drink of his coffee. "With Shipman's death, we may have another piece of the puzzle." He had explained to Chase on the phone about Ryan Shipman's murder and the man's vague connection to Mindy.

"I filled Hawk and Lissa in after you called," Chase said.

Jax went on to tell them the details of Ryan's death. "Shipman's body was buried. I don't think the killers expected it to be found, but apparently, wild animals dug up the grave. The thing is, he was tortured before they shot him."

"Oh, God," Mindy said.

Jax glanced her way, felt a pang at the pallor of her face.

"Payback or information?" Maddox asked.

"I'm thinking information," Jax said. "He was beaten, but they only got as far as taking a finger before he gave them what they wanted."

A muted sound slipped from Mindy's throat. He wished she didn't have to hear this, but her life was on the line.

Chase's attention swung to her. "I assume the work you did for Shipman involved bookkeeping." Part of her job at The Max.

"Yes. It was several months before I came to work here."

"A temp position while you were working for De-Marco Staffing?" Chase asked.

"No. I did it on the side to make a little extra. Susan referred me to Ryan as a favor to help him save money."

"What did Shipman do for a living?" Lissa asked.

"He owned a small construction company. He worked out of an office in his house. With the different subcontractors, it required a lot of bookkeeping, and he got behind."

"You work at his house or yours?" Jax asked.

"Both."

"His computer or yours?" he asked.

"I used my own. I worked off the flash drives he provided. He kept financial information on a number of them." Her eyes widened. "You don't think—"

"That could be the link," Jax said, shifting forward in his chair. "The only thing you found missing from your apartment after the break-in were your flash drives."

She looked up at him. "Maybe they think I have one that belonged to Ryan."

With Shipman dead and her apartment trashed, it wasn't that far-fetched.

Chase shook his head. "None of this makes sense. You worked for Shipman months ago. If the incidents are connected, why the delay? Why was Shipman killed now? And if his death is connected in some way to you, why did they wait so long to come after you?"

"Good question," Maddox said.

Jax sipped his coffee, his mind going over the problem. "Gunderson said Shipman had recently run up a gambling debt. Maybe he figured abducting Mindy for the ransom money was a way to pay off his debt."

"I never mentioned anything about my mother's trust," Mindy said. "There's no way he could have known about it."

"Let's back up a minute," Maddox said. "From the beginning, we've been following the premise that whoever went after Mindy wanted access to her mother's money. But what if that was never what the kidnappers wanted? Maybe they didn't even know about it."

It was an idea Jax had considered. "If this has something to do with the missing flash drives, maybe one of them has something on it the kidnappers want."

"Something worth money to someone else," Chase said.

"You're talking about blackmail," Lissa clarified.

Maddox grunted. "Yeah, instead of money, Shipman got three bullets from a .45 cal."

"I think Chase could be onto something," Lissa said. "Shipman was kidnapped, tortured and murdered. They certainly weren't after his money because he didn't have any."

"An unpaid gambling debt can sure as hell get you killed," Chase said, playing devil's advocate.

"True enough," Jax agreed, but he could feel the idea gaining momentum in his head. "For the moment, let's run with the blackmail theory. Say Shipman had something valuable on a flash drive and Mindy took it home with her by mistake. Maybe the drive got in with the ones that held Shipman's accounting records." Jax swiveled his chair around to look at her. "Is that possible?"

Excitement flushed her cheeks. "I took at least three or four drives home with me every time I went to his house. Each of Ryan's primary subcontractors had a flash drive solely for their own records. It's possible one of his personal drives could have had gotten mixed in with the others."

"I did a little digging on Shipman before I came in," Jax said. "The guy didn't have the best reputation. He was arrested a couple of times on white collar charges, one scam or another. But he always managed to walk. He'd been staying out of trouble for the past few years, but if he owed somebody money, he might have gotten desperate. Blackmail wouldn't be much of a stretch."

"If that's the case," Chase said, "we need the name of his victim and what Shipman had on them."

Jax's gaze returned to Mindy. "If you have that drive, honey, we need to find it. It could be what the kidnappers are after. If it is, they won't stop until they get it."

While Mindy went to search her desk, Maddox cornered Jax. Anger vibrated through every muscle in his big body. "What the hell, bro? She's family. You're supposed to be protecting her not fucking her."

Jax clenched his jaw. "Don't say that. That isn't what it was."

"The way you look at her—you think I wouldn't know?"

"I'm telling you it wasn't like that. Mindy's special. I knew it way before anything happened."

Some of the tension eased from Maddox's wide shoulders. "Son of a bitch. I had a hunch you were in over your head. You've had your eye on her ever since she started working here."

Jax released a slow breath. "I know she deserves someone better. I get that. I know it shouldn't have happened, but I've wanted her for so long. When I realized she wanted me, too, things just got out of hand."

Maddox squeezed Jax's shoulder. "Maybe it'll work out. If that's what you want, I hope it does."

Jax's felt a pinch in his chest. He shook his head. "I don't think so."

"Why not?"

"She doesn't think it could work and she's probably right."

Maddox's intense blue eyes locked on Jax. "You're a navy SEAL, dude. You want something, you go after it. You want it to work, you make it work."

Jax made no reply, but his heart had started beating faster. He was a SEAL. SEALs went after what they wanted.

"You gonna be able to get your head on straight enough to do your job?" Maddox asked.

Jax's features hardened. "Nobody's getting near her."

Hawk relaxed. "Okay, then. Your best bet is to focus on finding that flash drive."

CHAPTER TEN

MINDY SEARCHED HER space at the office, her desk and credenza, every drawer and cubbyhole, though she couldn't imagine how the drive—if there actually was one—could have gotten to The Max in the first place.

She had worked on Ryan's books in her apartment, and that had been months ago. But she *had* transported them back and forth from his place to hers.

She'd done a thorough search of her Volkswagen, still parked in the lot out behind. Ryan's drives were all same brand, she recalled, little silver Kingstons only about a quarter-inch thick and an inch or so long. Easy to lose, though she'd been careful and Ryan had never mentioned any of them missing.

But she could have picked up an extra. What if she had simply dropped it somewhere as she carried it from his house to her car, or her car to her apartment? What if it never showed up again? No way would the kidnappers believe she didn't have it. Not after the trouble they had gone through to get it back.

She thought of Ryan being tortured and killed. Was she partly responsible for his death? If she had accidentally taken the flash drive, was he dead because he couldn't hand it over to them? The notion sent a chill down her spine.

By the time she and Jax had finished searching the car, then her apartment again from top to bottom, it was dark and she was exhausted. She toed off her sneakers and sank down on the floral sofa in her living room. Muffin jumped up in her lap.

"Hello, sweetheart." She stroked a hand over the cat's glossy coat, and Muffin curled up and started to purr.

Jax walked back into the living room. For the past hour and a half, he had been working on his laptop on the desk in her bedroom. He took one look at her sagging shoulders and dejected expression and sat down on the sofa beside her.

Muffin, little hussy that she was, moved over to Jax's lap, and he absently started rubbing beneath her chin.

Mindy leaned against the sofa with a tired sigh. "I don't think it's here."

"You checked your laptop case, right?"

"Only half a dozen times." She looked up at him. "It could be anywhere, Jax. Maybe I never even had it. Maybe there's no such thing as a flash drive with valuable secret information. Maybe we're completely off base."

He shook his head. "I did a little more digging on Shipman, and I think Maddox could be right. The guy was always out for himself. Shipman Construction had a number of one-star reviews, jobs he never finished or didn't stand behind. This feels right. It's the only way all the odd-shaped pieces fit together."

She toyed with the hem of the pink T-shirt she was wearing. "We've looked everywhere and we didn't find it. If you're right, what do we do now?"

"I've been working on that. Something you said has been rolling around in my head. The only link you had to Ryan Shipman was through the owner of DeMarco Staffing."

"Susan DeMarco."

"She's Jonathan DeMarco's wife. Jonathan De-Marco—the billionaire owner of DeMarco Industries. She's the person who told Ryan to call you."

"That's right."

"So how were the two of them connected? I've seen pictures of her. Susan's a beautiful woman. Her husband's thirty years older—younger woman, older man. I had a feeling Chase would know something about them, since he runs in the same megarich social circles, so I called him."

Chase Garrett and his two younger brothers owned Garrett Enterprises, a billion-dollar oil and gas company. They were Dallas elite, just like the DeMarcos.

"According to Chase," Jax continued, "Susan isn't the saint her husband believes her to be. Chase says she's had half a dozen affairs behind her husband's back, but she's always been able to keep them secret. Chase says if DeMarco found out his wife was cheating, he'd divorce her in a heartbeat."

Mindy straightened on the sofa. "You think Susan was having an affair with Ryan?"

"You think it's possible?"

She thought of Ryan Shipman. Late thirties, sandy hair and blue eyes, a lean, athletic build. "As you said, Susan is beautiful, and Ryan was definitely good-looking."

"Yeah, I saw his photo on the internet—along with a couple of mug shots."

Ryan had always been pleasant, on the verge of charming. She couldn't imagine him in an orange jumpsuit. "Now that I think back on it, a couple of times while I was at his house, a woman called—I could tell by the way Ryan was talking to her. Once I remember him saying he would meet her that afternoon at the Westin hotel at the Galleria."

Jax started nodding. "That's good. I'll check it out, see if I can find something that links the two of them."

Mindy watched the gentle glide of Jax's hand over Muffin's fur. Last night, the way he'd touched her, she'd felt like purring herself.

"We're getting closer," Jax said. "I can feel it."

With a sigh, Mindy fell back against the sofa. "I don't know…it's an awful lot of ifs, I-don't-knows and maybes."

"You're right. At the moment it's all conjecture, but that's the way an investigation works. You follow a lead till it solves the puzzle or comes to a solid dead end. My gut is telling me to follow this one."

He glanced at the old-fashioned mahogany clock on the wall. "It's getting late. Tomorrow while you're at the office, I'll take a ride out to the Westin, see what I can find out." Setting Muffin aside, he stood up from the sofa.

Mindy stood up, too, her gaze going to the glass-fronted Bedford clock, the brass pendulum swinging back and forth with a soft ticktock she usually found comforting. It was bedtime. Or close enough.

When she looked over at Jax, she couldn't mistake the hunger in his eyes. He wanted her. He no longer bothered to hide it.

Heat tugged low in her belly, spread all the way down to her toes. The more time she spent with him, the more she wanted him. But the deeper she got involved, the more difficult it would be when it was over.

On the other hand, she'd never felt as alive as Jax made her feel.

"You rather we stay here or spend the night at my place?" he asked.

He wouldn't leave her. She never doubted it. He would protect her until the danger was over.

"I'd rather stay in my own home," she said.

He walked over to the door and checked the locks, took a walk around the apartment checking windows, making sure there was no one outside. She looked up to see him walking toward her, looking like the hero in an action movie, muscled chest beneath his snug T-shirt, jeans riding low on his hips, a pistol in the holster clipped to his waistband.

His eyes were dark and smoky as they moved over her body then returned to her face. "You said you liked a man who takes charge."

Her pulse kicked up. Soft heat slid into her core. "I—I meant in the bedroom."

A corner of his mouth edged up. "Then I guess that's where I'd better take you."

She gasped as he swept her into his arms, lifted her against his chest and carried her down the hall. He wasn't asking her to make some monumental decision. He was going to make the decision for her, going to make love to her and she was going to enjoy every moment.

Desire washed through her, hot as sin, sweet as honey. Jax carried her into her bedroom, closed and locked the door. Slowly, he released her, letting her body slide the length of his, letting her feel every muscle and sinew, letting her feel his arousal.

Unclipping his holster, he set the gun on the dresser, reached for her glasses and slipped them off her nose, set them next to the gun. His hands slid into her hair, tipping her head back. Mindy moaned as Jax leaned down and very thoroughly kissed her.

SHE WANTED A man who would take the lead? Well, by God, he was going to do just that. Maddox's words rang in his head. He was a SEAL. If he wanted something, he went after it. He had wanted Mindy Stewart for weeks. Months. He had only recently figured out it was more than her body he wanted.

Since he had to begin his campaign somewhere, sex was a good place to start. Jax kissed her until his pulse was pounding and Mindy was gasping for breath, then he paused long enough to strip off her jeans and panties.

He started kissing her again, lifted her as her arms slid up around his neck. He palmed her lush breasts, felt the tips grow hard in his hands.

"Wrap your legs around my waist," he commanded, pressing hot kisses against the side of her neck. His hands slid down her body, over the naked curve of her bottom, cupping each globe to hold her in place as he backed her against the wall.

She looked at him, her big blue eyes cloudy with desire and excitement. She was wet and ready. Jax was more than ready as he buzzed down his zipper and freed himself, took care of protection and eased himself inside.

A soft sigh slipped from her throat, and her hold tightened around his neck. Her breasts were round and heavy, sexy as hell. He loved the feel of her body gloving him so sweetly, loved the way she gave herself so totally into his care. He drove into her, taking his pleasure, stroking her as he moved, determined to make it good for her, good for both of them.

What seemed like seconds later, she started coming,

her body clamping around him so fiercely it was all he could do to hang on to his control. She was responsive to his every touch, every demand of his body. He had never been with a woman who aroused him more or suited him more perfectly.

She came again before he followed her to release, then he carried her over to the bed and stripped off the rest of her clothes.

A blush crept over her skin. "Oh my God, you're still dressed. I didn't even notice."

He chuckled. "I wanted you. I didn't want to wait. Any complaints?"

She smiled and shook her head, moving her heavy mane of hair. "Definitely not. Curt insisted we always make love in bed."

Jax grinned. "Then you're in for some surprises, honey. I promise you."

Mindy laughed, and Jax frowned. "Wait a minute. Curt wasn't the only guy—"

"No, of course not. But it had to be special, or it just wasn't worth it, and that hasn't happened very often."

He tried and failed not to be glad.

Jax headed for the bathroom. By the time he got back, Mindy was asleep. Jax joined her on the bed, snuggled her against him and kissed the top of her head.

She belonged to him. He had never felt that way about a woman before, but he could feel the rightness deep in his bones. All he had to do was convince Mindy.

Jax sighed into the darkness. First, he had to find the men who threatened her. Until then, he had to keep her safe.

CHAPTER ELEVEN

AFTER A SECOND night of glorious sex, Mindy went to work with Jax on Monday morning. Before he left her at the office to drive out to the Westin hotel, he checked with Jason Maddox to be sure his friend would protect her until his return.

It didn't sit well with Mindy. She might not be a former police detective like Lissa and Wolfe, or former military like Jax and Maddox and some of the other guys in the office, but she was smart, and she was used to taking care of herself.

She didn't want to be a burden to her friends. She was an independent woman and she wanted her life back.

Thinking about it as she sat behind the reception desk, her shoulders slumped. She would never have her life back exactly the way it was. She would have to quit her job as soon as this was over. No way could she come to the office every day, see Jax and not yearn to be with him.

But the two of them would never work. They were just too different. She was a bookkeeper-receptionist, planning to take night classes to get her CPA accounting degree. He was a hot navy SEAL, a private investigator who took perilous assignments, and did God only knew what else. He lived on danger, while she wanted a quiet life with a husband and kids.

There was no way she could be with him, and once she ended things, it would hurt too much to be around him. Jax Ryker was a very virile man. A man like that had needs, and she wasn't willing to be his booty call no matter how much she wanted him. Which meant he would turn to other women, and there was no way could she could handle that. She hadn't forgotten the crushing pain she'd felt when Candace had appeared at his door.

She forced her thoughts back to the ledgers she was working on, glanced up a few minutes later to see Lissa walking up to her desk. She stood half a foot taller than Mindy, around five-nine, slender, with short, softly curling blond hair.

"Want to take a walk?" Lissa asked. "Maddox can keep an eye on things, and I need a cup of coffee. How about you?"

She could certainly use a cup. "That sounds great." Rising, she followed Lissa into the break room. The smell of coffee hit her as Lissa filled a mug decorated with a cowboy hat on the side and handed it over. She poured a mug for herself, and they sat down at the round, Formica-topped table.

Lissa took a sip of coffee. "I thought the Sunday meeting was very productive, didn't you?"

Mindy sighed. "I guess. We still don't know what's going on."

"No, but we came up with a couple of solid working theories. Jax is tracking one of them down right now. I know Jason and Chase are both trying to come up with something useful."

"I know." Mindy's hands tightened around the mug. "I can't tell you how much I appreciate everyone's help. It's just… I feel so useless."

"Hey, we all have our strengths. Jax and the rest of

us—we're each involved in law enforcement in some form or another. That's what we do. We want to help you solve this."

Mindy took a drink of coffee and sat back with a sigh. "I hope it doesn't take too much longer."

Lissa smiled. "Just think of the time you get to spend with Jax." She lifted her mug, looked at Mindy over the rim. "How's that going, by the way?"

Surely Jax wouldn't have told Lissa. Surely not. "I'm not…not exactly sure what you're talking about."

"Seriously? You're going to take that route?"

Mindy straightened. "How did you know?"

"It wasn't hard to figure out. I could tell you were attracted to him when I saw the way you looked at him in the office. It's tough to hide that from another woman. When the two of you walked into that meeting yesterday morning, it was written all over your face."

Mindy stared down at the dark liquid in her mug. "I'll have to quit my job when this is over. I feel bad about that. I really like my job."

Lissa's features tightened. "Who says you have to quit? That's a load of bull crap. Just because you and Jax hooked up—"

"It's not that. Not exactly. Once it's over, I won't be able to remember what a great time we had and just let it go. I know that's what men do, women, too, but I'm just not that way."

Lissa studied Mindy's face and one of her blond eyebrows arched up. "You aren't falling in love with him, are you?"

Mindy managed not to glance away, but the truth must have shown in her face. What she felt for Jax went way beyond physical attraction. For months, she had watched the way he treated people, everyone from the delivery boy to Chase's wealthy friends. It made no difference to Jax.

She had noticed his intelligence, his honesty and courage, his loyalty to his friends. In the past few days, she had learned he was all the things he seemed and more.

Lissa reached over and squeezed her hand where it rested on the table. "It doesn't matter. This isn't over yet. Jax cares about you. I know he does. Give it some time. Who knows what could happen?"

But Mindy knew. She swallowed, wishing the conversation had never come up. She finished her coffee and stood. "I've got to get back to work. I've got some ledgers I need to bring up to date."

She walked over to the sink and washed out her mug, set it in the rack to dry. "I really do appreciate everyone's help." Turning, she walked out of the break room, back to her desk up in front.

JAX PARKED THE Dodge in the parking lot of The Westin Galleria and walked into the lobby. It wasn't a five-star luxury hotel, but with its open interior, modern design, sleek wood paneling, thick columns and beige marble floors, it was nice.

It was part of the Galleria shopping complex, a convenient place for shoppers to stay when they came to Dallas to spend their hard-earned money. It would also be a convenient place for a lovers' tryst, Jax thought, the perfect excuse to be in the area if either party happened to be spotted. *I was just out shopping, honey—no big deal.*

In a pair of tan slacks and a dark blue blazer, a white shirt open at the throat, Jax walked up to the front desk.

If you wanted information from a desk clerk, dressing well always gave you an edge.

"Checking in, sir?" the desk clerk asked. He was in his late thirties, wearing glasses and a dark brown sports coat.

"I just need a little information," Jax said. "I'm hoping you can help." Reaching inside his jacket, he pulled out a photo he'd printed off the internet and set it on the counter. "Any chance this guy looks familiar? His name is Ryan Shipman."

The clerk looked at the photo. "I'm afraid not. But even if he did, it's against our policy to give out a guest's personal information."

"The guy in the photo was murdered. Sooner or later the police will be asking you the same questions I'm asking you now."

"Are you a cop?"

Jax reached back into his pocket, pulled out his badge wallet and flipped it open. "Detective. I work private." He dug a folded hundred-dollar bill out of the wallet and smoothed it open on the counter. "How about any of the other employees? Like I said, the cops will be after the same information. I'm sure you'll want to cooperate with them, so the info's going to get out anyway."

The clerk eyed the hundred and picked up the photo. "I'll ask in the back." He disappeared behind the wall and came back a few minutes later with one of the other clerks, a young woman in her twenties with chocolate eyes, coarse black hair and an olive complexion.

"I've seen this man," she said. "But I don't remember his name. It was several months back. He came in a couple of times a week for at least two months. It was during my shift, so I was the one who checked him in."

"In the afternoon?"

"It would have been during the day. I don't work in the evenings."

"Was he by himself or with someone?"

"He was always alone. He was good-looking, a little flirty, a definite player type if you know what I mean. I was pretty sure he was meeting a woman."

"Do you remember if he paid for the room or if it was paid for by someone else?"

"It was always prepaid online. I just checked him in and handed him a room key."

Jax passed her the hundred. "If someone can give me a name or a decent description of the woman Shipman was meeting, there's another hundred in it." He took out a business card and handed one to each of the two clerks. "My cell number's there. Call me."

"I'll ask around." The young woman stuck the card in her jacket pocket and disappeared behind the wall.

Jax turned back to the male clerk, *Bob*, his name tag read. "Thanks for the help."

"What about the police?" Bob asked.

"I'm sure you'll be hearing from them sooner or later." He still didn't have enough to call Gunderson, but if his theory proved correct, eventually he would.

"You get someone to come up with the info on the woman, and I'll pony up a hundred for each of you."

The desk clerk's interest stirred. "I'll ask around." He tucked the card into his pocket as Jax turned and started walking.

At least they knew Shipman had been there, just as Mindy had said. Who he'd met was still speculation. Jax hoped he'd get a call from someone on the hotel staff, but time was of the essence. He needed to talk to Tabitha Love, the company computer whiz, get her to do

some digging, see if she could come up with the name
on the credit card used to pay for the room.

He quietly swore as he slid behind the wheel of the
Dodge. He had a couple of errands to run, some leads
he needed follow up on. It was going to take a couple
of hours when he needed to get back to the office, back
to Mindy. Even with Hawk Maddox there to protect
her, he worried.

The longer this dragged on, the more likely something would go wrong, and Mindy could get hurt.

By the time Jax pulled into the parking lot behind
The Max, the always efficient Tabitha Love had called
him with the information he needed.

"DeMarco Staffing," Tabby said. "Company credit
card, booked through the hotel webpage. You were right
on the money, Jax-man."

Jax could almost see her grinning, the silver hoop
in her sleek black eyebrow glinting. She was tall, with
short black hair shaved on the sides and moussed on
top. Tabby was uniquely her own person. Jax had never
met anyone like her—or anyone half as smart.

"Thanks, Tab, you're the best."

Tabby laughed. "Can't argue with that."

Jax chuckled as he ended the call.

As soon as he walked into the office, he collected
Mindy and Lissa, and pulled Maddox and Chase in for
a meeting. Since Wolfe had clients in the conference
room, they walked down the block to Clancy's, which
was quiet this late in the day.

The bartender, a string bean of a guy named Marty
O'Halloran, and a waitress named Bridget, were the
only ones working. Jax led the group to a long wooden
table in the corner, and they all sat down.

Bridget took their drink orders, iced tea for Jax and

Lissa, water for Mindy, beers for Jason and Chase. Once everyone had their drinks, he brought them up to speed on the case.

"Way it looks, Shipman and Susan DeMarco were definitely involved in an affair. According to one of the desk clerks, it was several months back, but Shipman checked in a couple of times a week, and the room was paid for with a DeMarco Staffing credit card."

"Now that I think about it," Mindy said, "Susan mentioned shopping at the Galleria more than once."

"Perfect cover if she ran into someone she knew," Chase said.

"Like her husband," Maddox added.

"Let's assume Shipman was blackmailing Susan," Jax said. "Threatening to go to her husband. He'd need proof of the affair."

Lissa sat forward. "Pictures of them together in a hotel room would certainly work."

"Better yet—nude photos or a sex video," Maddox drawled, sending color into Mindy's cheeks.

Jax nodded. "An insurance policy for when things started going south between them."

"Which, sooner or later, they would," Chase said. "Susan DeMarco isn't known for her fidelity. I did a little more digging. It isn't exactly common knowledge, but one of the caddies at the country club says she's damned fickle when it comes to her lovers. Unlike Shipman, they had the good sense to keep their mouths shut."

Maddox picked up his longneck bottle and took a swallow of beer. "Instead of fading quietly into the sunset, Shipman planned ahead. He made the flash drive in case he ever got into a financial bind."

"Like needing money to pay off a gambling debt," Chase said.

"He had proof he figured was worth big money," Lissa added.

"But why would anyone think I'm the one who has Ryan's sex video?"

Jax's dark eyes hardened. "Because while they were torturing him, Shipman told them you had it. By then he'd figured out he'd given it to you by mistake."

"Or accidentally given you a copy," Maddox said.

"Even more likely," Jax agreed. "Since he'd need something to sell in the first place."

Silence fell around the table. Just the sound of ice clinking in glasses and beer bottles being hoisted and set back down.

"Okay," Mindy said at last. "If we follow that logic, what happens next? The kidnappers still want the flash drive—and I still don't have it."

Jax took a drink of his tea, set the glass back down. "We can't find the drive, but the kidnappers don't know that. We'll send Susan a message, tell her we've got what she wants."

Mindy's eyes widened. "Set a trap?"

"Exactly. If we're right about all this, we won't have to go after Susan and whoever she hired to do her dirty work. We'll get them to come to us."

CHAPTER TWELVE

"THAT LITTLE TRAMP." Susan paced back and forth across the living room of Elliot's sleekly modern, seventeenth-floor apartment overlooking the city. She didn't come here often. She didn't want to risk being seen, but today was important.

"And to think I actually liked her." She turned, paced back the opposite way. "I helped her get the job working for Chase Garrett. I even gave her my cell number."

"You can't trust anyone these days," Elliot said mildly, taking a sip of his Bombay Sapphire martini.

Susan sighed and thought of the text she had received. "She wants to meet me at noon tomorrow at the Vietnam Memorial at Fair Park. She wants twenty-five thousand for her copy of the video."

"You're lucky. You thought she'd want a hundred."

"There's no way to be sure she hasn't made a dozen more copies. Twenty-five thousand now, fifty the next time. It'll never end until we get rid of her."

She paused in front of the window to look down at the traffic crawling along the street. "And what if she goes to Jonathan? He'd pay a king's ransom to keep the world from knowing he's a cuckold. His pride's too great for that. Jonathan has the best lawyers in the world. I'd get next to nothing."

"I told you I'll take care of her," Elliot said. "You just make sure she comes alone."

Susan thought of the phone call to Mindy that she had made using one of the disposable phones she kept to communicate with Elliot and anyone else she didn't want her husband to know about.

"I told her I'd meet her, but only if she came alone. I told her if she brought her SEAL boyfriend, the deal was off."

"And she agreed?"

"Only if I agreed to the same terms. You were right about the money. She can't wait to get her hands on it. The only stipulation is that I come by myself."

Elliot chuckled, sipped from his long-stemmed martini glass. "Only you won't be alone. I'll be close by, and my men will be in position to take the girl out."

"What about the police?"

"As soon as you have the flash drive, you'll leave. When they find her body, the girl will be in possession of twenty-five thousand dollars. It'll look like a drug deal gone bad. There's no way to connect you to any of this. You'll have the video, and Mindy Stewart will be dead before she gets back to her car."

MINDY SAT ON the brown tweed sofa in Jax's living room. The evening had settled in. The Chinese takeout they'd had for supper was gone, the dishes cleaned up and put away. After the text she had sent, and the return phone call she'd received from Susan, they knew they were on the right track.

Ryan Shipman had been blackmailing his ex-lover. Now he was dead, and Susan believed Mindy had a copy of the drive, for which she wanted twenty-five thousand dollars.

Since the stakes had just gotten dangerously higher, Jax had insisted they stay at his place where DeMarco and her crew were less likely to find them. Muffin was with them, perfectly at home, curled up in the middle of Jax's big bed.

Jason had arrived to help Jax flesh out the plan they had come up with earlier and now sat across from them, sprawled in an overstuffed chair.

"You have to bring in the cops," he argued. "You know it as well as I do. We try to handle this on our own, we'll end up killing some dickwad and winding up in jail."

Jax grunted. "At least Mindy would be safe."

"Stop it, Jax," Mindy demanded. "You need to listen to Jason."

It took another few minutes, but since Jax knew his friend was right, he had grudgingly conceded. They needed help. Lieutenant Gunderson was their best option. Jax called and filled him in as much as possible. The detective was on his way over now.

A knock sounded at the door. When Jax pulled it open, Gunderson walked into the living room. With faint circles beneath his eyes and his light brown hair mussed, he looked even more fatigued than usual.

"I was getting ready to call you anyway," Gunderson said, taking a seat in the empty chair while Jax sat back down on the sofa next to Mindy. "Looks like you've managed to get yourself in the middle of an ongoing homicide investigation."

"How's that?" Jax asked.

"CSI's found evidence that links the Shipman murder to the kidnapping attempt on Ms. Stewart."

Jax sat up straighter. It was the conclusion they had already drawn, but they had needed a way to prove it.

"Shoe print at the murder scene was made by a Giuseppe Zanotti high-top sneaker. Same shoe you reported the night of the attempted abduction. Also, there were tracks in the dirt that matched the tire tread on the white van."

"Son of a bitch," Jax said. Mindy felt a sweep of relief that they were definitely on the right track.

"We also got a print off the inside of the van door. It belongs to a scumbag named Walker Riley. Big bastard, tough and vicious, known for his skill with a knife. Got a bad scar on his right hand from a fight he nearly lost, but didn't. Sound familiar?"

Jax nodded. "Yeah."

"Riley hangs with a couple of ex-cons named A. J. Whiteman and Charley Burns. Burns is average height and weight with pale blue eyes, and Whiteman is tall and thin. Both fit the descriptions you gave of the men in the parking lot."

"Tell me they're in custody," Jax practically growled.

"They're walking around free as air," the detective said. "And if you'd get your head on straight, you'd understand why. These guys are nothing but low-level criminals. If we don't bring in the person who hired them to make the hit on Shipman—the same person behind the kidnapping attempt—Ms. Stewart will still be in danger."

"He's right," Jason said. "Plenty of scumballs ready to step in and do the job if the money's right."

Jax sighed. "That's for sure." He turned back to the detective. "After the phone call Mindy got from Susan DeMarco agreeing to the meet, it's pretty clear Shipman was blackmailing DeMarco for whatever is on the drive he accidentally gave to Mindy."

"Which unfortunately I managed to lose," Mindy said.

Gunderson shifted to face her. "Which is why we're

going to need you to be wearing a wire when you meet Susan DeMarco in the park tomorrow."

Jax shot up from the sofa. "No fucking way."

Gunderson remained unruffled. "Sorry, Ryker, but the only way we're bringing these people down is with hard evidence. We've got the shoe print, the fingerprint from the burned-up van and a hodgepodge of miscellaneous evidence, but it isn't enough. We need direct evidence against Susan DeMarco." He turned and looked straight at Mindy. "We're counting on you, Ms. Stewart, to get it."

"It's too dangerous," Jax argued, pinning the detective with a glare. "DeMarco won't come alone. She'll bring men with her, and their job will be to take Mindy out. We have to figure another way."

She reached over and slid her hand around a powerful bicep, felt the tension running through him. "We don't have time to figure out another way, Jax. We have to do this now while we have the chance. You know Lieutenant Gunderson is right. You and Jason both know it."

"Once we get what we need on DeMarco," the detective calmly continued, "we can round the whole bunch up and bring them in. They'll turn on each other like a pack of jackals. We'll have enough evidence to put them all away, and Mindy will be safe."

Jax scrubbed a hand over his face, making a rasping sound on the stubble along his jaw. Mindy could read his worry, anger and frustration. He knew the detective and Jason were right, and there was nothing he could do but go along with it.

"Okay, fine," he ground out. "She wears a wire. But Maddox and I are there to cover her. We're there and we're in on the op."

"That isn't the way it works," Gunderson said.

"That's the way it's going to work tomorrow—or it isn't going to happen. You want DeMarco for murder? We can get her for you. You just do whatever you need to in order to make your bosses happy."

A long silence fell. With a sigh, Gunderson rose and stalked off to make a phone call. When he returned, Mindy followed the men into the kitchen, and they all sat down at the table.

"You're in," Gunderson said. "Just make sure you don't kill anyone."

Jax eyed him darkly. "Unless, of course, it's self-defense."

Gunderson's mouth tightened, but he didn't argue, and Jax relaxed back in his chair.

The next hour was spent working out a strategy designed to protect Mindy and end up with a recorded confession from Susan DeMarco, along with the arrest of the men who had killed Ryan Shipman.

Mindy prayed it would work.

CHAPTER THIRTEEN

TWO MILES EAST of downtown Dallas, Fair Park encompassed 277 acres of beautifully landscaped ground. Built for the 1936 Texas Centennial Exposition, it contained a complex of museums, entertainment venues, monuments and landmarks, one of which was the Texas Vietnam Veterans Memorial.

The rendezvous was set to take place near the flagpole, in a granite seating area not far from the memorial wall. Trees and buildings surrounded the spot, enough to provide distant cover for SWAT team marksman and other MAX team members—or at least that was the plan.

Jax and Maddox would be closer, there for Mindy's protection if the exchange went wrong. She knew they would do everything in their power to keep her safe— even at the risk of their own lives.

She nervously fidgeted as she drove her little VW Bug down Parry Avenue, turned off the road onto a lane that led to the parking lot closest to the memorial.

Jax and Maddox had left for the park hours ago, as soon as the police arrived at the apartment to provide protection. They needed to recon the area, Jax said, find a secure location to be ready for her arrival at the rendezvous point. They planned to go after the men they were sure would be coming with Susan DeMarco and "quietly take them out."

Mindy didn't ask what that meant. She was pretty sure she didn't want to know.

After Maddox and Gunderson had departed last night, she and Jax had spent the remainder of the evening in bed, Jax making wild, possessive love to her. It was as if he wanted to absorb her into his skin, as if he couldn't get enough of her.

Mindy felt the same. Anything could happen. They both knew it, accepted it.

"I'm crazy about you," Jax had said during a particularly sweet interlude as he drew her down into his arms. "Tell me you feel the same about me."

She couldn't lie to him. If things went wrong tomorrow, she could be killed—or he could be—and they would never see each other again. She swallowed, forced herself to say the words that crowded her throat.

"I love you, Jax. You probably don't want to hear that, and it doesn't change anything, but—"

He came up over her swiftly, silenced her words with a fierce, demanding kiss. "I love you, too, honey. I've never said those words before. I don't want to lose you. I want us to work things out."

Her eyes teared. "Jax…"

"It can work, baby. We can make it work. We'll talk to Chase, convince him to let you keep your job. Say you love me enough to try."

She swallowed past the thick lump in her throat. It was insane. She had dreamed of Jaxon Ryker, dreamed of spending time with him, making love with him, dreamed he would look at her the way he was looking at her now, his dark eyes filled with yearning. But it was only a fantasy. *Wasn't it?*

But what if it wasn't? What if he loved her the way

he said? Because she knew in her heart that she was deeply in love with him.

"I don't want to lose you, either." It was as much as she was willing to say, and it was the truth. Now that she had been with him, giving him up would be the hardest thing she had ever done.

Jax ran a finger along her cheek, leaned down and softly kissed her, accepting the words as enough for now. He made love to her again, slowly and with tender care, and they finally fell asleep.

Morning came way too soon.

Now she was pulling her red VW into a parking space and turning off the engine, taking a couple of deep breaths for courage.

Unconsciously, she touched the wire she was wearing beneath her lavender print blouse. She had dressed in jean leggings and put on a pair of sneakers—in case she needed to run—pulled her long hair into a ponytail for the same reason. Determined to know as much as possible about what she would be doing, she had Googled audio surveillance that morning as soon as she had finished dressing.

Body wires were covert devices you could put in your pockets or on your body to send conversations to a radio surveillance receiver. With the receiver, you could either listen or connect to an audio recorder. The police would be doing both.

A female officer named Pamela Wrigley had brought the device to Jax's apartment, but she had rejected the notion of putting the wire in one of Mindy's pockets.

"Too easy to find," the officer said. She was tall and long-legged, her skin lightly weathered and darkly tanned. She taped the small device, about two and a half inches square, under Mindy's breasts.

"You're getting top-of-the-line equipment," Officer Wrigley said with a smile. "Model G1416. It's got a 300-megawatt power transmitter. They won't have any trouble hearing you."

"Good to know," Mindy said with only a touch of sarcasm.

The police would be listening to the conversation from inside a van disguised as a landscape maintenance truck. Jax and Maddox would both be wearing earbuds, linking them into the conversation.

Mindy tried not to look for the van as she climbed out of her car and started across the grass toward the rendezvous point. There weren't many people around, the reason the guys had chosen the spot, just a man sitting on a park bench with a baby stroller in front of him—a policeman in disguise—and a woman walking her dog in the distance. Perhaps another officer; Mindy didn't know.

She wondered where Jax was, resisted the urge to scan the area in search of him. He was out there somewhere. She trusted Jax and Maddox to keep her safe. Mindy kept walking.

WEARING CAMO CARGO pants and an olive-drab T-shirt beneath a tactical vest, Jax adjusted the eight-inch knife on his pistol belt next to his HK45. He moved into position behind the wide trunk of an oak tree, fixing his gaze on Charley Burns, aka Mr. Average, the guy with the pale blue eyes.

Easing silently closer, Jax stepped up behind him, locked an arm around Burns's neck and started to squeeze, at the same time jerking Burns's semiauto out of his hand and tossing it away. Burns struggled, clawed and tried to kick backward. Jax tightened his hold. Burns made a few wheezing noises and went limp.

Almost too easy.

Propping Burns against the tree trunk, Jax bound the man's wrists and ankles with plastic zip ties, slapped a piece of duct tape over his mouth and moved on to his next target.

Through his earbud, he could hear Mindy speaking to Susan DeMarco. She had just arrived at the rendezvous site. He felt a surge of pride at the calm control in her voice. It was followed by a shot of worry. She wasn't a police officer or a private detective. She had no law enforcement training. Anything could happen.

He clamped down on his fear and picked up his pace. He had a job to do, same as Mindy. Counting on Maddox to take care of Whiteman, the smoker in the Zanotti high-tops, Jax wove quietly through the trees and shrubs, making his way around behind the big man with the scar on the back of his hand.

In a lightweight trench coat, Walker Riley stood in the shadows, using the lower branch of a tree to steady the barrel of the .308 rifle he pointed toward the path leading back to Mindy's car.

Knowing he meant to kill the woman Jax loved, he felt a wave of fury so hot he had to clamp down hard to stay in control. He pulled his pistol, slipped up behind Riley and pressed the barrel against the side of his head. "One move and you're a dead man."

The rifle fell off the tree branch and landed with a thud on the soft green grass at Riley's feet. "I told them you'd be here. The fools didn't believe me. They thought the girl would do whatever they said to get the money. They figured she was as rotten as the rest of us."

"Put your hands behind your back."

Riley pretended to turn, feigned right and whirled left, his knife sliding into his hand at the same time he managed to dance away. Jax cursed. With the op still underway, there was no chance he could take a shot without giving them away and putting Mindy in even graver danger. He tossed his pistol and pulled his knife, jumped back as Riley's blade slashed toward his throat above the vest, missing him by inches.

The two men began to circle, silver blades flashing in the sunlight shining between the clouds. Time was running out. He needed to get to Mindy before something else went wrong.

He slashed and thrust, dodged a slicing attack that came from the right, felt the deadly blade rip down his arm and jumped back out of the way. Riley was good. Agile for a man his size.

Jax swore softly, thrust and parried, jumped back as a sharp pain sliced across his thigh. He prayed the blade hadn't nicked his femoral artery, knew he needed to make this end before Riley's superior knife skill cost him his life.

Whirling, he shot out a kick with his boot that knocked the blade out of Riley's big hand. Followed with an elbow to Riley's chin, drove a hard right into his face that knocked him backward, and punched him again, breaking his nose and sending a spray of blood into the air.

Riley turned to run, but Jax tackled him, taking him to the ground. In seconds, Walker Riley was on his stomach, his wrists and ankles bound, duct tape over his mouth, Jax on the move toward Mindy.

CHAPTER FOURTEEN

SHE'D WANTED TO get there early, be there before Susan arrived, but when she reached the granite conversation area near the flagpole, Susan rose to greet her. A leather satchel sat on the ground at her feet.

Mindy took a shaky breath. Plastering a fake smile on her face, she kept moving. The trick was to get Susan talking, get as much information as possible before it was time to take the money and leave.

Susan's smile was a parody of warmth. "Well...if it isn't my old ex-friend and employee, Mindy Stewart. You always played it so meek and mild. Who would have guessed what a ruthless little bitch you are."

Mindy walked up in front of her. "I guess we both have our secrets. Yours is going to cost you twenty-five thousand dollars."

A cold smile curved Susan's red-painted lips. "Ryan was a good fuck, but he wasn't worth twenty-five grand."

"For the information on this drive, I bet he wanted a lot more than that. Is that the reason you had him killed? Or maybe you were the scorned lover, and you killed him for revenge. Which was it?"

"He's dead because he tried to play me," Susan said. "Didn't work out very well for him. I guess we'll find out if it's going to work for you."

She should have been afraid but instead anger rolled

through her. "Are you threatening me? Because if you are, I'll turn around right now and walk away. I'll drive straight to your husband's office and hand the flash drive over to him. I imagine he'll be very grateful."

Susan's spine stiffened. "You little whore. You try to go against me and you'll be as dead as Ryan Shipman. I'll see to it personally."

"The way you did him?"

She smirked, but didn't answer.

Mindy looked down at the satchel. "You want the flash drive. I want the money. Let's get this over with."

"First I need to know if you brought the real drive. Hand it over."

A chill swept through her. They had talked about this last night, the possibility Susan might want to actually see what was on the drive before they made the exchange. Mindy needed to keep her talking.

"Fine, but first I want to be sure you brought the money."

Susan sat down on the granite bench, picked up the satchel and set it down on the bench beside her. She opened the case and tipped it so that Mindy could see stacks of bills held together with rubber bands.

She also saw the laptop.

"The money's all there," Susan said. "Now give me the drive. As soon as I verify the contents, the money is yours."

Her heart was beating, hammering away in her chest. She couldn't hold Susan off much longer. Mindy walked up beside her and held out a hand. The little silver Kingston flash drive glittered in her palm.

"You can look at it," she said. "But I don't see the point. How do you know I haven't made half a dozen more copies?"

Susan's features darkened with fury. She rose from the bench, her blue eyes cold as ice. "Because if you have, you're dead."

Mindy didn't look away. "Just like Ryan Shipman?"

"That's right." Susan grabbed the drive and stuck it in her pocket. Mindy gasped as a tiny revolver appeared in Susan's hand.

"I don't like the way this is going," Susan said. "We'll finish it somewhere else. Now start walking back the way you came."

Mindy's heart was pounding so hard she could feel it throbbing in her temples. She hadn't taken two steps when a man strode out from behind one of the granite walls, black-haired, dark and handsome, holding a big semiautomatic pistol pointed at Mindy's chest.

"Elliot," Susan said with a smile that actually looked sincere. "You always appear at exactly the right time."

"I'm glad you finally noticed." A look passed between them. Susan tucked the little revolver into the satchel and closed it up. Elliot's big black pistol didn't waver.

"The car's waiting at the end of the path," he said. He signaled toward Mindy. "Get moving."

"I didn't have a chance to look at the flash drive," Susan told him as they walked along.

"In a very short time, it won't matter," Elliot said. *Because Mindy will be dead*, were the unspoken words.

She glanced around, searching for Jax, but didn't see him. Her pulse hiked up even more, and her stomach quivered with nerves. Still no sign of Jax, not until they reached the dark green Jaguar idling in a handicapped spot at the near edge of the parking lot.

She stifled a cry as Jax rose up beside the car like a big dark shadow, shoving Susan out of the way hard enough to send her sprawling across the asphalt, disarming Elliot so fast Mindy almost missed it. One moment the man was aiming a gun at her, the next he was lying on the ground moaning and clutching his arm, which appeared to be broken.

Police swarmed out of nowhere, shouting orders, pistols drawn, pointing at Elliot and Susan. Maddox strode toward them across the grass. Mindy looked at Jax, saw blood running down his arm. One of his pant legs was soaked crimson.

"Jax!" She closed the distance between them, fear for him making her tremble. "Jax!"

He caught her against him. "It's all right. I'm okay, baby. It's not as bad as it looks."

"Oh God, Jax." Worry and all the blood made her light-headed.

Gunderson hurried up just then, took one look at Jax and started shouting. "Get a bus here, now!"

Maddox helped Jax strip off his tactical vest, guided him over to the edge of the parking lot and eased him down on the grass. He pulled his knife and sliced open Jax's bloody pant leg.

"Missed the femoral," Maddox said, some of his worry easing. "You're going to need a shit-ton of stitches, but you'll be okay."

"You took care of Whiteman?"

"Left him tied to a tree. Cops already picked him up." Maddox sliced off a piece of Jax's cotton T-shirt and ripped it into a strip, which he tied around the injured leg. He folded another strip into a rectangle and handed it to Mindy. Her hand trembled as she pressed it against the slice in Jax's arm.

A police officer ran up with a first-aid kit, and Maddox went to work taping up Jax's leg, repairing the damage enough to get him to the hospital, while Mindy bandaged Jax's arm.

"You did good, baby," he said as she worked. "You handled DeMarco like a pro. I'm really proud of you."

"I was so scared, Jax. I was afraid one of us would get killed, and we'd never see each other again."

Jax pulled her close and settled his good arm around her waist. Mindy rested her head on his shoulder. In the distance, she could hear an ambulance racing toward them.

"This is finally over and we're both still alive," he said. "Does that mean we'll be staying together?"

She looked up at him. He was covered in blood from fighting to protect her. He would have given his life for her. He was everything she wanted, and she was desperately in love with him.

Were they together?

"Is that what you want?" she asked.

His hard features softened. "You like a man who takes charge, right?"

If that man is you, she thought, but just nodded.

Jax kissed her. "Then I'm taking charge now and I'm never letting you go."

Mindy slid her arms around his neck. Her throat tightened, and her heart swelled with love for him.

"Okay," was all she said.

IT WAS A week before Jax was healed enough to go back to work, and things had calmed down enough for him to talk to Chase about the situation with Mindy. They both loved working at The Max. But if they had to, they would choose each other.

Fortunately, Chase being Chase, he already knew what was going on. When they walked into his office holding hands, he just grinned. "I wondered how long it would take you two to figure things out."

Jax felt a rush of relief. It was followed by a trickle of irritation. "How the hell did you know?"

"I've got eyes. Besides, I'm a detective, remember?"

Jax couldn't help smiling.

"So…um…everything's okay?" Mindy asked. "We get to keep our jobs?"

"Is that an engagement ring I see on your finger?" Chase asked.

Mindy looked down at the diamond solitaire they had picked out together.

"We're getting married," Jax answered for her. "We haven't set a date but I'm hoping it's soon."

"Congratulations. Yes, you can keep your jobs. I'm lucky to have you both."

Mindy smiled at Jax, and he felt the same kick he'd been feeling since she'd walked into the office on her first day of work. He leaned down and brushed a soft kiss on her lips. Mindy flushed. Damn, he was crazy about her.

"I guess you heard," Chase said. "Elliot and Susan both tried to turn State's evidence. They wanted desperately to testify against the other for a lighter sentence, but the DA turned down the deal. Thanks to you two, they had plenty of evidence without them. They're both going to jail for a good long time."

"I was hoping it would go down that way," Jax said.

Chase rose behind his desk. "Before I forget, Harper will probably want to host an engagement party. Any objections?"

"Not from me," Jax said, smiling.

"That would be wonderful," Mindy said.

"Great. I'll let her know."

They walked out of Chase's office together. They had work to do. Jax was on the Eleanor Donahue case again, and Mindy was needed up front. They smiled at each other before they parted.

It was a good day. And the future looked even brighter.

* * * * *

Don't miss the first book in the exciting
Maximum Security series from
New York Times bestselling author

KAT MARTIN

*Tension and passion raise when family ambition
turns deadly...*

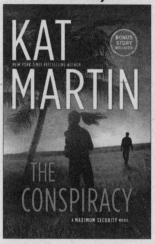

"Martin keeps the twists and turns coming in the sensuous
and spirited first Maximum Security romantic thriller."
—*Publishers Weekly*

Order your copy today!

HQNBooks.com

PHKMBPA10520